A CC

LORRIE FARRELLY—T
Lily Harmon's heart was captured when she adopted little Maddie, an orphan whose father was presumed killed in battle. But former Union Army Major Luke Cullinan is very much alive, and he's determined to reclaim his cherished daughter in Lorrie Farrelly's "The Longest Way Home."

LINDA CARROLL-BRADD—FORGED BY FIRE
Ivey Treadwell, cook at her family's boarding house, wants to accomplish something big. For now, she satisfies herself with improving on the traditional recipes for the boarders by adding herbs and spices she gathers. An incident with a broken pan causes her to see Berg Spengler, the town's blacksmith, in a new light.

Stigmatized for his huge size and blamed for his brother's injury, Berg has discovered being alone is safer for his heart. But when he sees interest spark in Ivey's eyes, he decides to take a chance and approach her. The pair discovers an attraction that heats up each time they are alone together. Will Ivey convince Berg his wandering days are over and home is here with her in Comfort?

AGNES ALEXANDER—SECOND CHANCE AT LOVE
Dr. Miles Kerry and his nurse, Cora Hilliard, have both given up on finding love again. But when Cora is asked to move out of the boarding house where she and her ten-year-old son Koby live, they have nowhere to go. Miles insists they move into the spare rooms in his house—an arrangement with no complications. But when Cora falls ill with a raging fever, she must rely on Miles as she never has before. Will Koby get the father he wants so badly? Will Miles and Cora get their **SECOND CHANCE AT LOVE**?

BEVERLY WELLS—BRIGHTER TOMORROWS
Five years ago, Callie Lynch fell in love, only to have her dreams shattered when she realized she'd been played the fool and used like a puppet. Bitter and shamed, trusting no man and determined to stand alone, she leaves Virginia to find new roots in Wyoming.

Three years ago, Marshal Chase Matlock lost the love of his life during a bank robbery and was left riddled with guilt for failing to protect her. For three years, he's tracked the scum of the earth—and this time, by God, he'll get his man.

Scars from the past run deep, but when these two bruised hearts and lost souls meet and desire runs strong, can they overcome their doubts as well as the madman who holds Callie's life in his hands?

ANGELA RAINES—NEVER HAD A CHANCE
Thomas Heath's sister, Clara, abandoned him to the cruelties of the people who were raising them. As a young man, he finally finds her—but she is on her way to getting married. Tom leaves in search of something to give him the stability he yearns for…but what?

Maria Bernal, pampered and coddled by her wealthy father, is on the verge of becoming a woman as her eighteenth birthday approaches. When a stranger shows up at their door and is wounded as he tries to protect her, she finds him more than a passing attraction—she's falling in love.

But Tom is the victim of a deadly trick, and can't remember who he is or why he's at the Bernal home. Will he regain his memory in time to prevent a second attack?

JULIA DANIELS—FOR THE LOVE OF GRACE
Poppy Stanton tracks down her mentally handicapped sister, Gracie, who has run off to become a mail-order bride. In the family way, Grace refuses to leave the dusty Wyoming town of Hope Springs, though she is married to an abusive husband.

Bachelor Reed Ridgeley and his mother live nearby, and invite Poppy to stay at their spacious ranch while she sorts out what to do about Gracie. Can Poppy convince her sister to come back home to Chicago with her before Reed can show her what a new future could look like for them in Hope Springs?

MEG MIMS—WINNER TAKES ALL
Cora Peterson is dead set on winning the Fourth of July Barrel Auction with her Mile High Apple Pie. She expects her rival might best her once again, but what she doesn't expect is a bid for love from the handsome newcomer to Cady Corners…

A COWBOY CELEBRATION

Lorrie Farrelly
Linda Carroll-Bradd
Agnes Alexander
Beverly Wells
Angela Raines
Julia Daniels
Meg Mims

A Cowboy Celebration
Copyright© 2015 Prairie Rose Publications
Cover Design Livia Reasoner
Prairie Rose Publications
www.prairierosepublications.com

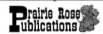

All rights reserved.
ISBN-13: 978-1514670323
ISBN-10: 1514670321

This is a work of fiction. The characters, incidents, and dialogues are products of the author's imagination and are not to be construed as real.

No part of this book may be used or reproduced in any manner whatsoever without written permission of the publisher, except in the case of brief quotations embodied in critical articles and reviews.

"The Longest Way Home" Copyright© 2015 Lorrie Farrelly
"Forged by Fire" Copyright© 2015 Linda Carroll-Bradd
"Second Chance at Love" Copyright© 2015 Agnes Alexander
"Brighter Tomorrows" Copyright© 2015 Beverly Wells
"Never Had a Chance" Copyright© 2015 Angela Raines
"For the Love of Grace" Copyright© 2015 Julia Daniels
"Winner Takes All" Copyright© 2015 Meg Mims

Table of Contents

The Longest Way Home By Lorrie Farrelly 1

Forged by Fire By Linda Carroll-Bradd..33

Second Chance at Love By Agnes Alexander....................................63

Brighter Tomorrows By Beverly Wells 88

Never Had a Chance By Angela Raines...128

For the Love of Grace By Julia Daniels 163

Winner Takes All By Meg Mims..207

    Recipes...237

        Lily's Berry And Apple Crisp Cobbler....................................238

        Buttermilk-Crispy Chicken 239

        Knee-Deep Dried Apple Stack Cake 240

        Lip Smackin' Good Corn Bread 242

        Green Corn Fritters 243

        Ma's Molasses Cookies 244

        Cora Peterson's Mile High Apple Pie......................................245

The Longest Way Home

By Lorrie Farrelly

Little Maddie, sent West on an orphan train, sets off fireworks between her young, widowed, adoptive mother and the angry man hot on their trail— Maddie's father—very much alive and determined to reclaim his daughter.

WANTED

Homes for Children

A company of homeless children from the East will arrive at
OMAHA, NEB. TERR., ON FRIDAY, JUNE 2nd, 1865

These children are of various ages and of both sexes, having been thrown friendless upon the world. Some have been orphaned by the tragic events of the Late War.

The community is asked to assist the agent in finding good homes for them. Persons taking these children shall treat them in every way as members of the family.

An address will be made by the agent.
COME SEE THE CHILDREN
AND HEAR THE ADDRESS.
Distribution will take place at the

HERNDON HOUSE Ninth and Farnam Streets
FRIDAY, JUNE 2, at 1:30 p.m.

The elegant, paneled dining room of the Herndon House Hotel was crowded and overwarm, and the din of chattering voices, many with a keen

THE LONGEST WAY HOME–LORRIE FARRELLY

edge of excitement and anticipation, did nothing to calm Lily Harmon's nerves. Her hands twisted together in her lap, betraying her anxiety. She took the deepest breath she could within the confines of her corset and willed herself to remain composed.

Her husband, Jonah, laid his hand on her arm, patting gently. "Don't you worry, now," he said, his tone a little too hearty. "Mrs. Trent said there'd be sixteen young'uns. We'll find us a sweet girl to help you with the cooking and washing and so on, so's the trip won't be so hard on you."

Lily sighed. Ever since she'd seen the adoptions announcement posted in storefront windows about town, she'd dreamed of a little girl of her own. She and Jonah had been trying for a baby since their marriage over two years earlier, but they hadn't been blessed. Jonah seemed untroubled about it; but then, he was untroubled about most things. He was not pessimistic by nature. In fact, Lily thought he tended to be rather more naively optimistic than situations warranted.

Turning to remind him–again–that she wanted a little child, not a servant, Lily caught herself as she saw his doting smile. Jonah continued patting her hand, his earnest, puppy-dog gaze uncomplicated and devoted. He obviously wanted to make her happy, and had, after all, readily agreed to "come and have a look-see" at the children today.

There suddenly seemed to be so many changes in their lives. This would be their last week in Omaha. Soon, they'd join with other families heading west to Wyoming, or maybe Oregon, where skilled saddlers like Jonah were needed and handsomely paid. Nearly stuttering with excitement, he'd shown her handbills advertising jobs for farriers, carpenters, blacksmiths, wheelwrights, and, yes, saddlers like himself. They could head up to Fort Laramie, a major trade and military outpost along the Mormon and Oregon Trails, and see what was what. If they didn't like Wyoming, well, then they could keep on going. Oregon, California–so many promised lands lay further on. In his mind, Jonah saw an uncomplicated future of boundless opportunity.

"You could open up a bake shop, Lily, like you've always wanted to," Jonah had said with a happy, widening grin. "Traveling folks and soldiers would buy up your pies and cobblers faster than you could make 'em, I bet."

Jonah's plan had quickly been settled. Lily's one request before they made ready to leave was that they attend today's adoption meeting. She knew in her heart that even a new start out west would still feel empty without a child of her own, and she was coming to fear they would never otherwise be blessed with a family. Jonah, filled with eager anticipation for their journey to a new land of

A COWBOY CELEBRATION

opportunity, readily agreed. He still thought, however, that Lily was not being entirely practical.

His brows furrowed above pale hazel eyes. "You sure you don't want someone older?" he asked. "A good chore-girl to help you?"

"Jonah…" Lily began, but the chatter in the room suddenly stilled as a line of children, Bibles tucked under their arms and small canvas bundles of meager belongings clutched in their hands, entered the dining room. Obediently, they followed a kindly-looking matron down a center aisle formed by several rows of chairs. As fifty pairs of curious, hopeful, assessing, and often pitying, eyes stared at them, the children marched doggedly toward a raised platform at the front of the room.

Lily swiveled in her chair, all but held her breath as the youngsters filed past her aisle chair. There were little ones, barely more than toddlers, as well as older children. Two of the tallest appeared to be twelve or thirteen years old.

The differing expressions on little faces, and attitudes from obviously very shy to nearly cocky left her both deeply touched and terribly curious. What were they thinking? How would it feel to be put on display, literally "put up" for adoption, on that small stage in front of so many strangers–strangers who might very well determine the course of all their days and years to come?

Lily searched their faces, not certain exactly what she was looking for. I'll know her when I see her, she thought. I'll know my little girl.

A boy of about ten, his ruddy hair bowl-cut and slicked down, gave her an irrepressible, cheeky grin as he marched by. Lily smiled in return, but couldn't help thinking: That one'll be a handful, but he'll keep things lively.

Her attention turned to the next children in line, a willowy, dark-haired girl of about ten who tenderly held the hand of a little boy of about three. The two looked much alike, and Lily's heart went out to them. Most people wanted just one child, so this young girl and her little brother would almost certainly be separated, never to see one another again.

Lily felt tears burn her eyes. Perhaps she and Jonah could find a way…

She was so lost in thought about the two children that she jumped when a vexed call of "Maddie! Come back here this minute!" startled her. A moment later, a little body clothed in a clean but ill-fitting blue frock cannonballed into her arms.

"What the—" Jonah exclaimed.

The flustered matron turned to the oldest girl. "Lizzie," she said quickly, "please see that the children stand in order."

When Lizzie nodded, murmured, "Yes'm," and began sorting the children

3

into a semicircle on the small stage, the matron started back down the aisle toward the wayward Maddie. Lily gave the woman an apologetic shrug, then looked back down at the little girl clinging to her with surprising strength. Bible and bundle had fallen, forgotten, to the floor. Nonplussed, Jonah bent down to gather them.

The matron took hold of the child's arms, gently tried to loosen her grip, but Maddie clung ever more tightly. Abruptly, the little face turned up, and Lily found herself looking into huge green eyes filled with both hope and despair. Then, suddenly, Maddie's face crumpled and tears began to well.

"Oh!" the child whispered, staring up into Lily's dark blue eyes. "Oh, you're not her! I thought you was her!"

Before Lily could think how to respond, the matron, still grasping the little girl's vice-like arms, said in embarrassment, "I'm so sorry, missus. She's usually quite well-behaved, she is." She stopped pulling on Maddie and stooped down until her face was nearly level with the child's.

"Maddie," she said in a patient but stern voice. "Maddie, you know the rules. You must come stand with the other children. Quickly, now. We'll have no more of this nonsense." The matron looked up as Jonah held out the Bible and canvas bundle.

"Here you are, miss. No harm done," he said pleasantly.

The matron thanked him. She took the simple items, tucked them under her arm, and rose to stand. Managing to clasp Maddie's hand, she tugged firmly and said, "Come, now. You must not make such a scene, Madeline. It's unseemly."

"It's all right," Lily blurted suddenly, surprising herself. "Please, let her stay. It's all right."

Both the matron and Jonah stared at her in astonishment, but Lily's gaze had found little Maddie's once more. Understanding passed between them, and in that moment, something she'd scarcely known she so deeply needed settled into place in Lily's heart.

"Please, Matron," she said again, her thumb gently stroking a tear from Maddie's cheek. "Let her stay with me."

♥ ♥ ♥

April 1866
Fort Laramie, Wyoming Territory

Tired, covered in trail dust, his leg, shoulder, and side aching like hell with the hide off, Luke Cullinan rode into Fort Laramie on a lineback dun nearly as weary as his rider. But no amount of weariness dulled Luke's vigilance in a

A COWBOY CELEBRATION

place as bustling as the fort on this crisp spring day. The chill blowing off the Big Horn Mountains was still sharp in the air, but it did nothing to dampen the hubbub of activity in and around the neat, low, wood and grout-lime buildings. Years in the army allowed Luke to identify headquarters, sutler's store, ordinance depot and magazine, barracks, hospital, guardhouse, and Quartermaster's building at little more than a glance.

Soldiers, emigrants, workmen, trappers, homesteaders, even quite a few Indians, clad in the leathers and skins of their Northern Plains tribes, went about their business. Many were gathered at the post trader's store, others busy at the workshops or farrier's, blacksmith's forge or saddler. A party of emigrants–Luke figured they were missionaries by the plain severity of their clothing and their solemn, purposeful demeanor–loaded supplies into a group of wagons lined up on the wide expanse of parade ground. Several large cargo wagons full-laden with cut lumber and sacks of coal stood waiting to be unloaded.

Luke turned in the saddle to look up the valley toward South Pass. Winter hadn't entirely lost its grip on the mountains, and that was the truth. He sighed, studied the stream of the Laramie River running silvery and cold. He'd have much rather camped alone in the wilderness than in this bustling crowd of humanity, but that wasn't an option. The war had left him badly hurt in more ways than one. Physically, certainly, but almost as much damage was done to his heart. He'd gone marching off to battle to the tunes of "Battle Cry of Freedom" and "Glory, Hallelujah!" But he'd come home, battered and scarred, to find he'd lost everything.

Almost everything, he reminded himself. He was here, in this place that had too many people for his liking, wary of everything around him, because there was a chance, a good chance, that his daughter might have passed this way. And though he scarcely dared to hope, there was a small chance she might, God willing, still be here.

He'd been gone so long, he knew the odds were stacked against him. But he couldn't–wouldn't–give up his search.

Nearly shot to pieces in a battle near Franklin, Tennessee, back in the late fall of '64, Luke had been confined in hospitals for close to a year thereafter. The first had been a Confederate field hospital where, as a prisoner of war, he'd lain barely conscious for long, agonizing days. Thankfully, he had little memory of that desperate time.

Rescued by the Union Army when the area was retaken less than three weeks later, he was moved from Franklin to Nashville, and then, finally, to

Washington. Only by a whisker and the grace of God did he still have all four limbs at the end of the ordeal. Weeks later he was finally able to write home. But Becky had never answered, nor had she ever come to see him.

He held out hope that his letters had simply gone astray, but as the months passed, he feared the worst. Finally arriving home to his Boston neighborhood confirmed what he'd known in his heart. Becky was gone. A kindly neighbor, Mrs. Larson, had fought tears as she'd told him of Becky's losing battle with the consumption that had also taken her parents a few years earlier. Luke's parents had passed as well, and his only brother had fallen at Gettysburg.

"With no one to care for her properly–We thought you long dead, Lucas, you see, and your young missus gone, too. I'd have taken in your wee tyke myself had not my John been doing so poorly…"

But Luke and Becky's daughter had been sent to the New England Home for Little Wanderers.

And from there, he'd learned to his gnawing frustration and despair, to Omaha, Nebraska, on a charity "orphan train," to be given into the hands of strangers.

The children's home had kept records, of course, but more than a dozen groups of orphans–most of whom, as his daughter had been thought to be, the sons and daughters of Union officers who'd lost their lives in the war–had gone west in the previous two years. The Little Wanderers administrator, kind and helpful as she tried to be, could not seem to locate the records Luke needed. She gave him an apologetic smile as she pulled out yet another file drawer and rifled through the packed cardboard folders.

"I'm very sorry this is taking so long, Major Cullinan…"

"Not 'Major,' ma'am. Not anymore. As I mentioned, I'm a civilian now."

"Oh, yes, of course. Forgive me. It's only that your daughter's records would have had your unit and rank on them, you see."

Luke nodded, trying to contain his impatience. The administrator withdrew a thick armload of folders and toted them to her desk.

"These documents are all from the past year, Mr. Cullinan. If I may beg your forbearance for a few more minutes, there should be something here…"

She sat down and began skimming through the papers. One folder after another was discarded and set aside, and another one opened.

Her brows knitted in a frown. "Sadly, we've had so very many displaced children since the war's end. I'm sure you can understand…"

Luke tensed, frustration a pounding ache in his head, but he continued to hold his temper with a tenacious grip. "Yes, ma'am, I do. But wouldn't the agent have sent a report with the names of the families that adopted children?"

She nodded again, still leafing through the papers. "Yes, yes. And Miss Lyndon is one of our most thorough and conscientious agents, so there has to be... Ah! I knew it! Here it is!" She held up several pages, written in a neat hand and pinned together.

Standing as quickly as his bad leg would allow, Luke leaned over her desk and held out his hand. The administrator hesitated–there were other families named on the list besides the family that took the Cullinan child, after all–but she was not unmoved by the desperation of the young man who'd fought so bravely for his country, and who now stood before her in such agonized suspense.

She handed over the list, but said, "I do ask your discretion, Mr. Cullinan."

It took Luke most of a week to reach Omaha, a city that seemed to be perpetually on the move. It was difficult enough to find anyone who'd been acquainted with the Harmons; obtaining any reliable information on where they'd gone when they'd left Omaha was nearly impossible. The months the Harmons had lived in this gateway town, with so many people passing through, might as well have been five minutes. Finally, however, he found a former neighbor who told him Jonah and Lily had planned to head up the Mormon Trail, along the North Platte, maybe as far as Fort Laramie, maybe all the way on to Oregon.

The neighbor did vividly remember the little girl who went with them. "Pretty little dark-haired thing, with big green eyes," she said. "Clung to her new mama like a cocklebur, she did. Lily got out of sight, that child wouldn't be comforted 'til she found her again."

Luke thanked the woman. Determination hardening in his heart like a stone, he saddled up Smoke, a sturdy, clean-boned lineback dun he'd bought at a reputable livery stable, and set out for Wyoming.

And now, some weeks later, here he was at Fort Laramie. But as he sat watching the throngs of people come and go at the fort, despair settled over him once more like a heavy black cloud. How was he going to find three travelers who just might have been here nearly a year ago, and who might just as likely have kept on going to God knew where?

From long practice commanding a cavalry unit in the war, Luke forced himself to think calmly. He was no good exhausted and keyed up like this. He'd need to settle in for a day or two and get his wits about him. He was more likely to get useful information if he didn't give his urgency free rein and pounce on people like a madman.

Nudging Smoke past the long Quartermaster's Building, with its workshops, storage rooms, and forges, Luke headed along the riverbank to the military bridge spanning the Laramie. On the far side stood Brown's Hotel, a large wood and sod establishment that still looked suspiciously like the hay shed it had once been. Nevertheless, after weeks on the trail, any place that offered a clean bed would be just fine with Luke. He reckoned a bath and a hot meal wouldn't come amiss, either. His bones felt just about rattled apart.

♥ ♥ ♥

An hour later, having seen to Smoke's care at the hotel stable, Luke procured a small–little more than a narrow bed and a washstand–but clean and serviceable room. He stowed his gear and indulged in an honest-to-God, blessedly warm bath. Shrugging into a clean shirt and vest, he headed for the hotel's dining establishment, a bustling room furnished with a few rows of handhewn tables and benches set end-to-end.

He paused in the doorway, suddenly stopped short by the most delicious aromas he'd inhaled since, well, since before the war, certainly. His mouth began to water and his stomach growled. Dang, but something smelled good! He nearly forgot his fatigue in his sudden, ravenous hunger.

He strode into the room, taking note of how many heaping platters and bowls were on the tables, and how rapidly they were being emptied, only to be replaced by new ones. For once, the crowd and din of boisterous chatter didn't raise his hackles; he was too intent on the sweet, savory, and succulent dishes luring him with their aromas. He found a space at a table near the kitchen and sat down just as a young woman, her dark, shining hair bound at her nape in a crocheted snood and her pretty face flushed with heat from the stove and ovens, came through the kitchen doorway carrying a large pan of hot, bubbling cobbler drenched in thick cream. She set the pan in the middle of a nearby table and, with a laugh, easily dodged a few diners who would have liked to taste her along with their dessert. A moment later she appeared at Luke's side.

"Howdy, mister," she smiled, a little breathlessly. "We've got pan-fried trout or roast venison today. Special for Saturday night. Cornmeal spoonbread, too, or grits and gravy if you'd rather, and three kinds of pie or strawberry and apple crisp cobbler for dessert. What'll you have?"

As Luke looked up at her, his heart nearly stopped, and he scarcely heard a word she said. Staring into eyes the color of the deepest mountain lake, he could think nothing more than *God in heaven, she looks so much like Becky!*

He suddenly realized she'd stopped talking and was waiting for his reply. When he still couldn't seem to wrap his tongue around a response, she cocked her head, her lips quirking into a gently wry smile.

"Cat got your tongue? Well, you'd best make up your mind while we still got something left. Business keeps up like this tonight, we'll be down to turnips and bread crumbs before another hour passes."

Luke swallowed, found his voice. "Yes, ma'am. Sorry. It all sounded so good. I'll have the venison and the spoonbread and the cobbler. Heap the plates high, please, ma'am, and keep 'em coming."

She laughed, and Luke felt his heart skip with a feeling he hardly recognized as enjoyment. Nodding, he said, "Much obliged, ma'am," and he meant it.

His reluctance to see her turn away and head back into the kitchen was as acute as his pleasure at seeing her return. As she approached his table, Luke stood and carefully took the plate, bowl, and utensils from her. Surprised, she said, "Thank you, that's very kind of you. Not every fella that comes in here is so much of a gentleman, Mr...."

"Cullinan," Luke said as he set the dishes on the table. "I'm Luke Cullinan, ma'am, and I'm very pleased to make your acquaintance."

A strange expression came over her face, as though a cloud had covered the sun. But it was gone in a flash, and she smiled again, a little too brightly. Still, he'd seen it, and he was certain that, for just an instant, her eyes had registered shock and a rush of fear. He'd seen that haunted expression in the eyes of many a soldier during battle, and he sure as shootin' knew it when he saw it.

"Is...is everything all right, ma'am?" he asked, his brow furrowing. Concerned, he reached down and took her hand.

She nodded, stammered a bit. "I...of course, it's just very busy tonight and I'm a bit distracted, I fear. But don't give it a second thought, Mr. Cullinan. Please, sit down and enjoy your meal." She extracted her hand from his gentle grip. "I'll be back in just a moment with some hot coffee for you."

Before Luke could ask her to sit with him for just a few minutes, she turned and hurried back to the kitchen. In fact, she almost seemed to run.

Cullinan! Oh, dear God, it couldn't be, could it? He couldn't be some long-lost relative here to take precious Maddie away from her, could he? Oh, please, no!

Lily leaned back against the wall of the kitchen, closed her eyes to shut out the steam and bustling frenzy of the cooks and helpers, pressed her hands against her mouth to hold back a sick rush of alarm and dread.

But his eyes–how could she not have caught the resemblance the instant he looked up at her? As green as a forest glade they were, clear as minerals in a silvery stream. And his hair–even damp as it was and slicked back, that sable color was so like Maddie's.

Oh, Lily thought, nearly in a blind panic, whatever was she going to do?

Calm down, calm down, she ordered herself. You don't know he's here for Maddie. He might not be her relation at all. The name is just a coincidence, that's all! Scores of folks come through every day. He'll likely move on in a day or two, just like so many others.

She took a deep breath, tried to steady her breathing. But his eyes...Oh, Lord, his eyes!

"Miz Harmon? Miz Harmon, are ye all right, then? Are ye feelin' poorly?"

Lily dropped her hands, opened her eyes, took a shaky breath and forced a thin smile.

"Yes. Yes, thank you, Mrs. O'Toole. I-I'm fine. A bit overcome by the heat, that's all. I'll be fine."

The plump, ruddy-cheeked cook squinted at her skeptically. "Yer tryin' ta do too much, ye are, Missus," she scolded. "Bakin' all mornin', runnin' about the dining room totin' platters and pans all afternoon an' evenin'. Ye need ta take a bit of a break, now. Sit yerself down an' have yerself a bowl of cobbler before that horde out there licks the pans clean!"

Lily relaxed a bit, and her smile was more genuine now. "It is that good, isn't it, Mrs. O'Toole? It was my mother's recipe, you know."

"Yes, Missus, that it is. Now, won't ye take a wee rest?"

Sighing, uncertain whether she should keep an eye on Luke Cullinan or run to "Granny" Grady's, grab Maddie, and light out for parts unknown, Lily managed to nod pleasantly.

"I will. Yes, thank you, Mrs. O'Toole. You're very kind. And please don't worry. I'll have plenty of rest tomorrow. Lt. Gordon's wife Sadie is going to come in to do the baking and serving, so I can have a whole day to spend with my daughter."

"Well," Mrs. O'Toole replied, "that's all well and good, it is, though we'll hear nothin' from the guests but grousin' that her pies can't hold a candle to yers. But never mind that; we'll manage all right. Now, ye need ta sit an' eat sumpin', ye do."

"All right. Just for a few minutes, though. There're more hungry bellies out there tonight than you could shake a stick at."

A COWBOY CELEBRATION

"An' ye'll not be rushin' out there again, Missus, until ye've finished that bowl, ye hear?"

Lily nodded again, but Mrs. O'Toole hovered until the younger woman obediently dropped into a chair at a small worktable and began to poke a bit at the dish of cobbler the cook set in front of her. Finally satisfied, Mrs. O'Toole returned to her duties, barking orders and waving her wooden spoon like a cavalry sword.

Giving up all pretense of eating, Lily propped her elbows on the table and wearily dropped her head into her hands. What in the world was she going to do?

She had to be honest with herself. If Luke Cullinan indeed proved to be Maddie's relative, didn't her daughter have a right to know? But what if he intended to take her away? Dear God, what if he could take her? Of course, Lily had an official paper that confirmed she and Jonah had legally adopted Maddie Cullinan, but with Jonah gone and she now the sole parent, would that document be enough?

Lily clung to the hope that if Cullinan were a relative, he was only a distant one. But what if he were a near cousin? Or worse, her uncle? Would the adoption hold up against the claim of a blood relation? That possibility struck sick fear in Lily's heart. She couldn't lose Maddie now. She simply couldn't!

Rubbing her eyes, Lily knew she was too exhausted and too panicky to think things through properly. She'd sleep on it tonight–or try to–and she'd hope that tomorrow, somehow, a plan would come to her to ensure Maddie's safety.

In the end, she slept not a wink, rising every little while to check on her daughter, sleeping so angelically on her little cot, innocently unaware of the dangerous storm that could even now be brewing. And as for a plan, Lily was no more certain what to do at dawn than she had been the night before.

But even if she had thought of a foolproof course of action, she'd have been out of time to set it in motion. For less than an hour after sunrise, Luke Cullinan came knocking at the door.

♥ ♥ ♥

Inside the small, tidy cabin, Lily opened the door just a sliver and peeked out. Her heart sank at the sight of Cullinan on her doorstep, his battered cavalry hat in hand. His tall, lanky form seemed to completely block the doorway. For a moment, she considered slamming the door and bolting it, then running to grab Jonah's Winchester. Fortunately, her common sense prevailed.

What are you thinking to do, Lily? she asked herself in disgust. Murder

11

him? And wouldn't that put you and Maddie in a pretty fix!

There was no help for it, and she knew it. She'd have to talk to this man. Squaring her shoulders, Lily pulled open the door and said coolly, "Good morning, Mr. Cullinan."

Luke's jaw dropped and he stared at her with undisguised disbelief.

"*You're* Mrs. Harmon?" he blurted. "Mrs. Lily Harmon?"

With as steady a voice as she could manage, she said stiffly, "I am Mrs. Harmon, yes."

Luke's mouth drew into a tight line and his surprise vanished in a black scowl. He leaned forward, tightened his fingers around the edge of the doorjamb as though he might any moment simply rip it from the wall.

"Where's my daughter, Mrs. Harmon? Madeline Cullinan. Where is she?" He tried to look past Lily into the interior of the cabin, but he stopped himself just short of physically pushing past her.

Despite her resolve to remain composed, Lily gasped. *Daughter!* How could that be? A shiver of cold fear ran along her spine. But my Maddie's an orphan! Of course she is! Still, doubt gnawed, and she felt a rush of sick alarm.

For Maddie's sake, I must stay calm! Lily thought desperately. I mustn't panic! Gathering every ounce of her courage, she lifted her chin and set her jaw stubbornly, though she still had to look up nearly a foot to meet Cullinan's glowering green eyes.

"Mister Cullinan..." she said slowly, stalling for time. "I'm afraid I don't know what you are talking about. My daughter is sleeping, and I will not have her disturbed. Now, if you will kindly..."

Lily tried to shut the door in his face, but Luke's large hand shot out to hold it open.

"Not a chance, lady," he snapped. "I know you have my daughter, and you'll by God let me in to see her!"

"Do you really think I'll let you, a complete stranger, into my house or anywhere near my daughter?" Panic flashed into hot anger. "How do I know you're even who you say you are?"

Luke glared at her for a long moment, then held up a hand, palm out. "Wait a minute," he growled. Lily stiffened when he reached inside his unbuttoned coat, but he simply pulled out a small metal case from an inside pocket. When he held it out to her, Lily recoiled, but he said insistently, "Open it, Mrs. Harmon. Take a good look."

Reluctantly, she took the case from his hand, opened it slowly, stared at the tintype photograph inside.

A COWBOY CELEBRATION

The tintype was of a young family–husband, wife, and little girl–taken perhaps as the husband was preparing to leave home to fight in the war. In the full dress uniform of a Union cavalry captain, he sat on a straight-backed chair, his long legs stretched out in front of him. Beside him stood a pale young woman in a light-colored, lace-trimmed day dress decorated with small fabric sprigs resembling rosebuds. She was very young, no more than eighteen or nineteen, and slender as a reed. There was no hint of the pudginess of adolescence in her delicate face. Her fair hair was pulled back and fashioned into a neat fall of curls at the crown, but the style only emphasized her fragility. She stared, a little warily, at the camera with unusually dark eyes that seemed far too large in her thin face.

The young couple's daughter, an adorable little dark-haired child scarcely out of toddlerhood–perhaps three years old–sat happily on her father's lap, one chubby little hand tenderly engulfed in her father's much larger one. She wore a delicate lawn dress intricately smocked at the bodice and embroidered with tiny flowers. Her hair, dark like her father's, was painstakingly curled into a mass of perfect ringlets. Both father and daughter gazed steadily at the camera with clear, light eyes.

Maddie's eyes. Pain squeezed Lily's heart, set it hammering in her chest. My sweet Maddie's eyes. And no matter how much she tried to convince herself it was not so, she could see without a doubt that they were Luke Cullinan's eyes, too. She felt the icy heat of his gaze as he waited, studying her, watching her every move, her every reaction.

Lily blew out a shaky sigh. "You...you don't look much like this man anymore, Mr. Cullinan," she said, though she knew in her heart that it was indeed him.

He shook his head. "It was a very long war, Mrs. Harmon. The day that photograph was taken feels like a hundred years ago, you want to know the truth. A man goes to see the elephant, he's not going to come back the same."

She swallowed, shook her head. "No," she murmured. "I suppose not. Well," she said finally, looking up at him once more, sighing as she realized there was no way around it. She had to deal with him. "I guess you'd best come in, then. But only for a minute."

Reluctantly, Lily took a step back, and without acknowledging her last attempt at controlling the situation, Luke stepped through the doorway.

He paused to let his eyes adjust to the dimmer interior light. When she extended the tintype to him, he took it, slipped it with care back into his pocket. Almost grudgingly, he grunted, "Obliged."

13

THE LONGEST WAY HOME–LORRIE FARRELLY

Then, his patience evaporated. "Where's Maddie?"

"I'll take you to her, Mr. Cullinan," Lily said warily. "But I won't have you frightening her with your ill temper. Please keep in mind that you are in this house only thanks to my forbearance. Do not make me regret my sympathy for you."

Luke glared at her for another long moment, then his stony expression eased a bit.

"My apologies, Mrs. Harmon," he said quietly. "It's…I haven't seen my daughter in more than two years. I promise I will be very careful with her. And I…" he paused, cleared his throat. Chagrined, he made an effort to speak civilly. "I, well, I'm grateful to you and Mr. Harmon for taking Maddie in. I truly am. But the thing is, Maddie should never have been given to you in the first place. It was a…a…"

Damn blasted ball-up was on the tip of Luke's tongue. He stumbled, searched for words that wouldn't scorch the lady's ears. "…a sorry chain of misfortunes and mistakes complicated by good intentions."

He blew out a breath. "It wasn't 'til I finally made it home, going into the end of '65, that I found out my wife had passed and Maddie'd been sent to the Children's Home. Seems everyone had thought I was dead, too."

His eyes hardened. "But she's all I've got left now, Mrs. Harmon, and I won't be leaving Fort Laramie without her. You understand that, ma'am?"

Lily met his eyes, drew herself up as straight and tall as she could. "I do understand, Mr. Cullinan. And while my heart goes out to you, Maddie is now legally my daughter, and I love her with all my heart. I promise you I won't give her up, to you or to anyone else. And you can stick that in your pocket and take it to the bank."

♥ ♥ ♥

Damned if she doesn't look like a gunman about to draw down on me. The thought struck Luke out of the blue, and despite his current fix, it also struck him as oddly funny, in a demented way. His fingers, clenched on the battered brim of his hat, began to relax. The tension in his shoulders eased as understanding dawned on him.

"You really do love her," he said slowly. "My Maddie. You really do love her, don't you, ma'am?"

♥ ♥ ♥

Lily blinked. For a moment, the dawning understanding in his eyes confused her. Was he giving in? A little warily, she nodded.

14

A COWBOY CELEBRATION

"Of course I do, Mr. Cullinan." He winced a bit when she added, "She's my daughter."

She expected him to argue. Instead, he nodded almost imperceptibly and fell silent. Lily could see warring emotions furrow his brow and tighten his lips. When he finally spoke, his quiet, almost gentle request caught her once more by surprise.

"May I see her now, ma'am?"

Though an inner voice warned, Be careful, Lily crossed to the cabin's single bedroom, silently opened the door, and allowed Luke Cullinan to pass through.

He moved across the room, past Lily's bed, her small bedside table, and a pine washstand, until he came to little Maddie's bedside. He said nothing, simply clutched his hat and stared down at the sleeping child.

Never taking her eyes off him, Lily closed the door behind her–just in case he tried to grab her daughter and bolt–and took up her guard again at the foot of Maddie's cot.

Luke made no move to touch the child, but his gaze swept over her, swiftly at first, then again with a slow, heart-breaking, lingering wonder. Finally, he settled on her face, angelic in sleep, one rosy cheek tucked against a well-worn, obviously well-loved, rag doll.

From his shaky breathing and rapt expression, Lily saw Luke's devotion and wonder. Her wariness eased, and when his eyes filled with unabashed tears, her heart ached, and then melted.

"Maddie had that little doll with her when she came to us," Lily offered quietly. "Tucked in this sad little bundle with a few scraps of clothing. It means so much to her. She…she calls it 'Becky'."

Slowly, Luke turned to look at her. There was something in his brimming eyes she couldn't define, but she saw a muscle kick hard in his jaw. He nodded, almost more to himself than to Lily, then he turned and dropped a little awkwardly to one knee beside Maddie's cot. Gently, almost reverently, he reached out with one trembling hand and lovingly tucked a wayward strand of fine hair behind her ear.

Maddie's long lashes fluttered, and her eyes opened. Still sleep-glazed and unfocused, she gazed into Luke's drawn face. Dreamily she lifted one hand and placed it on his cheek.

"Papa."

♥ ♥ ♥

"When you was away, my first mama got real sick, Papa," Maddie said,

15

and though fresh pain lanced Luke's heart, he kept his expression shuttered for his daughter's sake. "She went to sleep one day and she wouldn't wake up no matter what. A lady came and got me. I didn't want to go, but she said Mama couldn't take care of me and I had to go with her." She paused, looked up at her father. "I think Mama went away to heaven, and that's why I couldn't stay with her anymore."

Heartsick, Luke hugged his little girl, rested his chin on her soft hair. They sat together in a rough-hewn wooden rocking chair just outside the cabin door. Maddie was snuggled in Luke's lap as he pushed the rocker gently back and forth on the bare, hard, dusty ground with one booted foot. He was deeply grateful Mrs. Harmon had trusted him enough to let him have this time alone with his daughter.

"Yes, Bitsy, you're right," he agreed now, taking her hand gently in his and using his old pet name for her. "Your mama went up to heaven, but she still watches over you, you know. Every day and every night."

The child nodded. "Yes, I thought so," she said matter-of-factly. "The first time I saw Mama–my new mama, I mean–I thought my first mama had come back for me. I wasn't supposed to get out of line, but I did it anyway, 'cause I couldn't help it. I had to go see her."

Figuring he'd sort out Maddie's whole story with Lily Harmon later, Luke nodded as though he completely understood all she'd told him and said, "Yes. Mrs. Harmon reminds me very much of your mama, too, Maddie."

"She is my mama, now, Papa. The only one I got. She's awfully nice, and I reckon I love her a lot." She considered a moment, then added, "You know what? You should love her, too, Papa. Then, we could all be a family just like we used to!"

Luke drew back a bit, raised an arched brow.

"Well, now, don't you reckon Mr. Harmon might have something to say about that, Bitsy?" he asked drily.

Maddie shook her head. "No, Papa," she said solemnly. "See, Mr. Jonah went to heaven, too. It was when we was coming here in the wagons with the Wheelers and the Adamses and all the other folks. Me and some of the other kids got the measles, but most of the grown-ups didn't 'cause they already had it when they was kids. But Mr. Jonah hadn't got it when he was little, so he got sick, too. But he didn't get better like I did. He just got sicker and sicker, and then he died. Betsy Wheeler's papa and Jimmy Adams's papa, they buried him under the grass, and Mama made a marker by scratching his name on a rock."

"I'm sorry, Maddie," Luke said gently. "That must have been a very sad

A COWBOY CELEBRATION

day for you and Mrs. Harmon."

"Uh-huh. But it was sadder for Mama than me, 'cause I didn't know Mr. Jonah very well. He didn't talk to me much, and I wasn't with them very long when me and the others got sick."

Saying a silent prayer of gratitude that his daughter hadn't also taken a turn for the worse, Luke hugged her again. "Well, I'm sure glad you got all better, Bitsy. I'd've been mighty sad otherwise. Mighty sad, indeed."

Maddie nodded, but she had clearly lost interest in the story of the unfortunate Jonah and the measles. She thought a moment, then said brightly, "I can read now, Papa, did you know that? Granny says I'm the beatinest girl for reading she ever did see!"

"Granny?"

"Yes. Granny Grady. She lives over past the sutler's and takes care of me when Mama's over at the hotel cooking and such. Mama makes the best cobbler ever, and she always brings me home a bowl. She never forgets to save some for me, even if all the rest gets et up, 'cause it's my very favorite."

Then, with no warning, Maddie asked, "Why've you been gone so long, Papa? I've missed you something awful."

Luke swallowed. How could he explain to a seven-year-old about so many years of war and loss and pain? Then he realized she knew a thing or two about loss and grief as well, and his chest ached with that knowledge. He reached out, softly stroked her cheek. Maddie leaned into his palm, and that simple, trusting gesture went straight to his heart.

"Well..." Emotion caught in his throat, and he had to pause, swallow. "Um, you know there was a big war going on, Bitsy, and lots of soldiers were fighting for a long time..."

Maddie nodded, watching him intently, but she didn't speak. Luke took a breath and went on, searching for words his little girl might understand.

"Well, so, I was a soldier, too, you see, and I had to go fight in that war, so that other folks could be free and our country would stay together in one piece."

"Oh."

"Then one day, down in Tennessee, I got some hurt in the fighting, and I was in a hospital–a couple of hospitals, actually–for a long time. When I finally got back home, your mama had already gone to heaven and you'd been taken away. I've been looking for you for a long time, Bitsy Baby. For a very long time."

Maddie sighed, snuggled against him. "I'm real glad you found me, Papa." Then she sat up, looking her father in the eye, adding, "But I'm not a baby

17

anymore, Papa. I've been going to school here and everything. Miz Parsons gots me in the second primer and I'm nearly done with it already."

"My," Luke smiled, "don't that beat all. I'm mighty proud of you, Maddie."

"Thank you, Papa," she said, and snuggled once more against his chest. Together they gazed out past the straggling cottonwoods to the Laramie River beyond. A few minutes later, Maddie asked, "So, what are we gonna do now?"

Luke shook his head. Damned if I know, he thought. "Don't know, exactly, Bitsy," he said. "But I reckon we'll figure it out. You, me, and Mrs. ... I mean, your mama."

"Okay," she said, and together they sat and rocked and pondered.

"Maddie told me about your husband, Mrs. Harmon. I'm very sorry for your loss."

Luke, hunkered down at the hearth as he banked the evening's fire, replaced the poker and rose stiffly to his feet. Lily quietly closed the door to her daughter's room and crossed the few steps to sit at the worn table. Despite the obvious wear, everything in the small cabin was spotlessly clean.

"Thank you, Mr. Cullinan," she said. Sighing, she pushed a wayward strand of hair behind her ear. Somehow, Luke found the simple gesture far more appealing than he should have. He cleared his throat in embarrassment, but Lily misunderstood his ill ease, thinking he felt awkward at the mention of Jonah.

"That's kind of you. It was a very hard time, but Jonah is past suffering now, and Maddie and I are getting along quite well."

Yeah, as you run yourself ragged baking all morning and serving all evening at the hotel, Luke thought, but he said only, "Well, I do admire you, ma'am, and I'm mighty grateful for the kindness and care you've shown my daughter."

Lily's spine stiffened. "She is my daughter, too, Mr. Cullinan, and all things considered, she's been with me nearly as long as she was with you. How old was she when you went off to war? Two? Three?"

He frowned, but said evenly, "It was the summer of '61, so Maddie had to've been two. I was commissioned as captain of a volunteer cavalry unit, but we lost so many men at Gettysburg, there wasn't a unit anymore." His expression hardened and a muscle kicked along his jaw. "But experienced cavalry officers were sorely needed just about everywhere, so I was bumped up to major and put in command of a unit under General Hatch. By the fall of '64 we were down near Nashville, on the Harpeth River at Franklin."

Luke pulled out a rough-hewn chair, dropped into it opposite Lily. Her eyes

A COWBOY CELEBRATION

never left his face.

"Forrest's Reb cavalry tried to flank us. It was a hel—uh, *heck* of a fight. I got shot up pretty bad, was in hospitals for close to a year."

"I'm sorry, Mr. Cullinan," Lily said. "I know your separation from Maddie was not your fault. I apologize for insinuating you had a choice in the matter."

He shook his head. "No, you have a right to ask. Truth is, I only got home once," he went on. "At the end of '62. It was the last time I ever saw Becky, and until today, the last time I saw my daughter. But it doesn't make her any less mine, Mrs. Harmon, and now I'm here, there's no way I'm going anywhere without her."

Her back stiffening, Lily said, "Then, it seems we are in something of a fix, because I certainly do not intend to give her up, to you or to anyone else."

Luke leaned back in his chair, studied her, his mouth a tight line and his green eyes hard. Abruptly, he leaned forward again, placed his palms flat on the table. "All right, then," he said, his tone that of a man who has flatly made up his mind. "We'll take it straight from the mouth of babes. Marry me."

Lily's eyes widened. "Marry you?" she exclaimed. "Mr. Cullinan, I don't even know you!"

He shrugged. "I reckon you know enough. I won't beat you nor be unfaithful, if that's what you're worried about. And I have enough money to buy three, four hundred acres, build us a decent house, and start in a good herd of Morgan horses. Lots of fine grazing and alfalfa-growing bottom land just a few miles out, and the army's always in need of mounts."

She simply stared at him. "I should marry you because you have some money and you won't beat me?"

Sighing, Luke shook his head. "No, ma'am. You should marry me because you're Maddie's mother and I'm her father. And while you're getting used to the idea, you may as well call me Luke."

Lily's mouth opened, then snapped shut. After a long moment, she said slowly, "I appreciate your offer, Mr. ... I mean, Luke. And I admit that marrying you would solve more problems than one. But the simple fact is, we are little more than strangers, and we certainly do not love each other. What would Maddie and I be to you but a burden?"

Pushing to his feet, Luke said angrily, "My daughter will never be a burden to me, Mrs. Harmon."

Rising from her chair, Lily drew up to her full height. "And I? What would I be to you?"

Scowling. Luke shook his head. "For Maddie's sake, ma'am, I guess we'll find out."

♥ ♥ ♥

They married the next morning. Her hair bedecked with ribbons, Maddie barely contained her joy and excitement during the brief ceremony at the little church on the edge of the wide parade ground. She was too young and too happy to understand either the guarded look in her mother's eyes or the grimly determined look in her father's.

When the preacher pronounced Luke and Lily "man and wife," and gave Luke permission to kiss his new bride, there was a long moment of hesitation.

Luke looked down into Lily's eyes, saw warring emotions flicker there. A wary shyness battled heightened awareness and curiosity. Mentally crossing his fingers, Luke took advantage of the latter. Framing her face with his hands, he laid his lips on hers. And all at once got far more than he'd bargained for.

Something sparked between them, quick and hot. As his pulse began to pound in his ears, Luke found himself quickly in danger of completely losing his composure and scandalizing the preacher. With enormous reluctance, he forced himself to end the kiss. He drew back, his eyes wide with surprise. Lily gazed up at him, a kind of dreamy wonder in her eyes.

The preacher cleared his throat, held out his hand. "Congratulations, Mr. Cullinan." He turned to Lily. "And my very best wishes to you, Mrs. Cullinan."

"What?" Lily blinked, caught herself. Color rushed into her cheeks. "Oh, I—well, thank you, Reverend Pelley." She turned, reached down for her daughter's hand. "Come now, Maddie," she said.

But as she stepped forward, she felt Luke's hand on her arm. She stopped, looked up at him. A ghost of a smile tugged at the corner of his mouth as he offered her his arm. After the briefest of hesitations, she slipped her hand into the crook of his arm, and together, for better or for worse, they walked from the church as a family.

Perhaps everything will be all right after all, Lily thought as they strolled back across the parade ground and past the post trader's to the small cluster of cabins near the river. Luke—she reminded herself she must think of him as Luke—was an attractive man who loved Maddie with all his heart, and wasn't that a good start? Perhaps tonight he might begin to care a little for her as well.

That thought made her blush again, and Luke didn't miss her expression.

"What is it?" he asked.

"Nothing," Lily said quickly. "Nothing at all. Just a touch of nerves, that's all."

"Oh." A shadow passed over Luke's eyes. "Well, you and Maddie can take some time to rest while I go fetch Smoke. I'm gonna ride out tomorrow morning and take another look at some pretty country I passed through on my way here, just a few miles out. There's plenty of water, good drainage, and good land for grass and hay. It's close enough to the fort that we'd have supplies and protection, and Maddie can still go to school. I'll contract with the sawmill for lumber, and there's plenty of willing labor here to help me build the house and corrals and raise a barn."

Lily's fingers clenched on his arm. He paused, saw her watching him anxiously, worrying her lower lip. Aw, hell, he thought. We should've talked about all this last night. Here I am rushing her into a new life. She wants Maddie, I know, but that doesn't come close to meaning she wants me, too. And I've got so many scars…well, I reckon the best thing I can do for Lily is give her time to get used to me.

Luke pulled in a breath. "Anyway, ma'am, I'll stay at the hotel tonight so's I don't disturb you and Maddie when I leave in the morning. Oh, and I'll let 'em know at Brown's you won't be working there anymore."

"Mr. Cullinan, wait."

He frowned, and Lily quickly amended, "Luke. I…" Her voice faltered as her courage wavered. Was he running from her already? If they were to have any kind of life together, she simply couldn't let that happen. "Please, don't go to the hotel tonight. Couldn't…couldn't you stay in our cabin?" With me, she thought, but said, "With us?"

What? Astounded, dumbstruck as hope flared in his heart, Luke stared down into his wife's deep blue eyes. "In the cabin? That is, with you? I mean, as husband and wife? Are… are you sure, Lily? I don't want you to think I expect something from you that you aren't ready to give."

Lily's chin lifted. "I'm your wife now, Luke," she said quietly, her voice strengthening as she gathered her courage. "And I think…I think we must start as we mean to go on, don't you?"

Almost overwhelmed by relief and hope, Luke blew out a breath he hadn't even realized he'd been holding. As his pulse kicked hard, he patted her hand and nodded. "Yes, ma'am," he said. "I reckon I do, indeed."

Luke moved Maddie's cot into the cabin's main room, close enough to the banked fire to keep her warm, and she snuggled under the covers as soon as darkness fell, exhausted from the excitement of the day. Beset by a sudden attack of nerves, Lily lingered a bit as she tucked her daughter into bed.

When Luke realized her nervousness–and his, as well–grew more acute by the minute, he walked to her, took her hand, and led her to the bedroom.

Closing the door behind him, he could make out Lily opening the kerosene lamp on the little table beside the bed, intending to light the wick. A quick bolt of panic shot through him.

It was one thing for her to be able to feel the extent of his scars; quite another to be faced with them in the light.

"No, Lily," he said, a little too sharply. "Wait!"

Lily looked up at him, startled. "What? What's wrong?"

What could he say? *I was shot to hell and back, Lily. I look like that monster Mrs. Shelley wrote about. Oh, yes, that would go over well.*

Maybe he could ease into it so the thing he most dreaded, her appalled rejection, would not happen.

"It's—it's just that I prefer the dark."

When her brows knit in a bewildered frown, Luke took her hand, swallowed hard, tried to keep emotion from his voice.

"Look, Lily, there's…there's something I should tell you. About what I look like. I—I got shot up pretty bad in Tennessee. There's a lot…well, it's not pretty. I don't want you to be…" *Revolted.* The word speared his heart, but he managed to say, "…scared."

Lily shook her head, said, "You don't frighten me, Luke."

"Good. I don't ever want to." Gently, he took her face in his hands. "I won't hurt you, Lily. I'll never hurt you, I promise. You will always be safe with me."

She turned her head, kissed his palm. Luke felt his body tighten at the sweetness and trust of the gesture. When she reached up to cup his cheek with her hand, she said, "Of course I will, Luke. We'll be safe with each other."

When she rose to her toes, offering her lips to him, he bent his head and kissed her. As passion flared, their kisses grew hotter and deeper, Luke eased Lily's dress from her shoulders, trailed his lips along her throat to the swell of her breasts. The scent and taste of her, the smooth flesh beneath his searching hands, set his pulse racing and fogged his head with desire.

Lily's quick gasps and sweet, throaty moans echoed his own ragged breathing, and when she wrapped her arms tightly around him, fisting the back of his shirt in her fingers and pulling him even closer, he was lost. He set her on the side of the bed and stepped into the vee of her spread legs. Taking only a moment to free himself and grab enough ragged control to be sure he wouldn't hurt her, Luke gripped Lily's hips, raised her to him, and plunged.

Passion drove them until there was nothing but sensation, nothing but pleasure, nothing but the two of them in the dark. Lily had no idea she'd torn buttons from Luke's shirt as he sent her flying. She cried his name, and he followed her into a soaring free fall.

Luke opened his eyes in the dim dawn light, found himself gazing into Lily's face. She was weeping quietly, her hand clamped over her mouth. Her eyes, filled with what he thought was terrible pity–and was that horror, as well?–were clouded with pain.

"Oh, my God, Luke," she whispered. "Oh, my dear Lord."

She reached out a trembling hand, began to gingerly trace the jagged scars that made a patchwork of his shoulder and side. Though she could not see his battered leg beneath the blanket, she could see plenty of the damage to the rest of him. Humiliation and anger clenched in Luke's stomach.

"Don't! I don't need your pity, Lily. I sure as hell don't want it." Luke stumbled to his feet, began to drag on his clothes and boots.

"No, Luke, no." Lily said, scrubbing her cheeks with her palms. "Wait. Listen, please. You don't understand. I wasn't—"

"I do understand. I understand perfectly," he said, cutting her off, his tone flat and distant. "Take care of Maddie for me, Lily. I'll be gone a few days, maybe a week or two. There're a lot of arrangements to make. You and Maddie should stay here until I've got the land deed secured and a house built."

He paused, pick up his battered hat, studied it a moment as though it held the answer to some gnawing problem. Lily tried again, saying in a stricken voice, "Luke, wait, please. Listen to me for a minute. I didn't mean…."

He shook his head, cut her off again. "I doesn't matter. I'll be back when I can."

He slapped on his hat, nodded to her as though she were a complete stranger.

"Ma'am," he said without emotion, and then he was gone.

Lily occupied herself that morning with getting Maddie off to school and cleaning the cabin. Doubt and worry plagued her every minute: What had she done that had made Luke turn to stone before her eyes? Would he abandon them? No, no, surely not! But what if he never came back? How would she ever explain that to Maddie? Losing her father again would crush her daughter's heart.

That will not happen! He would never do that! Lily insisted to herself. But the doubts were clever, and they ambushed her from hidden corners of her mind and heart. Finally, she forced herself to believe that if she were steadfast and had faith in the future, Luke must surely do the same.

Before her misgivings could grow strong enough to distract her further, Lily grabbed her shawl and tied her bonnet, then marched down to the trading post to hammer out a property deal with the sutler. Steeling herself with her last ounce of determination and forcing a sweet smile, she negotiated the sale of the cabin and the tiny plot it sat on for a profit that would have thrilled Jonah, had he been alive to see it.

The sutler, secretly delighted to have an available property, small as it was, to gouge the next eager buyer, agreed to let the cabin back to the Cullinans for a reasonable monthly fee for as long as they needed it.

Afterward, Lily walked to Brown's Hotel. She confirmed her notice with the owner, but assured Mrs. O'Toole and the others in the kitchen that she would visit often. That afternoon she retrieved Maddie from school, and the two of them visited Granny Grady to break the news.

Then there was nothing to do but wait for Luke's return.

He would come back, wouldn't he? Surely he wouldn't abandon Maddie. Lily tormented herself with worry. She knew he had somehow mistaken her compassion for him, and her distress at his obvious suffering, for pity and repugnance. Now she realized that, while he may have loved her with tenderness and passion the night before, he hadn't really trusted her. Not enough, anyway. Not enough to believe that, once she'd seen what he obviously considered his disfigurement, she could still want him.

As the supper hour approached and evening began to fall, Maddie, barely able to contain her excitement and impatience, peppered Lily with questions. When would Papa come back? When would they go to their new home? Could she have a pony of her own?

Lily tried to reassure the little girl–and herself. Yes, Papa would be back soon, and she was quite sure he would allow her to have a pony one day soon. Satisfied, the little girl cheerfully helped her mother stir batter for spoonbread.

"Mama, can we make cobbler, too?" she asked, scooping up spoonfuls of batter and dribbling it back into the bowl.

"Don't play with the batter, Maddie," Lily scolded gently. "And we'll have to go find more wild strawberries to pick if we're to have cobbler."

"Tomorrow?"

"Perhaps." Trying to put on a smile for her daughter and distract herself from her anxiety as well, Lily said, a little too heartily, "Do you remember how to tell which berry plants are the right ones to pick?"

Maddie nodded eagerly. "Yes, Mama. The ones with the white flowers and the dangly little red berries."

"That's right. Good for you." Lily dropped a quick kiss atop Maddie's head. But despite her cheerful tone, her thoughts were dark and troubled.

"Well, aren't you a sorry sight. You know you never were one for rye whiskey, Luke," the saloon girl said. Startled, Luke looked up from his glass and the bottle he was nursing. He sat at a table in a dark corner of the bar at the notorious Sheep Ranch, a sprawling cluster of lime grout buildings a few miles from Fort Laramie. The Sheep Ranch was well know for miles around for having plenty of whiskey, rowdy gaming tables, and even rowdier sporting girls, but it was mighty short on actual sheep. In fact, there weren't any.

Luke had been gone for nearly three weeks. He'd selected and purchased a double land section, ridden west up to the sawmill near Laramie Peak to contract for lumber and carpenters, and purchased a farm wagon and team of big, sturdy, dappled Percheron geldings.

Finally, he started back, but the memory of the pity and revulsion he was sure he'd seen in Lily's eyes dug ever deeper into the gaping hole of his heart. When the buildings of the Sheep Ranch appeared over a rise on the road back to the fort, promising distraction and mindless sport, Luke impulsively turned the team toward them.

While the Percherons, Buddy and Chico, happily shared a trough of hay with Smoke, Luke strolled into the smoky, kerosene-lit bar, elbowed through the rowdy crowd of off-duty soldiers, miners, cowboys, and prostitutes, and found himself a table, a bottle, and a glass to stare morosely into. And he continued to do exactly that until a sporting girl in a crocheted black shawl trimmed in feathers, low cut red satin dress, and heavily rouged cheeks spoke to him.

He reared back in his chair, stared at her, unable to make sense of what he saw, of the impossible. The girl dropped into a chair and scooted it close to his. She pointed at the bottle with a long, garishly painted fingernail.

"That rye is just going to make you sick as a dog, Luke. So what do you think you're doing, sitting here all alone, with only that bottle for company?"

Luke's heart was suddenly in danger of hammering out of his chest, and he couldn't seem to draw breath. His mouth opened, snapped shut again. He

THE LONGEST WAY HOME–LORRIE FARRELLY

swallowed, finally managed to choke out, "Becky? My God, Becky! How—"

"It doesn't matter how, Luke. But I haven't got very long, and that does matter. It matters, too, that you have left our Maddie again, and your Lily, too. I know you had to leave me, but why aren't you tearing up the trail to get back to those who still live? They need you, Luke, and they love you."

"Love?" Luke snorted a bitter laugh. "How can Lily love me? She hardly knows me, and what she does know is a scarred-up mess."

Becky shook her head. "She loved you before she ever met you, Luke, because she loves Maddie. And our little girl has shown your Lily all she needs to know."

Heat and shame rose in Luke's throat. "Dang, Becky, if you'd seen her face the morning after we were married, when she saw me in the light…" He trailed off, realized he was talking to his dead wife about making love to his living one. Appalled at himself, he buried his head in his hands.

"Judas Priest! I'm sorry, Becky," he muttered. "I'm sorry for everything. I'm sorry I left you and Maddie alone, and I'm so, so sorry you got sick."

"I was sick for a long time, Luke," Becky said gently. "You know that. I never told you, but the doctor said I shouldn't have tried to have children."

"What?" Luke raised his head, horror in his eyes. "What? Why didn't you…For God's sake, why didn't you tell me?"

"Because you know you would have done just as he said, and then we would never have had our precious little girl. Would you really have preferred that?"

"I—I…no," Luke stammered. "No, of course not. But, Becky, if I'd known, maybe something could have been different. Maybe I could have done something differently, something to save you." He shook his head again, and his eyes burned with unshed tears. "I should never, never have left you."

She laid a hand on his arm. "Your staying home would not have saved me, Luke. And you know you had to go. Both you and I would have thought the less of you if you had not answered the call."

"Becky…" he began again, but he faltered, words failing him. He gripped her hand, held it to his heart. His breath shuddered out, and he tried to offer her a smile, sad though it was. "Red's not so much your color, honey," he said. He hadn't drunk very much, but perhaps he had had enough to make him hallucinate. Or, possibly, he had lost his mind.

Becky laughed, a soft, musical sound. "No, it certainly isn't, is it? But I'm afraid Dovey's very fond of it, and it is, after all, her body and dress I've borrowed."

26

"Dovey?" Luke repeated, and though he peered, squinting, into the sporting girl's face, he could see no one but Becky. He couldn't seem to wrap his mind around any logical explanation.

"Never mind, Luke, the name doesn't matter. But what you choose to do now does matter. It matters very much. Listen to me now, darling. You must set your fears aside and go back to your family with an open heart. The scars in your mind are far worse than the scars on your body. Do you understand? Despite what you may think, Lily can and does see past them. And so you must learn to see past them, too, Luke. If you cannot do this for yourself, then you must do it for me."

She gazed into his eyes, and his heart seemed to crack open. Grief, pain, and hope swirled together in a wave of emotion. "All right, Becky," he whispered. "I will try. For you."

Becky smiled, and her face filled with light. "And for Maddie and Lily, too, Lucas. Remember that," she said. Then she added gently, "This is all the time we shall have, Luke. You must go, and so must I."

"Wait!" he said quickly. "Wait, Becky! Please. I need to know. Are you … are you … all right?"

The light expanded into a brilliant fan of impossible color. From its glowing center, Luke heard, "Oh, yes. Yes, Luke. And when you think of me, you must always think of me with happiness."

He blinked, and the blowsy, over-rouged and over-used Dovey pushed herself up and away from the table. "Go on home now, mister," she said in a smoke-roughened voice. "That there rye's stronger'n a bucket of kerosene, and I reckon you've had more'n enough."

It was nearly midnight by the time Luke put up the horses at the Brown's Hotel stable, then made his way back across the bridge to the little cabin. Quietly, he opened the door and stepped inside. By the soft glow of the fireplace embers, he could see Maddie curled asleep in a blanket on her cot, her beloved rag doll pressed against her cheek.

Emotion swelled in his chest, and for a moment, all he could do was gaze at her. Then he shucked his jacket and hung it on a peg by the door. He sat at the table and pulled off his boots, then padded to Maddie's bedside and bent down to press a gentle kiss to her cheek. When he stroked her hair, she smiled in her sleep and murmured something in a sweet and dreamy little voice, but she did not wake.

Straightening, Luke took a long breath, then walked to the bedroom door and opened it.

Lily lay asleep with one arm across the side of the bed where he'd lain for one unforgettable night. But then the light of day had come. Gazing down at her, Luke finally began to understand that the emotions he'd seen in her eyes that miserable morning-after were his own grief and self-doubt, not hers.

Slowly, deliberately, he shucked the suspenders from his shoulders and unbuttoned his shirt. He pulled the shirttail from his trousers, then stopped. Taking a deep breath, he turned to the little bedside table and lit the kerosene lamp. He turned the flame high.

When Lily began to stir, he saw that her pillow was damp with tears, and a pang of deep remorse squeezed his heart. He sat down beside her on the bed, stroked her hair.

Lily sighed, and her eyes opened. For a long moment she gazed up at him as though he were, at last, her rescuer from unhappy dreams. Then she blinked. Her dawning smile disappeared, and she was instantly flustered.

"Luke! It's you!"

Lily scrambled up to a sitting position, shoving her hair back from her face. She could feel tears on her cheeks–Oh, Lord, she'd been crying again in her sleep! Mortified, she hastily scrubbed them away with her palms. Regret filled Luke's eyes.

"Did you think I wouldn't come back?" he asked.

"I ... um, no, of course not," Lily said, but in truth, and despite her certainty that her new husband was an honorable man, she hadn't been able to banish doubts and heartache from her sleep. In her nightmares, if Luke came back at all, he came back only to take Maddie away, leaving her heart shattered.

But now, he sat beside her, and Lily's thoughts scattered. Before she could think what more to say, Luke reached out and cupped her cheek with his hand.

"I hurt you, Lily," he said quietly. "I'm so sorry, sweetheart. I didn't trust you.... No. That's wrong. I didn't trust myself. I didn't believe love could look past so many scars."

Fresh tears welled in Lily's eyes as she pressed her cheek to his palm.

"It wasn't the scars from your wounds that saddened me, Luke," she said, seeing the pain in his eyes. "Those are badges of honor. It was the scars on your heart that I failed to see. I didn't realize how much they pained you."

"I know. I know that now, Lily. I was a fool not to see it from the start. You have never given my daughter anything but kindness and love, and you have given me the most hope and joy I've known in many years. I intend to spend the rest of my life repaying you in kind."

Now, Lily's eyes welled with fresh tears, but these were tears of happiness.

"Oh, Luke!" She threw her arms around his neck, hugged him tightly. Her face turned toward the lamp with its dancing flame. Realization struck her and she exclaimed, "You turned on the lamp!"

"Yes, ma'am," he said, grinning now. "I'm becoming very fond of the light."

Luke yanked his shirt over his head, dropped it on the floor beside the bed. "And I don't want to miss seeing a single thing." He pulled her close again, found her mouth with his. Passion flared, hot and fast.

When they broke apart, gasping for breath, Lily hastily began to unfasten the ribbons of her nightgown, her fingers trembling with eagerness.

"No, wait. Wait, Lily." Luke placed his hand over hers to still them, and she could feel his fingers trembling, too. But his eyes shone, and his voice was warm and deep as he said, "Let me, sweetheart."

♥ ♥ ♥

July 4, 1866
The Cullinan Ranch near Fort Laramie

The sun was high and hot as men climbed down from the frame of the barn they were raising and headed for the creek to wash up. Lily, along with Mrs. O'Toole, Granny Grady, and several other women from the fort and the hotel, laid platters heaped with fried chicken, cornmeal-battered pan-fried trout, mounds of potatoes drenched in butter, and sugar-glazed carrots on the long, rough-hewn tables set up outside the newly finished, four-room ranch house. More tables were so laden with pies and pans of Lily's cobbler that they threatened to collapse.

Children raced about everywhere. They splashed into the creek with shouts of delight and squeals of delicious shock from the still-icy water. They rode Smoke, Maddie's new pony Sugar, and some of the other horses around the corral, and squabbled happily over whose turn it was to work the dasher crank on a big wooden and metal-banded bucket. The bucket was stamped *White Mountain Ice-Cream Maker*, and it was the source of much excitement and impatience that day, and not only on the part of the children.

His hair still dripping from dunking his head in the creek, Luke came up behind Lily and wrapped his arms around her waist. He leaned down, nuzzled her ear as much as he could without scandalizing the guests, and whispered, "That ice cream ready yet?"

29

Lily laughed, batted playfully at him. "Luke! For heaven's sake! You're all wet!"

He kissed her cheek, grinned. When she turned in his arms, Lily realized his shirt hung open, the tails out, suspenders dangling. Beneath the cloth, his skin was tanned from working shirtless on long, warm summer days. Even in just the few weeks of their marriage, her talent for cooking and his steady outdoor work was working wonders. Luke had begun to gain some weight and muscle, and he already looked years younger. Lily shook her head, pushed him back, and began buttoning his shirt.

"We do dress for dinner around here, you know, Mr. Cullinan," she scolded. Luke laughed, began to tuck in his shirttail.

"Yes, ma'am. And dinner sure does look mighty good!"

He helped her onto a bench as the long tables began to fill up with friends, neighbors from the fort, ravenous children, and the even more ravenous young men Luke had hired to help with construction. As platters, bowls, and baskets of bread were passed from hand to hand, everyone seemed to be talking at once, but once plates were full, silence fell as folks dug in to their Independence Day feast with vigor.

Nothing, however, could match the exclamations of appreciation at Lily's cobbler, topped with the children's slightly runny, but still delicious, ice cream. The pans of cobbler emptied quickly, and by the end of the hour, there was not a scrap of pie remaining, either. Grumbling cheerfully about the work still to be done on the barn, the men rose and headed back to finish the job. The women and older girls began to clean up from dinner, while bigger boys tagged along after the men. The smallest children, their bellies full, curled up on blankets laid in the shade of the cottonwood trees and promptly fell asleep.

As Luke got to his feet, intending to head back to work on the barn, Lily took his arm. Without a word, she tugged him with her to a quiet corner behind the house, away from the others. His brow arched questioningly.

"What?" he asked, not sure whether to be amused or worried. "What's going on, Lily?"

"Oh, Luke!" she said, her voice hushed but full of wonder and happiness. "I didn't think I could. I thought I'd never, ever—"

"What?" he asked again, even more baffled.

Lily's hand's flew to her mouth as though to keep her joy from exploding. "Luke, I'm...I'm in the family way!"

Stunned, he stammered, "What? You're...really? Are you sure?"

Nodding so enthusiastically that she practically bounced, Lily said, "Yes!

A COWBOY CELEBRATION

I'm sure! Granny says we'll likely have a January baby. Maddie and I will have to start knitting up a storm!"

Luke laughed, then hauled her into his arms. "Lily, that's wonderful! My God, but I do love you!"

She looked up at him, her eyes glowing with happiness. "I love you, too, Luke. And I believe you mean it, I really do. But…"

She paused, feigned worry. Luke was instantly alarmed. "But what?"

"Well," Lily said thoughtfully, "I think it would be a proper precaution to make one hundred percent sure."

And reaching up, she framed his face and tugged his head down to her. Against his lips, she murmured, "It's always wise to make absolutely certain, don't you think?"

He nodded, his heart bursting with more joy than he'd thought possible. "Yes, ma'am, I do," he agreed. "Oh, I surely do."

He took her mouth with his, in celebration and in love. For Lily, Luke, and their little Maddie, the journey may have been long and winding, but they had all finally found their way home.

About Lorrie Farrelly

A Navy brat and graduate of the University of California, Santa Cruz, LORRIE FARRELLY is proud to be a Fightin' Banana Slug. Following graduate school at Northwestern University, she began a career in education that included teaching art to 4th graders, drama to 8th graders, and finally, math to high school students.

She's a three-time winner on the TV quiz show "Jeopardy!" She has shepherded wide-eyed foreign exchange students along Hollywood Blvd, and has happily curried and shoveled as a ranch hand at Disneyland's Circle D Ranch. And always, she writes.

Lorrie has won a Presidential Commendation for Excellence in Teaching Mathematics. She's been a Renaissance nominee for Teacher of the Year and a finalist for the Orange Rose Award in romantic fiction. Her novels have been awarded Readers' Favorite 5-Stars. TIMELAPSE and TERMS OF SURRENDER are winners in the 2014 READERS' FAVORITE INTERNATIONAL BOOK AWARDS, and TIMELAPSE is also a GOLD MEDALIST in the 2014 AUTHOR'S CAVE BOOK AWARDS, and is the TIME-TRAVEL NOVEL WINNER in the 2014 CYGNUS AWARDS. Lorrie

THE LONGEST WAY HOME–LORRIE FARRELLY

and her family live in Southern California.

AMAZON: http://www.amazon.com/Lorrie-Farrelly/e/B008P3LJ0O

BARNES & NOBLE: http://www.barnesandnoble.com/s/lorrie-farrelly?store=allproducts&keyword=lorrie+farrelly

Facebook: **https://www.facebook.com/LorrieFarrellyAuthor**

eNovel Authors at Work: http://enovelauthorsatwork.com/153-2/

Goodreads:

https://www.goodreads.com/author/show/4351229.Lorrie_Farrelly

Website: **https://sites.google.com/site/yourbestreads**

Twitter: **https://twitter.com/@lorriewrites**

Google+: **https://plus.google.com/u/0/+LorrieFarrelly/posts/p/pub**

LinkedIn: **http://www.linkedin.com/pub/lorrie-farrelly/27/5a0/64**

VIDEO BOOK TRAILERS for all Lorrie Farrelly novels can be seen at: https://www.youtube.com/results?search_query=Lorrie+Farrelly

Forged by Fire

By Linda Carroll-Bradd

Can a wounded soul find solace in the attentions of a cook who nurtures through her culinary creations?

Chapter One

Another day to endure in the solitary world under his control. Shimmering air danced before his eyes, and Berg Spengler leaned away from the heat blasting from the blazing fire. He swiped a thick forearm at the perspiration beading his forehead. Summer in central Texas was not his favorite time to be working the forge. But the time of year or temperature had no effect on when horses needed shoeing or wheels needed repairing. That was all part of being a blacksmith, and he had no argument over being the only one for a fifty-mile radius around Comfort.

Hoping to catch a breeze, he untied the strings holding up his leather apron, letting it flap forward, and stepped to the open double doors of the smithy shop. Flittering among the leaves of a nearby mesquite tree were a host of chirping birds, seeming to outdo each other for the loudest calls. Wind stirred a dirt devil along the road, and the swirling air cooled his bare arms and torso. A fly buzzed his ear, and he swatted at it with an impatient hand.

Over the breeze came a female voice singing notes from a high lilting melody. Berg recognized the sweet tones and tightened his grip on the wooden door. *Miss Ivey's voice.* The same one he heard from his doorway at the boarding house on Saturday nights. More often than not, he stood there on those evenings just to hear the harmonizing songs from her family, the Treadwells. Unable to resist, he leaned forward to catch a peek. Within seconds, she walked into view, sauntering along the road with a basket over her arm. Probably, she'd been out on the prairie collecting greens or berries that made the meals she cooked so tasty and different from any other place where he'd boarded.

A blue calico bonnet covered the hair Berg knew to be the prettiest shade of brown with hints of copper and gold from spending time in the sunlight. Today, she wore a green blouse with a dark skirt. His favorite was her yellow blouse with tatted lace along the collar that she wore to Sunday services.

As she drew abreast of the building, Ivey slowed and started to turn her head his way.

He stumbled backward a couple of steps until he was in full shadow. No need to offend her with the state of his sweaty and bared skin. His profession might be considered an honest one, but not many women sought out the items he created. His customers were mostly men, and the gender he was most comfortable being around.

Her steps hesitated, and she cocked her head at the open doorway. But she didn't move closer.

Is she looking for me? His chest tightened. With fumbling fingers, he drew up the leather thongs of the apron and tied them around his neck. From a hook inside the door, he grabbed a chambray shirt and shoved in his arms, dragging the sleeves across his damp skin. Did he have time to do up all the buttons? With propriety uppermost in his mind, he fidgeted with a couple. Three long strides brought him into the sunlight, but all he saw was her back about two rods distant as she walked toward her family's boarding house.

Just as well…a woman as fine as Ivey Treadwell didn't have much use for a big brute like him.

♥ ♥ ♥

Two hours later, Ivey was in the midst of finalizing dinner, and she moved in a triangle between the stove, the bin table, and the sideboard with practiced steps. A small ham sat on her mama's best china platter, waiting to be sliced. Peas picked from her garden were accented with wild baby onions she dug up on her morning stroll. She eyed the batch of steaming dandelion greens and worried she hadn't gathered enough.

Her mama, Ellen, rushed into the kitchen and looked around. "Are you about ready? What help do you need?"

"Soon, Mama." Ivey stopped to brush a strand of hair off her cheek and gave her mother a smile. "Get Maisie and Lydia to carry these dishes to the dining room. And ring the bell. The biscuits will be ready by the time the table is loaded and the boarders appear." The word *boarder* gave her pause. This morning on her way into Comfort, she'd hoped to spot Mr. Spengler. Not that she had anything in particular to say, but she liked watching him work. The rhythmic ringing of his hammer against the anvil was a sound that fit in the background of her daily activities.

Once, she'd gone to the blacksmith shop with her brother Penn to inquire about a harness chain that needed mending. The heated air from the glowing fire, the large, silent man wielding a huge hammer, and the display of strange tools had intrigued her. She'd done her sharing of peeking at the play of muscles in the blacksmith's massive arms as he pounded horseshoes into shape while discussing business details with her brother. A row of fire pokers with twisted handles had proved irresistible, and she'd run a finger along the curving spirals. What a wonderful talent he had to take slabs of plain metal and create new shapes and forms.

Fingers snapped in the air. "Ivey! I asked if you made gravy."

She shook her head to dispel the improper thoughts and stepped to the stove. "Of course. And I'm adding a secret ingredient."

"Oh, Ivey." Ellen tossed up her hands and then clasped them around her waist. "I wish you'd stick to the tried-and-true recipes I always used—and your granny back in England used at the family inn. The book is right there on the counter."

As she stirred the drippings into the sauce pan, Ivey bit her lip to keep from issuing a less-than-nice reply. A book that held instructions for dishes from sixty, seventy years ago didn't thrill her. She wanted new tastes. The world was expanding, and the Othmanns offered new items every month in their mercantile. This argument wasn't a new one, and Ivey was tired of having it over the past three months. Assigned the duty of head cook should mean she had the choice in how the food was served. Mama was constantly worried about keeping the rooms rented and that meant providing hearty meals that everyone liked. All well and good, but Ivey wanted to experiment with new tastes and combinations. What else did she have to occupy her time? "Mama, no more than five minutes remain until everything is ready."

"Goodness me." Ellen whirled and headed for the doorway. "Maisie, Lydia, time to serve." She dashed through the living room and out to the veranda to run the metal rod around the triangle.

The mixing of flour with cold water was so oft-repeated the action didn't take much thought. Ivey reached for the mortar and pestle in which she'd ground wild mustard pods and roasted peppercorns and lifted the marble bowl to her nose. Such a wonderful smell. She dumped two generous pinches into the bowl of flour paste, stirred until no streaks remained, and then dribbled the thin paste into the boiling drippings.

From behind came the sound of boots stamping on the back door step. Then the door squeaked open. "Gotta put some grease on those hinges. Hey, sis."

"Good day, Penn." She gave a quick glance over her shoulder at her older brother. "Do you know you make the same comment just about every day?"

A second but heavier set of footsteps sounded.

"Come on inside, Spengler. No need to be so formal by using the front door."

Hearing that the blacksmith was a few feet away was cause for her stomach to flutter. Ivey stiffened but kept stirring to avoid causing lumps in the gravy, bracing the pot with a thick wad of toweling. The last frenetic moments before serving a meal were often not the cook's most attractive. Why did Penn bring Mr. Spengler through here?

Maisie and Lydia hurried down the hallway, laughing. "We're here."

Without a second glance, Ivey started her orders. "Maisie, the biscuits smell ready. Could you please pull out the pan and fill the wicker basket? Lydia, put the ham at Penn's place and bring back a dish from the sideboard for the greens." She moved to the side of the oven to allow her younger sister access.

"Sure, Ivey. Good day, Mr. Spengler." Maisie grabbed a towel and opened the oven door.

"Ladies."

The single gruff word was the man's usual greeting. But Ivey savored the sound of his deep voice that always held such mystery. No Texas drawl stretched out his words. Instead, they were often clipped, and his sentences were short. She'd never heard anyone else who spoke like he did.

Penn poured water from the bucket he carried into the metal sink. He grabbed a bar of soap and set to washing his hands. "Sure smells good, Ivey. But isn't that gravy a strange color?"

Not in the mood for his teasing, she tossed her head and muttered, "Just like Mama." Filling the gravy boat was her last task before heading into the dining room. After giving the orangey-brown liquid a final stir, she secured the pad around the pot's thin bail and lifted. Two steps across the floor, she felt a jerk, and the pan tipped at a steep angle. "Oh no."

Mr. Spengler stepped close, his leg brushing against the side of her skirts, and reached for the bottom of the pan. "I've got it. Let go."

For a moment, she swayed from the impact of his solid body. "No, the pan's too hot." But her denial was pointless—either she let him take the pot, or the broken bail would drop the pan and its contents to the floor.

With a muffled grunt, he lifted the pan from her hands and carried it back to the stove.

Ivey's heart lurched. The sight of the pan that contained boiling hot gravy in Mr. Spengler's broad hands made her cry out. She rushed forward and grabbed onto his sleeve, dragging him toward the sink and the water bucket. Her feet skidded because he wasn't moving. "Hurry, we have to get your hands in cold water." Again, she tugged hard on his sleeve but her boots just slipped on the wooden floor.

The mountain of a man didn't budge. "I'm fine." He looked at her, one dark eyebrow winged upward.

"You can't be. Blisters must be forming as we waste time talking." She stepped next to him and reached for his hands, turning them so the palms faced upward. Leaning close, she inspected the surfaces, expecting to see reddened and bubbled skin. Instead, she saw thick calluses that ran in a bumpy line at the base of his fingers, and scars marked the surface of his palms in irregular patterns.

The man inhaled. "My hands are around heat all day long. Your pot was nowhere near that temperature."

Ivey straightened and looked up into Mr. Spengler's brown eyes. As dark as cocoa powder. Staring, she also saw little flecks like caramel bits. What he said made sense, but she'd never seen anyone touch a pan right off the stove and not get burned.

The sound of a throat clearing interrupted. "Is everything all right?"

Mama's voice. That should remind Ivey of a pending task. But for the life of her, she didn't know what that was. Rather, she was lost in the sensation of warm skin filling her hands and a twirling in her belly over being this close to the man she'd been having secret thoughts about since the day he settled in Comfort almost a year earlier.

Mr. Spengler moved his hands to his sides. "Yes, ma'am. Pot handle broke, but the gravy is saved." He dipped his chin toward Ivey, and then stepped across the room and disappeared down the hallway.

Ivey shook herself and wished for the opportunity to fan her face with her apron but that would clue Mama into her true feelings. "I'll get a ladle to fill the gravy boat and be right in, Mama."

Ellen pressed a hand to her shoulder. "Everyone is seated, and all are waiting on you."

"Uh-huh." Ivey couldn't get out any other words as she spooned out the steaming liquid. That man had certainly set her thoughts atwitter. One final glance around the counter and the bin table showed that her sisters had been in and out of the room, gathering all the cooked food. So they must have observed her standing in the middle of the kitchen, holding hands with the blacksmith. Letting out a big sigh, she untied her apron strings and smoothed a hand over the front of her green blouse. Gravy boat in hand, she strode down the hallway to the dining room and took her regular chair closest to the entrance. "Sorry for the delay, folks. Just a small mishap in the kitchen."

"If everyone would bow their heads for a brief blessing," Penn's voice filled the room.

Ivey barely heard what her brother said, because all of a sudden, she was too aware of the quiet man sitting not four feet away. She served herself as the bowls and plates of food made the circuit of the rectangular table. Present at this meal were her family members plus the regular boarders—Mr. Spengler, the schoolmarm Miss Fletcher, carpenter Morgan Shipley, barmaids Olivia Domingo and Sally Doolan. She leaned forward to catch her mother's eye. "Where's Mr. Baklanov?"

Frowning, Ellen buttered a biscuit and shrugged. "If he doesn't respond to the bell, he misses a meal."

Ivey knew her mother disliked the fact half of the permanent boarders worked at the Golden Door Saloon and kept late hours. A situation her father must have anticipated when he'd had the boarding house originally built, because four of the upstairs bedrooms had private access from exterior doors. A small town like Comfort with its less than one hundred residents meant business owners had a limited clientele from which to choose.

"Oh my, that's got quite a tang." Sally dabbed at her mouth and then reached for her glass of water.

"What's that?" Ivey glanced toward the red-haired woman on her right who used her fork to point at the gravy covering her slice of ham. "Really?" She cut a wedge from her slice, dipped it in the gravy pooling under her split biscuit, and popped the tidbit into her mouth. Immediately, the saltiness of the meat and the savory mustard assaulted her mouth, and she closed her eyes to focus. The blend was nice, and the flavors complimented each other. Then came the slow burn of the ground pepper. And the intensity built until Ivey's tongue tingled. She resisted sipping her water and instead broke off a piece of dry biscuit and chewed slowly. "Is the gravy too spicy for anyone else?"

Nodding, Ellen munched on a mouthful of peas, and Ivey's sisters blinked, watery-eyed, above the napkins they pressed to their mouths.

"Not for me." Miss Domingo used her biscuit to sop up a puddle of gravy.

"Quite piquant, but I like it." Miss Fletcher gave a quick smile.

Mr. Shipley shook his head and kept eating. With his mouth full, Penn just gave her a thumbs-up signal.

Mr. Spengler held her gaze. "I like things a bit fiery."

Chapter Two

Forget increasing the inventory of stock items. I must craft this...for Miss Ivey's safety. Berg tossed another piece of oak on the glowing fire and settled it atop the low flames. Although an hour has passed since the midday meal, he didn't think his heart rate was yet back to normal. The disaster that might have happened with a broken bail on Ivey's pot had stolen his breath. He couldn't bear the thought of scalding liquid marring her beautiful peaches-and-cream skin. Being close enough to smell her floral scent and having her hold his hands had only partially eased his worry.

In front of the raw material shelves, he sorted through the pile of rectangular lengths of slab metal until he found the two sizes he needed. Those he slid into the smoldering coals at the base of the fire and pumped his foot on the pedal to force air through the bellows. The resulting orange glow reminded him of Ivey's gravy. After the midday meal and being as secretive as he could, he'd removed the saucepan from the kitchen and ducked out the boarding house back door. Lucky for him, he'd still had half a loaf of bread tucked away and used that to sop up the remaining tasty gravy. Hesitant to take portions at mealtimes that would truly fill his stomach, he always kept fruit, bread, and hard cheese in the shop for when the hunger pangs hit.

Whistling an unnamed tune, he used tongs to move the heated bar to the anvil and pounded the yellow-orange metal to flatten the end. Plunging the hammered metal into a nearby barrel of water tempered the steel. Berg kept the image of the finished product in his mind as he pounded, molded, and shaped, then held the piece next to the pan. With quick movements perfected from years of practice, he bent the bar by tapping it over a curved wooden block, attached the second piece to complete the circle, and added a twist at the base of the handles. He couldn't fight back a prideful thought of how this collar handle would ensure Miss Ivey's safety.

Smiling, he remembered the time Ivey had run a finger along the spiral twists of his fireplace pokers. Her blue eyes had glistened in wonderment. Surely, this design would please her. But was he expecting too much from what he'd seen on that brief visit? The concern he'd seen today in her eyes in the kitchen had been true. Deserved or not, he'd let the awareness seep into his lonely soul. All through the meal, he'd been aware of her gentle movements and had been glad for the chance to voice an opinion on her gravy. Such satisfaction went through him at her widened gaze when he used the word 'fiery'.

Shaking his head, he re-focused on the implement. Each adjustment was checked to be sure this device fit like a tight collar under the pot's upper edge. Unable to resist, he worked a hot-metal chisel along the middle of each handle in a meandering line. Then he tapped a curved punch at a couple of spots along its length, reversing the metal piece to create a leaf shape. His final action was to tap the punch with his initials on the underside of the collar. Steam hissed into the warm afternoon air with the final plunge into the water barrel.

Pounding hoofbeats from an approaching horse team announced the arrival of the westbound Bain and Company stagecoach from San Antonio. Berg grabbed a nearby sheet of toweling to mop at his neck and face. He removed the leather guards he wore on his forearms, glad for the air on his skin. Curiosity drew him to the doorway in time to watch the driver halt the team in front of Othmann's Mercantile. Was this only a mail and supplies drop, or would the driver need his services?

From the corner of his eyes, he noticed movement from up the street and hoped for a glimpse of Miss Ivey. But Miss Maisie scurried from the boarding house toward the mercantile. Her braids flopped against her back as she fast-walked down the dirt road then hopped up to the boardwalk. *Must be checking the mail.*

Turning toward the water barrel, he leaned, grabbed out the finished implement, and wiped off the clinging droplets. The cool water felt good on his heated skin, and he anticipated taking a dip in the creek before supper.

"Hey, are you Spengler?" A man voice sounded from close by.

Berg edged backward and spotted the driver leading a pair of horses. "Yes, sir."

"Name's Henry Demmon, the new stage driver." He stepped into the doorway. "Each of these mares has a loose shoe. Can you put on a new shoe right away?"

"Sure, Mr. Demmon. One can be tied to the post in the middle and the other to the ring on the far wall." Berg hung the collar on the closest hook on the wall and moved to the black horse, running a hand over its damp back as he crooned. "Such a beauty you are." He eased his hand down the animal's front right leg, stopping on the fetlock to let the horse lift its own hoof.

"Mr. Spengler."

Berg jerked upright at the sound of the female voice. He turned and looked to where Miss Ivey stood in the doorway, one foot raised over the threshold, her

A COWBOY CELEBRATION

gaze flickering between him and the stage driver. "Yes, Miss Ivey?" He couldn't stop from glancing at the collar, then back to her.

"Oh, you have a customer." She looked down at a white porcelain dish decorated with pink flowers in her hands and then back in his direction.

"Good day, ma'am." Demmon lifted his hat and nodded then swung his gaze back to the blacksmith. "I need to speak to the man in the livery. Okay if I come back in ten or fifteen minutes?"

Ivey stepped all the way into the shop. "That's my brother, Penn. If you don't find him there, walk through to the corral. He mentioned currying the horses this afternoon."

"Obliged." Demmon walked outside and turned left.

Berg walked around the head of the black gelding so the animal wasn't between them. "I can explain about the missing pot."

"Missing pot?" She frowned and shook her head.

Well, he'd just spilled the beans about his little thievery. He fought to give her a convincing smile. "I needed it to make a new handle."

"You did?" A blush came up in her cheeks, and she looked around the shop, eyebrows raised. "That's so...thoughtful."

A pinch grabbed his throat, and he swallowed hard. She was so pretty and approachable, especially when she wasn't surrounded by everyone in her kitchen. He liked seeing her here, in his world.

"May I see it?"

He shook the silly notions from his head and moved toward the workbench. "Let me show you how to use it." He lifted the collar off the hook and placed it on the wooden surface. Then he set the pot in the open circle.

Ivey moved close and watched his movements.

For the second time today, he could smell a sweet floral scent, like the wildflowers in the fields when he took his solitary walks to the creek.

"There're two handles?"

"Right, for stability." He lifted the implement by the handles until it stopped at the lip of the pot. "This collar allows you to carry a hot pot to where you need it. The only time you're in danger of getting burned is when you insert the pot into the collar."

"That's ingenious." She turned and smiled, her blue eyes shining. "May I?" She reached to test the handle and brushed her fingers over the tops of his.

Berg almost closed his eyes at her light touch. How many times had he thought of them holding hands? *Too many for my own good.* He dropped his hands, stepped back, and watched her angle and tip the pot. She maneuvered it

41

well; the collar and pot combination worked precisely as it should. Now, if only his heart rate would slow to normal.

"Oh, Mr. Spengler, this is wonderful. I like the weight of the metal and"—she rubbed a thumb along the top surface—"the design is a nice touch." Her gaze lifted to connect with his for just a second and then dropped again. "Please, tell me what the charge is."

"None, this is a gift."

"Thank you." She smoothed a hand over the design one last time. "Seems today is a day for gifts. I have one for you."

Berg stilled. No one had given him anything since he'd left home at age sixteen. "What? Why?"

"I've spent years around hot stoves and ovens, and believe me, I've had my share of burns." Ivey set the ceramic dish on the workbench and lifted off the lid to expose a yellowish paste. "This is a salve I make and keep on hand for burns. I know you said your hands were tough, but I had to see for myself that blisters didn't erupt in the time since the accident."

She'd worried about him? A warm feeling settled in his chest. He extended his hands, palms up, and showed her that only a couple of tiny blisters had erupted. Nothing worse than he got from a flying spark when the hammer hit the hot metal. "See, still fine."

A gasp sounded, and Ivey grabbed his left hand. "Not true. There's a blister." She dabbed up a glob and smoothed it over a spot that wasn't much larger than a pea.

The goop stung before it soothed. "What's in that?"

"Beeswax, sweet oil and turpentine. Is the stinging bad?" She leaned forward and blew on the shiny spot at the base of his palm.

He'd put up with the mild ache with no complaints if she stayed close to minister in such a caring way. For the first time in a long time, Berg felt like his welfare mattered to another person. His throat tightened, and he didn't move, allowing her to fuss over him.

"You know, I learned how to make this salve from my granny who was a healer back in England."

"Hmm." He wondered if Ivey was aware she still stroked the area around the spot of medicine. Not that he minded—not one bit.

"Her house was in the middle of a thick woods, and she knew the use for just about every plant and tree growing nearby. I loved spending time there, wandering among the trees and hunting for this flower or that pod." She tilted her head and gazed at the coals. "I'd have a sketch of what she needed, and I'd

A COWBOY CELEBRATION

just keep looking until I found it. Like a treasure hunt."

The dreamy note in her voice drew him, and he wanted to share something of his past. One of the few happy memories.

"Ivey? Is that you?" A female voice sounded from the doorway.

"Oh." Ivey dropped his hand and spun in the same instant. "Maisie, you startled me. I'm just putting salve on Mr. Spengler's burn."

Berg stepped toward the horse and put his hand behind his back, to let the salve soak in. That's what he told himself. In truth, he curled his fingers to hold in her caresses.

Wearing a wide smile, Maisie waved a piece of stationery back and forth. "Dylan's coming for the Fourth of July celebration. He'll arrive on Monday, and he's bringing a stallion for Mr. Hawksen at Shady Oaks. But, of course, he'll be in town to see me." She rushed close and grasped her sister's hand. "And a friend of his is coming along. Wouldn't it be so much fun if maybe his friend escorted you to the activities?"

Ivey glanced over her shoulder, biting her lip. "I'll just leave the salve here for a couple of days. We'll let you get back to work now."

Hearing about the possibility of Ivey being with another man shot a chill through his body. "I appreciate you tending my blister, Miss Ivey." More than she could possibly know.

♥ ♥ ♥

As Ivey settled the last dry dish on the shelf, she couldn't resist running a finger over the wrought iron collar Mr. Spengler had made. The decoration he'd added had to be a sign of his personal interest. Didn't it? After all, twice in one day they'd been in a position to hold hands. Although, they hadn't done so. Not in the true sense of the act.

Tonight's supper had been a noisy event. Maisie was irrepressible over the news that her beau would arrive in a little more than a day. Fewer regulars were present because Olivia, Sally and Mr. Baklanov had left for the Golden Door Saloon. But several cowboys from outlying ranches were in town for their Saturday night revelry. That meant both double bunkrooms upstairs would be filled.

Ellen smiled and grinned now due to the extra coins in her money box. But she'd grumble at breakfast tomorrow about being awakened when the cowboys' boots clumped up the wooden stairs in the wee hours of the night.

"Ivey, Mama says time for the family singing." Lydia stood at the edge of the kitchen, twisting the end of her long strawberry-blonde braid.

Ivey couldn't stop the frown that settled in her brows. Thinking their

43

private conversations might make a difference, she'd been so hopeful when she invited Mr. Spengler to join them in the parlor after the meal. Maybe he felt their new and exciting connection. But just like every other Saturday night, he'd declined.

She pulled her thoughts from the blacksmith and said to Lydia, "Tonight, I want to hear you play."

"Oh, Ivey, do I have to? You're the most accomplished player."

"Flatterer." She laughed and rested her hands on her youngest sister's shoulders, turning her. "How will you ever improve if you don't practice?"

For the next hour, the sisters rotated playing popular tunes so the guests and family could sing together. "My Grandfather's Clock" followed "Carry Me Back to Ole Virginny" which rolled into the hand-clapping, thigh-slapping "Camptown Races." Because she couldn't fight the jealousy over the fact Maisie had a beau and she didn't, Ivey dug into the piano seat for the sheet music for the ballad "Remember Me." With the last chorus, she felt her throat getting thick. "Maisie, your turn to choose." Then she dashed out to the front veranda, hoping the cooler evening air would calm her turmoil. Off to her right, she heard a scuffling sound. "Who's there?"

"Mighty fine playing, Miss Ivey."

Squinting, she stepped away from the doorway and saw the silhouette of a familiar big man. "Mr. Spengler? Why didn't you join us inside?"

"I prefer to sit out here." He tapped a hand on the rocker made of tree branches and thick slats and set it moving.

Her father had made that rocker when the boarding house was new. He'd always complained her mother's parlor chairs were too dainty. As realization struck, Ivey sucked in a breath. Papa had been a big man, too. Was that why Mr. Spengler always refused her invitations? "Well, I'm glad you get to enjoy the music." Not even giving him a choice, she chose the chair next to his and sat.

"I do. Even tapped my boot in time to the ones I know."

"A chorus always needs a drummer." She smiled, not knowing if he could see it in the light shining through the windows. "I'm sure your percussive support was missed."

"No one misses a quiet brute like me."

"I wish you wouldn't speak of yourself like that." The part of her that needed to nurture everything around her ached when she heard such words.

"Just repeating what I've been told." The rocker moved faster now. "Since I was about ten, I've been bigger than others my age. Hardly seemed fair that I couldn't do the same things."

She noticed his low voice grew reflective and didn't ask him any questions for fear he'd stop with his recollections. Making sure to stare at the emerging stars, she rocked with a gentle movement.

"I told Arney to get on his own limb. Not my fault that stupid tree branch wouldn't hold us both. I was just a kid, too." He pounded a fist on the chair arm. "I shouldn't have been blamed for his busted leg or the resulting lameness."

Ivey blinked hard, willing her burning tears not to fall. This poor man had been estranged for a long time. At least now, he had the atmosphere of the boarding house to make him feel included. She wondered about a gesture to offer him comfort at this time. Inside the cookie jar were the last of the oatmeal cookies from Thursday's batch. Maybe a glass of lemonade, or would he prefer a cup of coffee?

Grumbling, he shoved himself to his feet. "Pay no mind to my foolish blathering." With jerky moves, he jumped to the street and stomped away into the darkness.

When she was truly alone, she let the tears fall for this giant of a man with a wounded soul.

Chapter Three

All during Sunday breakfast, Ivey stole glances across the table at Berg but he wouldn't meet her gaze. Sleep had been slow in coming the previous night because she kept running over in her mind what he'd shared about himself. And how he'd used so many words and such long sentences. That was the lengthiest conversation they'd ever had without being interrupted, and she savored what each statement revealed.

"Goodness, look at the time." Ellen stood and gathered her plate, silverware, and cup. "We must clear the table and get ourselves across town for church services."

"Mama." Lydia rolled her eyes and giggled. "You make the town sound so big. We walk to the corner and down two blocks, and we're there at the church."

Ivey stood and reached for the empty platter that had held eggs and bacon. "Remember, I'm meeting with the committee for the final details on the celebration. Most of the dishes for dinner are ready for you and the girls to heat up." She stacked the bread basket onto her plate and then added the butter dish to the top. "I should only be thirty minutes or so."

Everyone stood to make their way toward either the kitchen or the entry door.

Mr. Spengler stopped at her side and tugged the string tie at his thick neck. "Miss Ivey, will you allow me to escort you to the town celebration?"

Hearing his rushed words, she jerked and stared. Today, he wore a butternut-colored shirt that she hadn't seen before. His wavy hair was slicked close to his head, and the scents of coconut and custard wafted to her nose. If she wasn't mistaken, he'd used Macassar oil like Penn did on special occasions. She bit back a smile before speaking. "Why, that would be wonderful, Mr. Spengler."

"All right." He nodded and walked out of the room.

What a surprise. Gaping at his retreating back, Ivey shook her head and walked into the kitchen, although she doubted her feet even touched the floor. *I have a beau.*

Two hours later, the committee of six women settled themselves in the small living room of the parson's home. A divan upholstered in a fleur-de-lis pattern of beige and black was positioned along one wall where a painting of a

A COWBOY CELEBRATION

snowy mountain hung. Wooden chairs from the dining room faced the divan. The parson's wife, Gwynne Oswallt, set down the teapot on a low table next to a plate of sugar cookies. "Are we ready to begin, ladies?"

Ivey tucked her reticule at her feet and wondered which of the activities might be Mr. Spengler's favorite.

"Rhobert wanted everyone to know he has six good-sized watermelons for the melon eating contest." Gwynne looked at the pad of paper in her hand and made a check mark.

Alda Othmann, owner of the mercantile, lifted a hand. "I have the cloth strips ready for the three-legged races."

Beside Ivey, her friend Clari Rochester bounced in her chair, sending her reddish-brown curls bobbing. "Trevor asked me to make a starting flag for the horse races, and it's ready. Plus I've made the marker that goes around the tree at the halfway point."

Ivey leaned forward. "I've set aside two dozen eggs for the children's egg race. And my sisters and I are going blackberry picking tomorrow. That gives me plenty of time to make the six pies I promised. And Miss Fletcher asked me to report that she'll have her vanilla cake ready."

"My three Barbados cherry pies will make the dessert table of red, white, and blue items complete." Mrs. Oswallt held up her pencil. "Ladies, what did we decide at the last meeting about the foot races?"

As Ivey listened to the discussion, she realized Mr. Spengler wouldn't be comfortable entering any of the activities. All were aimed toward those who were fleet of foot or skilled on a fast horse. He would need a strength activity. She leaned forward, waiting for a break in the conversation. "What about a wood chopping event?"

Five gazes of various colored-eyes turned her way.

"Aye," Kathleen O'Hara, the town's laundress, spoke first. "I quite enjoy the sight of a brawny man with an axe."

"I'm not so sure." Mrs. Oswallt frowned and scanned her list. "Why change the activity roster at this late time?"

Ivey didn't want to call attention to her new interest but needed support for her suggestion. "Not all Americans honor Independence Day in the same way. I've read a few stories about different types of celebrations." She hoped for a nonchalant expression as she elbowed her friend who had a secret hobby of writing stories for dime novels.

"So true." Clari jerked and then reached for a sugar cookie. "I've heard Trevor talk about the logger competitions he and his brothers entered back in

47

Oregon. There's even a rolling contest where two men balance on a log in a pond."

Alda huffed out a breath. "Only stock ponds here in central Texas."

"I know just the place for the contest." Johanna Altbusser flashed a smile around the circle. She and her husband had volunteered a space on their ranch for the town's celebration. "Gerhard uses a couple of stumps out by the woodshed. I'm sure he'll be happy to supply the deadfall branches, as long as we keep what's been cut."

"That is small recompense for allowing us to use your pasture." Ivey couldn't hold back a wide grin. "I heard the barmaids from the Golden Door talking about Mr. O'Shea acquiring Roman candles for the festivities. Wouldn't that be wonderful?" A shiver ran over her skin.

Alda tsked and shook her head. "Those things scare me."

"Oh, Aunt Alda, the candles just make flashes of light and a little bit of noise." Clari waved a dismissive hand. "When I was a child back in Racine, my family would go to watch the fireworks display over Lake Michigan. They were like magic."

After a glance at the timepiece pinned on her dress front, Mrs. Oswallt stood. "I believe we have the day well planned. The parson and I have a call to make this afternoon at the Reynard ranch."

"Oh?" Mrs. O'Hara ran a hand over her skirt as she stood. "No one's ill, I hope."

"No illness, thank the Lord. Just a social visit to an outlying ranch." Mrs. Oswallt held her hands clasped at her waist and smiled. "See all of you on Wednesday at ten o'clock."

Ivey gathered her reticule and followed Clari from the room. They said their farewells in front of the mercantile, and Ivey walked on. Her mind raced with the idea of sharing the fireworks spectacle with a beau. *What a romantic idea.*

Around five o'clock, Ivey felt anything but romantic. Somehow, she'd forgotten to pierce the potatoes when she put them into the oven to roast. So instead of the split baked skins filled with a fluffy mixture of potatoes, cheese, chives and buttermilk, the potatoes would be plain old mashed tonight. No enough time remained for the oven to cool, so the remaining bits of burst potato on the oven walls and floor would smolder as the peach cobbler baked. She reached over the bowl of steaming potatoes for the wire masher, and her sleeve dragged against her skin. Pain shot from the underside of her wrist. A red blister had popped up where she must have touched the oven while scraping.

A COWBOY CELEBRATION

As she kneeled down to look under the sink for her tub of burn salve, she heard male voices on the veranda where her brother usually read on Sunday afternoons. Had Mr. Spengler joined him? She rearranged tins and cans around looking for the brown crock, each movement adding a stab to the throbbing blister.

"Maisie?" Penn called out as he came into the entryway.

Ivey leaned back on her heels. "She's visiting with Clari at the mercantile, I think." Then, she stretched her left hand to the far back, feeling for the crock, angling out her right leg for balance.

Bootsteps approached. "Well, sis, Dylan and his friend arrived a day early. He wanted to surprise her."

Surprise her? What about the cook? For just a moment, Ivey hung her head and pulled in a calming breath. Unexpected visitors right before a meal? Good thing, she usually cooked extra. She scooted backward and braced a hand to push herself upright, but was aided with a strong hand at her elbow. She turned and looked into the unfamiliar face of a very tan stranger. "Thank you."

"With much pleasure, ma'am."

Ivey turned to face her brother and the other visitor. "Good afternoon, Mr. MacInnes. Nice to see you again."

The tall dark-haired man pulled off his hat and grinned. "Same to you, Miss Treadwell. The gentleman still grasping your elbow is Gabrio Menendez. He's a cowhand on the ranch who wouldn't be denied when he heard about Comfort's celebration."

Stepping to the side, Ivey eased her arm from his hold. "Nice to meet you, Mr. Menendez. Welcome to Treadwell's Boarding House."

With a great flourish, Mr. Menendez swung his hat from his head and gave a sweeping bow. "*Mucho gusto, señorita.* I am very fortunate to have such a wonderful friend like Dylan who is willing to invite me along as his traveling companion." He smiled, and his dark eyes twinkled as he stepped closer. "I have heard many fine things about your cooking, and I look forward to tasting them all."

She couldn't help but return the jovial new arrival's wide smile. Well, this man certainly had no troubles putting his thoughts into words.

The back door opened with its accompanying squeak of the hinges.

With a gasp, Ivey whirled and connected with Mr. Spengler's wide-eyed gaze.

♥ ♥ ♥

Monday morning, Berg tramped through the wild, overgrown bushes that

49

edged the creek and grabbed another handful of blackberries. If he'd wanted to do an activity alone, he could have stayed at the smithy. But here he was in the hot sun picking berries to help Ivey, though they hadn't exchanged more than half a dozen words alone since they left town. That new guy, the one who wouldn't stop fawning over all the Treadwell women, hadn't let him close enough to Ivey for a private conversation.

If he didn't outweigh the man with the accent by a solid eighty to ninety pounds, he might be tempted to muscle his way close. But a stupid act like that would only cement his image as a brute. Had he misinterpreted the special moments on the veranda with Ivey on Saturday night? Was she sorry she'd agreed to attend the celebration with him?

"Hey there." A male voice hailed the group. "Where are you?"

"We're over here, Penn. Along the creek." Maisie bounced and waved a hand over her head.

Trying to evade Mr. Menendez's incessant chatter, Berg moved along the creek, grabbing the ripe berries as he went, and looked up to see Penn escorting Miss Olivia and Miss Sally down the slope. He caught a wave from Miss Sally and nodded in acknowledgement.

In the next minute, he realized the only sound he heard was the buzz of flying insects. *Such a relief.* He turned to where he'd last seen the group and spotted Mr. Menendez staring at Miss Olivia with his jaw dropped. *So that's what was needed to shut the man up.*

The bushes rustled and Ivey came into sight. "How is the picking over here?"

When had he begun thinking of her as just Ivey? When he decided to court her? Berg rattled his pail. "Fair."

She pulled several berries off the bush and then she glanced at him from under the bonnet brim. "The bushes over here could be stripped clean, and I'd still want to linger." Her lips twitched before she grinned. "Quiet enough to hear the hummingbirds. See, over there." She pointed and tilted her head.

Slowly, Berg turned his head and spotted a pair of green-blue birds not a rod away. The birds dipped their long beaks into blossoms of the purple plumeria and yellow Indian blanket plants. Their movements were synchronized, like they were dance partners and the beatings of their wings made the music. Before he had a moment to reflect on the meaning of that thought, he watched them flit away from the plants, hover, and then dart out of sight.

"Aren't they so graceful, like dancers?" Ivey gazed at the spot where they had disappeared, then turned to him with a smile.

He blinked a couple of times, absorbing that they'd shared the same thought. That had to mean something special. "I agree."

For the next thirty minutes, they moved up and down the creek bank, taking only the ripest berries. He picked a bit slower because he was content to watch her face as she worked. Once in a while, she hummed one of the tunes she played on Saturday nights, and he found himself echoing her at the parts he remembered. When needed, Berg offered his hand to help her climb the slope and passed off his partially empty can when hers became full. He'd be hard-pressed to remember a time of contentment in his adult life that compared equally with today.

"I think that's the last ripe berry I can see." Ivey dabbed a handkerchief over her face. "Shall we call this picking a success, Mr. Spengler?"

"Yes, I think so." He glanced at the flush to her cheeks. "Do you want to dip your feet in the water? It's real refreshing."

"I remember how good it feels from when I was a young girl. But how would it look?" She glanced over her shoulder and stretched to look for the others. "I don't know. The group is a ways distant."

He sat and tugged at the laces of his boots. "Well, I need to rest a spell. I might as well get some benefit. And the creek is my reward."

Tilting her head, she braced her hands on her hips. "I'd say a taste of blackberry pie will be a good reward."

Once his wool socks were off, he felt immediately cooler. He rolled up the hems of his denim overalls and then dunked his bared feet into the water swirling over smooth rocks. Ah, the sensation made him close his eyes and let out a long sigh.

The rustling of layers of clothes preceded the scent of Ivey's soap and her warmed skin. "Now I've got to experience what I'm missing." First, the bonnet was removed. She untied the laces of her over-the-ankle boots and eased them off. Next came her stockings, and then her dainty feet slipped into the water. "My, that's cold. But you're right, it's an invigorating cold."

Berg liked hearing the lighthearted tone in her voice. Sometimes, he worried about how much work she did to provide the meals. He knew how much stamina was needed to keep working in a heated space during the hot summer months.

Water swished and gurgled as they swung their feet against the current. Once, they accidentally touched the sides of each other's foot—an experience that he was sure brought color to his own cheeks.

She kicked her feet and giggled at the spray that the breeze blew onto her face. "I haven't felt this carefree in years. What a great suggestion this was." Then she leaned down, scooped up handfuls of water, and tossed them high. Jumping up, she held her skirts out of the water and waded a foot or so away.

Berg knew he should avert his gaze but what man didn't enjoy the curve of a shapely calf and the turn of a slender ankle?

"Uh-oh." Ivey stood rigid, her eyelids widening to show the whites all around her blue eyes.

"Is it a snake? Tell me where, and I'll get it." Berg jumped to his feet, grabbed the closest overhanging branch, and yanked it from the tree.

"Not a snake. But something is crawling up my leg, inside my…" She bit her lip and looked toward where the group was last seen. "Inside my unmentionables. Owww."

"What?" He charged into the water, scanning the surface for a snake. If it was a cottonmouth, they needed to know right away. "Talk to me."

"It stings. I think I've been stung by a bee."

"Show me."

She gasped and jerked her head. "I can't do that. Call for my sister. But hurry, this hurts." Her lower lip quivered.

That does it. "I don't know where they are." Berg swung her up into his arms and strode for the dry bank. "Penn! MacInnes! Help at the creek side!" He settled her on a rock away from the water. "We have to get out the stinger, Ivey. Which leg?"

The crashing of running footsteps grew louder. "Spengler, what's happening?"

Penn dashed up to them from along the water's edge. "Why are my sister's feet and legs bare?"

"We were dangling our feet and Ivey's been stung."

"Penn, where's Maisie?"

"She's already walking back to the house. I was almost to the back corral when I heard the yell." He crouched at Ivey's side and patted her hand. "What can I do? What would Granny use?"

"You're right. I'm not thinking straight. Look for either a plantain weed or wild garlic." She went on to describe the leaf shape and the color.

"Be back soon." Penn headed up the bank.

Berg pointed at Ivey's leg. "I'll turn my back but you have to expose enough skin to get to the stinger." He set his feet apart and angled his body so he was looking over the creek. "Make sure to get all of the stinger."

52

"Oh, this is so embarrassing. The sting's on the back of my knee and I can't see it."

"Are you asking for my help?"

"Yes."

When he turned, he saw she'd scrunched her eyes closed but her leg was angled to expose the back side. He dropped to his knees and saw the dark stinger against her pearly white skin. With his left hand, he pinched the surrounding skin and using the nails on his right thumb and pointer, he yanked it out. Close inspection showed it to be intact.

"Here, I was sure about the garlic." Penn jogged back and held out a thin green stalk with a bulb at the end. "Looks like you got the stinger."

"Berg did." She tossed her skirts over her exposed legs. "Crush a couple of cloves into a paste and then put it on the sting. Take one of my stockings, get it wet and then tie it around my leg to hold the garlic in place."

The men worked as a team and followed her instructions. Then Berg hurried to pull on his socks and boots.

Penn rinsed his hands in the creek and stood. "Can you walk, Ivey?"

"No need. I'll carry her back."

"That's not nec—"

Berg bent and scooped her up, cradling her high on his chest. "This is necessary. That poultice has to stay in place."

"Oh." After a moment's hesitation, she wrapped an arm around his neck and then pointed. "Penn, please grab my bonnet and shoes. Don't forget the buckets, too."

"Well, that bee sting didn't tame your bossiness any." Berg chuckled because he was relieved her injury hadn't been any worse.

She stiffened for a moment, and then she relaxed. The heat from her body blended with his, and a sense of contentment settled deep inside.

"You know, Ivey Treadwell, in some cultures, what just happened would mean we're betrothed."

Chapter Four

July 4, 1877 dawned sunny and the air heated as the sun climbed into the sky. During the past two days, Ivey had fluttered between numerous tasks in the kitchen, with barely a spare moment to think about the incident at the creek. Although her mother had plenty to say about the spectacle of *her* daughter being carried through the streets of Comfort. With her bare feet exposed, no less. Ivey chose to remember that walk as being the most romantic thing she'd ever experienced, and she'd hold its memory close to her heart forever. Besides, the swelling of the sting was down, and she barely noticed the sore spot unless she hit it against a chair as she sat.

Today, she'd worn a new blouse—white muslin with embroidered vines along the high neckline. The three-quarter length sleeves would hopefully keep her cool in the afternoon heat. She glanced at the clock and shook her head. *Never enough time.* The buttermilk-crispy chicken was still baking, but the rolls were wrapped in a cloth, and the potato salad filled the biggest ceramic bowl the household possessed. A jar of Mama's famous peppered pickles was tucked in the big wicker basket.

The back door hinges squeaked. Suddenly, Berg was there, filling the doorway with his solid size. "Good morning. Are you ready?"

Since the berry-picking day, she could only think of him by his given name. "Almost, Berg. Thank you again for bringing your horse and cart." A peek past him had confirmed a dappled-gray draft horse was hitched to the canopied buggy she'd seen him drive on occasion.

"An escort comes prepared." He reached to the side and lifted a tall, narrow box, framed on the longs sides with metal strips. "Here's a pie carrier." He set it on the bin table, turned the latch and opened it to reveal narrow shelves. Six, to be exact.

"Oh, my." Ivey scooted closer to examine the carrier. "I've never seen anything like this."

"I made it for today. Well, to be honest, Shipley provided the wooden pieces. But I gave him the specifications." He gestured toward the sides where the outline of a pie had been burned into the pale wood. Small holes were inset in the steam curlicues above the pie and along the base of the pie pan.

Ivey was thrilled and hoped her smile displayed her feelings. "Thank you.

Berg Spengler, you are a handy man to have around."

His huge body went rigid, and then a grin burst on his lips. "I like hearing that. Now, load up those pies and let me see if this is sized right."

"Didn't you steal one of my pie pans, too?" She pretended to be mad and narrowed her gaze as she crossed her arms over her middle.

"Remember, I like fiery things. Sassiness is another kind of fire."

His dark gaze connected with hers, and she felt it all the way to her toes. Turning, she hurried to the counter where the pies sat, covered with cloths. "Two more are on the sideboard in the dining room."

"I'll fetch them." Berg walked from the room, whistling.

Ivey sagged against the counter and pressed both hands to her cheeks. In such a short time, Berg had gone from a taciturn man to one who spoke his mind. What had she unleashed?

The holiday celebration was in full swing. Berg had helped Ivey deliver the food to the appointed tables and left her to picket his Percheron, Tier, with the other horses. Thankfully, Mrs. Treadwell encouraged them to wander around and enjoy the activities. Never had he felt so proud than when strolling the pasture with Ivey's hand tucked into his elbow. He acknowledged the men he knew with a dip of his chin and lifted his hat when Ivey introduced him to women. But he preferred their private moments of watching the children running a race while holding an egg on a spoon, or laughing together over the wildness of the watermelon eating contest.

Now, they'd moved to where folks were gathered to watch the horse racing.

"Are you sure you can see?" Berg positioned himself behind Ivey and had a clear view over her head.

"Yes, who do you think will win the race?" Ivey turned to look over the crowd. "I'm sure Clari and Maisie are close by, Clari is supposed to wave the start flag. I know both Mr. Driscoll and Mr. MacInnes talked about entering their favorite horses. Do you see them?"

Berg cringed inside. Ivey sounded so excited about this race, and he wished he was one of the entrants. Just to know she was in the crowd rooting for him would be special. "They're lining up now. Trevor's riding the black and Dylan's mount is the roan stallion he brought to town for Hawksen."

"Did I hear my name?" Kell Hawksen clapped a hand on Berg's shoulder. "Spengler, good to see you here."

Smiling, Berg turned and extended his hand. "Glad to be here today." The ranch owner of Shady Oaks had always been a good customer. He spotted the youngster with light brown hair and green eyes perched on Hawksen's shoulder had clamped an arm tighter around his papa's neck.

"Good afternoon, Kell." Ivey smiled up at the pair and reached out a hand to tickle the little guy's stomach. "Hey, Davin. You're getting so big. And wearing matching red shirts. Did your mama sew those?"

"Wait until you see Maeve. She'll be walking any day and then there'll be no stopping her." Kell chuckled.

With a pang that went straight to his heart, Berg realized what Kell described was exactly what he wanted—a wife and family.

"After the race, I'll have to find Vevina and see for myself." Ivey swung her hand that Davin had latched onto.

Just then a horn blew, and Parson Oswallt climbed up on a nearby tree stump. "Quiet, everyone. We're about to begin the horse race, and we want a fair start. The race is to the tree at the far edge of the meadow, around it, and back across this rope laid in the field. Miss Rochester, here, will drop the flag, and may the fastest horse win." He stepped down and held out a hand so Miss Rochester could climb up.

Clari held the red flag high and, with a last smile toward her beau, Trevor, she dropped her arm.

Six horses bolted forward and charged down the field. Berg admired the skill of the riders to guide their horses in a tight pack at a full gallop. Within seconds, the pack stretched out and after circling the tree, Trevor and Dylan vied for the lead.

In front of him, Ivey bounced and waved a hand in the air. "Come on, Trevor. Run, Blackie."

Her competitive spirit made him chuckle, but her enthusiasm was short-lived when Dylan's stallion pulled ahead in the last rod to take first place. They watched as the riders walked their sweating horses past Clari to receive the prize ribbons—blue for first, red for second, and white for third. Fitting prizes for today.

He leaned close to Ivey's ear. "Don't let your sister know you were cheering against her beau's horse."

Ivey glanced over her shoulder. "I know, that wasn't very kind of me. But I've met Blackie before, and I don't even know the name of Mr. MacInnes's horse."

"What's next?"

A wide smile spread her lips. "The event I've been waiting for all day."

56

A COWBOY CELEBRATION

He frowned but enjoyed the smile that made her blue eyes sparkle like the tips of flames in a forge. "I thought the race was the highlight."

"Nope. Next is a wood-chopping contest, and I entered you."

"Never heard of such a thing."

With a girlish giggle, she grabbed his forearm and squeezed. "Hurry and grab your axe from the buggy. I'll meet you near the wood shed over there." She pointed toward a small structure near the Altbusser's barn.

As he walked across the pasture, he fell in with others headed in that direction. For the first time in a long while, he didn't feel strange about being close with others. The Othmanns walked ahead of him and echoed his statement about the oddity of this type of contest.

"Don't you know? Ivey made the suggestion and Clari seconded it." Mrs. Othmann shook her head. "Says her Trevor competed in such contests out West."

Berg stopped. Ivey had done that for him? To make him feel part of the community? When he started walking again, he couldn't keep the swagger from his posture. He'd do his best to make a good showing—for her sake. By the time he retrieved his axe and hurried to the barn area, he saw quite a crowd had gathered.

Gerhard Altbusser, a tall wiry man with salt-and-pepper hair, stood atop one of the stumps next to the wood shed. "Folks, listen up. Competitors will have five minutes each, timed by my daddy's stopwatch." He waved the silver timepiece aloft. "We're looking for the man who chops these biscuits—precut by my ranch hands into stove-length round—into eight wedges each. Winner is the one with the most pieces within that time. No wedges are to be used, just axes and muscles. And before the contest starts, I want to extend my heartfelt thanks to all you young bucks for helping me get a head start on the winter's woodpile."

Laughter sounded from around the crowd.

Two names were called and the men who Berg recognized as hands on the Wallache ranch stepped up, axe handles held with both hands above their heads, stretching their muscles.

Gerhard held up the stopwatch then yelled, "Start!"

Berg moved to where he could see both men in action and watch their methods, and listened for their tallies. He did this with the next team, and noticed how Trevor compensated for his weak hand with making an initial chop on both sides. The last pair was called and he heard his name. He connected with Ivey's bright gaze and flashed a smile before stepping up to the closest

57

stump opposite Kell, acknowledging him with a curt nod. So far, 64 was the number to beat.

As he worked, he kept that number in mind. His strength allowed him to split the biscuit with a single blow, move the pieces a quarter turn, and repeat. Then four easy blows were needed to split the four wedges. The rhythm satisfied just like when he performed the task to replenish his own woodpile. Most people hadn't a clue the amount of wood a blacksmith used. With great effort, he kept a smile off his face while he worked.

When he heard Gerhard yell "stop", he could barely step for the pile of splits that surrounded his stump and his feet.

Ivey dashed up, beaming. "Oh, Berg. Look at all this."

Stepping away so the splits could be counted, he grabbed a bandanna from his back denims pocket and mopped at his forehead, finally allowing himself a satisfied smile. "It's nothing. I do this much chopping every week."

Shaking his head, Kell snorted. "Figured as much. Well done, Berg."

People milled about waiting for the official announcement, but everyone knew who'd won.

Gerhard climbed onto the stump and put his fingers into his mouth and whistled. "The winner is Berg Spengler with 96 splits, second place is Jake Adley with 80, and third is Trevor Driscoll with 72. Gents, collect your ribbons."

When he turned with ribbon in hand, Berg spotted the pride on Ivey's face, and his chest pinched. He wanted to always see that light in her eyes. The woman was as special to him as his next breath. His mouth dried, and he could only nod when she came up beside him, chattering away with compliments. But he knew she didn't mind his silence, and he was content to just have her at his side.

Hours later, Berg lay stretched on his side on one of the blankets belonging to the Treadwells. Ivey approached and set down a tin plate brimming with his meal.

He glanced at the chicken pieces, pickles, potato salad, corn and green beans. "Now, tell me what you made and I'll taste it first."

She sat, with her feet to one side and arranged her skirts before lifting her plate and pointing with her fork. "The crispy chicken and the potato salad came from my kitchen. Oh, and those are Mama's pickles, so be sure to compliment her."

Berg eyed the uniform chicken. "Why are the pieces the same size?"

"I deboned the pieces. Penn trapped a half-dozen prairie chickens so I could

A COWBOY CELEBRATION

choose the meatiest parts to use."

He took a big bite, and the flaky crust crunched in his mouth and the meat was tender and juicy. "Must be something special about this, because I taste a tang."

She shrugged. "I went back to the garlic patch Penn found and collected a bunch. So there's garlic mixed with the buttermilk that I soaked the meat in before I drug the pieces through the flour and bread crumb mixture. Plus some pepper, chili powder and mustard powder."

"Another recipe with ground mustard, huh? I'm learning to appreciate the flavor."

"The preparation took longer than regular fried chicken, but I like not worrying about bones." She tilted her head and smiled. "I also like how much you want to know about the dishes I concoct."

"Do you write these down? You should make a book of these."

Ivey stopped chewing and stared, wide-eyed. "Me, write a cookbook?"

For several minutes, they ate in silence, each lost in their own thoughts.

Vevina Hawksen rushed up, baby Maeve balanced on her hip. "Have you seen Davin and Timmy? I thought they be with Kell, but he just came back to the blanket without them."

Berg jumped to his feet and headed to where a group of men gathered.

Heart pounding, Ivey dropped her plate on top of Berg's and stood. "Don't worry, Vevina. They'll be found. They are probably playing with friends. Who might that be?"

Vevina shook her head, loosening wisps from her strawberry-blonde braid. "On the ranch, they just be having each other as best buddies. And the ranch hands, of course."

"Have you checked with Trevor or Jake?" Ivey rubbed a hand over the fretful woman's shoulder as she scanned the faces of the men in the group. Trevor and Jake were both there. Her stomach pinched.

The men split up and headed outward to cover all directions, yelling the boys' names.

From behind the house a small boy came running. Ivey recognized the red gingham shirt from earlier in the day. "Look, there's Davin." She pointed to where the men now raced. *That doesn't look good.*

"Here, take the baby." Wide-eyed, Vevina put the little girl in Ivey's arms, lifted the front of her skirts, and ran across the field.

Compelled to see what was happening, Ivey followed, walking as quickly as she could. Little Maeve must have sensed the tension because she started

59

wailing and holding out her arms to her fleeing mother. "You're all right, sweetie. We'll catch up in just a minute or two." When that didn't soothe the child, Ivey started singing a happy tune and put an extra bounce in her steps.

When she reached the house, Ivey heard someone call out that the boy had fallen into the well. Then, she spotted Berg run from the direction of the picketed horses with a rope slung over his shoulder. *What is he doing?* Her heart raced. *Surely, he's not going down the well.* She hurried forward, making her excuses as she pressed through the crowd, barely recognizing anyone's face.

Berg stood like he was carved from stone, the rope tied around his waist and looped over a shoulder, holding the rope taut.

Vevina sat on the stone edge, reaching a hand down toward her son. "We'll get you out, me brave boy. Don't move."

Timmy's frightened cries echoed within the round shaft.

Kell balanced on the top of the well, tying the other rope end around his waist. "Push back against the wall, Timmy. Papa's climbing down to get you." Hands grasping the stone edging, he lowered his feet over the side. "Ready, Spengler?"

Berg braced his feet a few more inches apart. "I am."

Kell moved over the side, his boots scraping against the stones.

Ivey circled to the opposite side of the well and leaned down to see how far Kell had to climb. Timmy was on a rock approximately a couple of rods down. She glanced up and shouted, "Berg, watch my signals." She raised her free hand and waved him closer. Each forward step Berg took dropped Kell lower. When she saw him draw even with Timmy, she moved her hand palm out and connected with Berg's gaze.

His shirt over his shoulders and arms strained from the bulged muscles beneath. Sweat ran down the sides of his face.

But that mountain of a man never wavered. He was a true hero. She felt pride and love build in her chest and clog her throat.

"I've got him. Pull us out." Kell's deep voice seemed to fly from the well.

Ivey glanced at the crowd and spotted her brother. "Penn, grab the rope and help."

Penn and Mr. MacInnes stepped to the rope and grabbed on. Slowly, on Berg's command, they backed up, and moments later, father and son appeared at the top of the well. Vevina scooped up her boy and smothered him with happy tear-drenched kisses.

Silently cheering Berg with her proud gaze, Ivey watched as the crowd

Second Chance at Love

By Agnes Alexander

A temporary living arrangement might not work when love enters the mix.

Cora Hilliard was upset, but she didn't want Doctor Kerry to know. She'd been his nurse for over six months, but she still didn't completely understand the man. Most of the time he was kind and efficient, but occasionally he'd fall into a melancholy mood. She was sure it was because he still grieved for his wife who had been run over and killed by a runaway horse and wagon. She'd heard that the doctor's wife was a lovely woman, and everybody in Rocky Ridge had liked her.

The door of the examining room opened and she looked around from the medicine shelf where she was placing the rolled bandages. Miles Kerry walked in and she couldn't help noticing his shoulders were slumped, and he had a grim look on his face. She feared the worst, but she asked, "How were things at the Claytons?"

He removed his Stetson, held it in his hand, then shook his head and dropped to one of the chairs beside the patient examining table. "The baby died about six o'clock this morning."

Cora moved beside the doctor. She had the urge to put her hand on his shoulder, but she didn't dare. "I'm glad you were there with the family. That way, they knew you did everything you could."

"I don't know, Cora. Sometimes, I think I'd rather be anything than a doctor. When one of my patients slips away, I feel like a failure." He looked up at her. "Are you and your son alright?"

"So far, we are." She didn't mean to add, "But I don't know what I'm going to do with him now."

"What do you mean?"

"Mrs. Miller told me this morning to find somewhere else to stay. I think she's afraid he'll get the fever and spread it to everybody else at the boarding house." She sighed.

He frowned. "That wasn't very Christian of Sadie Miller."

"I guess it wasn't." She forced a smile. "You look like you could use a cup

63

of coffee. I'll get you one."

He nodded and stood. "I'll be at my desk."

In a matter of minutes, Cora brought him a steaming cup of coffee and a piece of bread spread with butter and jelly on a plate. "I figured you hadn't eaten anything."

"You're right, I haven't." He gave her a wry smile. "By the way, where did you get homemade bread?"

She set the food and the coffee on the corner of his desk. "Things were kind of slow this morning, so I went into your kitchen and made the bread. I hope you don't mind."

"Of course I don't. I think it was a wonderful thing to do."

She smiled at him. "If you need anything else, let me know."

"Thank you, Cora. I will."

Cora picked up the hat he'd tossed on a chair and hung it on a peg beside the door as she went out. She then returned to her job of storing the medical supplies. As she worked, she couldn't help comparing her former husband to the gentle doctor. Though she'd thrown him out of the house when he beat their ten-year-old son almost to death, she knew Melvin Hilliard would have probably come after her if he hadn't been killed the next day during an attempted stage robbery. Melvin had never been much of a provider, and Cora had worked as a nurse in the Denver hospital to support herself and her son. After Melvin died, she wanted to keep her son from having to deal with the stigma of having an outlaw for a father, so she decided they would move away. When she saw Doctor Miles Kerry's ad in the Denver paper for a nurse to work in the small western town of Rocky Ridge, Nevada, she answered and was hired. Now that she'd worked here six months, and had a chance to see what a good man he was, she hoped she'd never have to look for another job to support herself and Koby. She figured asking God for a second chance at love would be asking for too much.

After finishing the medicines, she moved to the front desk. She supposed there would be people coming in, and she knew the doctor would expect her to greet them. She got out the ledger Miles had entrusted her to use to keep up with the accounts and began figuring out the expenses they'd had so far this month.

A short time later, the bell over the front door jangled and she looked up. "Good morning, Sybil."

"Hello, Cora. Is the doctor in?" Sybil Kingman, the eldest daughter of the family who owned the town's only hotel, walked up to the desk.

A COWBOY CELEBRATION

"Yes. Are you feeling poorly?"

"No. It isn't me. My brother, Gary, is getting sick, and Mama wanted me to come and ask the doctor to come by. Like everybody else, she's afraid it's the fever everyone is getting."

"Oh, dear. I hope not."

"So do I."

"I'll tell Doctor Kerry right away."

"Thank you, Cora. I'm sure he'll come to the hotel when he can, so I'm going to hurry back. I'm trying to help out as much as I can."

Cora got up from the chair and headed to Miles's office. She tapped lightly on the door, but there was no answer. Frowning, she eased the door open.

Miles was slumped over his desk, sound asleep. She noticed he'd eaten most of the bread and jelly and had finished his coffee. She hated to wake him, but she knew she had no choice. He'd want her to.

"Doctor Kerry," she said softly.

He didn't respond, so she said it a little louder. This time, he stirred. After calling one more time, she saw him open his eyes and yawn.

"I must be awfully tired. I didn't mean to go to sleep."

"After being up most of the night, you needed it."

"Is somebody here to see me?"

"Sybil Kingman came by. Seems the little Kingman boy is beginning to feel sick and his mother is afraid he's caught the fever."

"Oh, Lord, have mercy on us. I was hoping soon there'd be fewer cases of this fever." He stood and picked up his medical bag.

"Do you want me to come with you?"

"No. I can take care of it alone." He strode toward the door. She followed.

At the front door, he turned. "Cora, while I'm at the Kingmans', go back to Millers' Boarding House and pack your bags and get your son."

"What?"

"You heard me."

"Yes, but where are we going?"

"You're going to bring him here, for the time being. We'll talk about the next step later."

"But..."

"Don't argue. I can't let that woman put you and Koby out on the street, and knowing Sadie Miller, she'd do it, too."

"But what will people say if we stay here?"

"The hell with what people say. The health of your son is at stake." He

65

didn't wait for her to say anything else as he closed the door behind him.

Cora stood there for a long time, not sure of what to do, but after thinking it over, she knew Miles had offered her a way out of her dilemma. She squared her shoulders, put the "closed" sign in the office window, and headed to the boarding house to get her son.

When she and Koby returned to the doctor's house, he looked up at his mother and asked, "Why are we seeing the doctor? I'm not sick."

"I know you're not, honey, but you know how Mrs. Miller is. She was afraid you'd get the fever everyone seems to be catching."

"I feel fine. I thought I'd go see if Gary wanted to go fishing today. He said the other day that he wanted to go sometime this week."

She didn't want to tell him Gary might be getting sick. "We'll have to talk about that later."

"Mama, you act like you're hiding something from me. What's going on?"

"I'm sorry, son. I know I rushed you out of the boarding house, but Mrs. Miller was hurrying me." Cora chuckled. "She was worried about getting sick."

Cora took a deep breath and motioned to the bench in the doctor's office where patients usually sat as they waited. After they were seated, she said, "Now, I want you to listen to me and listen good. Out of the kindness of his heart, Doctor Kerry has said we can stay here until we find a suitable place to live. He has never had children, so he's not used to having one around. I want you to promise me that as long as we're here, you'll be good. I'll be very disappointed with you if you aren't."

"What would he do, Mama?" Koby asked. "Would he beat me like Papa used to?"

"Koby, your father wasn't a good man, but Dr. Kerry is a very nice one. He'll not beat you. Besides, if you remember, I promised you after your papa beat you the last time that nobody would ever beat you again."

"I remember."

The office door opened and the doctor stepped out into the waiting area. "What's this I hear about me beating children?"

Koby's eyes got big and he muttered, "Nothing, sir."

"I'm glad, because I don't want it spread around town that I beat the young ones. When they misbehave, I think it's a more fitting punishment to hang them by their ears on the clothesline. That's how my parents punished me."

"Really?" Koby's eyes grew larger.

"Sure. Look at this." Miles turned his head sideways and touched the top of his left ear. "See how crooked this ear is? It's a lot worse than the other one,

A COWBOY CELEBRATION

because when I was really bad, they didn't hang me by both ears. They only pinned me up with the left one."

"How long did they leave you hanging?" Koby whispered.

"Oh, sometimes it would be for a day or two. But if I was in real trouble, they'd let me hang there for as much as a week."

Koby frowned and whirled toward his mother. Her eyes twinkled and she was trying not to smile. He then turned back to the doctor who was also forcing back a smile. He gave the doctor a sheepish grin. "You're funning me, aren't you?"

Miles laughed. "Of course, I am, son. I try to keep all the children in town well and happy. I'd never think of punishing one. Though, I admit, there are a few in the area who could use a little swat on the behind now and then. But that's a parent's job. Not mine."

"For a minute I believed you," Koby said.

"Why, child, how could you believe a tale like that?"

Koby laughed out loud. "I only did for a minute."

Miles turned to Cora. "I talked with Kingman about you staying in the hotel, but we decided it would be better if you stayed away from there for a while."

"But…"

"As I said before, you're welcome to stay here. There are two bedrooms upstairs. The one at the end of the hall will be just right for Koby. You can sleep in the larger one."

"Koby can sleep on a cot and we'll only need one room. We've been doing that at Mrs. Miller's."

"That won't be necessary here. I have a room here on this floor where I often sleep. That way, if I have to tend patients during the night, you can come down and help me without disturbing Koby."

"If you're sure."

"I'm very sure. Now, why don't you go on upstairs and get settled in? Then, if you don't mind, you can use the kitchen down here to fix something for you and your son. I bet you haven't had dinner."

"How about you?"

"I'll grab a bite of something."

Cora stood. "No, you won't. You're kind enough to give us shelter. The least I can do is prepare the meals while we're here. I'm not a half bad cook."

"All right, Cora, if you insist on cooking, so be it. It would be good to have a hot meal now and then."

67

She nodded. "Let's get our things upstairs, Koby. Then we'll all help in the kitchen, and in no time, we'll have dinner on the table."

Within a week, things settled into a routine. The doctor went about his rounds and looked after patients, as usual. Koby went to school and either came home or spent some time with Gary Kingman, who had only had a cold and not the fever. They'd go fishing, or as they said, "just play around." Cora did her job and cooked their meals, and like everyone else in town, hoped this fever thing would end before May and June passed and July was upon them. July the Fourth was a big celebration in Rocky Ridge, and the whole town was praying for the disease to go away before then. Cora had never been involved in a celebration on the Fourth, but now that she seemed to be putting down roots in Rocky Ridge, it would be fun to join in the festivities.

On Wednesday, Cora saw the last patient out the door then returned to her chair behind the desk. She coughed and grabbed for her handkerchief. She'd had this cough and runny nose since waking up this morning, but she didn't feel she could let the doctor down and stay in bed. There were too many patients, and somebody had to be in the office to regulate access to the doctor, or they would all try to get to him at once. Now, the day was over, and she could relax. Maybe with a cup of hot tea. That always helped when she had the sniffles.

"Well, Cora," the doctor said as he walked into the front office, "I'm glad to be through with those who came in today. Now, I guess I'd better go check on some of the ones who are laid up at home. Thank goodness, there's not as many as there were. I think this malady is beginning to subside."

"I was getting ready to make some tea…" A cough interrupted what she was saying.

Miles frowned. "Are you alright?"

She nodded. "Just a bit of a cold, I think."

He walked to her desk and took hold of her chin, turning her face to him. He frowned again. "Come in my office and let me check you, Cora. I can tell by touching you, you have a fever."

"It's just…"

"Don't argue with the doctor, nurse. Come along."

Cora followed him into the examining room and submitted to his checking her over.

After the examination, he shook his head. "Cora, I want you to go straight to bed. I think you have more than a cold."

"Could it be—"

"I'm not sure, but from what I've learned, this illness starts with a cough and a fever. I hope I'm wrong, but we can't take any chances."

"Oh, Doctor Kerry, what about my son?"

"Don't worry. I'll see he's taken care of, but I don't think I'll let him be with you until we know what's wrong."

"But..."

"Don't argue. Now, get yourself to bed. I'll make the tea you wanted and bring it up to you."

"You don't have to bother. Koby can do it."

"Not this time. I'm not letting him come into your room until we find out what you've got."

She didn't argue, because she knew he was right. Koby didn't need to be around her until she was safe. She nodded and turned toward the hall leading to the stairs. It would feel good to lie down, even if the doctor was being too cautious. It could be a cold, after all.

As she started up the stairs, Koby came around the corner from the kitchen. "Mama, you don't look like you feel good. What's the matter?"

Cora straightened her back. "I'm just a little tired. Doctor Kerry insists I go to my room and rest for a bit."

"I thought I heard voices here." The doctor came into the hall. "Koby, your mother has worked too hard and I'm having her go to bed so she can get some rest."

"Want me to come and help you upstairs, Mama?"

"No," Cora and the doctor said at the same time.

Koby frowned. "Why not?"

"Cora, I think he has a right to know. You go on to bed and I'll explain it to him."

Cora nodded and went up the stairs. When she reached the landing she paused and listened to what the doctor was saying.

"There's a possibility your mother has contracted the sickness that's going around." The doctor's voice was gentle. "I don't want you being around her until we're sure."

"No. I don't want Mama to have it."

"Neither do I, but one thing's for sure; if she does, we're going to take good care of her so she can get over it quickly."

"You'll let me help you look after her, won't you?" Koby sounded doubtful.

"Yes. I'll let you help me fix things for her like tea and such, but I can't let you go into her room. Only I'll go in there. You can talk to her from the door, but only when she feels like talking. She's going to need a lot of rest."

"Well, I guess that's something."

"Maybe we better get in the kitchen and make some tea, then I'll take it up. I'll come right down and tell you how she's doing."

"Thank you, Doctor Kerry."

Cora sighed when she heard her son and the doctor move away from the foot of the stairs. Koby would be fine, and she trusted Miles to look after him. She moved down the hall and put everything else out of her mind as she looked forward to getting in the soft bed.

After Koby left for school the next day, Miles checked on Cora, then left to make his rounds in town. The last place he visited was the Gibson house. He left there with a smile on his lips. Their daughter was making a remarkable recovery, and it looked as if everything in that household was going to be fine.

He was passing the hotel when he saw Hattie Kingman sweeping the boardwalk. She said, "Hello, there, Miles. How're things going?"

"Things are fine, Hattie. Looks like the fever is on its way out of town and people are beginning to look forward to the coming months."

"I hope so. I'd sure hate it if we had to cancel the July Fourth celebration."

"I'm sure that won't happen."

"I hope you and Cora can keep things under control until then."

"Until today, Cora has been a lot of help to me. She handles the patients who walk in as well as I can."

"What do you mean, 'until today'?"

He sighed. "She came down with the fever last night. I've put her to bed."

"Oh, my. What about Koby?"

"He's fine. Been helping me keep the examining rooms clean and even helps with the cooking. I thought it best to keep him busy so he wouldn't worry about his mama."

"Would you like to send him here? I wouldn't mind, and I know Gary would love it."

"Thank you, Hattie, but I think he wants to stay close to his mother."

"I have an idea, Miles. When you think he needs to get away, why don't you send Koby here just to spend a little time with Gary? I'm having a hard time keeping him in since he turned out just to have a cold. He's almost well now. A visit will be good for both of them."

"Then, if he'll leave his mother, I'll let Koby come visit."

The next day, Miles placed his hand on Cora's forehead and her eyes popped open. She whispered, "Do I still have a fever?"

"Yes, but it seems to be coming down." He turned to a pan of cool water, wrung out the wash cloth and placed it on her head. "This is going to help it along."

"Is Koby behaving?"

"Of course. After he gets home from school, he's been helping me in my office and the examining room. Sybil Kingman came by to lend a hand in the front."

"Sybil's a nice young woman."

"Yes, she is. Everything's under control downstairs. Now, you lie back and rest so you can come back to work soon. You're missed."

She gave him a weak smile. "That's good to know. I wasn't sure the patients even liked me, the way they act sometimes."

"They're not used to being as organized as you have the office running. Besides, they're not the *only* ones who miss you."

She looked confused. "Oh?"

"Until you got sick I didn't realize how much I depend on you." He patted her arm. "I'm so glad you came to work here."

"I love working for you, Doctor Kerry. I've always loved nursing, and feel I'm really doing what I was meant to do in life. Coming to Rocky Ridge was one of the smartest moves I ever made."

"I think it was a good move for me, too." He took a deep breath. "As I said, you need to get some rest. I'll come back and check on you later this evening."

She closed her eyes. "Thank you."

Miles didn't say anything. He just watched her drift off to sleep and wondered what had happened to his thinking process. Why was he attracted to this woman? After all, he was forty-two years old. He'd had a wonderful wife, and he still missed her. He should be happy with his memories, but lately, they hadn't seemed to be enough. Things had changed only a few days ago. He could pinpoint it to the day Cora moved into his house with her son.

Yes, Cora Hilliard was a lovely woman and she was a good nurse. Well, not just *good*; she was *excellent*. She could diagnose a sickness almost as quickly as he could. Add that to the fact that she was efficient. She could accomplish a lot in a day. She proved this by the fact that she often cooked a delicious evening meal, as well as kept his office and the other rooms neat and clean. She was also a wonderful mother, and Koby adored her.

Why couldn't he simply appreciate all these things about her? Why was he sitting here picturing himself in this bed with her? Why did he have a sudden urge to lean down, take her in his arms and kiss her fevered lips? What gave him the right to want a second chance at love?

Before he could make a fool of himself, he stood and eased out of the room. He knew he had to watch his step, or she would guess he was having these crazy notions about her. That would never do. She might decide to quit and go back to Denver. If that happened…he'd be devastated.

At the bottom of the stairs, he turned toward the front office. Pausing in the door, he watched as Sybil carefully entered a patient's name on the sign-in book so they could be taken in order. There were three people waiting to see him.

"I'm ready to see the next patient," he said in his business voice.

Sybil grinned and looked at the pad. "You can go in, Mrs. Winsor."

"Come on in the examining room, Mrs. Winsor." Miles held the door for the one woman in town he felt sure was a hypochondriac. "What seems to be your problem today?"

"I want to be sure I ain't gettin' this fever thing. My neighbor has it, and I've heard it's awful catching."

"That, it is. Have you been with your neighbor?"

"No, but the wind blows from her house to mine and I was afraid the wind would blow it to me."

"Well, have a seat and let's see if you're in danger of catching it from the wind."

After a quick examination, Miles said, "Well, Mrs. Winsor, it looks like the good Lord is looking after you. You have no signs of the fever, but I found you're a little under efficient in your stamina. I'm going to give you a tonic that will take care of that. If you're afraid of the fever being blown to your house the only thing you can do is to keep your windows closed and only go into the back yard. I would use the back door instead of the front."

"Oh, thank you, Doctor Kerry. You're the best doctor in the world. I knew you'd know just what to do for me. How much do I owe you?"

"The regular fifty cents is plenty, Mrs. Winsor. You can pay Miss Sybil as you go out."

"I thank you again. I feel those fifty cents I give you every time I come are well spent." She stood. "I hope I won't have to come back any time soon."

A COWBOY CELEBRATION

"Take care of yourself and you won't have to." He opened the door for her and ushered her out.

Sybil came running into the room. "A man's been shot at the saloon. They're bringing him in."

Two cowboys came in, one holding the young man's shoulders and the other holding his feet. They deposited him on the table the doctor indicated.

"What happened?"

"There was an argument in the saloon and this fellow lost. The sheriff will be here as soon as he gets the shooter locked up," the taller of the two cowboys said.

The doctor nodded and took a quick look at the wounded cowboy. "Looks like the bullet's still in his side. Help me get his shirt off."

After the wounded man was undressed, the doctor said, "You two wait out front. Sybil, will you help me?"

"If I can."

"Wash your hands and put on that jacket over there."

"Yes, sir."

It didn't take the doctor long to get the bullet with one of his long probes. He glanced at Sybil. "Not gonna faint on me, are you?"

"I hope not."

He chuckled. "I forget sometimes that the public is not used to seeing all this blood."

"I'm sure your nurse could do a much better job."

"Cora could have done this without me."

Sybil smiled. "I see."

Miles frowned. "*What* do you see?"

"Only that Cora is special to you."

"Of course she is. She's the best nurse I've ever seen."

"She's a nice lady, too."

"Yes, she is." He glanced at her. "I've got his wound clean. Hand me the bandage—"

The door opened. "Well, I see you have a new nurse, Miles."

Miles looked up and saw the sheriff enter the room. "Come in, Ross. And yes, if Sybil ever decides to leave the family business at the hotel, I'd be more than happy to train her as a nurse."

"Sybil never ceases to amaze me with the things she can do."

Sybil blushed and changed the subject. "If I remember correctly this is the cowboy you had in jail a while back, didn't you, Sheriff Buckhorn?"

73

"Yes. He's the son of some rich man who's bought a ranch east of town."

"Well, he's a lucky man. If the bullet had been an inch closer to the liver, he wouldn't make it," Miles said.

"What happened?" Sybil looked at the sheriff.

"He was accused of cheating in a card game. When he tried to draw his gun, the gambler shot him."

"Did he cheat?"

"Probably."

"Well, he's patched up for now, and if you'll help me get him into one of the rooms where I have a bed, I'll try to get to my other patients."

"Is there anything else I can do to help you, Doc?" Sybil asked.

"You might check him occasionally. He'll probably wake up in a little while and try to get out of bed. He needs to stay still so he won't open up the wound again."

"Should I sit with him?"

"How many people do I have in the waiting room?"

"There were three when I came back here."

The sheriff butted in. "There are still three."

"Then, I guess I'd better see them."

Two days later, the man with the gunshot wound was picked up by his father. The doctor didn't think he should be moved, but his father insisted on taking him. There was nothing Miles could do but let him go.

After they left, Miles headed out to check on his other patients that couldn't get to the office.

Koby came into the entry. "Where did the doctor go?"

"He's gone to make his rounds to see the sick." Sybil stood. "I figure he'll be tied up for a while. Why don't you and I go and see what we can find to make for supper? I'm sure everyone is getting hungry. We've all had a rough day."

"I think I'll go check on Mama."

"Didn't I hear the doctor tell you that he'd check on her when he got back?"

"Yes, but he's not here. Somebody needs to check her now."

"Then, I'll do it."

"But you might get sick, Sybil."

"I don't think—"

"Doc lets me talk to her through the door."

"Then, you may come with me, but only as far as the door."

It turned out neither them talked with Cora. She was fast asleep. Instead, they went to the kitchen and cooked some beef with stewed potatoes.

"Let's cook some corn," Koby said. "Doc likes corn."

Sybil smiled at him. "Then we'll cook some corn for Doc."

By the time everything was finished, the doctor came back.

"You didn't have to do this, Sybil."

"I didn't mind. Koby was hungry and I thought you would be, too."

"I am, a little. It's been a busy day."

"How are your patients?"

"Doing pretty good." Miles smiled at her. "Why don't I look in on Cora and then we'll eat. We can talk then."

A big smile crossed Miles Kerry's face when he looked in on Cora and saw her smiling back at him. "Well, you look like you're feeling much better."

"I am. I feel so good, I think I'll get up and come downstairs."

"Are you sure you're able?"

She chuckled. "I'm sure. After all, if I start feeling bad, I have a reputable doctor in the house."

His eyes twinkled. "I guess that's true, and I'm sure you wouldn't have any trouble getting him to look after you."

She was a little embarrassed by his words and changed the subject. "Seriously, Doctor Kerry, I'm sorry I left you in the lurch. Has Koby been a bother to you?"

"Not at all. Sybil Kingman came to help in the front office, and Koby has kept the examining rooms clean." He grinned again. "I think he has an interest in medicine, which is good."

"He has been asking me a few questions, too, but I don't want him to get in the way of your work."

"He hasn't. I enjoy having him with me. It's a pleasure to see his curiosity about a procedure, and I want to encourage him in pursuing that interest."

"Just as long as he's no bother."

"He won't be. In fact, he's been a big help looking after the patient we had staying downstairs."

"Oh? What happened?"

"A young cowboy got shot in the saloon. It was touch and go for a while."

"How is he doing now?"

"Better, I hope. His pa came and took him home. I hope it didn't tear open everything I did."

"I'm sure you did such a good job that he'll be fine."

"Thanks for the compliment, but you never know."

Cora shook her head. "It doesn't look like I'm needed around here at all."

Miles took her arm. "Are you serious? You're the person who keeps this office running as it should. It wouldn't be right around here without you. Besides, I'd miss you more than you can imagine."

"Well, that does make me feel better." She moved to the side of the bed. "It does my heart good to know I'm needed."

"I don't know what I'd do without you, Cora. You bring not only reassurance to our patients, but you always have a nice smile for me…and I like that."

She blushed and wasn't sure what to say, so she changed the subject. "Then, if you'll excuse me, I'll get dressed and come see what kind of mess the two of you have made downstairs."

He nodded. "Alright, I'll let Koby know you're coming down, but you have to promise me you won't overdo."

"I promise."

He looked as if he wanted to say something else, but didn't. He only gave her a small smile and left the room.

For a minute, Cora sat on the bed and stared at the closed door. Why did she get the feeling Miles had implied more than his words said? Did he only miss her presence in the office, or did he miss her being there with him? Could it be possible he was saying he really needed her, not only as a nurse, but as a woman… It was exciting to think there could be the possibility he actually missed her on a personal level. But was she only getting her hopes up that he was a little interested in her?

She bit her lip. She knew she'd let him know she thought he was a wonderful doctor, but had she somehow let it slip that she also thought he was a wonderful man? A man that made her heart pound a little harder every time he stepped into the room. A man who she watched when he didn't know she was observing him. A man who she wondered how it would feel to be in his arms. A man she secretly wanted to notice her as a woman—not just a nurse.

Stop it, Cora Hilliard. Doctor Kerry has been good to you and Koby. What you're feeling is only gratitude. Get romance off your mind. You'll be thirty-two years old on your birthday. It's time you accepted you'll never have another man in your life. Now, get your mind off the doctor, and go downstairs. Koby's missed you, and you've missed him.

A COWBOY CELEBRATION

Moving as quickly as she could, she got up from the bed and dressed. Maybe seeing Koby again would help her accept how her life would be from now on. No matter what, it was a good life. Being a nurse and a mother were respected occupations, and she could make herself content with that. She had to. There was no other choice, and she might as well quit dreaming about something that could never come true.

♥ ♥ ♥

On Friday, Miles couldn't help being happy there were no patients waiting to see him. Cora was busy in the kitchen, and Gary Kingman had come by earlier. Koby hadn't wasted any time getting his fishing gear together to head to the creek on the edge of town to spend some time with his buddy. Miles smiled to himself. It was as if they were a real family, with each one busy with their own pursuits, knowing they'd gather together again at the supper table. It made him feel good inside, but he wasn't sure how much longer it would last. Now that the fever had all but subsided in Rocky Ridge, Cora had hinted that she needed to find another place for her and Koby to live. Lord, how he hated to see them go. His life would be like it was when he lost his wife. He'd be left drifting from one day to the next without knowing or much caring what he'd do. He knew he'd see her every day she worked, but it wasn't the same as having her and her son in the house all the time.

Sighing, he decided he might as well catch up on some of his reading. They were always coming up with new procedures in medicine, and he liked to keep himself informed as much as he could when he had the time. It looked like today would be a good time to do some catching up.

He'd put most of the papers he'd received from his medical school back east on the top shelf of the bookcase in his office. Pulling the step-stool over, he didn't notice he'd placed it on an uneven board in front of the almost ceiling-high bookcase. When he stepped up on the stool, it wobbled and tipped to one side. He instinctively grabbed toward the bookcase, sending books crashing to the floor as he fell.

The next thing he knew, he was lying on his back in the middle of the floor and Cora was bending over him. She patted his face with her cool soft hand. "Please wake up, Miles," she said in a frightened voice. "I need to see if you've broken anything."

He couldn't respond, but he liked the sound of her voice and the feel of her hand on his face.

"Mama, is he hurt bad?" Koby sounded concerned.

"I don't know, honey. I hope not." She continued to pat Miles's face.

77

"I hope he's not hurt too bad. I like Doctor Kerry."

"I like him, too, Koby."

And I like you and Koby, too. He wanted to say it aloud, but his mouth didn't seem to be working.

"I don't think there are any broken bones. It looks like he just bumped his head and knocked himself out."

"Will he die, Mama?"

"No, honey. He's not going to die, but I bet he'll have one bad headache when he comes to."

"Good." Koby laughed. "I don't mean about the headache. I mean that he's not going to die. Mama, I like it here. I want you to marry Doctor Miles so we can be a real family."

Cora stared at him. "What are you saying, child?"

"Oh, Mama. You know my real pa was…mean to me—and to you! But Doctor Miles acts like he likes me. Do you think he likes you enough to marry you so he can be my new pa?"

"Oh, honey. Miles has been so kind to us, but marriage is a big step, and I'm not sure he'd want that—"

"You don't know, Mama. Have you asked him?"

"Of course not! A woman doesn't ask a man such things."

"Why? Don't you like him?"

"Yes, Koby, I like him a lot."

"Then why don't you marry him?"

"I *can't* marry him, honey. He hasn't asked me to."

"If he asked you, would you marry him?"

"Yes, Koby. I'd marry him if he asked me. In fact, I wish—" She broke off quickly. "Shh. Don't say anything else. I think he's waking up."

Cora was stunned when the first words Miles said were, "There's nothing I'd like more than to marry you, Cora Hilliard. Will you be my wife?"

Koby grinned from ear to ear

♥ ♥ ♥

Later that evening Cora came into Miles's office with two cups of coffee. "I thought you might like to have coffee with me."

He smiled at her and took it. "I sure would." He took a sip. "Is Koby asleep?"

"Finally. He was so worked up it was hard to get him to settle down."

"Well, it's not every day that he learns he's going to get a stepfather."

"No, it's not." She took a chair beside his desk. "I never dreamed he'd be so ecstatic about it, but I'm glad."

"I'm overjoyed he's so happy." Miles reached out and took her hand. "I just hope his mother is as happy."

"His mother is thrilled. She never dreamed she'd be lucky enough to marry again, much less to a man she loves."

His eyes twinkled. "I love you, too, Cora. You're the most desirable woman I know, and I want you as my wife as soon as we can arrange it. I realize I'm not a young, handsome man, but I'll be a good husband. I'll love you, and I'll take care of you and your son as long as I live."

"I know, Miles and I appreciate it, but that's not the reason I'm marrying you. Not only are you the most kind and gentle man I've ever known, but you must understand that, to me, you're one of the handsomest. A man who makes my heart flutter every time I look at him and a man who makes me think thoughts I haven't permitted to enter my mind in years. Some of those thoughts aren't so pure, but—I can't help it."

He took a deep breath and almost whispered, "Then Miz Cora Hilliard, I suggest we make plans to get married right away, because I'm having an impure thought about you and me right this very minute."

Before she could reply, there was a loud banging on the front door.

"Damn. Of all times for an interruption." He shook his head. "Must be an emergency this time of night."

"Let's go, Miles. It's our duty." She stood and reached for his hand.

When he opened the door, he saw Baily Odgon standing there. He knew the fifth Odgon baby had decided to make an appearance.

"I'll get your bag, doctor." Cora gave him a knowing smile and turned.

When she returned with the bag, he took it and squeezed her hand. "I'll be back when I can."

When he returned the next morning, he found Cora working on a ledger at the desk behind the small partition in the reception area. He couldn't help the smile that crossed his face. He couldn't wait to make her his own. After losing his first wife a couple of years ago, he never dreamed he'd be happy again. He felt he was so old no woman would ever love him, but Cora did. She didn't care that he was forty-two. She simply loved him as a man, and she'd showed him in many little ways. Soon, she would show him as his wife.

She glanced up and asked, "Why are you staring at me?"

"I'm merely letting your beauty sink in, and I can't help wondering why a woman with your looks settled for an old has-been doctor like me."

"You silly man. You know I don't know what to say when you come out with things like that. All I can answer is that I love you, Miles Kerry, and I'm looking forward to being your wife."

"And I love you right back. I can hardly wait for the day we say our vows."

She grinned. "I'm glad of that."

He walked around the reception table, pulled Cora to her feet and kissed her on the cheek. "I was thinking on the way home from the Ogdons' today. What do you think about us getting married at the Fourth of July celebration?"

"That's a wonderful idea." She put her arms around his waist. "I have the most wonderful future husband in the world."

"Now, who's saying silly things?"

He didn't answer. He simply lowered his mouth to hers and gave her a passionate kiss.

"Yuck!" came from the door leading into the hall behind the front room.

They laughed and broke apart. Miles looked at his soon-to-be stepson. "You might as well get used to it, my boy. I love your mother and I intend to let her, you, and everyone else around know it."

Koby shook his head. "I think everybody already knows. Everybody is talking about it."

"Where have you been, Koby?" his mother asked.

"After school, Gary and me went down to the creek and did a little fishing. I brought six back with me. You wanna to cook 'em for supper?" He sounded hopeful.

"Fresh fish will be tasty." His mother looked at him. "Did you clean them?"

Koby came into the room and looked at his mother. "Not yet. I thought maybe Doc would help me. He's good with a knife."

Miles put his hand on Koby's shoulder. "I don't see why I can't help you. Are they big enough to make a meal for all three of us?"

"I think so."

"I hope you're right. You know a hungry man can eat a lot of fish."

"Ah, Doc." Koby grinned. "Let's go clean them. They're in a bucket in the back yard."

"Did you catch all of them yourself?"

"Nah. Gary caught three and I caught three, but he said he didn't want his three 'cause they wouldn't cook such a small amount at the hotel."

Cora butted in. "Don't make a mess, Koby."

Miles shook his head and grinned as he followed Koby down the hall and then veered to the right where the kitchen was located. "Something smells good

A COWBOY CELEBRATION

in here. It looks like your ma has already got supper started."

"Good. It won't take her so long to get everything done. I'm hungry."

Miles ruffled the boy's hair. "Son, you're always hungry."

They had about half the fish cleaned when Koby looked up at him and said, "I like when you do that."

"Do what? Clean fish?"

"No." He giggled. "When you mess up my hair like you did."

Miles was touched, but he kept his voice even when he said, "I'm glad, because I was afraid it made you mad."

"Oh, no it don't. My dad never did nothing like that. If he touched me at all it was with the back of his hand or most of the time, it was with his belt."

Miles wondered what Koby had been through, but he didn't want to ask. He knew he hadn't been in the boy's life long enough to gain his complete trust, but he wanted to keep doing it slowly. This was the first time Koby had talked to him like this. He didn't want to say the wrong thing. "Koby, you do know I'd never hit you like that, don't you?"

"When we first come here to stay, I thought you might be like my pa was." He laughed again.

"What's funny?"

"I remember how you told me you didn't believe in hitting kids, but you punished them by pinning them to the clothes line by their ears."

"I think I recall saying that. You believed me for a bit, didn't you?"

"Yeah, but only for a minute. But then I knew you were funning me."

They had finished the fish, put them in a pan of water and carried them into the kitchen. Cora was waiting there. "Looks like you boys did a good job. As soon as I get these fried, we'll eat. In the meantime, Koby, would you go lock the front door and put the closed sign in the window?"

"Yes, ma'am." He trotted off toward the front room

Miles walked up to Cora and put his arm around her. "Ah, a minute alone with my beautiful woman."

"I do declare, Miles. How do you expect me to cook when—"

A yell came from the front office.

Miles took off in a run. Cora was on his heels.

The doctor turned cold inside when he saw a heavy-set cowboy standing in front of the desk with a gun drawn on Koby. The boy looked terrified.

"What's the meaning of this?" Miles shouted.

"I want my son."

Miles stared at him, then turned to Koby. "Son, come over here with your

81

mother. She's going to take you into the kitchen while I deal with this man."

"She ain't taking the kid nowhere."

"Do like I say, Koby."

Koby ran to his mother's open arms.

Cora hugged him to her, glaring at the man. "What do you want?"

"I want my son, ma'am. Where is he? In your examining room?"

"Couldn't you have asked that question without pulling a gun on a child?" Miles continued to stare the man down.

For a few seconds, the cowboy looked a little embarrassed, but it passed. "Where's my boy?"

"You're pitiful, Gaston."

"How do you know my name?"

"Not only are you a coward, you're slow in the head."

Gaston turned his gun on Miles.

Cora let out a little scream.

Koby squirmed away from his mother and ran up beside Miles. "Don't you shoot my pa, you big, fat, ugly old man! He ain't done nothing to you."

Though Miles was trying his best to figure a way out of the situation, he didn't miss the fact that Koby had called him his pa. He couldn't help feeling proud. He cleared his throat. "I know your name because I treated your son when he was shot in the saloon. You came in here throwing your weight around and demanding your boy go home before he was ready. Who would forget the name of a man who acts like you do?"

"And you've treated him this time, too. So where is he?"

"I haven't seen your son."

Gaston's eyes narrowed. "You're lying." He looked toward the boy. "What he'd do with him, kid?"

Koby moved closer to Miles. "I don't know."

"I told you I haven't seen your son."

"I don't believe you. He has to be here. He was shot again, and where else would he go?" Without warning, Gaston slammed the gun in his holster and yelled, "I'll see for myself. Get out of my way."

"If you wanted to look in the examining rooms, why didn't you just ask?" Miles turned to Cora. "Dear, please take Koby out of here."

Cora didn't hesitate. She put a hand on Koby's shoulder and ushered him out.

"Now, Gaston, if you'll come this way, you can look in the main examination room, and the spare ones."

After searching not only the rooms the doctor used for patients, Gaston searched the kitchen, the pantry, then the bedrooms upstairs, with Miles shadowing him. When they got back to the front entrance, he turned to the doctor. "He's not here, but I'd bet my last penny you know where he is."

"Then you'd be a pauper, Gaston. I haven't seen your son, and furthermore, I don't care to ever see him again. He was nothing but trouble when he was here, and I suggest you get out of here."

Gaston didn't say anything, but he turned on his heels and stomped out the door.

Miles watched the man leave his house. He then turned and walked into the kitchen. "It's all over. He won't be back."

Cora ran to him. "Thank you for your cool head. You saved our family."

Koby put his arms around both of them. "You're the best pa in the world."

Miles felt as if his heart was going to burst out of his chest, he was so happy.

The next day, word came that the Gaston boy was killed when he tried to break into the hotel. It seemed he'd been intrigued with Sybil Kingman and had planned to kidnap her.

Sheriff Ross Burkhorn happened to be checking doors at the time, and caught the man half-in and half-out of the hotel's front door. A gunfight ensued and young Gaston lost. Nobody had bothered to come for the doctor. The body was immediately sent to the undertaker.

In a matter of days, the Gaston family sold their spread and left the area. Nobody seemed to care.

The July Fourth celebration finally arrived. Cora put on her best dress, and Miles wore his usual suit and tie.

The three of them climbed in the buggy with the box of food Cora had made and headed to the creek that ran behind most of the town, where the tables and games had been set up.

Miles grinned at Cora. "You've sure got something in that box that smells good."

Cora smiled. "I know how you and Koby like to eat. I made extra."

"That doesn't tell me what you cooked."

"Oh, it's just the usual. Chicken, beans, bread—and a surprise."

"The *surprise* is what I'm interested in."

Koby broke in. "It's a cake, Pa. She only makes it on special occasions, so I guess this is one."

"Oh?" Miles looked at Cora.

"What woman *wouldn't* consider her wedding day special?"

"I know it's special," Koby put in, "'cause I'm going to get to spend the night with Gary tonight. Thanks for saying 'yes' when they asked you if I could, Mama."

"You're welcome, son."

Miles brushed her shoulder with his. "Now that we know you've made a special cake, tell me what it is?"

"Oh, alright. It's one my mother used to make during the holidays. It's called a Knee-Deep Dried Apple Stack Cake." He frowned, and she went on. "It's made of thin cake layers with an apple mixture between each layer."

"Sounds good. I like apples."

"I know. That's why I make so many apple pies."

"What possessed you to make this knee-high thing today?"

"With twelve layers, it's a tall cake, and—I—well, I thought since it was such a special day, it would serve as a wedding cake."

"Hey, there, Koby." Gary came running up to the buggy. "It's about time you all got here. We can't start the games 'till your ma and the doc get married."

"Hear that, Pa? Let me get out. I'll run the rest of the way with Gary and tell them you're coming."

The buggy stopped and Koby climbed out. Cora and Miles watched as the two boys ran toward the waiting crowd.

"Well, sweetheart, shall we hurry along so our friends and family can *really* celebrate the Fourth of July?"

"Yes, Miles. Let's hurry. I'm anxious to start celebrating, too."

"So am I, but I bet I'm looking more forward to the celebration that awaits us at home tonight."

Cora blushed. "Miles. You shouldn't talk like that."

"I can't help it. There's three things I want to do today."

"Oh, what's that?"

"I want to celebrate with everyone here to show I support this wonderful country of ours, then I want to eat some of that knee-deep cake, and last of all, I want to go home and close the door and make love to my beautiful wife."

Cora blushed again and would have agreed, but they had reached the picnic area.

"My goodness, Cora," Hattie Kingman said. "You need to come sit in the shade a minute before you pass out. You're as red as the strawberries on the table."

Cora nodded and followed her friend, after looking back at Miles.

He was grinning, and before she turned around, he winked at her and reached to get her box of food to carry to the table.

The ceremony was simple, but Cora and Miles wouldn't have had it any other way. They were hugged and patted and served a mountain of food. Cora's cake was a big hit among the desserts, and though it was a huge twelve layers, it disappeared quickly.

There were horse races, three-legged races, a pie-eating contest, target shooting, and many other games, but the highlight was the fireworks.

As Cora and Miles headed for home, she leaned on his shoulder and said, "It was a wonderful day. How many women can say she had fireworks for her wedding day?"

"Those aren't the only fireworks, my love."

"What do you mean?"

"As soon as I get over the fact that I didn't get any of our knee-deep wedding cake, we're going to start making fireworks of our own."

Cora giggled and held to his arm. "If I promise to make you a knee-deep cake all your own, will you start lighting the fuse?"

He stared down at her and laughed. "Cora, I can't believe you said that."

"Why not? I happen to be in love with my husband, and I want to show him how much."

"I'll meet you in our room as soon as I put up this horse and buggy."

"I'll be waiting."

And she was. She was sitting on the side of the bed wearing a lovely silk nightgown. A gift from Hattie Kingman, she said.

Miles leaned down and kissed her as he began to unbutton his shirt. She reached up to help him.

In a matter of minutes, they were in each other's arms. Their kisses were passionate, and his need became obvious against her.

"Oh, Cora. I didn't think this night would ever come."

"But it has, and we're here together. Oh, Miles, I pray we'll never be separated again."

He lifted her up in his arms and lay her on the bed. Bending over her, he let his hands roam up and down the body he'd wanted to possess, hardly believing he'd have her tonight.

A loud pounding sounded on the front door.

A look of concern crossed Cora's face. "Oh, no. Who could that be?"

"Surely, nobody would bother us tonight."

"Unless something terrible had happened."

"You're not going to relax until I see what's happening, are you, Cora?"

"It could be something about Koby."

Miles stood and slipped into his pants then grabbed his shirt. "I'll be right back."

Cora stood and put her arms in her robe. "I'll come with you."

When Miles opened the front door, a young man of about fourteen with panic written on his face stared at him. "Are you the doc?"

"Yes, I am. What can I do for you?"

"It's my pa. He fell out of the barn and almost tore his leg off. He needs a doctor bad."

"Where is your father, son?"

"Out at the ranch. We was afraid to move him. Will you come and see to him?"

Miles glanced at Cora.

She smiled at him. "I'll get your bag, dear."

"While I get ready, son, how about going to the barn in the back and hitching up my buggy? I'll be ready by the time it is."

"Yes, sir." The young man bounded off the steps.

Miles looked back at Cora. "I'm sorry, honey, but you know I have to go."

"I know, and don't be sorry, Miles. I knew things like this would happen if I married a doctor."

"Don't give up on me. Please be here when I get back."

"I'll be here with my arms open, waiting for you, Miles. I love you, my husband. Now, come, and let's get you ready to go. Make sure your bag has the things you'll need in it."

"I love you, too, Cora. I always will."

The boy appeared with the buggy, and Miles was ready and waiting on the porch. He slid his arm around Cora and kissed her lips. "I'll be back as soon as I can."

"I know." She watched him climb into the buggy and head out of town. She couldn't help smiling. Miles was such a good man. Though their wedding night hadn't ended the way she wanted it to, she knew there would be many nights to follow.

In the distance, she heard firecrackers, and knew the celebration was still going on. She might as well celebrate this second chance God had given her and her new husband. She closed the front door and headed to the kitchen. When Miles came home, she'd see that he got his other two wishes. The Fourth of July celebration had been all she could have asked for—not only celebrating their great nation's freedoms with him and their neighbors, but also becoming his wife. She began to gather the ingredients to make another Knee-Deep Dried Apple Stack Cake. This time, they'd share it, even if it was for breakfast!

And the other—that last wish he'd voiced? She smiled. They had a lifetime ahead of them to spend together…a second chance at love for them both.

About Agnes Alexander

Agnes Alexander's first Western Historical Romance was published in 2012. She now has 9 published and has another one under contract. Second Chance at Love is her first short story in this genre. Her website is www.Agnesalexander.com

Brighter Tomorrows

By Beverly Wells

A tale of fate, new beginnings and a recipe for love: Mix one distrustful, scorned woman with a widowed marshal riddled with guilt, add potent desire, two generous dollops of trust, stir in a sinister bank robber, and you have everlasting love.

Chapter One

Hallings, Wyoming Wednesday, June 28, 1882

Three years ago he'd proudly visited the bank to draw money and left devastated and heartbroken. This time he'd be tickled pink as a swine wallowin' in a foot of muck to sashay inside and kill a man.

So engrossed was he in his musing, Chase Matlock's long, even strides across Main Street had barely stirred up the dust when he made the mistake of glancing upward. His booted footfalls froze and his chest tightened until he gasped for air.

Dammit all! He'd warned himself not to look up until he reached the stoop. He had thought he had prepared himself for the gut-wrenching dread when he cast eyes upon his worst nightmare. But no way in holy hell had he anticipated this cannon blast to his heart, soul, and mind. Only by the grace of God did he remain upright before all six-foot-three of him toppled into a crumpled pile of mush on the sun-baked, hard dirt.

The building looked the same. Most likely, the inside hadn't changed; other than the blood from the victims who had been at the mercy of malicious outlaws.

He willed himself to relax, knowing he had to keep a level head and strong determination to finish the job. Three long, frustrating years; this time was way past due by his calculation.

He nodded to the building as if greeting a long lost acquaintance, letting him know that he would finally set the wrongs to right. And he would, by God, or he would die trying.

Descending the stairway from the second floor, Callie whisked the kerchief from her head and sighed in relief as the weighty confinement of her hair spilled down her back. As her foot touched the floor, the front door bell clanged several times.

She eyed her paint-spattered, tattered dress, her fingers covered in a lovely shade of sage. *Lord love a duck!* Whoever it was might either die of fright or laugh themselves silly. Despite her appearance, she hurried. She would never be so rude as to not answer her door and possibly discourage future business.

Opening the door, she smiled a warm greeting—and nearly swallowed her tongue. The tall stranger was one very handsome man. He had the brightest blue eyes she had ever seen. Sparkling and compelling. Her embarrassment skyrocketed, knowing she looked worse than a complete slob. When his eyebrows arched, she realized her hair must resemble a flying witch's mop. *Heavenly saints, put me six feet under.*

"Good afternoon. Are you Miss Lynch?"

She longed to bury her head under the hall runner. Swallowing down the lump in her throat, she squeezed the kerchief. "Yes. I'm Callie Lynch."

Removing his Stetson, he held it in one hand and tipped his head in greeting. "Name's Jonathan Tate, and I'd like a room—if you have one available."

Hoping to disguise her embarrassment, she offered a tentative smile to the dark-haired stranger. "I'm very sorry Mr. Tate, but I'm under renovations. I'm not taking in boarders at this time. The Hotel Royale is a lovely hotel." She regretted refusing any boarder, especially one so pleasing to the eyes. She might be resistant to any man's charm, but she appreciated a handsome face and well-muscled physique.

He tapped his Stetson against his thigh, and compressed his lips. His intense eyes scrutinized her through the screen. "Miss Lynch, I'd greatly appreciate you allowin' me to stay here. I prefer your house to the hotel. I'm willin' to pay you double. Promise to stay out of your way."

Stymied by his extravagant offer, suspicion flared. Why her house? At double the cost? His gaze remained steadfast, yet far from threatening. If he wanted to rob her, he'd be disappointed. She kept her money in the bank. Her curiosity enthralled her to no end.

"Your offer is appealing, but the paint fumes are strong. I have drop cloths everywhere, curtains down, and ladders up. Besides, I've no time to fuss with meals three times a day. You'd be much happier at the Royale."

"Miss Lynch, I see I'll have to convince you otherwise."

Callie stiffened in defense. If it wasn't for his slight grin, she would've slammed the door and bolted the lock. Instinct told her there was no threat.

"You see, you'd be helpin' the law by lettin' me stay here. And I need to stay here so I can walk the main road several times every day without people wonderin' why. If you'd come outside so we can talk, we could discuss it further. Talkin' through the screen is a bit difficult if you don't mind me sayin' so."

She winced in embarrassment. Her inquisitiveness spiked tenfold. "I beg your pardon, Mr. Tate. I hadn't thought our conversation would be so lengthy. Please, make yourself comfortable on one of the chairs. I'll gather us some lemonade and won't be a minute."

"That won't be necessary. I need to talk to some other people shortly, so if you wouldn't mind coming out, we could talk, quick like, Miss Lynch."

Beneath his unbuttoned suit jacket he wore a holster with a gun resting low on each hip. But those twinkling blue eyes and smile held no malevolence. He had mentioned helping the law. That had to count. She would hear him out, then send him on his way and her life could return to normal.

As she pushed the door open, Chase opened it further. Good manners were called for. Once she sat, he wiggled his butt in the wicker chair to readjust the thin cushion. Obviously the pad had been fashioned to suit a slighter person. Miss Lynch wasn't necessarily small, maybe five-eight, and nicely rounded in all the right spots, but hardly equaled half his weight. And she was as leery as a doe facing a double-barreled shotgun.

Chapter Two

They faced each other across the small wicker table. "Mr. Tate, let's cut to the chase to make it simple. Why is it necessary for you to stay here?"

His eyes twinkled and a slight grin surfaced, as if he found her directness humorous. For five years, Callie had strengthened her backbone, lived by her rules, and valued friends above all else.

He nodded and leaned back. "For the time being, I need to keep my true identity a secret to everyone, other than the few in town who know who I am and why I'm here. I'll tell you if you'll give me your word you'll not divulge anything I say until my job is finished."

Nothing existed that was more intriguing than a secret—and a plot to go with it. That's why Callie's one vice in life consisted of reading dime novels with suspense, twists, villains and the heroes who saved the day.

She took a calming breath. "I assure you, if it's not against the law, and you said I'd be helping the law, I certainly won't divulge your name or purpose. Please, do tell, Mr. Tate."

He scrutinized her. Was he judging her words for merit? "It's been a long time since I've gone by 'mister'. It's U.S. Marshal Matlock—Chase Matlock."

She let the words, title, and enormity of it all sink in. *Holy smoke and cows jumping over the moon!* She had been telling herself she needed something in her humdrum life to add a bit of zing. Who would have thought something as deliriously tantalizing as a marshal on a covert mission in her town would fall in her lap? *Thank you, Fairy Godmother!*

She started to speak and stopped before she let go a roaring 'whoop-de-doo'. She composed herself. "You need to stay at my home because…"

"Outlaws are goin' to visit the bank soon. I need to scout the town several times a day to listen, see if others are joinin' them, and set up plans with my team without the locals questionin' why I'm meanderin' around town too often. That's what could happen if I stay at the hotel. If I stay here, no one will think twice about me comin' and goin'."

Her mind whirled like a cumulative cyclone, yet sounded like music to her ears. She'd have extra money, be aiding the law, and have a fine time watching this plot unfold.

He'd be underfoot—*he'd be out most of the time.* It'd be inconvenient to fix him three meals—*she had to eat anyway.* He was far too handsome to have around—*she was profoundly immune to any good-for-nothing species of the male gender with their overly-excitable libidos, a viper's tongue, and mush for brains.*

As exciting and tempting as it sounded, she curbed her adventurous side. "Marshal, I'd like to help you, but I don't see how you can stay—"

"I believe I can stay here very easily, Miss Lynch." The slight grin before blossomed into an incredible smile. Her heart might be hardened, but she definitely appreciated the raw sensuality of this man. No man alive should be this attractive…

"But—"

"No buts about it." He leaned forward. "I'll shoot straight with you. Don't mind paint odor, tarps, and I'm willin' to fix my meals or offer a hand to help. If I ate at the restaurant or café all the time, someone might wonder. I'll stay out of your way, and with any luck, I'll be on my way within a week. And I will pay you double for the trouble. What do you say?"

Silence hung in the air as she lost herself in his incredible eyes. His handsome face, square chin, broad shoulders and wavy black hair weren't bad, either. As far as his trying to charm her? Trusting a man or having faith in him enough to open her heart was as farfetched as her jumping over the moon. It would not happen.

"What do you say, Miss Lynch?"

"Since you're paying double, I'll cook your meals. They'll be filling and wholesome, but they'll be simple. As far as meal times, we can decide each morning, depending on our schedules, if you like. My barn only holds my horse and wagon. The stall is fairly big and Freedom is a sweetie, but I don't believe she'd share space. Is that a problem?"

He pushed back his chair and stood, and darn if that smidgeon of a grin didn't make her smile. "I knew I could count on you. Sounds fine. The livery will be fine." He stood tall and straight like a towering pine. "By the way, as Jonathan Tate from Texas, I'm a land speculator and investor lookin' to buy parcels or invest in potential enterprises. I'll grab lunch at the café, then see David Millett and his deputy before checkin' around. I can grab supper tonight at the restaurant, if it's too much bother."

She admired his large hands as he fingered the rim of his Stetson. His suit coat gave him a business-like appearance, while the denims hugged his thick thighs. "I'll bake a chicken. You do like chicken?"

"I like anything as long as it doesn't move or talk back. What time's supper?"

She calculated the time to finish upstairs, fix supper, and look half-way clean and presentable. "How's six-thirty or seven?"

"Let's say seven." With that, he turned and strode across the porch, down the three steps, and across the front lawn to where he untied his big, chestnut gelding at the hitching rail. Lithely, he mounted and glanced her way. "See you at seven, Miss Lynch."

The café's greasy beef stew wasn't so bad as long as he reminisced about his meeting with Callie. Pretty thing, even covered in paint splatters. He chuckled as he pictured her looking in a mirror. Would she blush when she saw green smudges on her face? Or howl when she saw her rat's nest?

He sipped his coffee. Though he knew he'd never love again, he still appreciated a lovely woman. He admired her direct attitude, her gumption. He liked that she hadn't batted her eyes or acted coy. When females flaunted themselves, he ran as fast as his legs or horse could carry him.

♥ ♥ ♥

Securing the reins in front of the Hotel Royale, Chase peered across the stoop. He nodded to the man leaning against building. Matt Tremayne's lanky six foot frame belied his rough, tough persona while his fair features and persistent smile gave his recruit in training a younger look than twenty-four. When it came to bluffin' the bad guys, Matt appeared innocent and a harmless bystander.

People milled along the stoop. Matt ambled toward the sheriff's office, as planned, while he strolled around the side of the hotel and toward the rear entrance of the same destination. A man could never be too cautious.

Chapter Three

Callie had one big fearful question for the marshal. She had to know. She prayed it was a coincidence as she placed the utensils on the dining room table. Golden brown chicken and mashed potatoes sat in the warming oven while green beans simmered. She heard him come in and go into the parlor.

Brushing down the folds of her apron as she passed his Stetson and gun belt hanging on the hall tree, she entered the parlor.

He stood, feet apart, arms at his sides, and stared out the large front window. At the swish of her skirt, he spun around.

"Miss Lynch, good evening. I hope I haven't rushed you." His eyes lacked the previous sparkle. She missed that slight smile. Should she blurt out her question? Would he think her insincere?

"Good evening, marshal." She gave a welcoming smile. "You didn't rush me at all. Everything is ready, but can be kept warm if you'd enjoy a drink before dinner. I keep whiskey on the credenza for the gentlemen," she nodded to the right, "so please help yourself."

My stars! That devilish gleam in those bright blue eyes accompanied by a cheeky grin held her spellbound. A lightning bolt couldn't be more potent.

"Thank you, Miss Lynch. If you don't mind, I prefer one after dinner—if I have one at all."

Finding that he rationed his drinking surprised her…and satisfied her.

"That would be fine, marshal. I have no dessert to offer tonight unless you'd like an apple or canned peaches. So you may like that drink after dinner." Dare she ask her question?

"Sounds fine, Miss Lynch," he tipped his head. Their gazes locked and she had to inhale before she fell over. He seemed to stare into her hollow soul. She felt stripped naked, as if he could see how empty, bitter, hurt, and distrustful of being manipulated, as …

Defensiveness reared its head, instantly. She had to shield herself. No one could know how vulnerable, how unsure of herself she really felt. Her sane existence depended on her portraying a strong constitution. No one would tread over her heart and soul ever again. That's why she had come here three years ago. To find a new life, a new purpose; to be her own person.

"Marshal, you said your real name is Chase Matlock. Matlock sounded so familiar that all afternoon I tried to remember why. Am I correct that, a little

A COWBOY CELEBRATION

over three years ago, just before I moved to Hallings, a woman by that name was killed in a bank robbery? It would have been—"

"Three years, four months and nine days ago to be exact, Miss Lynch." His clipped words punctured the air like the jolt of a clashing cymbal. "What else would you like to know? You want details? I can give them to you. I—"

"Please, stop!" She pressed her palms to her lips. Her face ignited. She feared she might vomit. "I am so very sorry; I shouldn't have been so forward and rude. Please, forgive me. I don't usually—"

"Now, you stop, Miss Lynch." He spoke with authority, yet surprisingly, he had not bellowed as she had expected. His jaw flexed, his hands fisted at his sides, and then fell slack. "I realize you were inquisitive, didn't mean any harm."

"It was none of my business. I apologize for dredging up bad memories." Obviously, the woman *had been* a relative. Callie decided to say no more before she made it any worse. Thank the good Lord the marshal had controlled his temper.

"May I offer you that drink before supper, if I've ruined your appetite for now?" What an unfeeling, stupid person she'd become! She strove to maintain independence. She had no right to cause others harm or pain. Shame seemed to follow her no matter where she lived or what she did. Always due to the same reason. Stupidity. First, her naivety—pure stupidity—now, her inquisitiveness. Her mouth flapped before she thought through the entire matter. Would she ever learn?

He managed a faint grin. "Lead the way Miss Lynch. My appetite's fine."

Settled at the dining room table, they agreed to share a bit of their background. She explained she'd lived in Virginia, lost her parents in a fire just before having a falling out with her beau—she almost stumbled on that toned-down, flippant version—and decided to start fresh elsewhere. Her brother—five years older—his wife, and two children lived in South Carolina and raised tobacco on his in-laws' plantation.

"When I arrived in Hallings, I instantly felt drawn to its warm-hearted people and the size of the town—not too large, nor too small. I had money from selling my father's business to last for a while before I'd have to find a means of support. The moment I saw this old place for sale—it was the old Bardwell Estate—with the apple orchards out back, I knew I had to have it. I couldn't wait to rip into it, restore its beauty and charm, and open it as a boarding home. I never questioned my decision." His eyebrows arched and he cocked his head. She smiled.

"My father owned a lumber yard, but his passion and expertise was in carpentry." She hesitated to reveal she enjoyed a man's world. Then, she reminded herself to be proud of what she could do, what she enjoyed. "I followed him around from the time I could walk, carried a hammer as soon as I could lift it, and grew up being his right-hand man. I loved every minute."

His grin had those blue eyes twinkling. "I've never met a lady carpenter." His eyes canvassed the golden hickory wainscot, hardwood floors, hand-tooled crown moldings, and fine window casings.

"You restored this room...as well as the others?" He set his fork down and looked amazed at such a feat.

She dabbed her lips with her napkin. "I can't take full credit. Tom Wallace is a hard working young man. He works at the hardware store, dabbles in carpentry, but he's a handyman. Since he had a new wife and baby, he'd been looking for some extra money. I did most of the woodwork while he hauled lumber, sawed, nailed. We worked well together."

He eased back in the chair. "How do you take in boarders if you're always under construction?"

She grinned this time. "It took us a year to finish the first floor, other than my bedroom down the hall. It'll be last. The upstairs I cleaned, painted, and furnished to suffice so I could open and start bringing in money. Now, I take one room at a time. Next year, I'll tackle the last one upstairs."

"You're amazing, Miss Lynch. You do superior work. And it's very relaxing and homey. I wish you much success with your business and your home." *Classy, but not so ornate that it overpowers.*

"Thank you. I'm far from amazing, but I do feel blessed. I thoroughly enjoy cooking and making this my home, but most of all, catering to my wonderful boarders. I have the best friends in the world and the community here is close-knit and more like a family." Seeing he had finished his chicken, yet had potatoes and vegetables, she retrieved the platter. "More chicken, Marshal?"

He laughed. "Don't mind if I do." He took another piece. "You continue to call me 'Marshal' and that's fine here. But, if we're in public, will it be difficult to call me Mr. Tate?"

"Not at all. It won't be that often, but you can rest assured I'll remember."

"Good girl. I should fill you in on what's goin' on and who I'm workin' with so you don't have any surprises."

She had no idea what those surprises might be. Maybe one of his men running through her home with guns blazing? She nearly laughed, yet found herself delighted to be part of the adventure. His "good girl" had her heart

A COWBOY CELEBRATION

leaping and her face blushing.

"Not that I'm not eager to hear about your mission, because I am chomping at the bit to hear more. To an easterner like me, it's more than thrilling. But you're supposed to tell me about yourself, too." She refilled their cups.

"All right." He forked the last of his potatoes in his mouth and swallowed. "I'll tell you about me first, and then you'll understand more about my mission."

He set his fork down. "Not much to tell, really. During my last year at college for law and finance, my father died. My younger brother took over running our cattle ranch in Texas. When I graduated, I helped Jeff until he got his feet under him. Didn't take long to realize I liked law enforcement better than ranchin'. I accepted the local sheriff's position. Since a few investments I'd made started payin' off, I bought a place in town, helped out Jeff when needed, and married my long-time sweetheart."

Callie heard the pride in his success and saw his satisfaction as well. The fact he wore no wedding band, had had a relative murdered here, and now, an instant later, glowered as if he fought to hold back his rage, hit her like a hurtling boulder. Suspecting who he'd most likely lost here, her breath hitched. She didn't want to hear him say it.

Chapter Four

Discomfited, Callie hopped up. With trembling hands, she started stacking plates and silverware.

"Yes, Miss Lynch, my wife, Bethany, was one of the six victims who were shot and killed three years ago."

Her chest felt as if it would burst. Praying for composure, for his sake as well as hers, she raised her bowed chin and nodded once.

She wanted to say so much, yet her tongue cemented itself to her dry mouth. She knew the devastation and unbearable pain of losing a loved one. Their circumstances were different, yet so very alike. She never wanted to go down that path again— Couldn't, and keep her sanity.

Their woeful gazes met. She recognized his agony, suffered his anguish. She felt a bond form between them, much like kindred spirits; two wounded hearts and lost souls floundering in the cold, cruel world. Relating to him added to her torment. It reopened past raw wounds to sting anew. Inhaling deeply, she fortified her mettle and vowed to remain strong for him during his mission. She'd have time later to again lick her own reopened wounds.

She'd let him know she could relate to his loss. "You have my deepest sympathy, Marshal. I know what it's like to lose one you've deeply loved, and I empathize with you. They say time heals all. You must give it time before you feel peace once more within your heart, and allow your soul to heal. Someone once said, 'believe in the Lord and he shall help you set the world aright again'."

"Yeah? Well he can't bring my wife back—or our unborn child she carried. It's taken me this long to stick to his trail like glue, but this time around, I'll make it right. Amos Marten and his three misfits will never harm anyone again," he said, his voice full of bitter conviction.

At hearing his added loss, his words blasted her heart, deep and painful. She needed to help him be strong. He desperately needed his faith restored, to reconcile with a past that could not be changed. "You can't change the past, but you can learn from it, deal with it and then go on and strive to become wiser and stronger because of it."

His mouth twisted wryly. "You're a very wise, sincere woman, Miss Lynch. Did you ever contemplate preaching in your spare time? You could turn a few lost souls into God's children."

A retort stung the end of her tongue, ready and willing to spring free—

"Thank you," he said with a tentative smile. "I meant what I said as a compliment. If I could be reminded of that more often, I might be able to see the brighter side of life."

His words meandered over her like a gentle flowing stream warmed by the summer sun, his smile as intimate as a kiss. *Lord help me and keep me safe. This man's smile could melt a rock into molasses.*

"I'd be happy to remind you every chance I get." She found it impossible not to return his smile. Yet, she'd not offer more than friendship. She only dared the most minuscule affection to any male. No matter how devastatingly handsome, well-muscled, or well mannered he might be.

After Callie refused help tidying up after breakfast, Chase sat on the front porch swing finishing his coffee and gazed across the broad expanse of front lawn. A pretty white church sat across the street down aways. His gaze followed toward the town proper. Birds chirped their good mornings from tall tree tops as the early morning sun peeked through the wispy clouds and a faint breeze gave promise to temper the afternoon heat. Planting his boots flat against the floor, he pushed the swing leisurely back and forth. Four potted green leafy plants sat throughout the porch. The relaxing and peaceful ambience Callie's porch offered lulled him. He liked the name Callie. It suited her.

The screen door creaked opened. "Dishes all done," she said, holding a broom. Her eyes twinkled as she watched him swing.

"This swing is incredible. More comfortable than I thought. I haven't enjoyed sitting and admiring such a peaceful morning in a very long time. Town has sure changed since I was here last. Please, come join me for the few minutes I have before I have to leave." He stopped swinging, set his cup on the wooden stand and stretched his left arm out along the top of the swing.

She hesitated and gripped the broom tight. She resembled a mouse staring into the eyes of a big ol' Tom cat. Chase still had his moments, dealing with his wife's and unborn child's deaths, but this lady had fears to beat all. Had she been abused? Or, did she just fear a man's touch? Either would be a crying shame.

"I don't bite. I don't usually holler—much—and I'm not a molester. Does that help?"

"It's me, not you. I didn't mean to offend you," she said as a blush appeared. "Let me sweep the porch right quick and then I'll join you." She started sweeping. "Why were you here...last? You have relatives here?"

He was silent a moment. Then, "We were visiting some friends in the area—I...haven't been back here since then. And they've since moved away."

"I see..."

Silence fell again, with the soft "whisk whisk" of the broom the only noise.

"You always sweep your porch when there's no more than a fine dusting?" Chase asked.

"Marianne claims I'm possessed with cleanliness," she laughed, sashaying across the porch, making efficient sweeps. "I simply like things neat. Every morning, I set the porch to rights. It has to always look charming, homey and say a strong welcome to everyone."

He scanned the two large clay pots at the bottom of the steps with their red and purple blossoms, the painted "WELCOME" sign to the left of the porch. Even the arched sign that read, "Apple Grove Inn", attached to the front of the roof, greeted strangers warmly. She'd done an excellent job.

When she finished, she opened the screen, stood the broom inside, and joined him on the swing. He again set the swing into a steady motion. When she relaxed and leaned back fully, the mere touch of her thick hair and back against his coat sleeve warmed his blood. Realizing she hadn't flinched, he knew an inner satisfaction he hadn't felt in a long time.

"Everyone comments on this swing. It turned out better than I'd imagined." She focused on the doves and pigeons pecking around the base of the big cottonwood tree.

"Do not tell me you made this." Shaking his head, he glanced her way. He continued rocking back and forth.

"All right, I won't take full credit," her eyes twinkled. "Clive Horner, our cooper, can bevel a stave to perfection in minutes. He slightly curved the staves where your backside sits for more comfort. Our blacksmith, Evan Burrows, made the wrought iron braces, the hooks and chains. I took them my plans, they did their part. I stained and varnished the staves, and then Tom helped me put it together and hang it."

She was one smart cookie and an enterprising one at that. "Y'all did an outstanding job. You're a great team; you should go into business together and produce these." His burdened heart lightened as she beamed from his praise. He gave her shoulder a slight squeeze. The instant he felt her stiffen, he lifted his hand. His intent had been to let her know he offered no threat as well as...

A COWBOY CELEBRATION

Well, hell, he came here to see Bethany's killer apprehended, not to start something he would never be able to offer.

She acted as if nothing had happened. "We gave it some thought after several people commented on it." She looked him in the eye and grinned. "If it comes to fruition, we may need an investor to get it off the ground. Do you think you might be interested, Mr. Tate?"

♥ ♥ ♥

When Chase burst out laughing, an infectious deep belly laugh at that, Callie joined in with him. The man's hearty guffaws and smile could turn a nasty, grouchy, old biddy into kicking up her heels and asking for a dance. While she doubted she would ever trust another man with her affections, she, from the very first, appreciated his devilishly handsome face, and all the other attributes. She found herself extremely conscious of his virile appeal. And the blasted man had a sense of humor. *Well, shoot!* That made him twice as hard to resist.

Chase stopped the motion of the swing, stood and turned to her. "I better skedaddle. I don't anticipate them before two or three days, but I can't take any chances." He reached for his Stetson. "And I don't want to hold you up from your paintin'." His wink sent a warmth scurrying through her. He turned, made his way down the steps, and strode down the road.

She might live by the code to never take interest in or trust a man again, but she found herself admiring his vitality, and again, sensed some bond between them. Maybe it was the fact they had simply loved and lost. She needed to remember the pain, the insult, the sheer agony a man could cause a woman without a second thought.

♥ ♥ ♥

Lunch and supper passed with both relating the day's events. Callie had finished the painting, and now concentrated on rearranging furniture and adding new draperies. Chase had reviewed plans and schedules with Sheriff Millet, Deputy Hollis, Matt, and several others. Though Callie flinched and worried over his casual "showdown" and what that might entail, they both laughed as he reenacted how his young recruit had become moon-struck upon meeting Callie's friend, Marianne Grover.

Callie lay in bed agonizing over the strange attraction. For years, she had resisted the pull to any man, no matter how handsome or how nice. So, why now? And why would she suddenly feel her heart yearn for a man who still

101

loved his deceased wife? She wouldn't repeat her mistake of believing she could take another's place. When she punched her pillow, she cried, but no tears came. They never did.

Chapter Five

Callie leaned back in her chair and enjoyed watching Chase devour the last of his breakfast. It always pleased her to watch a man fully appreciate something she had cooked.

"I've shopping to do, so I may see you in town," she said, setting down her coffee cup.

He glanced up. "Be happy to get what you need and save you a trip."

"I appreciate your offer, but I'll need the wagon. I need several odds and ends, plus a lot more flour and corn meal for the corn bread I'm making for the Fourth's celebration. I should stop to see Marianne, and then Laura at the Chat-a-While, too. I've neglected them all week."

"They your two best friends? Heard tell the Chat-a-While serves the best pie in Wyoming and more," he said with a bright grin.

"They're both like sisters. And you better believe it. Laura serves good food, but her pies are absolutely scrumptious. She'll have five or six kinds at the celebration. You'll want try them all."

"Coming from you, I'll do that. Love pie, any kind. Sheriff Millet said they do up a quite a big shindig here for the Fourth."

"They sure do. All afternoon, there's games and contests, crafts sales, and socializing. Supper goes on forever. At dusk, the music and dancing start, followed by fireworks. Lots and lots of fireworks."

"I can tell you like the fireworks the best," he said with a chuckle. "Will you save me a dance, pretty lady?"

His compliment arrowed straight to her heart. She trembled in anticipation of dancing with him, and that was surprising. And only four more days. "I certainly will, but I thought you'd be guarding the bank. Don't robbers prefer to break in when no one's there?"

"You read too many dime novels?" he asked with a twinkle in his eye. "If no one's there, they'd have to blast it. Takes way more time, more brains than they have, and before the boom stopped there'd be people swarmin' the place. Nope, they'll plan it the day before or after the holiday. We'll take turns watching the bank throughout the fourth but only as a precaution. Got men trackin' their progress."

"Would you like more coffee, Marshal?" she asked as she sipped the last of hers.

"I'm full to the brim, but thank you, Miss L—" He shook his head. "You said you like to cut to the chase, so let's do it. I'd more than welcome you calling me Chase when it's just the two of us. And I'd be honored if you'd allow me to call you Callie. Callie short for another name?"

"Calinda," she almost gagged, "is my given name, but I prefer Callie, please." She hadn't meant to sound curt, but she hated the memories attached to the other.

She noted his intense eyes probing, sharp and assessing. "And will you let me hear you say 'Chase' before I leave?" His lips curved slightly as he pushed back from the table.

"Chase." Her heart hammered at the intimacy.

"I like hearing my name on your lips, Callie," he said as he stood, gathered his plate and utensils and took them to the kitchen.

"I'll hitch your wagon before I leave. At lunch, I'll carry in the heavy things for you, so just leave them in the wagon."

"Thank you, but you don't ha—"

"I know I don't. Let me have the pleasure of helping." He flashed that darn wink and left. The July heat in no way matched her bloodstream.

Once Callie made all her purchases at Harper's and Jacob had loaded them in the wagon, she ran across the street to chat with Laura over coffee.

A little while later, Callie drew her wagon up in front of Grover's Sweet Scents and rushed inside to greet Marianne. At twenty-one, Marianne had lost her mother years ago and her father just last year. Keeping the house, she sold off most of the farm land, cattle, and horses, but continued to raise rabbits and ducks for sale. She had three cats and two dogs and, of course, one cow and a buckskin mare. She had opened Sweet Scents where she made and sold her perfumes and colognes, soaps, lotions, candles, herbs and potions. With her new Singer sewing machine, she offered ready-made dresses, gloves and hats. She now stocked men's and women's boots and shoes that were more stylish than what Harper's carried.

The two chatted like magpies while they dusted the front window displays. Marianne turned dreamy-eyed and her smile widened. Callie felt a laugh try to escape when Marianne's next words stopped her cold.

"Oh, Callie, I met the handsomest, nicest man two days ago. His name is Matt Tremayne and he's passing through to a new job on a ranch north of here, but he...oh Lord, he set my heart to pounding when he first looked at me. He's only twenty-four, but he seems so much more mature, and his voice—" She broke off, and in a moment, went on shyly, "Just to hear him talk sent thrills through me to my toes like I've never felt before. And he never once commented on my gimpy leg."

Callie saw red. With hands fisted on hips, she glared. "I'll say it again; a lame leg doesn't make you any less of a person. All Timothy wanted was a wife who could work his farm from sunup till sundown, and when he realized you couldn't, he showed his true colors. He wasn't worth your time."

Marianne burst out laughing. "My staunch defender. My guardian angel. My—"

"Oh, stop," Callie spat. "I'm just saying it like it was. Howard wanted a rich wife. When he found out you weren't as rich as he thought, he hightailed it. You're too good for someone like either of them."

Marianne scowled. "If it hadn't been for my gimp leg—"

"I'm telling you, your leg shouldn't make a difference," Callie snapped.

"That's fine for you to say. You don't want a man. I do. I want love, laughter… and a few cuddles."

Callie raised her brows. "Only a few cuddles? Really?" When their gazes met, they started laughing with a spate of shared giggles just as the overhead bell jingled.

"Shucks, Matt, I think we just missed a good joke." Chase grinned at the two lovely women in the throes of merriment. Callie's allure robbed his breath, and his desires flamed as hot as a raging camp fire. His growing feelings scared the hell out of him. He hadn't wanted to care again.

They jumped and turned. Their mutual rounded-eyed surprise looked as if they had been caught smoking a cigar. "Why…Mr. Tate," Callie stammered as her cheeks turned a delightful shade of rose. "I didn't expect to see you here." Her eyes sparkled. Pleasure he knew he should not allow crept through him.

"Met young Tremayne, here, and he wanted to stop and say hello to Miss Grover."

"I couldn't walk past your shop without saying good morning, Marianne," Matt said, his firm, deep voice once again surprising Chase. Matt had matured ten years before his eyes. After only two days, they were on first-name basis, Matt and Marianne. Chase smiled. The kid had it bad. Who the hell was he to talk?

"That's so nice to hear, Matt. I welcome your visits anytime," Miss Grover said sweetly as she crossed the room.

Chase noticed her slight limp.

"Have you met my dear friend, Miss Callie Lynch? She runs the boarding house, Apple Grove Inn." Miss Grover smiled at Matt.

"No, I haven't," Matt replied. "It's a pleasure," he tipped his head in greeting.

"Thank you, Mr. Tremayne. It's a pleasure to meet you. Marianne mentioned she'd met you. Have you seen her animals? If you like cats, dogs, ducks, and rabbits, you're in for a treat." She offered a congenial smile, yet Chase noted her eagle eye as she awaited Matt's reply. *Hmm.*

Matt's eyebrows arched as his eyes went round. He glanced at Marianne. "You never mentioned animals. Are they here?" The minute his grin turned into a wide, open smile, Chase noted Callie's satisfied smile—a smile that just about completely disarmed him. *Get a grip, Matlock!*

Marianne shook her head. "They're at home. Sometimes, I bring Hunter and Millie, my two dogs, but not too often. They're happier at home." She beamed at Matt, and Chase figured the two lovebirds had totally forgotten two other people were present.

"I love animals. I'd enjoy seeing them sometime," Matt eagerly offered.

"You can visit any time," Marianne returned with equal zeal.

"Please excuse me, but I need to be on my way." He nodded. "Miss Grover, Miss Lynch." He leveled Matt with a scowl he hoped told the young'un to hustle so they could meet the others. As he exited, he heard Matt offer his apology to Marianne for leaving so soon.

"How do you know Mr. Tate? And who is he?" Marianne asked with a curious glint in her eyes as she leaned against the main counter.

"He's a land speculator and investor. He's also a boarder," Callie answered feeling like a nervous, naughty child. She loved Marianne like a sister, but she didn't have any answers, and she didn't want to talk about their relationship—actually, their non-relationship.

"Oh?" Marianne tapped her chin with her finger. "You mean a boarder like the ones you weren't accepting until you finished remodeling?" Marianne smiled a knowing smile. Rats!

"He…he wasn't comfortable staying at the hotel, and I had nearly finished most of the painting and messy things." She avoided eye contact.

Marianne actually laughed aloud! Callie cringed at Marianne's hilarity her friend gasped for breath. "Oh, this is too good to be true."

"Get whatever thoughts are plaguing that nutty brain of yours out of there. I gave him a room." She regretted she had to lie to protect Chase and the others.

Yet, she also knew she fibbed about her developing feelings.

"All right, just because he's gorgeous and nice why should I think anything of it? Is that what you're saying?"

"Marianne, I love you dearly, but I have a hundred things to do. Yes, he's gorgeous, and I'm fighting my attraction with every ounce of strength I have. He's my boarder. If you're truly my friend, you won't nag. I don't want more from him than his board."

Callie hugged her, kissed her cheek and stepped back. "I like your Matt. Just don't set your cap to high for him until you know him better." Dear God, how she wished she could warn her friend not to invest her time in Matt. His life would be in jeopardy every day as a marshal. He would be gone soon. Her heart curled into a tight ball. Chase would be leaving, too.

Saturday morning arrived with Chase explaining he would not be back until supper, and after they had eaten, he'd join a poker game at the saloon to glean new information and touch base with a few of his team. Although he failed to go into details, he did say he planned to check with a few scouts that were tracking the outlaws' progress. He would also be making arrangements for various people to play their parts.

She laughed as he described several lawmen that had the right physique and with some added stuffing here and there and wigs would portray lovely ladies. Throughout the day they would be in and out of the bank, or meander throughout the shops close by. When he informed her he'd mostly be inside the bank, she hid the anxiety that lanced her chest as her stomach clenched tight.

Surprisingly, she found herself downhearted. When he left, she would miss their talks, their banter, and his nearness. In four short days, she had become more than fond of him. She longed for so much more. Yet, she realized a relationship would be beyond any dream. Dreams were meant for children, not sinners. No matter how much she now longed to trust, she wasn't sure she dared.

The mid-afternoon temperature outside the Thirsty Goat Saloon neared ninety, but the sun's extreme brilliance threatened to ignite a fire. Chase knew about fire; he played with it every time he flirted with Callie. Alone at a table in the far corner, he leaned back in the chair, welcomed another cool sip of beer, then pretended to be engrossed in the newspaper. No sense in drawing attention of the other two patrons at the bar while he waited for what he hoped to be a positive report from Henry Boll.

He knew he should resist toying with Callie; yet, he was drawn to her. And to add to his foolishness, he had, a few times, recognized her reciprocal response. How her big, brown eyes would glaze over with a soft dreaminess, or sparkle with a hint of desire she so obviously and desperately fought to resist.

He longed to ask what had happened to her. If he did, she'd rant and rave until the roof blew off, then throw him out on his rude and mettlesome ass. He wanted to help her. The next best thing would be to force her hand. She needed to deal with her haunts.

Hell, who was he kidding? He found himself wanting something from her that he had never in a hundred years thought he would feel again. He desired her friendship as a start, but if what had wormed its way into his blood, his mind, and had started to burrow its way into his heart was meant to be—he couldn't afford to spook her.

She tried so hard to act as if she was a cool cucumber when she was as skittish as a hen with a fox nippin' at her tail feathers, ready to run as fast as she could or jump ten feet in the air.

The saloon door squeaked, and booted footfalls scuffed across planks to the bar. Without turning, he folded the newspaper and laid it across from him on the table. He heard a triple whiskey ordered, then steps draw near. Henry might be a good twenty years older than his thirty-two, but the man had the stamina of a young mule.

"If yur done with that there paper, mister, might I take a gander at what's happenin' around here?" Henry's voice brought music to his ears. If he carried good news, within the next two or three days, all hell would break loose. He was more than ready.

"You're welcome to it. Have a seat if you want. Name's John Tate."

"Why thanks, Tate, that's mighty obligin'," he tipped his head in greeting. "Henry Boll. Don't mind joinin' ya. Been travelin' all day, and need to sit my sorry ass." Henry set his glass down, pulled out a chair across from him and plunked into it.

They lowered their voices as Henry talked in coded language that only Chase would how to interpret. When Henry finished, Chase stood and slapped Henry on the back

"I'll do that and buy you a whiskey to celebrate, *ol' man*." Chase nodded, then sauntered out of the saloon one happy man. Let the fireworks begin. And he wasn't thinking about the Fourth, but the day before—or, more likely, the day after—depending on tomorrow's ride.

A COWBOY CELEBRATION

Henry had let him know the gang en route consisted of four, and would arrive to camp outside Hallings in one day; two, at the most. Not only did he ascertain he would be available for the duration, but when the time came, there would also be six more armed lawmen dressed as women. Three would hover in or by the bank while three would mill around town. Others would stand by.

If the gang made good time, they'd arrive tomorrow; but more than likely, they'd arrive on the fourth and attack on the fifth. With their very own fireworks—far more deadly.

Chapter Six

Sunday morning arrived with Callie dressed and ready to attend church. Chase bowed out, stating he preferred not being cornered when everyone lingered afterward. He expected the gang to be camped right outside the town by tomorrow night—or, if running ahead of schedule, by nightfall; he needed to do some more checking.

When she asked why he didn't attack them at their camp instead of having them come into town, he explained three previous attempts to do exactly that had resulted in them hightailing away. Two of their members had been killed, but the other four scurried away like a pack of rats. Their plan involved having them away from their horses. And this time, they wouldn't fail.

"That was one of the best ham dinners I've ever had, Callie," Chase said, carrying a stack of dishes into the kitchen. "Since I've stuffed myself on applesauce and you've told me how neglected the orchard had become, I'd love to see it. If I help you finish up here, would you have time for a tour before dark?"

Callie poured hot water from the kettle into the dish pan. "I'm glad you enjoyed the meal. I thought maybe I bored you with all the details of the orchard. When I get started about pruning, protecting against diseases, bugs, and simply maintaining them, I guess my mouth runs away with itself."

He took the washed plate from her and rinsed it in the rinse basin. "You could never bore me. Will you walk with me?" Standing so close, her scent of lavender tantalized him until he thought he would go mad. He longed to lean down and kiss the tempting curve of her neck.

"I'd love to. They're not only pretty trees that bear the sweetest apples, but when you're in the orchard it's like another world; peaceful, pleasant, pure nature."

She led him through the small back mud room, passed a wall of shelves lined with canned goods, boxes and sacks of dry goods. Along the other wall sat two wash tubs, a laundry basket and a long, flat table. Everything was neat and orderly; especially her narrow waist and obviously nubile fine hips that gently swayed under her gingham dress. He pictured those long legs, shapely and taut as they wrapped...*Whoa boy. Down, down.*

As they exited the back door, he pulled his gaze from the sweet temptation to suppress his rising desire and his breath hitched at viewing such a picturesque sight. Four straight rows of apple trees, a twelve-foot wide grassy path between each, seemed to go on forever and mirrored an artist's exquisite creation.

Standing twenty-some feet tall, their crooked branches resembled twisted, outstretched arms, lush with rich green leaves glistening under the descending sun. Sheltered by those leaves were an amazing abundance of small developing fruits, each splashed with various shades of green, yellow and rose. Down the length of the middle path, four black wrought-iron garden benches had been strategically placed. He pictured Callie relaxing on one in any given evening.

"You were right, it's fantastic. From what you described when you bought the place, I applaud you on the remarkable revival to such a healthy and productive state," he said, as he eyed her with a calculating expression. Callie felt as though she had missed something.

He held out his right hand. "Let's take a stroll down that middle path so I can see more."

She stared at the hand, longing to take it; every fiber in her body warned her against it. It had been too long. "Take my hand, Callie. I told you, I don't bite. Whoever hurt you, I can go after him when I finish here."

She glanced up wanting to laugh, yet too distrustful of him and afraid of her own fortitude. Their gazes locked, the blue depths questioning and full of concern. Her heart raced.

"I'm going to take your hand. No more than that...at least, for now," he reassured. "I'd never hurt you, Callie." Instead of cupping her palm, he laced his fingers through hers and gently pressed palms together. The potent intimacy fired through her like a flash of lightning. Her breath caught. For sure, he had to have felt her quake and probably believed it from fright.

"Let's walk," he said as he guided her across the small lawn and casually down the middle pathway. As they past each tree, he seemed to marvel at it.

"How do you pick all these before they rot?"

"Reverend Fields and his two teenage sons help during picking time. Actually, they prune, care for the trees, anything that needs to be done throughout the year. I could never do it without them. The reverend doesn't make much from donations, so they benefit, quite well."

They passed the first bench on the left. "Can you sell all of them?" he asked, sounding incredulous.

She relaxed and realized she enjoyed holding hands, of breathing in the scent of his light, spicy aftershave, horse and his own masculinity. Her pulse danced.

"I sell quite a bit to Harper's as well to two stores in two towns close by. Laura buys for pies and breads. Marianne buys some for candles, potions and lotions. Three families, each with a passel of children that live quite a ways out north, barely have enough to survive. Periodically, I send a bushel to each. As an added payment, the reverend and his family have all they can eat. Then there's me. I love eating apples and I can put up apple butter, applesauce, and slices for desserts. There's a large underground fruit cellar built into the side of a knoll by the barn."

"The two business are a little goldmine," he said, passing the second bench.

"It's not just the income, but the challenge and the enjoyment from both. Oh, I almost forgot," she added, content to have his warm hand linked with hers, "there are the badly bruised apples. The grass around the trees and on the pathways is to soften their fall, but half the time they fall hard. A good heavy wind or rainstorm takes more down. If I can't cut the bruises out, I put them aside for Freedom or take them to the livery."

"Lucky horses," he winked, and he surprised her as his expressive face changed and became almost somber. "Why'd you name her Freedom?"

He caught her off guard with the change of subject, and she halted. He followed suit and their gazes met. She had never been much for lying.

"Mr. Talley said it nearly drove him crazy to see her so neglected and beaten by her drunken owner. So he bought her and nursed her back to good health as well as restoring her spirit. He had her for sale when I arrived. Since I was starting a new life— a freedom of sorts—I figured she was, too."

She should not have included herself in that story. She read his multitude of questions as well as genuine concern in his now-cobalt eyes. Her skin heated and tingled as he gently rubbed his thumb back and forth across her hand.

"He really hurt you."

She realized when he spoke those words that she had to disclose more truthful facts so he would understand nothing could ever develop between them. That thought ripped through her heart until she thought she might scream.

She felt the need to move, and started to walk. "Yes, he hurt me, but not physically. Without going into nasty details, I never want another man in my life. He took my heart and threw it in the dirt like garbage, then stomped on my soul until it was battered beyond repair." Regret swamped her. She had not

A COWBOY CELEBRATION

cried in five years, she would not start now.

"Give me his name." His grip tightened. "You can't judge others by what he did. Don't throw your life away just because of one horse's ass."

At the third bench, he stirred her toward it. "Let's sit." When he released her hand, she sat, peering at the ground. He joined her

His thumb and forefinger cupped her chin and raised it. She trembled, thrilled by his mere touch. When their gazes locked, despair washed over her at seeing his smolder. "Callie, I've only known you five days, and it might be because we've spent hours together every day, but I've come to care very much for you."

Her voice quivered. "I vowed to never trust another man with my heart. And I most certainly would never, *ever again*, pin my hopes on a man who pined for another woman."

"You think I'm still in love with my wife?" His baritone raised an octave as his fingers pulled away. His eyes drilled hers. "I loved Bethany with all my heart. I regret our life together was cut short. And I'll treasure what we had and her memory forever. But I do not pine for her. I carry tremendous guilt because I failed to protect her. For three years, I've avoided any relationship with any woman because I feared I'd somehow fail to protect her. Until now. I want to look forward to brighter tomorrows. Maybe we could have them if you would trust me…if you'd give us a chance."

The air hung silent. She longed to trust him, yet she instinctively fought to keep under stern restraint. If she lost at love a second time, she would lose her mind, certainly. His blue eyes softened to match a quiet lake warmed by the sun, offering soothing caresses if one dared venture into the waiting water. Reading the sincerity, the honesty that drew her in like a magnet, she longed to surrender. If he knew her shameful story, he would walk away. She had sinned. Now, she would pay the price. Oh, yes, fear was a potent force for both of them, but withholding the truthful entirety would rock any foundation they might try to build together.

Glancing down, she studied the ground and found courage. "He didn't simply walk away and break my heart. You're a good man, and you need to know the truth so you can find someone worthy of you. After I explain, if you would not say anything and just go inside, it will be easier for both of us. Tomorrow, we can pretend tonight never happen. You'll do your job, leave, and I'll continue—as always."

A slight breeze chilled her, and she realized perspiration coated her skin. Her heart beat a tattoo on her rib cage. She could do this…

113

Chase caught her bitterness and hurt, understood her distrust and fear to give her heart again. But there could only be one reason she would feel unworthy. He ached for her. It took all his willpower not to drag her into his arms. She needed to share the pain, vent her woes—or she would never be able to accept what he wanted to offer. She needed to resurrect her trust, rebuild her self-esteem—if he'd guessed his cards correctly—and open her heart to a new beginning. He avoided agreeing to her terms.

She leaned back against the bench as dusk settled in and the orange glow off in the distance fell to just above those tree tops.

"Robert courted me for almost two years. I knew he carried a flame for another. We even discussed someday having a family. I thought he'd get over Linda's rebuff and I believed he loved me, though he never said the words. Over the next six months, we…we became intimate." She clutched her hands together.

"One night, he'd had a few drinks and we were…together. He called me Linda. I convinced myself I heard wrong." She swallowed. "The next week, when the same thing happened more clearly, I became angry, but thought he'd finally realize he wanted me—not her."

She focused on the trees ahead. "Several weeks went by and…again, in a heated moment, he finally said he loved me." She made a fist and rubbed it with her other hand. "I knew joy as never before…until he followed it with 'Linda'." She bowed her head.

"I felt as if my heart had been savagely ripped out of my chest. What I had believed as being in love, making love that was gratifying and meaningful, turned into nothing more than sex—dirty and vulgar. Then, realization hit me. For two years, he had used me…used me as a substitute. Every time he kissed me, held my hand, made love…he had been thinking of her.

"So, now I'm distrustful and have chosen the life I've accepted. I'm used merchandise. I refused to be walked on, lied to, and hurt like that ever again. For two years, I contended with scorn from those who believed me a fallen woman, or pitying glances from others. Ashamed, I sold my father's business and moved here. I hate my own name—Calinda."

Silence hung heavy as wet snow. He felt the leashed tension build inside her. She would shatter into a hundred broken pieces if he allowed her to continue on this dangerous course.

She ran her palms up and down her forearms, trembling as if she were ice cold. "Please go in, I'd like to sit out here for awhile. Tomorrow, we'll go on as

A COWBOY CELEBRATION

before."

She tried to be tough. But she wasn't, not deep down. She wore a smiling face every day for others; yet inside, deep down, she continued to shed tears. And he loved her all the more.

He took her two hands within his, brought them to his lips and kissed them. She gasped, and quaked. She looked like a frightened rabbit staring an eagle in the eye. Releasing her hands in one deft motion, he pulled her into his embrace, and cradled the back of her head against his chest.

"Now, you'll hear me out."

She stiffened within his embrace.

"I'm sorry he used you, wronged you, and hurt you. But his selfish thoughtlessness in no way reflects on you. He may have taken your innocence, but you are the same caring, ambitious, talented woman you've always been. You made a mistake; we all have. We're human. You gave him your love, every way you knew how. Most men would be honored by such a show of love."

She leaned back, peering up at him. "Not many could overlook I'm not a...virgin."

"If you were a widow, it wouldn't be an issue. It's not as if you slept around. You gave your innocence in good faith. That's the difference. Besides, I'm not any man. And what I see, I like...inside, even more." He brushed back a strand of hair from her forehead.

"You make is it sound so simple."

"It is, if we're willing to try. If I work on putting my fear of losing you aside, are you willing to see if you can trust me? We might have something very special if we give it time."

Her lips quivered, and tears pool in her eyes. A tear slowly leaked out and ran down her cheek. "I haven't cried in five years." She swatted the moisture from her cheek. "I'm...scared."

Again, he lifted her chin. "Let's see if there is more to this." His lips found hers. He went gently, so she would not take flight.

His good intentions flew away as if they rode a mounting gust across the prairie. Her lips tasted sweet as her applesauce and felt soft as rose petals. When she leaned into him, returning the kiss with equal pressure, he battled not to devour her.

Pulling back, he ended the sheer bliss. Her tears released as if a flood had burst through a dam. She shuddered as a gut-wrenching sob tore from her lips. When she buried her tear-streaked face into his chest, wrapping her arms

115

around him, he held her tight, rubbing her back and rocking her as she wept softly. His chest expanded as he realized she had found solace in him enough to release all her pent up torment.

♥ ♥ ♥

After ambling back to the house hand-in-hand, Callie extinguished the oil lamps, other than the one each of them carried, while Chase bolted the front door for the night. She wondered if he would treat her to another feverish kiss. She longed to see if it was as potent as the last. As they stood at the bottom of the staircase saying goodnight, the outside bell clanged. Callie jumped, making Chase laugh.

"Easy, sweetheart. I doubt anyone up to no good would be ringin' the bell." He nonetheless, drew his gun, placed his lamp on the flat-top newel and pushed the door's curtain back. "It's all right. It's one of my men." Opening the door, he ushered Henry inside. Chase made the introductions and assured Henry he could speak freely.

"Sorry to disturb ya, but I thought ya'd wanna know they're jist the other side of the south ridge. Figure they might take a notion ta pay us a visit tomorrow since they got here early. What do ya think?"

The man appeared so calm you would have thought they were discussing her apple orchard.

"I think you're right, Henry. If they got here late tomorrow like we thought, they'd wait until after the Fourth and strike. It sure as hell wouldn't make sense for them sit it out for an extra day. I'll come with you to make sure everyone's aware and ready to party first thing tomorrow." Henry nodded as Chase turned to her.

"You have an extra key I can take? That way, you can leave the bolt off and lock the door so I can get in, if it's real late."

Fear at what would happen tomorrow sunk in like a lead ball to her chest. "Yes…I'll get it." She scooted down the hall, returning in less than a minute.

"Henry, give us a minute, and I'll be right out."

"Meet ya out on the porch." He nodded to Callie. "Nice to meet ya, ma'am," he said, making a beeline through the doorway.

Their gazes met and Chase cupped her face between his palms, his fingers gently caressing her cheeks. "There's nothing to worry about. We're only going to make sure everyone knows their parts. I may be back late, so don't wait up. I'll need to get up before sunrise so I can coordinate everything before the bank opens at nine."

"I have a Seth Thomas alarm clock I brought from Virginia. I'll set it for five—if that's all right with you—then fix you breakfast before you leave. I'll need to see you before you go. Please."

"I'd like that. Just seeing your face before I leave will start my day off right." He kissed her, slow and gentle. Her heartbeat fluttered.

"Hmmm," she murmured, wrapping her arms around him and leaning against him. Feeling his arousal, her blood surged hot and wild through her veins.

"We'll resume this discussion another time. I need to leave now, or I won't leave at all." He gave her a peck on the lips, winked and grabbed his Stetson. "Sweet dreams, sweetheart."

Chapter Seven

"Another cup of coffee?" Callie asked, covering her mouth as she yawned.

Chase pushed back his chair and stood. "No thanks, but I appreciate you getting up to fix me breakfast. Henry'll be here any minute. He's bringing my horse in case we need to ride."

They walked down the hall and stopped by the hall tree. He already wore his guns, and had forgone wearing his suit coat today. He looked good either way, but oh my, he looked so very much more the Texan without the coat.

He turned toward her. "You bakin' your corn bread today?"

She shook her head. "I'm going to do loads of laundry, and lots of cleaning so I don't have to think. I won't bake the bread until tomorrow afternoon. That way, I can cover the pans with a quilt and they'll stay warm. I'll go watch the games and visit for an hour or two in the afternoon, then come back to bake."

"Sounds like you've got it down to a science." He hesitated. "Just promise you'll stay out of town today. For me."

Their gazes met, each saying a thousand words silently.

"I promise. And you be careful. For me. Will you have someone tell me when it's over?" Her attempt to smile failed.

"I will. Most shop owners do their banking first thing, and others, usually right after lunch. If I have him pegged correctly, he'll wait until late morning or early afternoon, when the crowd is thinner."

He crushed her to him, devouring her lips, robbing her of all thought. She matched his passion. He pulled back and gazed at her with so much emotion she trembled. "Henry should be outside by now. Hold all your thoughts till I get back."

He turned, placed his Stetson. She followed him out to road. She greeted Henry, and Chase mounted. She watched the two walk their horses toward town.

Ready to turn and go inside, Callie stopped when she saw Chase halt and twist in the saddle. "Just in case," he yelled so loud the birds overhead took flight, "I love you. More than life itself. Just sayin'…so you know." His grin matched that of a cocky, pleased little boy.

Her heart almost took flight with the birds. "It's a helluva time to tell me," she bellowed loud enough for anyone down the road to hear. "I love you too, and you better come back to me. Just sayin'."

Chase and Henry both hooted and set their mounts to jogging.

Callie scrubbed clothes to lessen her rioting nerves. As she hung out the towels, she sputtered. Of all the times to profess his love, he had to yell it while going off to a shootout. She smiled, remembering the look on his face, his laughter. *Don't you leave me now.*

"Well, now, ain't that the purdiest sight," a voice, scratchy and sinister, sneered from ten feet behind her.

Callie's fingers froze against the line. Sheer black fright ran through her. If this was Amos Marten, why would he be here, now, unless…unless he had been following Chase's moves. *Dear Heavenly Father. Please help me…help Chase…the others.*

"Was that smile fer me, sweet cheeks, or Chasey-boy?"

Her fear turned to fury. This vile vermin had no right to slander her love for Chase. She wouldn't step aside and allow him to hurt him or use her to curtail Chase's mission. Somehow, she had to get a message to Chase—or figure out how to best this creature herself. Think.

"You look at me, woman. I was countin' on diddlin' ya but I jist as soon put a bullet in ya if ya don't behave better. Ya hear?"

That did it! She'd kill the slug herself before the sun had time to set. No one would use her for their own purpose ever again. He had signed his death warrant with Chase years ago, with plenty more, too; and now, he'd just added one more to the roster.

She turned and nearly threw up. His pinched face, wizened from years of hard-core living, resembled a rat—not hard to believe—his scruffy beard and straggly filthy brown hair were sure to be infested with lice, having a rip-roaring field day. Cold, black eyes leered as threatening as a coiled rattler.

He glared, and she returned the favor. She needed to think, to somehow foil his plan. "What do you want?"

"Well, now that's right nice to ask."

She was tempted to throw caution to the wind.

"I be wantin' what yuv been givin' ta the boy. "

Vulgar monster! "It isn't like that."

"Oowee! Ya don't say. Never had me no virgin before. Hot damn!" He slapped his thigh with his left hand. "Hit the jackpot on this one. Now, ya stop that glarin' and let's you and me go inside and get real cozy-like."

She glanced at the basket of clothes.

"I meant now. Don't git me riled."

"Fine, but I'm taking the clothes. Anyone, even animals, could take them." She picked up the basket, marched around the side and to the front. On the porch, she set the basket down. "Thank you. They're wet, so I'll leave them here, except these." She grabbed two towels so she'd have an excuse to go to the kitchen. Would anyone realize the basket was her distress signal?

Fifteen men dispersed throughout the town on a mission most were not privy to.

At two minutes to nine, Chase and Matt tied their horses in front of Harper's and ambled toward the bank. Marianne, holding a small leather satchel, stood behind an elderly couple.

"Good morning, Miss Grover. Nice to see you again." Matt, grinning like a fool, spoke and nodded.

"Good morning to both of you. Time got away from me yesterday and I didn't make it to the bank. I need change before I open." Marianne glanced up at Matt and Chase, smiling.

The bank president, Mr. Williams, opened the door, called out a greeting, and announced they were open for business.

"I think Callie is mighty keyed-up about finishing her upstairs. I never thought to see anything mar her porch." She moved up to the teller window as the couple finished.

A warning whispered in Chase's head. As soon as Marianne stuffed her money in her satchel, Chase directed her to the far corner. "What about Callie's porch?"

"She left a laundry basket, full of clothes, right in the middle of the porch above the steps. I wish I'd had time to stop and tease her, but I needed to get the bank before I opened."

His blood iced over thicker than on a pond in February. Fear like he had never known seized his heart.

Marianne's eyes widened. "What's going on?"

"There's no time. We'll take care of Callie. Promise you'll go to your shop and stay there."

"I…promise."

Callie led him to the kitchen and set the towels on the counter. Could she grab a knife? Her mind spun.

"Sure smells good in here. Bacon's my favorite. Ya got some left? I could

A COWBOY CELEBRATION

eat me some before I take my fill of you."

"I can fry some in a minute. Eggs, too."

He eyed her. "Well now, ain't that obligin'." He plunked down on the chair at the work table and kept his gun pointed in her direction. "Two eggs, three bacons. Make it quick. My pecker needs carin' for before I gotta take care of business. Name's Amos Marten. Ya oughta know who's gonna diddle ya."

Vulgar...She set a cup of coffee in front of him. She'd love to serve him hot grease. When the bacon sizzled, she stared. As young teenagers, her brother had taught her to flick. They had contests using plates, and fry pans, lighter with shallower sides than cast. Could she do it?

She placed a table setting in front of him. After cracking two eggs into another pan, she lifted the skillet with a pot holder, wiggled her wrist to test the weight. She'd use two hands today due to the added weight. A possible life with Chase and many other lives depended on her. Those incentives boosted her fortitude to hurl a blacksmith's anvil.

After serving his eggs, she returned to the stove. Tightening her grip on the handle, she hefted the skillet using two hands. "I don't want to splatter you. I'll hold the pan, if you'll remove the three strips with your fork."

As soon as he finished, he held his fork in his left hand and kept the gun in his right. She took two steps toward the stove, then turned her head to see him chomp bacon. Tipping the pan to what she prayed was the correct angle for the grease to slosh out freely, she gave the pan handle the hardest flick she had ever done.

Hot grease spewed through the air like a thin horizontal waterfall. Marten shrieked as the scalding oil reddened and instantly blistered patches across his face. His gun zoomed through the air like an arrow. As if painted blazing red, his hands swelled before her frightened eyes. His shirt and pants were coated, and looked melted to his skin. Scrambling to his feet, quaking and shaking as if convulsing, he fought to pull the material from his heated skin. He howled and screeched.

Before she could reconsider, she swung the pan like a stick of wood, full force. A direct hit to his head. He went down like a flimsy rag doll. Callie stood silent, frozen in place at what she had done. She had not thought she could be so vicious. *Dear God, forgive me for what I have done.*

♥ ♥ ♥

Once Chase made sure the bank was covered by others, he and Matt mounted and raced toward Callie's. Chase would go in the front; Matt would enter the back.

BRIGHTER TOMORROW—BEVERLY WELLS

His gun drawn, Chase silently opened the door. He eyed the vacant parlor to his left, then crept down the hall, his mind alert. He checked the dining room to the left, Callie's bedroom to the right. *All empty.*

Nearing the kitchen, he saw her. She stood still, facing left. Relief swelled in his heart, yet he listened for voices, any movement. *Nothing.* With pot holders, she gripped a fry pan in both hands, in front of her. His instincts went on alert. He took a step.

Below the table a man, unmoving, lay prone, arms and legs contorted at different angles.

Spotting Matt with his gun aimed, peeking from the entryway, Chase tilted his head toward the table. Matt's eyes widened. Chase scanned the room, found nothing, and breathed a huge sigh. He holstered his gun and held up a hand to hold Matt at bay.

"Callie."

She remained silent, ashen. He moved slowly, stepped in front of her.

"Callie, it's Chase. I'm going to take the pan from you."

"Hot," she said in a stoic voice. Taking a frank look at him, her brown eyes softened.

That's my girl.

"I think I killed him." She went to the stove and set the pan down. He followed her.

"Matt, check and see if he's breathin'," Chase directed.

From behind, Chase wrapped his arms around her and inhaled her apple scent as he buried his face in her hair. "Let me hold you. Did he hurt you, sweetheart?" He held his breath while his heart thudded.

She turned within his arms, laid her head against his chest, and wrapped her arms around his torso. "He was vulgar. He said he'd…he'd—you know…after he ate, but he didn't hurt me. He laughed when he told me he'd been watching you."

They clung to each other, both content to merely savor the moment. Chase knew he would have gone mad had Marten physically hurt or violated her. *Thank you, God, from us both.*

"It's Amos Marten all right, and he's still breathin'…for now," Matt said. "He's a mess, Chase. He needs a doc bad. He's out cold."

Let him rot on the floor.

Chase turned his head. "Get the doc. Have him bring a stretcher and men. Then, bring Marianne to stay with Callie. Tell doc to hurry, we need the rest of the gang."

122

A Cowboy Celebration

Matt vanished.

Chase preferred to take Callie to the parlor, but Marten's ankles and wrists were so red and blistered he could not add more injury by cuffing the heinous beast to the table. Neither could he leave him unattended.

He sat on a kitchen chair in the far corner with Callie nestled on his lap. Sometimes, bad situations had their benefits. He insisted she needed to talk about it. She recounted the events of the morning.

Doctor Swithers, accompanied by four strong men toted Marten away. When Marianne arrived, Chase and Matt hightailed it to town to help round up the other four. As they left, they heard Marianne insisting Callie start at the beginning—and this time, she wanted the particulars—how long Callie had known John…Chase…whoever.

The late afternoon breeze ruffled Callie's hair as she sat in the swing awaiting Chase. After convincing Marianne she was fine, her friend agreed to go home to her animals. Her stomach growled just as Chase strode toward her house. Hiking up her skirt, she ran across the yard and bear-hugged him. Their lips clung before his deep belly laugh erupted. "I believe you missed me."

"You know I did." She drank in his raw masculinity and wondered how she'd gotten so lucky.

"I've brought food for sustenance," he said holding up the crushed bag. "I stopped at the Chat-a-While and had Laura pack us some supper. Have you eaten?"

"No. Marianne cleaned up the kitchen before she left. I wasn't hungry before."

"Good."

While Callie opened containers, Chase washed up.

As they ate, he related how the three other outlaws had been in a tizzy waiting for Marten to show up. They were to meet behind Harper's. Two of them, at intervals, would leave to look for the fool. They'd been sitting ducks. It'd taken all day to process the men, send telegraphs to authorities and thank all involved, drop off his horse, and grab the supper.

After eating their fill, they sat on the swing, him with a whiskey, she pillowing her head on his shoulder and enjoying the feel of his arm around her shoulders.

She glanced up. "What a horrible way to say you love me. You yelled it down the street."

His eyes glittered. "Oh yeah? You screeched like an ol' washerwoman, and it meant just as much to me."

His words warmed her. "I hate that you're a marshal."

"May not be a marshal for long."

She glanced up. "Why not?"

"David Millet said he's gettin' tired. Been wantin' to move to Cheyenne to be with his family since his wife died. He offered me the sheriff position."

"Would you even consider it?"

He sipped his whiskey. "Might, but only if the town approved two deputies. If one gets sick or hurt, I'd be stuck; two in a sticky situation is always better. I'm tired of movin' around. Be nice to stay in one place. He'll talk to the town fathers."

"What about your brother, your house?"

He shrugged. "Jeff doesn't need me. We'd stay in touch. I'd sell the house. I think there's more attraction here." When he winked, her heart twittered.

She met his gaze. "Make love to me."

"Sweetheart, there is nothing in the world I'd like better. But not tonight. We're both exhausted. And you're more than vulnerable. When we make love, we both need to know it's because of what's in our hearts, not to wash away today's horror." His voice hinted of anguish.

"Tell me what's wrong. You say you love me; that you might move here; and then, you refuse my offer. Don't lie or lead me on. I couldn't take that."

"You could have been raped or murdered. I failed to protect you, just like I failed Bethany."

Anger surged, yet she caught herself, realizing that reinforcement of his worth, understanding, and love would make him see the truth.

"You did protect me. With your love, you gave me the fortitude to fight adversity. I was determined nothing would stand in my way to see what lies ahead for us. Otherwise, I would've folded and given in. Had I lived, I'd be forever floundering. Thank you, my love, for being my backbone, fortress, savior—and my true love.

His eyes glistened. "You humble me." He kissed her tenderly, and that kiss alone said everything, even without his next words. "I love you so much, Callie. I didn't refuse, I only postponed. Tonight, I'll hold you in my arms and kiss you until we're both breathless. *I need* to show you I love you and will never use you. After tonight…you're fair game."

By early afternoon, Chase joined Callie at the celebration. They strolled past tables set in long rows with snacks, beverages, sandwiches, and fresh cut

A COWBOY CELEBRATION

vegetables. They laughed as children of all ages grabbed bags of popcorn, or chose taffy, fudge or cookies off the tables, then run to catch up with friends.

They shared popcorn while shouting encouragement to contestants throughout different events. Chase won the shooting contest easily, while Ben Tucker, the postmaster, won at archery. By three-thirty, they left so Callie could bake corn bread.

♥ ♥ ♥

Since Callie had most everything premeasured and organized on the kitchen table, she made simple work out of mixing the batter. Chase opened jars of canned corn.

"Do you buy this or make it?" Chase asked smelling the bowl of sour cream.

She broke eggs into a bowl. "You can buy cultured, but I mix milk, vinegar, and heavy cream. It has to set, covered for twenty-four hours, then chilled until used."

He started greasing the pans as she'd instructed. "Why use it?"

Callie stirred the corn meal into the mix. "It adds richer flavor, and cakes and breads bake more level instead of doming."

They worked side by side until six pans of corn bread were baked, covered with a quilt in the wagon and the kitchen was tidy. Callie changed into a navy blue gingham dress and pulled her hair back with a bright red-and-white ribbon. Chase wore denim pants and a dark blue shirt.

As the wagon rolled along to the celebration grounds, Chase said, "You look lovely. Of course, you always do."

She blushed. "Thank you. You look very handsome, as well."

He winked, and her blush deepened. He flicked the reins and said, "So, you like to watch the children run and play. Do you want children?"

Their gazes met, and she actually glowed. "I'd love a houseful. More, if I were so blessed."

The grin he gave her said he would do his best to oblige.

♥ ♥ ♥

Hand-in-hand, they milled around the grounds after eating their fill of supper. Chase praised her corn bread repeatedly. He'd chucked down four pieces. The festivities were in full swing, with baseball at one end and crochet at the other. Men pitched horseshoes while women tended their younger children.

While Matt and Chase played a game of horseshoes, the two women

125

watched. Marianne turned to Callie. "Matt said he has months of training and wants to write to me. He asked that I do the same. Do you think I'm crazy?"

Callie smiled. "No, you're not crazy at all. Sounds like you might have actually found someone worthy of you. Follow your heart. If he's the one, it'll be worth the wait."

Sheriff Millet clapped Chase's back. "Had time to talk you up to most of the board. Most feel two deputies could work. Looks like the job's yours, if you want it."

"Sounds great. Thanks, Sheriff. Let's talk tomorrow before I haul those three to Cheyenne." They shook hands, and David tipped his head to Callie.

"Congratulations." She gave his cheek a peck. He took her hand and began walking.

An hour before dusk, the band started playing. Chase led Callie to that area and they danced three dances. He led her to the side, again among the crowd.

He turned to her and squeezed her hand. Keeping his voice low he said, "I feel our bond is so strong because I now know the value of such a precious gift and treasure it. I'm blessed you love me, and I'm so thankful you could trust me enough to find your heart and soul again."

He held her left hand and went down on one knee. "I love you and I want that house of children to share our lives and love with. I want those brighter tomorrows with you. Callie, will you marry me?"

Silent tears slipped down her cheeks, and love beamed from her eyes. He held up a ring. His gaze captured hers—and the rest of the world ceased to exist.

"This ring was my mother's. I ask you if you'll accept this ring as a token of my love and fidelity. If you prefer another, I'll—"

"Oh, Chase…it's beautiful…Yes—I'm honored to accept this ring." She smiled. "And yes, I will marry you."

Chase placed the ring on her finger, stood, and kissed her lightly on the lips. Then, he whispered, "I love you."

She repeated his words. The crowd roared.

Finding a spot away from the crowd, Chase explained he and Matt would be leaving tomorrow to take the three prisoners to Cheyenne.

"We'll be gone two weeks…I'm wondering if that'll be time enough to plan a wedding?"

Callie's heart soared. "That will be just about perfect."

Another boom rent the air, and the sky lit up with a brilliant display. Callie leaned back against Chase, savoring being held within his arms. Shouts from the crowd went up around them as a multitude of colors, sparkling and more dazzling than each one before, exploded overhead to shower down like colorful falling stars.

Chase tipped his head down and his breath fanned her ear. "What do you say to going home to make our own fireworks?"

About Beverly Wells

For years Beverly Wells worked a hectic pace as a Public Health Nurse in Homecare while also serving on the Medical Reserve Corps for Homeland Security. Little did she know when she decided to escape from reality and write a historical romance it would set another whirlwind to swirling. Now as an award-winning author, she devotes her full time to making writing her career. Bev enjoys writing humorous, sensuous historical romance while including a lesson learned or raising awareness of a heartfelt issue, or just a darn good heartwarming tale.

She feels blessed not only to live on one of the Finger Lakes in NYS with her husband (who patiently puts up with her crazy writing world) and her devoted walking buddy, Jamie, a rescued black lab mix, but to have a wonderful and loving son, daughter-in law and two fantastic granddaughters plus oodles of treasured friends. She enjoys all lake activity, Nascar, volunteering at the local shelter, flower gardening(so she can get her hands good and dirty) and cooking for gathered friends.

For more information regarding Bev, visit her at *Prairie Rose Publications author page*, her website *@www.beverlywellsauthor.com*, *FB*, *twitter*, *blog @beverlywellsauthor.wordpress.com* or gmail her *@beverlywellsauthor@gmail.com* She'd love to hear from you.

Never Had a Chance

(An Agate Gulch Story)

By Angela Raines

How can a deadly trick bring two people from different worlds the love they didn't know they needed?

Chapter 1

"My sister, my dear sweet sister," Tom slurred. "Here's to my sister. May she have a long, happy, married life, damn her."

Tom had been sitting in the bar in Pueblo for the whole afternoon, drinking. He'd had a fight with his sister and soon to be brother–in–law. They'd wanted him to help out at the ranch, maybe run errands. He'd wanted to relax, spend time with his new friends in Agate Gulch. Truth was, Tom was feeling out of place. He'd been surprised when he finally recovered from his beating at the hands of Oliver's gang, to find that his sister, who'd deserted him, was living in the town where he'd run.

"Something happening?" the bartender asked, as he wiped the scarred bar top.

"She's getting married. I finally found her—and she's getting married," Tom answered, throwing back the rest of his drink. He did love his sister, but her leaving him to Oliver's tender care still did not sit well.

Two men moved to sit next to Tom, listening to his slurred words. Exchanging looks at the bang of Tom's glass, they nodded.

"Sounds like you're having a tough day," the short one said. "How's about I buy you a drink?"

"Why you want to—" Tom started.

"Hey, just being friendly, no offense," the tall one said.

"Sorry," Tom said, "but you gotta have one with me, seein' as you're being so friendly."

"But, of course. Bartender, drinks all around," the short one said, throwing coins on the bar.

A COWBOY CELEBRATION

"Thank you," Tom said, raising the fresh drink to his lips. "So, who do I owe?"

"You can call me Pete," said the short one, "and this tall galoot, you can call George."

"Well, Pete, George, here's to your good health," Tom said, lifting yet another drink to his lips, most of it dribbling out of the corner of his mouth, down his shirt and onto the sticky floor. "How's about I buy the next round?" Tom asked, pulling money from his pocket. Although he had trouble focusing, anyone could tell he must have started out with a fair amount, considering how much he still had on hand.

"I think maybe you're about to run out of room for any more, young man," said the bartender. He liked the kid; he had promise, and just needed to get past whatever was bothering him. Plus, the other two were trouble, if he knew anything about it, and with his years behind the bar, he had a fair to middling knowledge of trouble.

Pete glared at the bartender. "Seems to me you'd not limit a man who obviously could use some sympathy," he questioned the bartender's pronouncement.

"Yeah. What *he* said," Tom agreed, his head falling onto his chest, his body swaying forward.

"How about we go find someplace else?" George asked, catching Tom before he fell to the floor.

"I think that'd be a good idea," Tom said, trying to straighten up, but instead, slumping against George who, with the help of Pete, escorted the woozy Tom out the door into the heat of the summer night.

"I know just the thing to cheer you up, friend," Pete whispered into Tom's ear.

"Whassat?" Tom asked, turning his head, eyes trying their best to focus on the man holding him upright.

Catching the eyes of George, Pete repeated, "I know just the thing to cheer you up. What you need, friend, is some female companionship."

"No, no females, they're nothing but trouble," Tom insisted.

"You're looking at it all wrong. Best way to get over it is to…"

Tom shook his head; in fact, he would have fallen had they not been holding him up. Even then, the alcohol in his stomach rebelled, and soon he felt as if he would retch.

With effort, Pete and George helped Tom stand up. He stumbled as they walked along a wooden fence. Confused, Tom followed their lead, embarrassed

129

at his lapse, his inability to hold his liquor. His stomach rolled again, noisily.

"Sorry," he started.

"Think nothing of it," George said.

"Where we going? Why aren't we riding? Oh, wait, I don't have a horse." Tom tried to laugh, but it trailed off.

"We're taking you to see Mary. Once you see her, everything will be okay," Pete explained.

"How can seein' Mary make everything okay?" Tom asked, eyeing Pete, then George. He was trying to figure something out, but his brain was so foggy the thought wouldn't take hold. The fence they were following was ending. Tom could almost make out the outlines of a two-story house.

"Where you taking me?" Tom asked again.

"To see Mary. She's one of the special girls," Pete replied.

Slowly, the two helped Tom up the steps, knocking on the door and walking backward into the shadow. The two made it into the darkness just as the door opened. Light streaming out from the door outlined a young girl, a girl with curves and substance.

"You must be Mary," Tom said, looking into intelligent and curious brown eyes. "I'm supposed to see you." With those words, he grabbed at the girl, throwing his arms around her. Faintly he heard laughter and snickers behind him. Heard, but they were not registering. The only thing that registered was the feel of this young girl in his arms, with a figure made to be held. He bent his head, but she turned her face away quickly.

Tom gloried in her beauty, trying to pull her closer, his lips brushing hers. Then, for an instant, he felt her response…just before the realization hit him that this girl was not one of the "ladies" as he'd been led to believe. He found himself quickly sobering up. The girl, whatever her name was, pushed against his chest. At the same time, Tom heard a man's voice calling, "Maria, who is it?"

Letting loose of her, Tom moved back, shame coloring his face. He pulled his hat from his head, lowering his eyes to the girl. "I'm sorry—" he said, breaking off when he heard the voices behind him.

"There the bastard is," Pete whispered.

"We'll get him this time," responded George, as the click of hammers reached Tom's ears.

Tom, at first confused, saw an older Spanish gentleman move toward the door, then realized the man was a target. Fear for the girl and the man completed his sobering process as he pushed her toward the man and, drawing

A COWBOY CELEBRATION

his own gun, stepped in front of both.

"What the hell do you think you are doing?" challenged Tom just as the two guns flashed out of the dark. He felt a double blow, but managed to get his own gun into play, firing at the flashes. He went to give chase, and managed to get down the first two steps when his right leg gave out.

"Damn, I've been taken for a sucker, and I don't—" Tom began. But his head hit the ground, bouncing off a rock, and then—there was nothing but darkness.

Chapter 2

Maria stood over the bed. The man looked younger, except for the growth on his face. Her fingers traced the line of her lips, feeling again the kiss.

When he first grabbed her, he had called her *Mary*. The overpowering smell of alcohol on his breath had caused her to try to pull away. His strong arms prevented her escape. Then this man, lying here, captured a kiss. He'd been demanding as the kiss started, but it soon changed to a gentle probing, a request for a return kiss.

Dropping her hand from her mouth, she gasped at her thoughts. Leaning in, her lips brushed his. She whispered in his ear, "Thank you, I enjoyed it."

She didn't know if he heard her or not, but it seemed important that he know. That she tell him before someone caught her in his room. It might be different if he were awake, but she wasn't waiting.

"What do you look like without your beard, what color are your eyes? Why—or what— brought you to our door?" she asked the unconscious man lying so still. He looked dead, except for the rise and fall of the sheet covering him.

Watching the sheet, its gentle rise and fall, intrigued her. What did he look like? Glancing around to make sure no one was near, she tentatively touched the sheet.

"Father will be furious," she muttered, but it didn't still her hand.

Pulling the sheet up, her eyes studied the chest that she'd been crushed against. The arms, so strong, yet gentle. Reaching out, she traced the hair sloping toward his waist, the bandage binding his arm to his body, the almost invisible scars across his chest and sides, then down toward his legs.

"So many whys and whats, yet you cannot answer, cannot tell me how you received these scars," Maria said as she continued her exploration, enjoying the beauty of Tom's form. "What would it be like to..." she started, then caught herself. Time for answering that was in her own room where detection wasn't likely. She'd have the leisure to explore her thoughts there.

At almost eighteen, there had been boys who had wanted to court her, but never had she been given the chance to really study anyone in the manner she was doing now.

"How scandalous, but..." With a sigh, Maria drew back, smiling as she gently pulled the sheet over Tom.

A COWBOY CELEBRATION

"I'm sorry, I should not have done that, but I have a feeling I may get to know you better as time passes," she said, looking back again at the man in the bed as she silently left the room.

Maria returned to her room where she sat on her bed, thinking, remembering the moment when her father had called out, asking who was at the door. She had turned to answer when he'd pushed her back behind him.

"Stay back," he had shouted, but to whom? Who had he shouted that command to? How quickly the night had split with a thunderstorm of gunfire and flashes. Who'd started the firing she didn't know, but the actions of the man lying unconscious in their home had saved their lives, of that she was certain.

Her father had caught her, immediately asking, "Are you all right?" while pushing her even farther back into the house. As the stranger had started out the door, he had shouted something to her father, then staggered as bullets hit his body. Hand to mouth, she'd tried to scream, but no sound had come out. Fear for her father overrode everything else as she'd moved forward, only to be pushed back again by her father. The man, instead of falling, had taken off after the culprits, only to fall and hit his head on the rock by the steps.

"We will take him inside. Go get one of the servants," her father had ordered. She had hurried to the man's aide, to find out more, but her father's voice brooked not argument. She did not have far to go, the gunshots having drawn the servants to the scene more quickly than she had expected. They'd brought the man into the room where he now lay. Young Esteban had hurried out to get the doctor and sheriff, once they had the man settled.

She'd wanted to stay and help, but her father would not hear of it. "You are a young girl, you have no business being in the room with such a man," her father declared. It was so like him. Since her mother had died ten years ago, he had treated her like she would break. Nothing was too good for her, but at the same time, no one was good enough.

But Maria managed to work her way around her father most of the time, and she was very determined to have her way with this situation. Maria smiled to herself, thinking again of how the man's skin felt under her fingertips.

Chapter 3

Tom struggled against the pressure on his chest. A hot breeze blew across his sweat–drenched face; a buzz of noise, unclear sounds, assaulting his ears. Even as he continued his struggle, the pain lancing through his left arm brought focus and the noise broke into intelligent words.

"Does anyone know his name, where he came from?" an authoritative voice asked.

"He came and knocked on the door," a soft female voice answered.

"I do not know who he is, or his reason for coming to my door in the middle of the night, but his part in what happened, *quién sabe*—who knows?" another man interrupted.

"Who, what?" Tom coughed. Then his breath caught, the pain returning to his chest tenfold, and the darkness claimed him again.

The smell of unfamiliar food cooking pulled Tom back from oblivion. His mind tried to process what he was smelling; a pungent, smoky smell. Immediately, his stomach started growling as though it had been empty for some time. Moving to rise and follow the smells, Tom found his left arm tied to his chest. A pain shot through his upper left chest and shoulder, followed by a stinging in his right leg; but none of those irritants compared to the throbbing behind his eyes, up through the top of his head and down the back of his neck. He took a deep breath to calm the panic he was beginning to feel.

Where was he, why was he restrained? That thought was swiftly followed with the question that pushed Tom into full panic. *Who was he?*

Fighting the pain, Tom rolled to the right, moving to the edge of the bed. He was in a bed. The knowledge calmed him somewhat, but he still needed to find the answers to his questions. He'd almost made it to a sitting position when the door opened.

"So, you are awake," the male voice stated. A voice with a Spanish accent. "I will send for the doctor; in the meantime, you lie back down," he continued, as he pushed Tom back toward the pillow. "Please, stay here until the doctor says otherwise. I do not want you doing anything that will require you to stay longer." So saying, the man quickly went out the door, closing it firmly.

Tom stared at the closed door. More questions fought for dominance in his brain. The pain and exhaustion he felt soon overwhelmed him, and he entered the dark of sleep once again.

About an hour later, Tom awoke and lay staring at the ceiling, the lack of memory weighing on him almost as much as the pain he felt in his body. *When would he remember? Would he ever remember?* Those two questions played tag with each other as they circled his brain.

The door opened and a man, maybe the doctor, walked in. "Mr. Berñal told me you were awake," was his jovial greeting.

"I am now," Tom replied. He wondered if he should confide in the doctor, tell him he had no memory of anything. Perhaps a few discreet questions might help him jog his memory. It was worth the try, Tom thought. Anything was better than not knowing.

"How long have I been here?" Tom asked the doctor. It seemed a safe question.

"You were shot about three days ago. While serious wounds, they were not life-threatening, unless infection sets in, and it doesn't look like that's going to happen. It was the head wound that concerned me—you being unconscious for three days," the doctor answered. "How are you feeling?"

"I hurt, but I..." Tom paused, hesitant to continue, but realizing he would get nowhere if he didn't say something. Sighing, he continued. "It's the lack of memory, the not knowing that worries me. It's like everything is just beyond the edge of my vision." Now that he had said it, he felt relieved. Perhaps the doctor could give him an opinion as to how long he might be a blank page.

"So, do you know your name? Why you were here?" the doctor questioned as he continued to examine Tom's head. He'd finished cleaning and dressing the other wounds, making satisfied sounds while working.

"There's nothing. I don't know who shot me—which I assume is what happened—or why anyone would want to do such a thing. By the way, where am I?" Tom asked, frustration coloring his voice, making the gruffness even more pronounced.

"Relax," the doctor said. "It's not uncommon for someone to temporarily lose their memory with some head wounds. I would say you must've hit that rock at just the right angle."

"So...you think I'll remember?" Tom asked, hope in his voice.

"There's a good chance, but when? That's the big question. Otherwise, you seem to be healing nicely," the doctor proclaimed as he finished. "You just continue getting well and let nature take care of the memory."

"Thank you," Tom started, but the next question went unasked as the man who'd found him awake returned.

"Mr. Berñal," the doctor said, "your guest is doing well."

"He is *not* my guest," Berñal huffed. "When can he leave?"

If the man didn't want him here, why was he lying in a fine bed in this house? The image of someone back in the shadows played across his mind, just beyond reach. Try as he might, nothing came into focus. For some reason, this man was a part of the puzzle Tom was trying to piece together.

"In a few days," the doctor replied to the question. "We don't want to rush things."

"A few days is too many, I have guests and a celebration to attend to, not some tramp," Berñal said, standing straight and tall, belying the image of his medium height.

Tom watched, puzzled even further by the man called Berñal and his reaction. Who was he, to be called "tramp"? What had he done? Nothing would come into his mind. Frustration, and anger at Berñal, the doctor, and himself, made Tom attempt to move out of the bed.

"Now, you lie down; don't let Mr. Berñal upset you. Get some rest," the doctor said, gently pushing Tom back down.

The doctor turned to Berñal. "Let's go out into the hall. We need to let the patient have quiet."

"Very well," Berñal conceded as the two left the room, Berñal closing the door firmly behind him.

Chapter 4

Maria stared at the sky. Blue, a turquoise blue that appeared artificial. Clouds slowly traveled from north to south, covering and uncovering the golden light from the sun as she watched out the window. She was in the kitchen making the green corn fritters. With each step in the process, she remembered her mother showing her how they were made.

"I made these for your father, little one, when I decided to marry him."

"Did he want to marry you?" Maria had asked.

"No, it took a bit of persuading, but in the end he was glad he pursued me," her mother had laughed.

"How did you know, and why green corn fritters?" Maria had wanted to know.

"I knew the minute I saw him that he was the one for me. And the fritters, they are an old family recipe, and if you make them with love, the one who eats them loves you back."

Maria missed her mother, having someone to share secrets with, someone of whom she could ask questions… The servants were kind, but it was not the same. Sighing, she grabbed her small tray with the fritters, and headed to the young man's room. Perhaps she was being foolish, giving the stranger the fritters, but if they had helped her mother catch her father, she could do no less.

When she reached his door, she glanced right, left, and behind her. Seeing no one, she turned the knob. Cracking the door, she squeezed into the darkened room, just as she had every day since the shooting. No matter what anyone said, she knew she must be with this man lying on the bed. Her heart told her this was the one for her, and she would do whatever it took to make him understand she was for him.

The figure in the bed was quiet. *Perhaps he is still asleep*, she thought. She moved to the window and grabbed the curtains, throwing them back to allow the light to blaze into the room. After all, she'd heard her father and the doctor say he'd awakened. She wanted to see what color his eyes were. To see if the sight of her would bring back any memories. She'd heard them say he couldn't remember. It bothered her that he could not remember, especially the kiss, for it was so special to her.

Expecting a shout at the sudden brightness, the room remained silent. Glancing back to the bed she saw eyes, the color of the same skies she'd enjoyed, following her movements.

"What do you think you're doing?" the hoarse voice asked.

"Letting in some sunshine, and bringing you food," Maria replied with a bright smile.

Silence greeted her reply. The clock in the main part of the house chimed two, but all else remained quiet.

Hesitating but a moment, Maria moved toward the bed and its occupant, and she set the food on a side table. Her patient's uncertain thoughts played across his face, and she loved him and felt sorry for him at the same time. She intended to marry him. His kiss, it had started her thinking, and her resolve only deepened every time she came near him.

The same hoarse voice broke the silence as he looked up at her. "Who are you?"

Her voice sounded familiar to Tom, but from where, he had no recollection. She appeared comfortable in the room, in his presence. Was she a servant, a nurse? Of course, there were pretty servants, but not dressed in such a fine quality of fabric. The thought that she might be related to his host made him uneasy. The man didn't like him, and if this was a relative, he needed to find out, and make plans accordingly. But who was he? He needed to find that out, first.

"I am Maria, but you called me Mary," was the saucy answer, a flirting response.

"I'm sorry, but am I supposed to know you?" It seemed safer to keep a distance, but with a face like that, it would be hard to do.

"You kissed me, do not you remember?" Maria replied, a sweet, knowing smile on her face.

"No offense, for you are stunning, but if I kissed you—I would remember that," Tom replied with conviction, but his thoughts were troubled, as he struggled to remember.

"A very nice compliment, but at the same time…you are calling me a liar?" she questioned, hands on her hips.

"No, ma'am."

"It is *señorita*."

"No, *señorita*," Tom corrected. "I wouldn't call you a liar, but…I don't remember kissing you," he insisted.

Maria laughed, a gentle laugh, leaning in toward Tom. "Oh, *señor*, I am giving you a difficult time. I am aware that you do not remember anything, for I

A COWBOY CELEBRATION

heard my father and the doctor talking. But you *did* kiss me, and very thoroughly, I will add."

Tom sighed. The story that he had kissed this beauty startled him. *But I wish I knew for sure,* he thought. *How those eyes sparkle...and her rose-colored lips... I would remember that.* Tom stopped himself. He had no business thinking such thoughts. He didn't even know who he was or where he had been, or— This beauty deserved the best, and somehow, he didn't think he was that person.

Maria laughed. "Shall I show you what you do not remember?" she asked, as she leaned in.

Tom's arms started to move, but the pain of his confined arm brought him back to his senses. He felt a feather-like touch on his cheek, a familiar touch. Frustrated at his limitations and lack of memory, Tom's voice was harsher than he intended as he looked at Maria, saying, "I can't decide if you are trying to irritate me, embarrass me, or cheer me up."

Maria smiled a knowing smile. "Now, let me fluff your pillows. You need to get well so that you can attend my birthday celebration." She jumped at loud voices outside the door.

"Bernardo, my friend, you mean you have a criminal under your roof?" Fin Merrick asked his friend Bernál.

"Now, Finaldo, we do not know anything for sure," Mr. Bernál's voice sounded, "but the doctor does not want him moved. Besides, here is the sheriff, so there is nothing to worry about."

Looking at Tom, Maria grimaced at the conversation. She leaned toward him and whispered, "That is my father's friend Finaldo Merrick. He always thinks he knows best, and I think he wants to court me. But he is such an old man!"

The door opened, and Mr. Bernál, followed by a man with a star on his chest and another who could only be Merrick, entered the room.

"Maria, what are you doing here? We have servants who take care of such things," Bernál roared.

"You see what can happen," Merrick said, giving Maria a stern look.

Tom watched from the bed. This was a complication he didn't need. Seeing Merrick, Tom took an instant dislike to him. If this man was wanting to court Maria...well, it was criminal. Still, it was none of his business. He needed to get well and regain his memory so that he could leave.

"I choose to do this, to help with this man's care," Maria replied, her eyes flashing.

139

"No daughter of mine will act the trollop with a saddle tramp," her father stated, moving to escort Maria from the room.

Maria jerked her arm away saying, "You do not know he is, as you call him, a saddle tramp; that is Finaldo's influence!" She stamped her foot for emphasis. "And I, Maria Teresita Sandoval Bernál, say you are wrong!"

God, she is beautiful, Tom thought and it humbled him to see her belief in him was so strong. *Perhaps she is telling the truth, and I did kiss her. I just wish I could remember something like that.*

"I will leave, not because you order it, but because I choose to. I believe Sheriff Desmond wishes to speak with him," Maria continued, walking through the door, head held high and hips swaying. "And you, Finaldo Merrick, will stop interfering in things you know nothing about," she said, glaring at her father and Merrick.

Tom watched Bernál follow Maria out, neither saying anything.

Merrick gave a sly smile as he informed Tom, "This is Sheriff Patrick Desmond. He is not only the sheriff, but a member of the Rocky Mountain Detective Association. He is known for the skill with which he catches criminals. Now, I shall take my leave. Sheriff Desmond, good day."

Sheriff Desmond watched Merrick leave, then turned and asked, "Do you remember anything?"

Tom shook his head, the food Maria had brought forgotten.

Chapter 5

Frustration continued to cloud Tom's thoughts. It had been five days since he regained consciousness, and he was still no closer to solving his puzzle. He was using a cane, but his leg was healing nicely according to the doctor. He had some use of his left arm but he still had no idea who he was, or why he was at the Berñal place that night. The June heat giving way to July's inferno contributed to his unease.

"I know," Tom muttered, "I *know* there was something I was going to do, but what?"

No one had been asking about him, and that thought left him empty. It didn't feel right. Maria had been all that was helpful, and even her father was starting to tolerate him. He supposed he had Maria to thank for that.

"A blank page, that's what I am...a blank page," Tom said aloud.

"And what do you plan to write on that page?" the sheriff asked, walking into the room.

The sheriff had been to visit every day since he regained consciousness. It was both comforting and confining. Still, Tom admitted the sheriff was helpful, almost like the father he never had growing up. The thought brought him up short. *How did I know that?*

"I don't know sheriff. I still remember nothing. Who was I, what kind of thoughts did I think? Was someone trying to kill me? If so, why? What if I'm just as bad as those who tried to kill me?" Tom asked in a rush, frustrated.

"Do you really believe that?" Desmond asked. "Do you think you're as bad as those who shot you that night?"

"I really don't know, but my feeling is, I was just being a fool—and now, well, now..." Tom sighed.

"You just keep following your instincts," Sheriff Desmond suggested. "I've the feeling they'll aim you right."

"I hope so. This not knowing—wondering what really happened that night...who I am..." Tom said, his right fist hitting the bed post, followed with a grunt of pain.

"Guess that was pretty stupid," Tom grinned sheepishly.

The sheriff laughed, a deep belly laugh. "I'll keep my thoughts to myself," he said. "If you feel up to it, care to take a walk to where it happened?"

Desmond continued.

"Anything to help," Tom replied. "Besides, I could use some fresh air. Being confined to this room, well, I'm sure you can guess. Do you think the doctor will be upset?" Tom asked.

"It's okay, I checked with him before I stopped by. It seems to me you're making great progress. You must've been in pretty good shape before all this happened."

Tom wasn't so sure about that. Lately, there had been a couple of dreams where he was being beaten, but the doctor had made no comment about any other injuries.

"You know, you've been good for Maria, young man," the sheriff said, walking alongside Tom. "I think a lot of that young lady, but her father—well, we won't go into that."

"She is wonderful," Tom said, smiling, "and has helped pass the time." She'd been more than helpful. He'd gotten used to her coming in and fussing over him. But the thoughts he'd tried to keep in check were fast getting out of control. He needed to find out who he was and what had happened. Then, he would leave before he ended up hurting Maria. She was too special, and the last thing he wanted was to see her hurt.

The sheriff pulled out his watch. It was an elegant-looking timepiece, engraving covering the lid. Tom watched, observing the sheriff, how he handled the watch with such care.

Seeing Tom watching him, Sheriff Desmond smiled. "My wife Ann gave this to me on our wedding day. And in a couple of days we will both be here for the celebration."

"Celebration? What are the Berñals celebrating?" Tom asked.

"Well, besides the Fourth of July, it's Maria's birthday," the sheriff replied, closing his watch, carefully returning it to its pocket, straightening the chain that secured it to his vest.

"She's quite the determined young lady," Tom said. "How old will she be?"

"Older than you might believe, and younger than most," the sheriff returned as he helped Tom maneuver through the door to the house. "Does any of this look familiar?"

Tom stared about him. The porch, steps, the path leading to the house—nothing was familiar. Yet, there was a nagging suspicion they were being watched, but he saw no one. He shook his head. "Nothing, nothing is familiar.

Damn!"

"I know you're frustrated son, but careful of that temper. It might cause you to do something sudden that you'll end up regretting."

Chapter 6

The shed was gloomy; Pete and George didn't look happy. They'd sneaked out during the night to get some food and drink. The time spent watching the house hadn't been easy. Conversation, which never was prolific, had almost come to a standstill.

"You know," George whispered, taking another swig of the bottle, "there's talk that you are an evil person."

"Who says I'm evil?" Pete asked. "Who has that right?"

"Now, Pete, no need to get upset. They were just talking," George placated, handing the bottle back to Pete.

"I'd like to know what they think is evil? Is it evil to kill a rattlesnake before it bites you?"

"Maybe they just don't think it's right you kill folks for a living," George said.

"And maybe some folks just need to be eliminated! Did they ever think of that? What's their rules for right and wrong?" he asked slamming the bottle down.

"Well, maybe they think it's wrong to take money for it?" George wondered, his eyes trying to focus on Pete, hoping to get the bottle back before Pete's temper broke it, or he drained it.

"If you're good at what you do, shouldn't you be paid for it? And I'm good." Pete smiled.

"You are, that," George said, slapping Pete on the back.

Pete whirled on George, grabbing the offending arm and shoving him away. "Don't you never touch me again."

George cowered back, rubbing his sore arm. He'd only been trying to pass the time, make some conversation. He'd never expected his friend to hurt him. He had hurt other people, but never him. It must be the suspense that made Pete short-tempered.

"Now, let's get back to business," Pete said, "and keep the noise down. Do you want to get caught hiding out in this shed?"

Pete and George returned to watching the house. They'd seen the sheriff visit at least once each day for the past five days.

"Whatcha think is going on?" asked George.

A COWBOY CELEBRATION

"You know as much as I do," replied Pete with a frustrated sigh. "Maybe they've checked, and didn't find anything…moved on," Pete mumbled.

"But what happened to that young feller we shot? You think he's dead?" continued George.

"He might be, but I doubt it. Now, shut up. Someone's coming out."

The two ducked back further into the shed where they'd been hiding. George couldn't figure out why no one had thought to look in such an obvious place. But they hadn't stayed there the whole time after shooting the kid.

"Pete, why are we staying around here? They're sure to find us," whined George.

"Shut up, George. You know why we can't leave. We have a job to finish; the boss gave us half and we want to collect the rest."

George shook his head. Everything had gone wrong since that night. He was tired of sneaking around in the dark. He hated the shed they hid in while spying on the house. Most of all, he hated not knowing. It was one thing to kill someone that you were getting paid for, but that young man…well, George felt he'd jinxed the whole thing; that Pete had made a mistake changing the plan all sudden-like.

He was just getting ready to say so to Pete, when the door opened and out walked the sheriff holding the young man up as they moved to the chairs on the porch. George felt they'd lost.

Now what? he thought. *Well, I can end it now.* George took aim, slowly pulling back on the trigger. At this distance, he wouldn't miss, and he could maybe get the sheriff, also. Smiling, sure Pete would be pleased, he hesitated as he heard voices nearby.

Pete turned toward the sound, seeing the gun in George's hand. Quickly, he grabbed at the gun, almost tearing George's hand off in the process. *"What the hell do you think you're doing?"*

"I figured I'd get rid of the kid and the sheriff at the same time. Then, we could do our job and get back to Kansas. That way, we could get the boss off our backs."

"Of all the dumb—" Pete started, when the voices George had heard caught his attention.

"It will be a big celebration. It is the *señorita's* birthday, and July four, also. Many people will be coming. We will have much food and lots of work, but fun, too," the deep Spanish voice said.

"Oh, the *señorita*, she has been planning some surprise, and I do not think her father will be too happy, but who can say no to her?" answered a female

145

voice as the two moved away from the shed.

Pete turned to George, a big grin on his face, "There's the answer to our problems."

Chapter 7

Tom watched the crowd sway to the music floating across the open space behind the house. He'd never seen such a grand event as this party and celebration. But how did he know that? There was no indication his memory had returned, just those glimmers at unexpected moments. He studied his reaction to the scene he was seeing. In his heart, he truly felt this was a new experience.

Standing back, almost at the edge of the light, he hoped no one would engage him in conversation. There were only so many times you could say "I don't know". He was enjoying watching Maria swaying to the music, dancing with the young men. Turning his head away, he noticed two shadows moving furtively around the edge of the party, away from someone who reminded him of Merrick. Before he had the chance to investigate further, Maria walked over, a devilish smile dancing in her eyes.

"Are you ready to dance with me?" she asked.

Tom softly replied, pushing his cane out in front of him, "I don't think the doctor would approve."

"Very well, I shall keep you company until the dance is over," Maria declared, seemingly unwilling to let the chance pass to spend time with him.

"Are you sure that's a good idea? I don't think your father would approve. He may have accepted that I didn't try to harm you or himself, but he still doesn't trust me," Tom replied as he moved slowly away from Maria.

The farther he moved away, the closer she moved toward him, until her hand shot out, covering the one holding the cane.

"Come, at least you can eat, can you not?" Maria smiled, leading Tom slowly through the crowd toward the food tables.

The closer they came, the more Tom realized he really was hungry. He'd held back, concern for his hesitant host keeping him from even remotely enjoying himself. It took the determined young woman at his side to pull him out of his self-imposed solitude.

"This all looks and smells so good. I do think there are some new things here for me to try." Tom laughed.

"Then, I shall be your guide, answer any questions you may have. But first, you must have one of the green corn fritters, since you did not eat them when I brought them to your room," Maria grinned, pulling the food from the small

NEVER HAD A CHANCE—ANGELA RAINES

basket she picked up from a servant. "They are from a family recipe, and I made them myself."

He took a bite. "These are really good, and I'm sorry now I missed eating them sooner. You must love cooking." *Now that was a stupid thing to say*, Tom thought to himself. "I mean, the love you put into these," he stammered.

Maria laughed, a joyous sound that traveled across the area. "I put a lot of love into many things."

Tom grinned to hide his embarrassment, not minding that she found his efforts funny. He was finding there was a lot he didn't mind about Maria, as down the line of food-laden tables the two traversed. Tom sampled one aromatic dish after another, occasionally grimacing at the fire on his tongue from some of the spices. Laughter and a lot of good-natured joking accompanied the two. For Tom and Maria, everything else faded completely into the background.

Slowly, Maria guided Tom toward the front of the house, laughing and talking the whole way. When Tom realized where they were, he stopped, concern for Maria clouding his mind.

"Hadn't we better get back to your party?" Tom asked. "They still haven't found who took those shots."

"I feel safe with you," Maria said, snuggling close. "Besides, I have decided that I will marry you."

"You what?"

"I am going to marry you," Maria stated, her arms going about his waist.

"I don't think that's a good idea, you don't know me. *I* don't know me," Tom protested, fear and concern warring with amazement at Maria declaration.

"That is nonsense. You protected me and my father at great cost to yourself. You have been all that is kind and considerate."

"But—"

"No buts, and I suggest you seal our engagement with a kiss, like the one you gave me when we met."

"I didn't—I couldn't—"

Maria pulled Tom forward onto the porch, toward the door. She silenced his protest, pulling his head down and placing a tender kiss on his lips.

Tom responded, his arms circling her waist, the kiss deepening into something more demanding. Tom felt Maria respond, moving closer to meld her form into his. Tom inhaled the sweet smell of Maria, the taste of the food they'd just enjoyed mixing with a response in himself. Tom pulled her tighter, demanding even more. Suddenly, he halted the kiss, afraid of...

148

The world spun, memories flooding back.

"Oh, my God," Tom said.

He grabbed Maria's hand, and moving as fast as his wounded leg would let him, he headed back to the party.

Chapter 8

Tom slowed as he neared the edge of the lights at the party. Pulling Maria close, he whispered, "Quietly, go find the sheriff and ask him to come talk to me. And tell him to make it look natural."

"What is going on?" Maria whispered back, fear at what was happening tying knots in her stomach.

"I'll tell you later, right now, I need you to trust me, please," Tom replied, placing a hand over hers and giving it a gentle squeeze.

Maria hesitated, but the urgency in Tom's voice concerned her. Placing her left hand on Tom's chest, she reached up with her right hand and pulled Tom's head down, kissing him lightly on the lips.

Tom's arms went around her, pulling her closer, deepening the kiss. Lights went off in his brain again, throwing him back to reality. Stepping back, he smiled, kissing Maria's forehead. "Please, go. It's important."

Maria patted Tom's chest, returning his smile, as she moved into the crowd in search of the sheriff.

Tom turned back toward the front of the house, heading to his room to pick up his gun. He might not need it; in fact, he hoped he wouldn't. Leaving his cane by the bed, Tom slowly returned to where he'd left Maria. Without the cane, his balance was a bit off, but that couldn't be helped. He needed to be unencumbered, just in case.

Walking up to Tom, the sheriff said, "Maria said you wanted to—" Noticing the gun on Tom's right thigh, the lack of cane, his eyes narrowed. "What's this?"

"I remember everything," Tom said. "I'll be glad to tell you all I remember, but right now we need to protect Mr. Berñal. I thought I saw a glimpse of those who shot me. I think it was Berñal they were after, all along."

"You mean—"

"I think they were after Berñal with me as a decoy," Tom continued, answering the sheriff's implied question.

"If that's the case, we don't want to spook them," Sheriff Desmond stated, checking his own pistol.

"My thought exactly," Tom said, placing his weight on his good leg. The exertion, along with the blast of memory, was sapping his strength. If he could hold on until this was over... He quailed at the thought that Maria or her father might be hurt.

"Perhaps I could be a decoy again," Tom said.

"What?" the sheriff asked, his eyes taking in the guests at the party as he looked for Berñal.

"Maybe if we let it be known I remember, and place myself where the two will come after me," Tom began.

"And get yourself shot again, maybe killed this time?"

"Listen sheriff, if we panic everyone, Pete and George—that's their names—will have a greater chance of finishing what they started. If they focus on me, then we can get the Berñals to safety without anyone the wiser. Plus, we might get lucky and catch those two, find out what this is all about."

Sheriff Desmond listened, shaking his head. "Might work, but I'm worried for your safety in all this."

"I'll be all right. I know who I'm looking for, now."

Walking back towards the party, Desmond was greeting people as he made his way to Mr. Berñal. Fortunately, Berñal had been surrounded by his friends most of the day and evening.

"You can always count on a big shindig," the sheriff said to Merrick as he passed by.

"That, you can sheriff, that you can," Merrick replied, scanning the crowd.

"Looking for someone?" Desmond asked.

"I thought I saw Maria, but then she disappeared. Wanted to wish her a pleasant birthday before I left."

"Last I saw her, she was heading back to where her father was," the sheriff replied.

"Thanks," Merrick said as he started moving toward Mr. Berñal.

"I'm headed that way myself."

Tom watched the sheriff move away, stopping to talk with different people. When about five minutes had passed, Tom slowly made his way to the outer area. There, the light of the party met the surrounding darkness. He was amazed at the energy of the revelers, for he was tiring fast. It had been a long day, and his leg and shoulder were bothering him. Walking was even harder without his cane, but it would have just been in the way if he had to use his pistol.

"Soon, they will set off the firecrackers," a nearby voice exclaimed excitedly.

"*Sí*, it is good that the *señorita's* birthday coincides with such a festive occasion."

Firecrackers. That would be the time they would strike, Tom thought. He needed to hurry, but wasn't sure where the two would be. Carefully, Tom continued moving around the perimeter. As he approached the halfway point, he glanced toward Mr. Berñal. Maria was there with her father, the sheriff, and Merrick. Merrick's presence triggered his subconscious, then a certainty in Tom.

"Merrick," whispered Tom, taking in Merrick's profile, "he was talking to the two in the shadows earlier."

Merrick glanced to his left, about ten yards from where Tom stood. Suddenly, he nodded, as the firecrackers went off. Merrick moved Maria aside, and Mr. Berñal was totally exposed. Where was the sheriff? He'd been there just a few moments ago. But Tom realized the moment had come. Taking a deep breath he shouted, "Hey, Pete! Hey, George!" He pulled his pistol. "You want to try to finish what you started?"

Two shadows detached themselves from the darkness. The noise of the firecrackers stilled as the tableau took form in front of the guests. The sheriff suddenly appeared again in front of Berñal, but it wasn't necessary. Pete and George were focused on Tom, their thumbs pulling back on the hammers of their own pistols, suddenly loud in the silence.

"Well, lookie who's here," sneered Pete. "You talkin' to us?"

A COWBOY CELEBRATION

Chapter 9

Maria knew Tom's memory must have returned. It hurt that he wanted to send her away, for the kiss was just as wonderful as the first one. She wanted to stay with him, ask him questions, but the urgency in his voice moved her forward toward Sheriff Desmond.

Spying the sheriff by the food tables, Maria walked as quickly as possible, while trying to appear calm. Many of their friends stopped her progress, talking of the party, of her birthday, and all the while, she grew more and more irritated.

"Maria, happy birthday," cried one woman.

"What a wonderful celebration," from another.

Even little Ava grabbed at her skirt. "Miss Bernãl, when do we shoot off the firecrackers?"

Stopping, despite her agitation, she knelt down. "It will not be long, but you must promise me you will stay a safe distance away," Maria informed her, patting Ava on the shoulder as she stood to move away.

"I promise, and happy birthday. Have you made a wish?" little Ava asked stalling Maria's leave.

"Not yet," Maria grinned as she replied.

"Well, don't forget, but don't tell it or it won't come true," Ava ordered.

"Yes, ma'am," Maria saluted, trying again to locate the sheriff. He hadn't moved. Shortly, Maria was by his side.

"Sheriff, our patient wants to talk with you. He asked that we be calm, but I think that he has remembered something."

"What makes you say that?" Desmond asked.

"Just the way he asked me to find you, and to be calm. I think he believes something is going to happen."

"Well, you'd best go over to your father. If necessary, I'll let you know what's going on," the sheriff said as he started to move away.

"I insist you let me know," Maria informed him.

Her look of determination quirked the sheriff's lips, then he sobered quickly. "I'll try," he answered, moving away.

Now that her task was finished, Maria was torn as to what to do next: Go to her father, or defy orders and return to Tom. Her heart demanded she return to Tom, be by his side; but her head told her she would only be a distraction.

153

With this unhappy decision, Maria moved toward her father, a smile plastered on her lips, but she couldn't keep her eyes from looking toward Tom and the sheriff.

"What has you preoccupied?" Merrick asked as he placed a familiar arm around her shoulders.

"All these people, and wondering when the firecrackers are going to go off," she replied, deftly moving away from his arm and further contact.

"Then let me escort you away from the crowd," Merrick offered, this time offering his arm instead of grabbing her.

"Why would I want to leave my own party?"

"Maria, I'm just trying to make you comfortable. Trying to give you some protection," Merrick answered, moving a restraining arm around her waist, guiding her toward the edge of the light, away from her father.

"What are you doing? Let me go," Maria demanded, her voice low and angry.

"You are coming with me. There will be no more discussion," Merrick stated, his grip even harsher.

Maria glanced back and around. Her father was talking with friends, people were laughing, children running around. She didn't see the sheriff, who had just been there, but she knew he had to be close. She was filling her lungs to scream, her leg tensing to kick Merrick when her eyes saw Tom, a gun belt around his waist.

Opening her mouth, she started her scream just as the firecrackers went off. Jerking, she attempted to break loose, but Merrick simply tightened his grip. Twisting, Maria swung only to be stymied yet again. She was preparing for another assault, when into the silence after the firecrackers, came the words, "Well, lookie who's here. You talkin' to us?"

Maria followed the sound of the voice to find Tom confronting two men. She stood still, her heart in her throat, her voice silenced.

Beside her, she heard Merrick mumble, "Those fools." Merrick's words didn't make sense, but she was terrified for Tom.

"I wish that he be safe, that is my birthday wish. And please, God, *keep* him safe," she whispered.

Chapter 10

The silence lasted about fifteen seconds, but it seemed both shorter and longer to Tom. A breeze started, blowing the smell of the firecrackers away. The crowd, once free of its shock at the events suddenly taking place, started moving. Tom wanted to look around, make sure Maria and her father were safe, but to do so would mean certain death.

It wasn't as if Tom couldn't quickly draw and fire. He was fast; Oliver had made sure of that with every crack of the whip. Many a time, Tom had wanted to kill him, but Oliver never put anything but blanks in the pistol Tom used. Oliver tried to encourage him to take part in their lawlessness, but no amount of beatings accomplished that. Oliver found creative ways of keeping him captive, until finally he managed to escape. When Oliver had gone to take care of some personal business in Colorado, Tom saw his chance, but not before Oliver's boys did some pretty hefty bodily damage.

"Well, what's it to be?" Tom responded. "Of course, you have the advantage: two guns against one, just like that other night." The perspiration started to bead on his forehead as his energy began slipping away.

"Yeah, you still managed to sting me," Pete growled, "and for that, I should plug you right now."

"In front of these witnesses?" How long he could remain upright, Tom didn't know, but he had to see this through. Maria and her father needed to remain safe.

Pete slanted his eyes, watching as George turned completely away, taking in the retreating crowd.

"Hey, boss, what you doing with the girl?" he shouted.

"You damn fool," Merrick growled.

"So I *was* right. I thought I'd seen you before with these two," Tom said to Merrick, never taking his eyes off the two in front of him. "Now, I think you two should give yourselves up. You're in a no-win situation. You might get me, but you won't get away."

"Pete, what are we going to do?" George whined.

Pete stood stock still.

Tom watched the thoughts flow across Pete's face. He believed they were going to give up. Then, Pete's finger tightened on the trigger. Thumbing back the hammer, Tom fired, striking Pete's gun.

He escaped the shot from George's gun, by the grace of his leg giving out. Before George could fire again, the sheriff came up from behind, knocking him over the head with the butt of his pistol, then quickly reversing it.

"You two are under arrest," the sheriff announced. "Don't try anything," he said, pointing his gun at Pete.

Tom struggled with his leg, managing to get up to help the sheriff. They'd been so focused on Pete and George, they were startled when a screaming oath rent the air.

"You bitch!"

"You were our friend. Why?" Maria shouted as she pulled out of Merrick's grip.

Merrick lunged after her, attempting to regain his hold and silence her, but she was moving too swiftly, wise to his plans.

"What do you know, you foolish, willful child?" he sneered. "Your father spoiled you, flaunted his wealth, while the rest of us struggled."

"You had the same choices he did. You were unwilling to work," she shot back. "You wanted to play the great Don, instead of learning and working with others."

"Lies! You lie!" was the snarling reply.

"Do I, Finaldo?" Maria questioned.

"And it would have all worked out, if your *friend* hadn't spoiled it all," Merrick shrieked, trying again to grab Maria and flee.

George and Pete took advantage of the disruption to escape. The sheriff turned and Tom raised his pistol. Firing, he hit George in the leg but Pete swiftly dodged and was soon lost in the darkness.

The partygoers were returning. Many were confused and a few were whispering at Merrick's confession.

"There's the real culprit," Tom said to the sheriff, pointing his pistol in Merrick's direction. "What about Pete? Do we take off after him?"

"That one isn't going very far," Sheriff Desmond said. "Some of you help that miscreant to the jail." He pointed to George, ordering some men nearby, "And get the doctor. As for you, Mr. Merrick, you can join your friend in jail."

"You cannot arrest me," Merrick shouted as he rushed into the darkness.

The sheriff took off after Merrick. Before Tom could move to follow, Maria was in his arms, touching his face, making sure he was okay.

"My poor love," she cried, moving her arms to his waist. "You were so brave, yet again."

Tom tightened his hold, then placing a hand under her chin, he raised her

A COWBOY CELEBRATION

head, leaning in to place a gentle kiss on her lips. "Happy birthday, Maria. It has been a day. Now, I think you should go to your father. He's had quite a blow, and I need to go find the sheriff."

"I will go with you," Maria stated.

"No, it's better this way. And, you can call me Tom."

"Tom, Thomas, I like the sound," Maria smiled.

"You're a beautiful, wonderful woman," Tom said, kissing her with the kiss of a man who regretted what he'd done with his life and wanted to remember something precious.

"Better go see to your father," Tom said, breaking the kiss and giving Maria a gentle shove.

He watched Maria embrace her father; then, turning, he moved off in the direction the sheriff had headed, meeting him just as he was returning with Merrick.

Chapter 11

July moved into August. Tom was apprehensive about returning to Pueblo to testify at Merrick's and George's trial. They had postponed the proceedings when it was learned former President Grant was arriving in Pueblo. Pete was still on the loose. It wasn't the trial, but the possibility of seeing Maria that bothered Tom. He admitted to himself he was a coward, but he was not the one for Maria. She needed someone who didn't have an outlaw past, who didn't run away when things got tough.

When he'd returned to Agate Gulch, Tom sat down with his sister, Clara, and brother-in-law, Sam, telling them all that had happened. He left out his feelings for Maria, keeping those to himself. Yet, he did give vent to his frustration, the reason he'd taken off in the first place. Tom continued, "There's one thing I want to do before I begin. I want to retire."

"Now, what do you mean by that?" Sam asked.

"I've spent my life at the whim of Oliver and his sadistic hatred of life. When I finally managed to get away, I found my long-lost sister. It's not that I don't love you, sis," Tom said, reaching over to grab Clara's hands, "but I've had no chance to just be me, whoever *me* is. Even when I tried, I messed that up. I just want to quit, retire from what everyone expects of me, and find *me*."

Tom expected anger or denial; instead, he was given a sad smile and encouragement.

"Sometimes, we have to shed the expectations we think everyone asks of us," Sam told him. "Fact is, those expectations are self-imposed. We just have to realize it." Sam leaned over to give his wife a knowing smile and a quick hug.

"Tom, you take as much time as you need. I just want you to know there will always be a place here for you," Clara told him.

He would've taken off right away, but there was still the trial. The sheriff rode up a couple of times to speak with him, let him know their lack of success in finding Pete. Tom was hoping Pete had left the country, but his instinct told him that was not the case.

Riding the trails at the ranch, helping Sam with the cattle, Tom was still trying to work out where he stood in the scheme of things after his talk with his sister and Sam. Being outdoors had always helped him think. The slow, steady

A COWBOY CELEBRATION

pace of his horse as he rode along the trail lulled him into a peaceful state. That was one thing he loved about the ranch. It gave him a place away from town and friendly, but prying, people.

He had two days left to figure out what he wanted to do. Two days before he needed to return to Pueblo for the trial. He cared for Maria and was hoping by staying away she would forget the whole incident, forget him. He was a poor orphan, with nothing, and she was a wealthy young woman. Her family had land, a place in the community.

Still, every time he thought of her, he remembered how wonderful she felt in his arms. That first kiss had been a surprise, but the others... He admitted to himself he'd taken the coward's way out when he took off that night.

"Yes, a coward, Thomas Heath. You are a coward," he mumbled.

After telling his story, Tom had asked the sheriff to tell Maria and her father thank you for everything. He'd packed up and headed back to his sister and Agate Gulch.

So lost in thought was he in the memories of Maria, it took a bit for him to realize a horse was approaching behind him. Jerking around, expecting to see Sam, he was surprised to see Maria.

It's a mirage. You were thinking of her. But no, she was real—and riding toward him. Panic took hold, but there was no escape. With a sigh, he prepared to bite the bullet and end this once and for all.

"Thomas," Maria greeted him warmly.

"What are you doing here?"

The smile faded from Maria's eyes, soon filling with question, followed by anger. Tom watch the emotions play across her features, bracing himself for what was to come, but it never materialized. Instead, her eyes slanted behind him, fear replacing everything else.

Tom started to turn, the click of a drawn-back hammer stilling his movement.

"Just stay still cowboy," a familiar, yet dreaded voice intoned.

"What do you want? You had better be careful. The sheriff is looking for you," Maria declared, her voice steady.

Tom knew what the gunman wanted and his fear for Maria threatened to consume him. Could he stay between the two and still get off a shot, before taking a blow himself? If he had to, he would. The decision now made, Tom became calm, awaiting his break.

Tom slightly turned his head, and knew Pete had realized who he was by his chortling laugh.

159

"Oh, this is rich."

"Come to finish what you started, Pete?" Tom asked, carefully turning his horse to face the man. "There's no profit in it, you know."

"What do you know about the life?" Pete answered. "About reputation, that is,"

"More than you might guess," Tom responded.

Tom was now facing Pete, blocking him from Maria. Tom hoped she'd remain still. There was no telling with her. After all, she had followed and found him here. He wondered how—and, more importantly—*why*. His heart hoped for one reason that came to him, but his head couldn't comprehend.

"And what do you know?" Pete sneered, hand steady as he watched Tom.

"Ever heard of Ollie Hellyer?" Tom asked. "He raised me."

The name stilled Pete's hand. The knowledge made him less sure. Tom had wanted to tell Maria in a gentler way. The sheriff knew, and he had promised Tom that he would let Tom tell the Bernals. Now, the story was out. A girl like Maria had no business with someone like him, but, at least, he could keep her and her father safe. He owed them that much. Maria was young; she might think she loved him, but Tom also knew he loved her...loved her enough to let her go.

"So you see Pete, I know all about reputation. Know what Ollie's reputation got him? An unmarked spot in the mountains."

"Well, that was him, I'm going to be different. I'll take care of you two, then—" Pete began.

"Then what?" Maria demanded boldly. "You will have nothing. You will simply be a killer who shoots defenseless victims. What kind of reputation is that? A sneak killer."

Tom could hear the contempt in Maria's voice. Did she think that of him? He hoped she didn't hate him. But one thing her words were doing was taking Pete's attention away from him. It was the opportunity he'd been waiting for.

He spurred his horse, and the animal jumped forward into Pete's. The action startled Pete, and he fired too fast. Tom felt the air of the bullet as it flew past his face. At the same time, he pulled and fired, watching as the bullet entered Pete's skull through his left eye. Pete fell sideways to the ground.

Turning quickly, he moved to see if Maria had been hit by the stray bullet. Seeing her safe, he slumped his shoulders, preparing himself for the look of contempt in her eyes. Still, he didn't want her to see Pete as he was now. "Don't look," he commanded.

"You were wonderful," she said. "I was so frightened."

160

A COWBOY CELEBRATION

Startled at her reaction, Tom sighed. "It's all over now."

Tom's hand shook as he thought of how close Maria had come to being harmed. "We'd better head back to Agate Gulch and let them know what happened," he suggested, moving his horse toward Maria's.

Maria moved in front of him. "You are going nowhere until you agree to our marriage," she declared.

"Maria, I'm not the kind of man—"

"You *are*, and my mind is made up."

"But—"

Maria leaned over to kiss Tom, to end his protest, but her horse moved and she fell to the ground. Almost before she hit, Tom was out of the saddle, bending to scoop her into his arms.

"Are you hurt? Why did you try a stunt like that? Anyone who marries you will have his hands full," Tom scolded as he searched her face for any sign of pain. What he found was a smile and eyes shining with love.

"It seems to me you are doing a pretty good job of it. I think you are hired," Maria said taking Tom's face in her hands, her lips meeting his.

"You know, I will always be your Mary," Maria said with a teasing laugh as their lips parted.

"You're not going to let me to forget that, are you?" Tom asked as he laughed with her.

"Never, for if you had not come to the house that night, I would never have found the love of my life."

"You mean that? I mean—I love you...no, more than that—I adore you. But I never believed someone like—"

Maria stopped him with a finger to his lips. "You are you...the most wonderful man I know. And besides, you ate my green corn fritters. So, that is settled. Let us go back and tell your family."

"My family? Corn Fritters?"

"Yes, I told them I was going to fetch you so we could finally be married." Maria laughed. "Did I not tell you that eating the fritters was the same as agreeing to marry me?"

"I guess I didn't stand a chance." Tom grinned.

"None whatsoever."

About Angela Raines

Doris McCraw, who writes fiction under the name Angela Raines, has always loved telling stories. From an early age, she was writing and producing plays for her neighborhood. This allowed her to pursue both of her loves, writing and acting/performing. This love has continued into adulthood. Finding a home with Prairie Rose Publications, she now gets to share the stories dreamed she would be telling growing up in the Midwest.

For the Love of Grace

By Julia Daniels

For the love of her runaway sister, Poppy travels into the Wyoming Territory. She not only finds Grace, but her own happily-ever-after, too.

Chapter 1

"This here is Hope Springs, ma'am."

Miss Penelope "Poppy" Stanton looked up from her book, surprised how fast this leg of her trip had passed. She smiled at the kindly old man who'd kept her company for this part of the journey, and then glanced out the window as the stagecoach gradually slowed to a halt. The town was rather what she had expected to find in the middle of Wyoming Territory, not so unlike the small towns she'd passed on her way across the prairie in her journey from Chicago.

"Once we stop, I'll point you to a man that will see you out to your sister's place." His moustache twitched as he smiled.

"Thank you, Walt." He'd let her use his first name, because everyone did.

She packed away the sack of food she'd brought as a snack, and her book, just as the coach stopped. The driver popped the door open and helped her step down. She looked around the dusty western town as she stretched. It would be good to have a real bed after her week of travels

"Right over there, miss. Rodney Baker's Mercantile." Walt pointed to the store just a few doors down. "Tom, there," he pointed to a young man approaching the coach, "will carry your trunk, and Baker should be able to arrange transport."

"Thank you for your help. I'm sure all will be well." She gave him a smile.

"You too." He tipped his hat and left her.

"Well, Tom, let's go fetch my bag and get me on my way to my sister!"

She followed the boy down the street. A few people looked at her curiously, but no one spoke to her. She'd expected to see cowboys in the western town, but there wasn't a single one in view.

When Tom set her trunk outside the door of Baker's Mercantile, she

FOR THE LOVE OF GRACE—JULIA DANIELS

handed him a tip, and off he ran.

She took a deep breath and walked through the door of Baker's, hopeful she would soon be reunited with her sister, Gracie. It had been a long six months of disappointments as the investigators she'd hired to locate the runaway continually came up empty.

"Hello, miss. Can I help you?" A young woman, about Poppy's age, greeted her the minute she walked through the door.

"Hello," Poppy returned. "I've just arrived on the stagecoach from Cheyenne. A gentleman told me I could arrange transport from here?"

"Yes." The lady nodded, with a smile. She moved from behind the glass counter and held out her hand. "I'm Elizabeth Baker. My father owns this place and he often takes visitors where they need to go. I'm sorry to say he's gone for the afternoon, though."

"Oh." *Now what?* "That's a shame, I was hoping to get to my sister's."

"Well, who is your sister?" Elizabeth asked with a frown.

"How rude of me, I'm sorry!" Poppy chuckled. "I'm Gracie Timmerman's sister. My name is Poppy Stanton."

Elizabeth's mouth formed a perfect "O" before she cleared her throat. "I see."

"Is something wrong?" Poppy was hit by a sudden bout of panic as she studied the other woman's expression.

"Oh, no." She shook her head. "It's just…well, we've all wondered for some time where Miss Gracie came from, how her kin could let a woman of her…ability…travel so far by herself."

"I see." Poppy had anticipated this. "She ran away from home. As I understand it, she made up her mind to be married, and ended up here as a mail-order bride."

"But surely you know…she's not quite right in the head?" Elizabeth tapped her temple.

"Yes." Poppy sighed. "She is *very* simple minded. I took care of her all my life, until I went to teach, and then she ran away."

"Well, this makes sense now. You know she's carrying?"

"Yes. That's how we found her, finally. I've had investigators looking for her. She finally wrote a letter to me, and we traced it back here. It's been a very long search."

Elizabeth scratched her head and frowned, as if in deep thought. "My brother could run you out to the Timmerman's. It's not so far from here."

"Alright. Thank you." Poppy began to feel hopeful again.

164

A COWBOY CELEBRATION

"Let me go find Mitch. He works at the bank, and can probably get away to run you out to their place."

"I don't want to impose. I can wait until your father returns."

"I think you've been waiting long enough, don't you?"

Poppy nodded.

Within the hour, Mitch and Elizabeth Baker loaded Poppy into their father's wagon and drove her the short distance to the Timmerman place. Mitch was a good looking, well-dressed man in his mid-thirties, and hadn't minded closing the bank for a short time to drive the wagon. As they passed his house, Poppy learned he was married and had three children.

"Tom, the boy that helped with your trunk, is my eldest son."

Poppy wanted to ask why he wasn't in school, but she let it pass.

The Bakers were good conversationalists, and Poppy learned much about the town called Hope Springs. There was general excitement about the upcoming Fourth of July celebration as it also marked the twenty-fifth anniversary of the founding of their small town. Elizabeth was to marry during that celebration week, so the Bakers were in high spirits.

"If you stay until Miss Gracie has her baby, you'll be here for the celebration!"

"That's what I plan to do." She nodded. "How many people are in Hope Springs?"

"Oh, just about three hundred. Most came for the government land, and we've slowly added more people as time has gone along."

"I was the first child born here." Elizabeth smiled with pride.

"How amazing! Growing up in Chicago, I hardly knew my neighbors, but I would guess with only a few hundred people. You must know everyone in these parts!"

"Yes, we do." Mitch nodded, glancing at her briefly. "It helps that Pa has the mercantile and I run the bank, but I think we'd still know everyone."

Poppy wanted to ask more, but suddenly Mitch said, "Here we are."

He pulled down a short driveway off the main wagon-rutted trail, and soon they reached the hovel her sister had chosen to live in.

"*This* is her home?" To Poppy it looked like a ramshackle hut.

"I'm sorry, Poppy, I should have prepared you better for this." Elizabeth grimaced and patted Poppy's hand.

Poppy swallowed, struggling to picture her delicate sister living in such a situation.

Mitch pulled right up to the door, and called out, "Timmerman!"

FOR THE LOVE OF GRACE—JULIA DANIELS

When no one answered his call, Mitch hopped off the wagon seat and climbed the rickety stairs before knocking on the door. Poppy watched with bated breath, hoping her sister would appear in the doorway.

"Miss Gracie, how do you do?" Mitch's voice carried to where they sat waiting. "I've brought someone out here to see you."

Poppy jumped down, and rushed up the stairs to hug her sister, who'd just opened the door. Gracie looked awful, filthy, but Poppy didn't care. She pulled her older sister into her arms and held her, mindful of her rounded tummy.

"Oh, Gracie I have missed you so much!" Poppy whispered.

Tears streamed from Poppy's eyes as she held her sister. She was alive! Six long months of searching and she was here!

"Poppy, how did you find me?" Gracie pulled away, confusion etched on her face. "I didn't want you to find me."

"Yes, I know. You made it hard, too." Poppy smiled at her sister and swiped some stringy, greasy hair from Gracie's eyes. "May I come in?"

Gracie nodded.

"We'll leave your trunk here on the porch, Miss Stanton." Mitch set it down. "Good day to you."

"Oh, wait!" Poppy turned from her sister and reached for her bag. "I must pay you."

"No charge, ma'am," Mitch said with a slight shake to his head. "I reckon we'll all be glad to know someone is here to see to Miss Gracie."

"Thank you." She waved to Elizabeth who had remained in their wagon and then turned to follow Grace inside the house.

166

Chapter 2

"There now, you look a hundred times better!" Poppy studied her sister with a gentle smile.

Grace had badly needed a bath, and her hair washed. Now that she was clean, with some fresh clothes on, she looked so much better...more like herself, rather than a street urchin.

The house was horribly dirty, cluttered with used dishes and soiled clothing. Mice were running willy-nilly along the walls, and there was an odd smell Poppy couldn't readily identify. Seeing to Grace had been her priority, but now Poppy would shift her efforts to straightening the house.

She'd realized quickly there was no way she could stay with Gracie in this house. The place had no interior walls, it was just one large room, with a narrow bed in the corner of one area.

"Shall we change the sheets on your bed and see to that part first?"

Grace shrugged. "He don't seem to care."

Poppy bit her tongue as she was about to correct her sister's grammar. Gracie led her to a box under the bed where some sheets and blankets were stored.

"I can't get down that low no more."

"No, I suppose not." Poppy chuckled. "I'm going to be an aunt! I am so very excited for you."

"Yeah."

"You aren't excited?" Poppy began to strip the sheets from the bed. "Tell me about your Mr. Timmerman."

Gracie shrugged. "He's not so nice."

Poppy felt like someone kicked her in the gut. "Oh?"

She wanted to ask why she stayed with him, but it occurred to her that Gracie could hardly leave on her own, and she hadn't wanted their family to know where she was. Looking around, Poppy could easily understand why Gracie might not want anyone to know where she'd ended up. Having grown up in a fine home in Chicago, this was quite a comedown for Grace.

"Yeah. He yells a lot, calls me bad names."

Now, she wanted to throw-up. Her poor sister.

Anger seeped into Poppy's bones. Anger toward their father who didn't hire a helper, and who refused to look after his daughter because she was too much of a strain on him. Anger toward this Mr. Timmerman fellow who treated such a simple, unassuming soul with cruelty.

"Does he hit you?" Poppy asked quietly.

"Sometimes." She frowned. "And he throws things."

Poppy set aside the sheet she was unfolding and took Gracie in her arms.

"Do you want to leave?"

Gracie shrugged. "I can't leave my husband."

"We can go, Gracie." Poppy squeezed her hand. "You must come back to Chicago with me."

"No." She caressed her stomach with her free hand. "I can't go home."

"You can," Poppy said. "We can live together."

"You left me," Gracie whispered.

Here it comes. The guilt.

"I went to teach," Poppy explained. "Papa said he would find a companion for you."

"You left me," Gracie repeated.

"That's why you came here?"

"I wanted to have a baby, like Emily. She told me how to get one, and then helped me find a man."

So it was Emily Schneider who wrote the letters! Poppy never suspected her. No one knew exactly how Gracie had written to the man, when she was completely illiterate. When they'd found all the papers with the mail-order brides ads circled, they knew what Grace had done, but not where she had gone.

Poppy didn't know what to say. She piled all the dirty laundry into the corner, along with the dirty clothing that had been strewn all over the floor. Tomorrow, she would tackle that chore.

"Let's clean up the kitchen shall we?"

"Poppy where will you stay? We can't all sleep in one bed."

If Gracie's face weren't so serious, Poppy would have laughed.

"I suppose I'll go back to town tonight, if Mr. Timmerman will take me?"

"I don't know if he'll be back today. He never says."

Where would he go? "What does he do for a living, Gracie?"

"He kills little animals." Gracie shook her head. "I don't think it's very nice."

Hunting? Trapping? "Well, you have to eat, right?"

"Yeah." Grace sat on the edge of the bed, watching Poppy.

"I'm going out to get some water and do your dishes." Poppy grabbed the

A COWBOY CELEBRATION

pail and headed toward the door. "Can you clear off the table? Make a pile of things to throw out and I'll carry them to be burned."

"Yeah."

Poppy went outside to their pump to fill the bucket with water. She'd have to heat the water on their dirty stove and then maybe with the kitchen clean, the house would feel a little better. As she'd cleaned, time had gotten away from her. The sun was setting. Had Gracie learned to light lamps? She'd never been allowed to do that at home because she caused a fire once.

Poppy filled up the bucket and had just turned off the spigot when she heard heavy footsteps stop just behind her. She turned, curious who might be sneaking up behind her.

"Well, now, who do we have here?"

A disheveled, bearded man, reeking of alcohol and body odor stood just a foot in front of her.

"Who are you?" she asked boldly, feigning more courage than she felt.

He wasn't any taller than her, or much bigger in terms of weight. If she needed to, she could run.

He snorted. "It's my land you're on and you're asking who I am?" He snorted again.

"Mr. Timmerman?"

Another snort. "No one calls me that. Buck's my name. And who might you be?"

"Your wife's sister. Penelope Stanton."

"Well, aren't you a fine looking *lady*?" he sneered, and then walked within inches of her person. "Have you come to take her place?"

She wanted to spit at him, but instead she swallowed back the fear and anger and took a step back.

"No, I've come to look after her." Poppy took another step backward and found herself flush against the pump. She sidestepped him and walked back toward the house, hoping he wouldn't follow.

Once inside, she plastered a false smile on her face for her sister. "Let's get this heated up to wash the dishes, and then we'll get dinner started."

Poppy poured the water into a large pot and lit the stovetop.

"Buck's home," Gracie stated in a flat voice as he tromped in the door.

"Yep, I damn well am, and again, no food on the table for me. Woman, I think I've decided to trade you in for this fine lookin' sister 'a yers."

Poppy cringed as he neared her. "I've come to help Gracie with the baby and make sure she is being cared for as she needs to be."

169

FOR THE LOVE OF GRACE—JULIA DANIELS

"What about me, *Penelope*?" He slurred her name. "I got me some needs, too."

"Leave her alone, Buck."

"Oh, lookie there, the simpleton defending her high and mighty sister." He snorted. That seemed to be his favorite sound.

"How dare you talk to your wife that way!"

He shrugged. "She don't mind, why should you? If you wanna stay here, that's fine by me, but you gotta earn yer keep."

"And just want do you mean by that, Mr. Timmerman?" She hesitated to ask, afraid she knew exactly what he was referring to.

"One bed, two girls. Now *that* is what I mean."

What a disgusting man.

"We can't all fit in the bed. I told Poppy that." Gracie's face was blank, oblivious to what the pig was suggesting.

"Gracie, I need to go." She glanced at Buck's leering face before she kissed her sister's round cheek. "I'll be back to see you tomorrow."

Gracie grabbed her arm. "He said you could stay. Where are you going?"

"I'll stay in town tonight." Poppy walked out the door.

She didn't care if the fire on the stove burned down the house, she just needed to get away from that man.

Gracie followed her onto the porch. "You can't walk that far! It's almost dark."

Poppy stopped. "Where else could I stay tonight?" she asked.

"Mabel Ridgeley's. Come on."

Poppy looked back, saw Buck standing on the porch, still leering at her and decided *anywhere* would be better than here.

"Who is that?" Poppy started walking after Gracie.

"She lives just over yonder." Gracie pointed somewhere in the distance.

They didn't speak on the short walk to the Ridgeley place. As they neared, Poppy could see a lovely large, two-story house in the distance. This was what Poppy had expected to find in Wyoming, not her sister living in squalor.

"You're sure she'll let me stay?"

"Yeah."

Poppy didn't feel right just dropping in, especially because it was almost dark. But, what choice did she have? She could hardly go back to see Buck and follow through with his warped fantasies.

Grace marched up on the front porch and knocked on the door.

It didn't take long for an older woman to arrive at the door, a wide smile on

170

her face for Gracie.

"Well, Miss Gracie! How are you this fine evening?" She opened the screened porch door and welcomed them into the well-lit foyer. "You look lovely, did you fix your hair different? Who might this pretty lady with you be?"

"This is my sister, Poppy." Grace introduced her.

"So *you're* Poppy! Miss Gracie has talked about you often enough." Mabel looked her up and down. "You are a fine-looking young lady. Fine indeed." She walked in a full circle around Poppy. "When did you arrive in Hope Springs?"

"Just this afternoon." Poppy glanced at Gracie.

"Can she stay here, Mrs. Ridgeley? She don't want to sleep with me and Buck."

Mrs. Ridgeley's face turned white. "No dear, I don't suppose she does." She looked quickly at Poppy and then back to Gracie. "Of course she can stay." She nodded in agreement. "I've got plenty of room. Plenty of room."

"Thank you." Poppy smiled. "I left my trunk there. I don't suppose you have a wagon so we could go fetch it?"

"I do." She nodded. "But I'll wait until my son Reed gets home and I'll have him go get it. In the meantime, why don't we have some lemonade?"

"I gotta get back, Mrs. Ridgeley." Gracie pointed over her shoulder. "Buck don't let me out after dark."

"Alright," Mrs. Ridgeley said. "I'll drive you back home. You can wait here, Miss Stanton."

"Call me Poppy, please. And thank you very much for letting me stay with you tonight."

"Oh, honey you can stay as long as you like. This is a mighty big house for just me and Reed. When I had the other boys at home, and my man, Frank, it was just big enough, but now… well, now there's just a lot of quiet."

"Thank you." Poppy smiled at her.

"You go on into the kitchen and make yourself at home." She waved toward the back of the house. "I made a plate of sandwiches for my son, you go ahead and help yourself. I'll be back in just a few minutes."

"Thank you. You're very kind."

"I'd do anything to help Miss Gracie. If that means keeping you here, that's the least I can do." She looked Poppy up and down again. "Yes, you'll do quite well."

She didn't know what to make of that comment, so she let it slide. The two ladies left, and Poppy promised to visit Gracie again in the morning. Maybe

171

Mr. Timmerman wouldn't be drunk and disorderly by then, or maybe he'd just be out doing whatever he did to fill his days.

Poppy walked through the house, peeking in the rooms as she walked down the hallway. She could help Grace get ready for the baby. She wasn't familiar with pregnant women, but given the fact Grace had been gone from home for almost eight months, she could be due in just a few weeks. Poppy hadn't seen any baby clothes or furniture, or anything that suggested Grace was ready for the birth.

The sound of a door closing at the back of the house drew her from her reverie. Poppy made her way toward the noise, shocked to find a tall man pouring himself a glass of lemonade.

She cleared her throat.

He shifted his gaze toward her, and her breath caught. He was the most handsome man she had ever set her eyes upon. Until he frowned, and then, she got a little nervous.

"Who are you?" he demanded. "Where is my mother?"

He stalked toward her, and she felt herself backing up, much like she had done with the fool down the road. He looked like a *real* cowboy, even had a Stetson hat.

"I'm Penelope Stanton," she said, as if that explained everything.

"And?"

"Oh, yes…" Her mouth went dry the closer he came. He had the bluest eyes she'd ever seen. "I'm Gracie Timmerman's sister."

"And?"

"Your mother took her home and will return shortly."

"And?"

"I think I answered your questions," she said, a bit breathless.

"If she left with Miss Gracie, why are *you* still here?"

"Ah, I see." She cleared her throat. "They don't have room for me there."

"And we do here."

"So your mother thinks."

"I'll bet she does." He studied her, much in the same way his mother had. "I'm Reed."

"So I gathered."

"You're not exactly what I pictured a *Poppy* to look like."

"I'm sorry to hear that. I think." She pointed behind him. "Mrs. Ridgeley said she had made sandwiches for you."

He glanced over his shoulder and then back at her.

She held up her hands. "I promise not to steal anything."

A smile covered his face. Then, he broke out in a chuckle.

Whatever he'd expected his neighbor's sister to be like, it wasn't this beauty in front of him. He found the plate of sandwiches and placed them on the center of the table.

"Would you like one?" He pointed to the plate.

She eyed him warily, but joined him at the table anyway.

"How about some lemonade?" He held up an empty glass. "Ma makes the best."

"Yes, please."

"I'm relieved someone has come for her. No one here understood how someone with her... limits... arrived here on her own."

"We didn't know where she was," Poppy said quietly. "She ran away, without word."

He nodded in understanding. "She wouldn't tell us much about her family. You're the only one she ever mentioned. When she asked Ma to write you a letter about the baby, we were all hoping you'd come."

"I wondered who she had write. I would have been here so much sooner, had I known. I had planned to stay with her, but their house is so..."

"Dirty?"

"Well, I worked on that today," Poppy said. "It's much better already. I was going to say 'small'."

"Did you meet Buck?"

"Yes." She looked down at her folded hands on the table.

He stood as he heard a wagon pull up to the back door. With a glance out the window, he said, "Ma's back."

When he turned, he caught Poppy staring at him. Could she be as attracted to him as he was to her? Now, wouldn't that be a fine thing?

Reed looked down at his sandwich, holding back a smile. She was still looking at him when glanced up again. Early twenties, he would guess, with large brown eyes and a nice figure. She was taller than Gracie, fuller in the bust and hips.

"That Buck is something else!" His mother stormed through the back door. "I thought you were teasing about what he expected you to do, Miss Poppy!"

She blushed.

"What?"

"Mr. Timmerman asked me to do something...immoral...and when I said I

FOR THE LOVE OF GRACE—JULIA DANIELS

wouldn't... he got angry," Poppy answered.

"Immoral?" Reed asked.

"He wanted me to share his bed," Poppy said, not meeting his eyes.

"What!" He wouldn't have expected such a thing from Buck.

"You stay here, girl," Ma said. She patted Poppy's shoulder. "We'll keep an eye on you, and you can visit Miss Gracie during the day when that husband of hers is gone."

"Can you ride?" Reed asked.

"A horse? No." Poppy shook her head.

"I'll teach you tomorrow," he offered. He swallowed a gulp of lemonade. "If you'll be going back and forth to help Miss Gracie, you'll need to be able to ride."

"I can walk," Poppy argued.

"No." He shook his head. So, she was a stubborn one. "I will teach you to ride." He finished his lemonade.

"Poppy's trunk is still on the Timmerman's porch," Ma said.

"I'll go get it." Reed wiped his mouth, and then stood.

174

Chapter 3

He walked back out the door and down the back steps. Untethering the horses, he climbed up in the wagon and headed the short distance to the Timmermans'. Gracie met him at the door.

"I came for Poppy's trunk," he told Gracie. "She'll be safe with my mother, and she'll be here to help when the baby comes."

Buck joined them on the porch, smelling like a still.

"I came to get Miss Poppy's trunk."

"You taking her on, then?" He snorted. "Don't blame you, she's a damn fine looking woman."

Reed frowned and glanced toward Gracie.

"She's staying with my mother."

"Sure she is…"

Reed wanted to punch the man in his throat.

"I'll take her trunk. Miss Gracie, I'll bring Miss Poppy tomorrow. I'm teaching her how to ride."

"Ride? Ride in a wagon?" She laughed. "Poppy knows how to do that."

Lord, but the girl was slow.

"A horse, Miss Gracie. That way, she can come see you as often as you want her to."

She smiled. "I love Poppy. She always helps me. I didn't know she was coming, but I'm glad she's here."

"Is this her trunk?" Reed pointed to the luggage on the porch.

Gracie nodded.

"'Night, Miss Gracie."

"Thank you, Reed." She waved and walked back into the house.

"You can't blame me. Can you?" Buck slurred. "Poppy wasn't here ten minutes and I was so damn hard I had to leave the house."

Reed swallowed back the anger brewing in his chest. He'd known Buck longer than just about any other man he wasn't related to. Alcohol and bitterness had turned him into a disgusting mess of a man.

"You see to your wife now, Buck. Poppy will help when Miss Grace's time comes."

"Don't tell me you don't want her, Ridgeley." Buck punched his shoulder. "No man alive would pass up her sweet little ass."

175

Reed ignored him. "Poppy came to help her sister, not get mauled by you. You leave her alone, or you'll be answering to me... and my brothers."

Reed climbed in the wagon again, leaving Buck to imagine whatever he wanted to. He did find Poppy attractive, but he wasn't some animal that couldn't control his desire. The girl had come to help her sister. Ma had taken her in, and by God, he would treat her with all the respect a young woman like her was due!

At that very moment, back at the Ridgeley house, Poppy was settling in.

"Well now, it'll be nice to have a girl in the house." Mabel Ridgeley was putting away the dishes. "I have three sons. I had a wonderful husband, but not a daughter. I reckon you and me, we'll be getting on just fine."

"Thank you. I never expected anything like this to happen." Unexpectedly, Poppy began to cry. "I've missed Gracie. Here she's gone and gotten married to some man with dirty, evil thoughts."

Mabel cackled. "Darlin', all men have dirty, evil thoughts. Most are able to control them, but the thoughts are there, just the same."

"You're probably right." Poppy laughed, her tears dissipating.

"I know I am." She topped off her glass of lemonade and sat back at the table with her. "Now, then. We got seven bachelors here in Hope Springs. My Reed is probably the oldest, at thirty-two. But, all of them are decent, God-fearing men who'd make ya a fine husband. I think you oughta pick one after church on Sunday. If you don't pick one right away, they'll start arguing over you, and that won't end well."

"But, I'm not staying, Mabel. I have a job in Chicago." Poppy argued. "I didn't come here to wed."

"Well, don't you wanna have a husband and kids?"

"Yes, but..."

"And if you got hitched out here, you could watch your niece or nephew grow up and keep an eye on Miss Gracie."

"Yes, but..."

"You just think about choosing one of them men."

"Picking out a man isn't as easy as choosing a new dress or a pair of shoes."

Mabel sighed. "In a lot of ways it's easier." She laughed. "We're havin' a social after services on Sunday to celebrate plantin' being done, and pickin' a date to put up my boy's barn."

"Reed's?"

A COWBOY CELEBRATION

Mabel shook her white head. "My youngest, Matthew. He lives just up the road." Footsteps on the porch steps interrupted whatever else she was going to say. "Sounds like Reed's home."

Poppy rushed to open the door for him as he struggled through with her case.

"Ma, where you want Miss Poppy's things?"

"She can take Lucas's room," Mabel said. "Poppy, why don't you go ahead on up to bed? You've had quite the rough day, young lady."

More like a rough *six months*! She wasn't certain she'd slept a full night since Gracie disappeared. Every time the investigator gave her bad news about leads that didn't pan out, it got worse.

"I should help you with something," Poppy offered weakly. The small bed upstairs was very appealing at the moment.

"No, no. There will be plenty of things to do once you wake up. You go on ahead and have sweet dreams." Mabel plopped a loaf into a bread pan, before starting on a second lump of dough. "Make that room your home sweet home."

"Very well," Poppy agreed.

Poppy followed the tall, dark, and handsome Reed out of the cheery kitchen down the hallway, and up the flight of stairs to the back of the house. He carried the heavy trunk like it was light as air. He finally shouldered open a door, and she followed him inside. She found the lamp and lit it, casting a reflection of their shadows against the wall.

"Thank you, Mr. Ridgeley. I appreciate your help." She wanted to hug him, which wasn't normal for her. "Was Grace alright?"

"She looked to be fine," he answered. "You best be calling me Reed. I reckon we'll be around each other enough. Just as well be friendly."

They stared at each other. He stepped forward and she held her breath, wondering if he might hug her. Instead, he walked past her to go out the door.

"Excuse me…"

His body grazed hers as he passed, causing goosebumps to form on her arms.

She shook her head at her craziness. Of course he wouldn't hug her. He'd just met her. She closed the bedroom door after he left and plopped on the bed, exhausted.

177

Chapter 4

"I'm sorry we don't have a sidesaddle for you," Reed told Poppy as he finished saddling a horse for her.

Their lessons were later in the day than expected. He'd gone off to do chores in the morning, and she and Mabel had whipped the Timmerman house into fine shape. Gracie was happy, even singing and laughing as she used to do back home. Mabel shared that she'd never heard Gracie sing, even when she first arrived and joined them at church, she was as quiet as a mouse.

"Now, put your left foot it the stirrup, and grab the saddle horn," Reed told her.

Poppy hiked up her skirt and did as he said.

"Good. Now, step into the stirrup, and lift your right leg over the saddle."

She was up on the first try.

"Well, that was fine, Miss Poppy. Fine indeed." He smiled. "I'll adjust the stirrups now to match the length of your legs."

"Teachers can learn too," she quipped.

It was odd being up so high. She wasn't sure she liked the idea of something moving underneath her.

"I never said you couldn't, ma'am." He winked at her, making her pulse race. "There. You're all set now."

She watched as he climbed aboard his mount, lean and lithe like a cat. She supposed most cowboys would be like him, all toned and muscular. He was a fine looking man!

"Give her a little kick with your heels to get her moving. We call her Lady, by the way."

"Alright Lady, let's get moving." She gave the horse a light nudge and sure enough, she started walking.

"We'll just walk today. You use the reins to direct her which way to go."

She did pretty well, but she stayed close to Reed's side, still feeling rather uncertain.

After a short time, he said, "There's a nice little spot up ahead with some trees where we can practice getting off. Sometimes, getting off is harder than getting on."

She followed his lead and when he stopped, she pulled back on her reins. It *was* a nice little spot to stop. He got off his horse quickly and moved to help her down.

"Now, you do everything backwards."

She tried it, got so far as getting her right leg over, but her left leg got stuck in the stirrups, and if he hadn't been there, she would have fallen on her behind. Instead, she landed in his strong arms.

"Thank you," she whispered.

Warmth spread throughout her body as he cradled her. Oh, he smelled nice; all male and leather and some spicy fragrance she couldn't identify.

"Slip your foot out." He held her as she removed her foot from the stirrup, glad the horse wasn't spooked.

"Lady is an awfully calm horse." Her voice sounded thick, like she'd just swallowed a whole jar of honey.

Once her foot was free, he set her down on the ground, but allowed his hand to remain at the back of her waist.

"I've had her a long time," he whispered close to her ear. "We should try it again. Back up and down."

"Alright."

She climbed up easily on Lady's back. This time, as she dismounted, she kicked out her left foot and hopped to the ground with a laugh, and landed against him.

He supported her shoulders with his hands. "Nice job, Poppy. I think you've got it figured out." He took a step back.

By the time she turned around, a big smile of accomplishment on her face, he was already back at his horse, reaching for something from the saddle bags.

"I brought along a snack for us. I wasn't sure how long we'd be out."

"I'll bet you've got some of your mother's cookies." She smiled at him. She'd smelled them baking just before she went to change for their lessons.

"Yes, ma'am. Ma bakes the best molasses cookies."

"I would say you may be just a bit biased."

"It's possible." He nodded.

In addition to the food, he had a blanket, which he quickly opened and spread on the ground.

"Have a seat," he invited.

She joined him on the ground.

She had planned only for a short ride so she could become accustomed to traveling by horse. Now, it seemed they were sharing an evening, which was quite alright with her.

"I enjoy watching the sunset," he said.

"It's a lovely evening," she agreed. "My father's home in Chicago is near Lake Michigan. On nice nights, such as this, Gracie and I would have walked down to the lake to watch the birds." She smiled at him.

"Here, you can judge for yourself." He handed her a cookie.

"Thank you." She took a bite of the thick molasses cookie. "Very good. I like sweets."

"I do, too." He shifted on the blanket, leaning against the trunk of the tree and extending his legs forward. "I imagine Hope Springs is very different for you."

Understatement of the decade! "It is," she agreed. She turned sideways so she could look at him. "I'm happy I found my sister, and I can be here for the baby."

She finished her cookie while they sat in silence.

Eventually, he cleared his throat and spoke up. "You think you might like to stay here? Or are you set on going back to Chicago?"

"It's early days, yet," she answered. "I love teaching. I'm not certain I'm willing to give that up."

"What if you didn't have to?" he asked.

"What do you mean?"

"We haven't had the need for a school in Hope Springs. It's been suggested by the town board that we look for a teacher."

"What are you suggesting? That I offer to be the teacher for Hope Springs?" She smiled, warming up to the idea.

"Sure. You'd be able to keep an eye on your sister and her baby, and still be able to teach as you wish."

Not a bad idea. It wasn't Chicago, had none of the conveniences she was accustomed to, but that didn't mean she couldn't be happy here.

"Who is the head of the town board?" she asked. "I could speak to him."

He smiled. "Go ahead. You're looking at him."

"Oh!" Her eyes widened. "You? I had no idea!"

"You seem surprised."

"Oh, I just expected someone older, I suppose."

They sat in companionable silence for a while. She would look at him, then blush when he looked at her. He handed her another cookie and she accepted it.

"What do you like to do in your free time?" she asked.

"I don't get too much of that. Seems like I'm ranching from waking up in the morning to when I go to sleep at night." He leaned his head against the tree and closed his eyes.

A COWBOY CELEBRATION

"Surely you must do something for entertainment? Do you read?"

His eyes popped open. "I *can* read if that's what you're asking. I suppose you'll find out in time. I enjoy writing poetry."

"Poetry? How wonderful!" she said.

"Yeah?"

"Of course!" She shifted closer to him, getting into the topic. Finally, something they could discuss! "I like Whitman."

"I do, too. Cather, though, is my favorite. She's from Nebraska, understands life out here."

"May I read some of yours?"

"I don't know about that." He shrugged. "Maybe."

Writing was a personal thing, she supposed.

"Hope Springs has a lot of single men," he said, shifting on their blanket. "I expect when you go to church, you will meet most of them. Ma said she mentioned this to you."

"Yes, she did."

"Well," he cleared his throat and pinned her with his beautiful blue eyes. "I'd be honored if you'd consider allowing me to get to know you better."

"It's inevitable isn't it? I *am* staying under the same roof as you." She knew what he meant, was being deliberately obtuse.

He sighed. "I would like to spend more time alone with you, like this…getting to know you."

"So, courting?" she asked. She smiled, excited about the idea.

"I suppose you would call it that, yes. I'd like to see if you and I might suit for marriage."

"Oh, my," she breathed.

"Too soon, huh?" He laughed. "Well, I figured I should put my intentions out there and let you decide if I'm worthy of your time."

"Worthy of my time? You make me sound like a princess," she scoffed. "I'm not certain I could stay here forever, Reed."

"But Grace is here," he argued.

"Yes, Grace is here. But, I'm hoping to convince her to leave with me. She would have a better life in Chicago."

"But she's *married*," he argued. "She can hardly pick up and leave her husband."

"After two days I can see he's not a good man, surely you know this, too?"

"But she is *married*, Poppy." He shook his head. "She won't leave him, no matter how awful he is."

181

He was probably right, when Grace made a decision she was stubborn about it.

"Perhaps it's time to go home." She abruptly stood.

"If you'd like," he said. He slowly gained his full height. "I'm sorry if I offended you. I'm an honest person, I tell it like it is." He folded the blanket and put away the rest of the cookies in the sack and then stuffed them in his saddlebags.

"I like that in a person," she said.

She climbed back up on Lady without a hitch and waited for him to do the same.

"You sure you've never been on a horse before?"

"No. Just Lady, here." She patted the neck of the horse.

"You're a mighty quick study."

As they slowly made their way back to the house, he described the subtle changes in the landscape of the area, his family background, his ranching plans and his vision for the future of Hope Springs. As they went, he drew her a picture of what life could be like for her if she decided to stay there, be with her dearest sister and, maybe, just maybe…with him.

Chapter 5

Poppy looked even prettier than usual, sitting in the pew between his mother and Miss Gracie. They hadn't spoken about his courtship suggestion since their evening ride three days earlier, but the more time he spent with Poppy, even in the company of others, the more he knew he wanted her to stay in Hope Springs—with him.

She was funny, clever and loving. She'd done so much for Gracie since coming, he didn't know how she could even consider leaving. Grace looked better than ever, and Poppy had even gotten her to come back to church, something not even his sweet mother had been able to do.

The night before, his brothers Lucas and Matthew along with Lucas's wife, Suzy had come to the house for dinner and they ended up playing cards until the wee hours of the morning. Poppy had shared detailed, silly stories of her classroom, the naughty boys leaving frogs and snakes in her desk drawers, and the girls crying over getting muddy or a teasing. He could tell, just by how she described the scenes that she was a good teacher, that she enjoyed children. After last night, he was even more determined to convince her to consider staying on, taking the teaching position the township board wanted to create.

He easily imagined many such evenings, especially on the cold winter Wyoming nights, when there was little to do other than read and play cards. Unless a person were married, and then he imagined there were much more enjoyable ways to spend a quiet night at home.

He'd begun to consider *that* aspect of marriage much more since Poppy arrived. The idea of kissing her when he wanted to, holding her when she was close, was so very appealing. He glanced at her profile as she listened intently to their minister discussing some verse from the Bible. If someone offered him a hundred dollars, he wouldn't be able to tell them what the service was about that day. Poppy had his mind—and heart—tied in knots.

He glanced around and noticed he wasn't the only one looking at her. The other single men were staring at her as much as he was. He knew there would be fierce competition, which was why he brought up the idea of a courtship on their ride.

"And I would like to welcome Miss Penelope Stanton from Chicago. She's here visiting Miss Gracie until the baby arrives later this summer. Welcome, Miss Poppy."

She smiled and nodded toward the minister.

"Now, let us end the service with *Onward Christian Soldiers*."

After the song ended, people filtered out into the late June sun. Miss Poppy was quickly greeted by Mitch Baker, his wife, Sarah, and their three youngsters. A few men with guts walked up to Poppy and introduced themselves. Reed noticed his brother Matt hung back, but was taking in the whole scene. How would Poppy react when she learned the truth about Matthew?

"You need to get over there, son," Ma whispered to him. "She's being pursued already."

"Why do *I* need to do anything?" He'd already offered to spend time with her and she rejected him. At least, he thought she had. "Seems like she's holding her own."

"I thought you were trying to keep her attention for yourself."

"I think she said no." He shrugged.

He really didn't know what she thought about him. He liked her…a lot…but, he had no reason to think the feelings were reciprocated.

"You asked already?" Ma sputtered.

"Yeah, the night I taught her to ride."

"Oh. I didn't know." She frowned.

"I didn't exactly wish to share my failure."

"She watches you a lot." She chuckled. "When you aren't looking at her, she's looking at you."

"I think you're imagining it."

"Nope. I'm sure I ain't. Noticed it in church today, even."

Poppy broke from the clump of fellas she was talking with, and threaded her arm through Miss Grace's to head toward them.

He knew Buck was leaving Poppy alone. He asked Poppy every day when she returned home, as he unsaddled her mount. She said Buck was never around when she was.

"We're gonna meet in the church hall and discuss the building days. Folks have all brought food for lunch, so we'll eat here and then figure out the details."

"Miss Gracie, you are looking fine today," Reed said.

"Thank you. Poppy is taking care of me." The lady smiled at Poppy, a look of pure adoration evident on her face.

"Come with me, Gracie." His mother coaxed her away. "You can help me set out the molasses cookies and lemon bars."

A COWBOY CELEBRATION

"Yes, ma'am."

Dutifully, Miss Gracie followed, leaving him alone with Poppy. He had a feeling their departure was an intentional ploy to get the two of them alone.

"You must be so happy to be with her," he started.

"Of course! But, I'm not convinced she's safe with Mr. Timmerman."

"Have you uncovered how she ended up here?"

"A family friend…well, I *believed* her to be a friend…helped her write the letters. The friend had just had a baby, and Gracie got it in her head she wanted one, too. I don't believe for a minute she will be able to care for a child. She can hardly care for herself."

"You're planning to stay, then?"

"If she won't leave with me, then I must." She shrugged. "I have no real choice in the matter. When my mother died, in her last minutes of life, she made me promise I would look after Gracie. I can't go back on that promise."

"How old were you?"

"Only twelve." She grinned at him and his heart did an odd flip-flop in his chest. "I had already done so much looking out for her, it seemed natural that I continue. My father married very soon after her passing and my step-mother wasn't willing to cope with Gracie's extra needs. My father is a decent man, but sort of forgot about Gracie and me after he remarried. Papa was supposed to hire a companion when I left to teach, but he never did, and Gracie's incapable of living without help; surely you see this?"

"I do. Ma did, too. She's tried her best to help your sister."

"Thank you for any help you've given Gracie." She stopped walking and looked up at him. "You are a good man, Reed Ridgeley."

If they were alone, back in that special spot he'd taken her when she learned to ride, he'd kiss her.

"I try my best, ma'am." He leaned forward and dropped his voice. "You're pretty darn special yourself."

She looked away and started walking toward the church hall again. "Your mother reminded me to pick one of the single men today so there wouldn't be any fighting or hurt feelings over me." She laughed.

"You sound like you don't think that's exactly what would happen. Women are *scarce* out here. Point of fact, Elizabeth Baker is the only lady of marriage age available in all of Hope Springs." He tipped back his Stetson and scratched his forehead. "LeRoy made it known when Elizabeth was sixteen that she was his. Ma isn't exaggerating. I'm surprised you haven't been pursued, as beautiful as you are."

She stilled. "You think I'm pretty?"

He raised his eyebrows and smiled. "Surely, you've looked in a mirror?"

A small grin crept across her face as she resumed her walk to the hall.

He knew the other men were concerned that, being sisters, Poppy might be as slow as Gracie, and that was likely what was holding some of them back from pursuing Poppy. Gracie was pretty, but slow. They might think the same was true of Poppy. It was to his advantage that she was staying with Ma, but that didn't mean she would choose him.

She cleared her throat and glanced over at him. "So, let's just suppose I've chosen to stay here, and I think I must, given Gracie's situation. How would I go about telling someone that I am interested in getting to know them better?"

"Well," he blew out a sigh, "I suppose you could simply explain that of all the bachelors in town, he is the most interesting to you. I think any man would like to be told he'd been your first choice."

"I see."

That's all they had time to discuss before being joined by his brother, Matt, just outside of the church hall. Matthew trailed after them. Reed knew he was cautious about spending too much time with Poppy, worried what would happen when she found out his secret.

The rest of the afternoon was hell on Reed's nerves as he watched men giving Poppy attention. All the bachelors except for Matt spent considerable time talking with her. She was the center of attention, but didn't look particularly comfortable with it. Jealousy bit at his gut, but Reed put on a good face, and tried to appear that her interactions with the others didn't trouble him. In reality, it was eating him up inside.

At one point, Matthew came and sat next to him. "You gonna marry her, aren't you?"

Reed hadn't been certain if it was a question or a statement, and instead of answering, he'd just nodded.

It took only a short time to plan for the building of the barn. They would start the following Tuesday evening and work full days until it was built. Matthew offered to host Elizabeth and LeRoy's wedding dance in the brand new barn. It was perfect timing, and by the time everyone climbed into their rigs to head home, all were excited about the upcoming events.

On the ride home, it started to drizzle. People had been talking about a much-needed rain for days, and it was finally here. He pushed the horses harder to get them home before getting drenched. They dropped off his mother first, and then he and Poppy took Gracie home.

A COWBOY CELEBRATION

When they got to the Timmerman house, Gracie refused to go in. "I don't want to, Poppy. Please, don't make me."

"You know I'm just down the road, Gracie," Poppy soothed. "You have to go in or you'll catch cold, and that would hardly be good for the baby."

Gracie rubbed her belly. "Yeah." She nodded and let Reed help her off the wagon.

"I'll be here tomorrow morning again," Poppy told her.

"Alright."

He helped Gracie walk up the rickety stairs and waited until she was inside before he returned to the wagon to take Poppy to the ranch.

"She could have come with us."

"I don't want to make Buck mad," Poppy said. "I hope...well, I don't know what I hope. I don't know what to do, or how this is all going to work. I'm trying to be strong, because that's what she expects from me, but I don't know what to do this time. Gracie can hardly care for the baby...and I can't live in that house." She sounded defeated.

"You have time," he said. "Ma thinks she's about seven months along."

"I wondered." She looked up at the sky. "It's coming down heavier now."

"You won't melt will you?" He smiled at her, pleased when she laughed.

He didn't like to see her unhappy and worried about Grace. He knew everything would work out for the best. It sounded like she'd chosen one of the bachelors, he hoped it was him, but even if it wasn't, whomever she chose would help her see to Gracie's needs.

He clicked the reins and pushed the horses on. If he went much faster, they'd not only be wet, but covered in mud, too. Finally, they pulled up to his house and he helped her down.

"Thank you!" Abruptly, Poppy leaned forward and kissed his cheek before she ran into the house, giggling.

His mouth hung open. Had she kissed him as a mere "thank you" or from true affection? He shivered, not sure if it was from the chill of the wet air or from the kiss. A smile spread across his face and he started whistling as he hopped back on the wagon to put it and the horses in the barn.

187

Chapter 6

Her bedroom window looked out onto the barn. After Reed dropped her off, she'd gone up to her room to change from her wet clothes. Since then, almost an hour already, she'd sat at the window, waiting to see a light go on in the barn.

She knew he was in there, working in the tack room, tinkering with one of the machines he'd showed her days ago when she'd gone with him to unharness Lady. He had a nice workshop, very neat and tidy, with all sorts of tools and interesting things she'd never seen before.

If he put a light on, she would go talk to him. She'd decided on the ride home she wanted to talk with him privately, because, having met all the bachelors the town had to offer, it was clear the only man remotely interesting to her was now in that barn. She didn't know what she would say, or how she would say it, but somehow, she would let him know she was interested in a courtship. And she had kissed him! How brazen was she to do that so unexpectedly! She wondered what he thought of that.

"Ah, there it is." She smiled as the glow from a gas lamp shone through the window. "Now, how to get by Mabel without answering too many questions?"

As luck would have it, as Poppy passed the parlor, Mabel was snoozing in her chair. "Excellent!" she whispered to herself, tiptoeing passed her.

Once outside the back door, she sprinted to the barn and flew inside, laughing like a loon. She shook off some of the water from her head and then listened, surprised to hear singing coming from the back of the barn. She silently moved to the room where he stored his supplies, enjoying the deep baritone of his voice.

Just before she reached the door, she called out, "Reed? Are you in here?" She didn't want to catch him totally off-guard.

The singing immediately stopped. She smiled.

"Yeah, back here," he called out.

"Hi." She said with a smile for him as she walked in the door. "House is kind of quiet, I thought I'd come see what you were up to."

"I see." His Adam's apple bobbed. Did she make him nervous? "Just drying off the leather to prevent rot."

"Do you do that every time it gets wet?"

"Try to." He shifted on his stool and reached for another rein. "Ma's got

188

A COWBOY CELEBRATION

some books to read, if you're interested. I'm sure she'd let you borrow them."

"I would rather talk with you, if that's alright." She still wasn't quite certain how to say what she wanted to say to him.

"Have a seat." He hooked his boot on the bottom of the extra stool and scooted it over her direction.

"Thanks." She sat.

"What would you like to talk about?" he asked.

He looked up briefly from his job and then focused again on the leather in his hands.

She took a deep breath. This was going to be a challenge. She was never forward with men, never approached them, and when they talked with her, she always acted with modesty. But she'd kissed him!

"A few things, actually." She shifted on the short stool. "First, I want to ask when the next township board meeting is, and if you might bring me along to discuss starting the school."

He looked disappointed. "We meet the first Monday of the month, so that'll be next week. Being right before the big Fourth of July Celebration, I'm not sure the others will want to discuss it or not."

She raised her brows and smiled at him. "Surely, being president, you can bring it up?"

"Yes, I suppose I can." He nodded. "I'll suggest it when I see them at Matt's barn raising."

"That's terrific!" She clapped.

"Well, it's time Hope Springs had a school." He shrugged. "I just have to convince the bachelors to cough up some money."

"I see."

"Don't look so down. We'll figure it out." He reached out, took her hand to comfort her, and she squeezed it.

"I like that you said *we*," she said. "I don't feel so alone if I know you're willing to help me."

"I am willing to do more than that." He dropped her hand. "I told you that when we went riding."

He stood up and hung the reins on their proper hook.

"That was the second thing I wished to talk with you about." She tried to remember how he had phrased it earlier as they walked from the church to the hall. "Reed, you're my first choice." She smiled at the surprised look on his face. "You are my *only* choice."

"I don't know about that," he said. "You sure garnered a lot of attention

189

today."

"Jealous?" she teased.

"Maybe." He turned away and fidgeted with something on his workbench.

"Well, if you noticed, they came to me; I didn't go to them." He came back to the stool, moved it closer to her and sat down. "It would have been impolite to ignore them," she continued. "If I plan to stay here, these gentlemen will be my neighbors, maybe friends." She reached for his hand. "If we had met on Michigan Avenue in Chicago instead of in your Ma's kitchen, would you even have noticed me?"

"Hell, yes, I would have. But, I would have been too chicken to talk to you." He chuckled. "You're all fancy and sophisticated and I'm just a cow wrangler. I can't imagine you'd choose me when you got the town lawyer and doctor both talking to you."

"Talk is just talk." She waved her hand in the air. "You've shown me your wonderful character by how you treated my sister and how you treat your mother. But, beyond that, I want a marriage based on love, and I think…I *hope* you and I can have that." She smiled.

"I want that, as well." He scooted even closer. "My parents had a very happy marriage for over thirty years. So," he caressed her cheek, "how about you let me court you right and proper and we'll see how it goes?"

"I like that idea." She smiled.

He leaned forward, and she knew he was about to kiss her. Her eyelids closed and butterflies started fluttering in her tummy. The pressure from his lips was soft. She tasted coffee on his breath, smelled the leather of the room, and sighed as his hands cupped her face and pulled her even closer to him.

"Reed! Reed are you in here? Is Poppy with you? Reed, you have to come quickly!" Mabel's voice cut through the haze of their kissing.

"Yeah, Ma." He backed up his stool and grinned at her. "We're back here."

"Oh, thank God!" Mabel rushed in the room. "It's Gracie. That fool husband of hers has beat her up. Come quick!"

They rushed through the barn, through the rain, in the back door of the house and into the kitchen where Gracie was sitting at the table, softly crying. Poppy went down to her knees and pulled her sister into her arms.

Gracie's lip was ripped open and her eye was already starting to swell. Poppy didn't say anything, she just held her.

"Told you I didn't want to go."

"I'm so sorry, Gracie. I should have listened."

"Poppy, you take her up to your room and lay her down," Mabel said. "I'll be right there to help you get her cleaned up."

"Alright." She nodded. "Come along, Gracie."

Poppy heard Mabel tell Reed to go fetch the sheriff and the doctor. Poppy wasn't certain what the sheriff could do, and she hoped that Grace wouldn't need the doctor for the baby.

"So? What did the doctor say?"

Reed was standing at the sink in the kitchen, having waited for over an hour for word from the ladies upstairs about Gracie. Instead of answering his question, Poppy threw herself into his arms, and rested her cheek against his chest. He gladly pulled her close and held her tightly, surprised how tense and tight her slender body felt. Yeah, he was doomed. He loved her.

"He thinks the baby is well. He said he felt it move," she whispered into his chest. "She can't go back to Timmerman. Reed, what am I to do?"

"What are *we* to do?"

"Yes." She pulled away and smiled up at him. "*We*. Thank you."

He bent his head and kissed her forehead, still holding her against him.

"Can you take her to Chicago to escape him?" As much as it hurt him to suggest that, maybe it was for the best.

"She just told me she won't leave here. She won't go back home, no matter what."

"She'd go back to him?" He was shocked. He was sure his voice showed that. "Even after what he did to her?"

"No." She shook her head. "Grace wants to stay in Hope Springs, but not with him."

"I'm confused."

"Let's sit," she said.

They moved over to the table and sat close to each other. He took her hands in his.

"She wants me to settle here," Poppy explained, "and she wants to live with me."

"I see," he said quietly.

He let thoughts of the future filter through his mind. His mother would live with him the rest of her life. If Poppy agreed, she would live with him, which meant Gracie would too, along with her child, and any children he and Poppy might have. It was a lot to consider.

"What did the sheriff say?" she asked.

"He couldn't find Buck, but he'll be out looking for him. I'll be locking the doors of the house tonight." He squeezed her hand. "I've never had to do that before, but I want you and Gracie and Ma to be safe."

Ma joined them a few minutes later.

"Gracie's sleeping." She looked at Poppy. "I made up Lucas's bed for you. It's right next door to Gracie. You'll be able to hear her cry out."

"Thanks, Mabel." Poppy stood up. "It's been quite a day. I'll go on up to bed now. Thank you both for your help."

"Don't you worry yourself about nothing," Ma told her. "You get a good night's sleep and we'll worry about everything in the morning."

"Good night." She smiled gently at Reed before leaving the room.

After Poppy left, Ma turned on him.

"That Buck is one hell of a character. I wish I could get my hands on him!" Ma rarely cursed, and never threatened.

"You and me both, Ma. You and me both."

She sat in the chair Poppy had occupied.

"Did I interrupt something in the tack room?"

"I kissed her." He grinned. "Of course, she kissed me first. We're going to try courting, see if we suit."

"And you said she rejected you! Ha!"

"I guess I don't know much about women."

"It'll be best to learn it from your woman than any other anyway." She slowly stood up. "I reckon I'll be hitting the hay now, too. Might wanna load a gun. Just in case."

"I already did." He sighed. What was this world coming to? "Locked the doors up, too."

She patted him on the shoulder. "You always were a smart one."

He watched her walk from the room, still thinking about living with a household full of people. Growing up, he'd imagined having his own family, but as he got older, as he realized the shortage of available women, he let that hope and dream fade away.

Until Poppy.

Chapter 7

"Are you ready?" Reed asked her.

Poppy watched him adjust the sleeve of his fancy suitcoat in what looked like a nervous gesture. They were about to enter the building where the township board was meeting. Poppy was invited to plead her case for the need of a school.

She had spent the greater portion of the day preparing her speech. Gracie was all but healed after a week of good care by Mabel. She was settling into the house well, hadn't mentioned going back to Buck a single time. The doctor said the baby was fine and would likely make an appearance in less than four weeks.

Poppy and Reed had spent hours upon hours together, laughing, flirting, and playing in the dirt. She'd followed him around doing chores, and he'd given her a tour of the farm. Matthew's barn was up, and almost ready for the wedding dance in just five days. She missed a lot about Chicago, but here she had Gracie, and had gained a good man she was falling in love with.

"I am ready, yes." She smiled.

He helped her down from the wagon seat and allowed his hand to remain at the back of her waist. Their courtship became common knowledge when everyone was out at Matt's barn raising.

"Good luck, honey," he whispered. "I'd give you a kiss but I might scandalize the town."

"And you *are* the President of the Board." She winked at him.

They'd shared plenty of kisses over the past week, were getting closer by the day. She no longer worried about staying in Hope Springs. Even if the board didn't accept her idea of the school. Poppy was confident she's have plenty to occupy her time in the future.

Reed opened the door for her and guided her to a seat on the side of the room, before joining the other men already gathered at the center table. She was the only woman in whole room!

Minutes were read, the agenda was passed and old business was tabled. Suddenly, she was on center stage, being called forward to discuss why a school would be good for Hope Springs and why she would be the perfect candidate.

"Good evening, gentleman." She smiled, hoping it would soften some of their faces. "I've met all of you already, but I'm not certain you all know that I am a teacher in Illinois. I have had my own classroom in a small town near Chicago. When I came here to Hope Springs, I had hoped to simply find my sister. After I arrived, and learned that a school had not been created yet, even though we are about to celebrate your twenty-fifth anniversary, I was very surprised. It seems with the number of children I have seen at church on Sundays, there is a sufficient number of pupils to start a school."

Reed smiled at her, and nodded his encouragement.

"What happens when you get married?" Mitch asked again, shooting a sideways glance toward Reed.

"I would hope that her husband would allow her to continue at the school," Reed answered, staring at her the whole time. "At least, until her own children were to arrive, and then perhaps at that time she might consider concentrating on her home."

She smiled broadly at him. That was exactly what she wanted. Was he saying it because he knew that's what she wanted to hear or because he believed that, too?

A neighboring farmer, one she'd met at the barn raising, snorted. "I find it hard to believe she would marry the brother of the man who jilted her sister."

She frowned. "What do you mean, Mr. Watkins?"

"Oh? Haven't you told her yet, Ridgeley?" Watkins mocked.

"It didn't come up." Reed looked sheepishly at her. "This is hardly the place…"

"No, please tell me." She cornered him with her eyes. "What does he mean, your brother jilted Gracie?"

"I will tell you after the meeting," Reed said quietly. "This is family business, surely you don't want this aired here."

"Apparently everyone knows." She looked around the room, and wasn't surprised when all the men nodded at her.

"Fine." He sighed. "Matthew was the man who placed the advertisement for a bride. When Miss Grace arrived, Matt decided they wouldn't suit. He offered to send her home, but she refused. He wouldn't marry her, so Buck did."

"I see."

She wanted to yell at him for keeping such a thing secret, but *that* she'd save for later.

"Well, gentlemen, as I am here to discuss the school, I would just like to close by saying a school fosters a sense of community and unifies a town like nothing else can. Students will be taught with the same goal of making Hope

A COWBOY CELEBRATION

Springs a prosperous community well into the future." She smiled at each of the men at the table, except for Reed. "I thank you for your time."

She left the building without another word, making her way into the beautiful early July evening and over through the park, looking neither right nor left at the women who were there decorating for the upcoming celebration.

♥ ♥ ♥

After the meeting adjourned, Reed found Poppy sitting in the park on a bench, watching the kids running around, playing tag, and leapfrog as the sun was setting in the western sky. He sat down next to her and stretched out his legs.

"Shall we go home?" he asked.

"I don't know." She folded her hands in her lap and then pinned him with her hurt gaze. "If Watkins hadn't opened his big mouth? Would you have ever told me?"

This was going to be their first argument.

"It wasn't my story to tell," he answered quietly. "I don't know what Matthew had arranged with Gracie through their letters. He was very tight-lipped about it all, but I know he was excited for her to come. He bought that house he's in now to start their lives together. I know she wasn't what he expected and didn't feel he could support her as she needed."

"But he thought Buck could?"

"Fair argument." He crossed his legs at the ankles, and turned his head to the side. "I tried to stay out of the situation, but I can say for certain Matthew had every intention of paying for her return to Chicago, and she refused. We didn't realize your people didn't know she was here."

She didn't answer right away and he wondered what she might be thinking. They watched in the waning light as the children were rounded up by their mothers, the decorations left to be finished the following day.

"In one way," she began, "I wish none of this would ever have happened. I wish Gracie was still home. But, by like token, I have to think that maybe everything happens for a reason, and this was the only way you and I would ever meet each other."

He reached over and took her hand, pleased she wasn't as angry with him as he'd anticipated.

"Do you wish to know what the board decided?" he asked.

"Yes."

"Hmmm... I wonder if I should tell you?" he teased.

"Yes! I hate secrets!" She pushed against his shoulder.

195

"Alright." He sighed dramatically. "Well, we have decided that after the celebration is over, we would do a census of the number of school-age children. The board liked your speech, and they asked me to collect references, if you want the job."

She smiled. "That's excellent news!"

"I thought it would make you happy." He kissed her hand. "Are you still mad at me?"

"No. I wasn't really *mad*, just confused as to why you wouldn't have told me. Of course, Gracie never said anything either, but that isn't a surprise." She shook her head.

"So, you'll get those references for me so we can hire you?" he prodded.

She nodded. "Promise me no more secrets in the future, alright?"

"No. No more secrets, Poppy. So, we have a future?" he asked with a chuckle.

"If you'll accept I'm a package deal," she said. "Even if Timmerman shows up, Gracie will only go back to him over my dead body."

"We don't want that." He chuckled. "The sheriff will find him, eventually, and he'll get his just due."

"There *is* one more thing," she said.

"What's that?"

"You'll have to keep writing me poetry." She smiled at him.

"You liked the one from this morning?"

"It was beautiful." She gave him an adoring look. "You have such a way with words."

"Not as beautiful as you." He kissed her hand again. "Let's go home."

Chapter 8

"Looks like everyone in town has showed up!"

Poppy glanced around the town square. Although she'd seen plenty of people at church services and while visiting at Baker's Mercantile, there were dozens of new faces for the celebration of Hope Springs's anniversary.

"Look at all the decorations!" Gracie squealed from the back of the wagon.

"It's very festive!" Poppy agreed.

"You look very patriotic," Reed told her.

She'd worn a navy blue skirt, white blouse and red ribbons in her hair.

"You look rather handsome yourself." He looked so wonderful, she just wanted to sit and look at him.

"Well, I do have to ride in the parade." He chuckled. "I could hardly wear my work clothes." He hopped off the wagon seat and helped her down first before going to the back and, together with Poppy, helping Gracie down.

"I'm so fat!" Gracie said.

"That means you and the baby are healthy." Poppy threaded her arm through her sister's.

"You look remarkably healthy since Poppy arrived," he said.

"She takes good care of me. She always has."

"And she always will." He met Poppy's eyes over the top of Gracie's head. "I see Lucas and Suzy with Ma over there." He pointed to a spot where blankets had already been settled on the ground.

Gracie walked ahead of them.

"She's like a different person when you're around. Much more confident."

"She feels safe and secure," Poppy told him. "She knows I love her and always will."

"I'd like to know that, too." He bent forward, inches from her face. "I'd like to feel your love, and have you make me feel safe and secure."

She didn't know what to say, but she was saved from answering when Matthew came up to greet them, and slapped Reed on the back.

"Ma and Lucas are over there." Reed nodded toward the spot Grace had gone. "If you want to sit with us, that's where we're headed." He held out his elbow for Poppy.

"I think I'll wander a bit before the ceremony starts, then I'll join you," Matt said.

FOR THE LOVE OF GRACE—JULIA DANIELS

"Ceremony?" Poppy asked.

"Oh, maybe you haven't heard. Elizabeth and LeRoy decided to get married in the square at noon." He tipped his head in greeting to someone she didn't recognize as he led her toward his family.

"Ah! You're here." His mother patted the ground next to her. "Come and join us, I was just about to pull out the food."

"It was hard to smell the chicken all morning and not eat it," Reed told her. "I'm starving."

Poppy helped Mabel set out the plates and food for everyone to help themselves. It was a perfect, sunny day for a picnic, with only a slight breeze. If she were honest, she was starving, too. She'd helped Mabel set up the baskets with food that morning. Poppy had created the green corn pudding, and made the white cake while Mabel worked on more of her delicious molasses cookies.

She handed Reed the bowl with chicken, and then gave Lucas the potatoes. Suzy passed the food she'd brought, a broccoli salad with cucumbers and tomatoes and two loaves of fresh bread. She'd also brought some of her canned peaches, which she declared were her husband's favorite.

"I feel guilty I haven't brought anything," Poppy said.

"You made the cake," Mabel said, "and peeled all the taters."

"True." Poppy nodded as she took a bite of the chicken leg.

"So, you can bake, huh?" he whispered softly.

"I can, yes." She smirked.

"Good to know."

She looked back at the rest of them and noticed Gracie staring at her. She smiled, but her sister looked away, an odd look upon her face.

"Is it this elaborate each year?" Poppy asked.

"No. We have a parade and families make picnics, but no one has ever gotten married."

"Oh, I almost forgot about Elizabeth's wedding dance!" She raised her brows and asked him, "Can you dance, Mr. Ridgeley?"

"Absolutely, Miss Stanton," he said, a wide smile on his face. "I sure hope you can, 'cuz you'll have plenty of partners tonight."

"I won't go tonight," Gracie said.

"Don't you feel well?" Poppy asked.

"I'm fine."

Again, Poppy wasn't certain what was going through Gracie's mind. She was acting odd.

"I think you'd enjoy it. For a bit, anyway." She smiled. "Don't you want to

198

A COWBOY CELEBRATION

see Reed dance?" Poppy teased.

"No." She looked away.

Poppy frowned, wondering what she could do to figure out what was wrong with Gracie.

"Miss Gracie, I'd sure be honored if you'd dance with me," Reed said.

"Alright." Her face was blank. Was she pleased? "But you should dance with Poppy. I think she loves you."

Poppy choked on her lemonade.

"Is that right, Miss Gracie?" His smiled widened. "Think Miss Poppy has fallen in love with me?"

"Yeah."

"Is she right, Penelope Stanton?" he whispered for her ears alone. "Have I caught your heart?"

His eyes twinkled with mirth.

"Maybe." She could hardly admit such a thing in the middle of a picnic with his family not two feet away.

"Will you dance with me, ma'am?" he asked her.

"Yes, I certainly will."

A commotion at the front drew their eyes. It was time for the wedding to start. LeRoy and his brother, were standing under a decorated arch, waiting for Elizabeth and her Matron of Honor to arrive. Someone with a violin began to play the wedding march, and Elizabeth, dressed in a fine dress and carrying a lovely bouquet of yellow and white flowers, walked down the makeshift aisle to greet her man.

"I've never been to an outdoor wedding," Poppy told Reed.

"Me, either. I'm not so certain I'd like all these eyes on me."

"No?"

"Nope. I'd be happy with just family looking on."

She studied him before looking away. Back home, she'd be expected to have a massive wedding, with all the best families of Chicago present, highlighting her father's wealth and standing in the community.

The ceremony wasn't very long, but Elizabeth looked radiant, and LeRoy was glowing, and after fifteen minutes, they were legally man and wife. LeRoy took Elizabeth in his arms and gave her a long kiss, which had people clapping and laughing along with them in their happiness. Leroy lifted her in his arms and carried her to his wagon, which someone had decorated with ribbons and papers. They trailed off, leaving their guests to meet them at the barn later that evening.

199

"When is the parade?" Mabel asked.

"I reckon they'll start lining us up soon. You gonna watch?" he asked Poppy.

"Of course! If you're lucky, I might even wave!"

He laughed.

Three hours later, the picnic lunch had been cleaned up, the parade had pulled down Main Street, children had played water games and raced around the park in feed sacks, and now she and Gracie were headed with Reed to the barn dance at Matthew's house.

"I don't want to go," Gracie said.

"Is it because of Matthew?" Poppy asked.

Gracie nodded mutely. She wouldn't meet Poppy's eyes.

"I don't want to leave you alone," Poppy said. "Reed, just drop us off on the way."

She didn't like his frown.

"I can't leave her alone, not with Buck still at large," Poppy said.

"Can't you come for a little bit? It's for Elizabeth, Miss Gracie," he asked.

"No," Gracie answered.

"Why must you always be so stubborn?" Poppy shook her head, frustrated that her sister didn't ever consider anyone but herself.

"I must go to the wedding dance, Poppy," Reed said.

"Of course." She sighed, regretting they couldn't spend the dance together. "Just drop us at your home."

"Very well."

Obviously, he was unhappy. He didn't say anther word unto they got to the Ridgeley house and stopped in front of the door.

"I'd be lying if I said I wasn't disappointed. I was looking forward to dancing with you," he whispered in Poppy's ear helping her down.

"I am, too, Reed."

They helped Gracie out of the wagon, just as they had at the park, and once she was out of earshot, Reed turned to Poppy.

"Will it always be like this?" he asked. "Will Gracie always come first?"

She frowned. She hadn't thought of it that way, but she supposed that's how it looked to him.

"For tonight."

"What about tomorrow, and all the rest of your days?" He demanded. She was shocked at the anger in his voice, on his face. "Will you ever put yourself first?"

"I promised my mother…"

"Penelope, she didn't expect you to give up everything *you* wanted to take care of Gracie," he shouted.

"How do you know what my mother wanted?" she yelled back.

He shook his head. "I'm sorry, I shouldn't shout at you." He lowered his voice before running a hand through his hair. "I have to go."

He stalked away from her, mounted the wagon seat and took off without looking back.

"Who else will care for Gracie?" she whispered.

Reed was right, Mama *wouldn't* have wanted her to give up her dreams. Reed was telling her he wanted to be first in her life, but how could she meet the needs of everyone, especially her own?

Chapter 9

A single light was burning in the front parlor as Reed staggered up to the house. He'd had a little too much happy juice at the wedding. He wasn't certain, but it sure felt like the world was spinning in his head.

He thumped through the back door and landed heavily onto a kitchen chair. He couldn't quite get off his boots. As he leaned over, his feet seemed so far away, his arms weren't long enough to reach them. No matter how hard he tried, his foot just kept moving away, thudding on the kitchen floor. He gave up and leaned against the chair, a wave of nausea overcoming him.

"Your mother said you were lit up like a lantern." Poppy's voice sounded so far away and slow like the words were being pulled from her mouth.

"Naw, I'm just fine," he argued.

She snorted. "If you're *fine*, I'm President Cleveland."

He pried open his eyelids. "You look mighty fine, Grover."

She snorted again. "You are looped, Mr. Ridgeley," she laughed. "Come along, I'll help you to bed."

She held out her hand to help him up, but instead, he was too fast for her. He pulled her onto his lap and into his strong arms. She squealed.

"Oh, Miss Poppy, I love you so." His lips found her neck, and although she knew she should push him away, she couldn't, it felt too good.

"I think it's the alcohol talking," she whispered.

"Oh, no." He pulled away and blinked a few times. "I had plans to ask you to marry me tonight." His voice was so slurred she couldn't be sure that's really what he said. "Marry me, would you?" That was unmistakable.

She shook her head. She would hardly accept a proposal from a drunk man.

Suddenly, he stood up, cradling her in his arms. He set her back down on the chair and got down on one knee. "I need you as much as Gracie does. Woman, I've fallen in love with you. I love everything about you. Please, do me the honor of becoming my wife."

"But…it's so soon…"

"You plannin' to go back to Chicago? 'Cuz if you aren't, you're gonna have to marry someone here. Just as well be me! We got the rest of our lives to get to know each other better."

He was getting all agitated, and it made her uncomfortable. She kissed the hand that had been holding hers. "Let's discuss this in the morning," she said.

"My mind isn't gonna change overnight," he stammered.

"I would hope not, but your approach might be a bit more... acceptable...then."

"Fine." He stumbled as he stood up. "I'll see you to your room."

"Actually," she said, threading her arm around his waist. "I best see you to yours."

"Will you stay with me?"

She laughed lightly. "Not tonight, cowboy."

Pounding woke Reed the next morning. He thought someone was banging on his door, but it was in his head. The minute he moved, his stomach revolted and he rushed to the chamber pot, avoiding a mess he'd have to clean up himself. Ma wasn't supportive of any of them when they imbibed too much.

He retched, and then retched again, losing everything from his stomach. To say he felt as bad as cow dung smelled would be an understatement. He'd been so frustrated that Poppy had stayed with her sister instead of going to the wedding dance with him, he'd been stupid and drank far too much.

He remembered talking with Poppy before falling into bed, had a feeling he may have proposed, but he couldn't be for certain if it really happened—or if it was a dream. He still wore the clothes from the night before, minus his suitcoat and boots, which he couldn't recall removing.

With a deep moan from somewhere low in his gut, he stood and slowly crept back to his bed, where he collapsed. His head continued to pound, his eyes felt as if he'd been punched, and his mouth was as dry as what he imagined the desert might feel like.

"Oh, hell." He leaned over the side of the bed and threw up some more, into the trash can near the bed. Again, he leaned back against his pillows, closed his eyes tightly, and took some deep breaths, hoping to calm his stomach. "What an idiot!"

More pounding came. No matter how many deep breaths he took, he couldn't shake the pounding from his head. Then came the yelling; his mother's voice, yelling at him, asking if he was all right?

He was in hell.

Gingerly, he sat on the edge of the bed and rubbed the sleep from his eyes with the heels of his hands. How he was going to get anything done today, he wasn't quite sure, but maybe if he got some fresh air, he'd feel better.

He washed his face and changed his clothes, holding onto his bureau as he did so. Nothing seemed very solid to him. Everything seemed to want to move.

Never Had a Chance—Angela Raines

Finally, clad in proper attire for his chores, he left his room carrying the offending trash can that had to be cleaned. He hoped he could make it outside without being noticed. The scent of bacon and eggs frying made his stomach roll and he had to stop in the middle of the hallway to take more deep breaths. This was not good.

♥ ♥ ♥

Poppy hid a smile behind her napkin as Reed finally joined them in the kitchen.

"How you feeling this morning, Reed?" she asked. He looked horrible.

"I've been better."

She laughed at his sour expression. "You seemed to be in a fine mood last night."

"I'm paying for that this morning."

"They caught Buck," his mother said as she set a plate of food in front of him.

"That's good news." He pushed the plate away. "Does Gracie know?"

"I told her right away," Poppy said. She filled up their coffee cups.

He sat back in his chair and rubbed a hand across his face. "Will they lock him up?"

"They said they would if he didn't leave town," Mabel told him. "He's got relatives in Nebraska, so I gave the sheriff money and told him to send him on the next train east."

"You didn't tell me that," Poppy said.

"It wouldn't do no good to have Gracie go through a trial, would it?"

"Oh, no!" Poppy said. "Of course not, but I would have given you the money to get the man away from town and out of her life for good!"

"Nonsense!" Mabel waved at the air. "I used the money Matt was going to give Gracie to go back to Chicago. He gave it to me to hold it if she ever changed her mind."

Things began to make a little more sense to Poppy. Mabel was extra nice to Gracie, not only because Gracie was slow, but Mabel felt guilty about how Matthew had treated her. Reed was generally a nice man, but he'd been even gentler and kinder than necessary with Gracie. Poppy had noticed that right from the beginning.

They finished their breakfasts, each lost in their own thoughts.

"I suppose she and I will move back to her house now," Poppy said, sipping on her coffee.

As much as she hated to say it, Poppy knew they should.

204

A COWBOY CELEBRATION

"You'll do no such thing. You'll stay right here," Mabel declared. "I think we should burn their house."

"Burn it?" Poppy squawked.

"Grace can't have many good memories from her time there," Reed said. "No reason to leave a shack like that standing."

"We'll let Gracie decide," Mabel said.

Reed pushed back from the table. Poppy noticed he was wobbly.

"Poppy, will you walk out to the barn with me?" he asked.

"Sure."

She figured it was a good idea to go with him, if nothing else to make certain he didn't fall over in a dung heap.

"See ya later, Ma." He kissed Mabel's cheek and took Poppy's hand.

"Do you have a job for me?" she asked as he led her from the house.

"Yep." He grabbed his hat from the shelf in the mud room. "I'll tell you about in the tack room."

"Are you going to be alright today?" she asked. "You still look rather peaked. You should have eaten something."

"I'll get by." He smiled, and squeezed her hand.

He let her go ahead of him into the barn, and with a hand at her waist, guided her to the back room. He seated her on a stool and then sat across from her.

"Last night when I came home, I was a bit intoxicated."

"Just a bit," she agreed with a smile.

"I don't drink often, but I was angry you chose Grace over me."

"I understand how you see it that way, but I was worried about her. She told me last night she was scared that if you and I married, we wouldn't want her anymore."

"What did you tell her?"

She took his hand. "That I can love more than one person."

"And do you?"

"Yes." She smiled broadly. "I do love you, Reed Ridgeley. Last night you said you loved everything about me. It's the same for me. I love everything about you, too."

"You'll stay in Hope Springs and marry me?"

She nodded briskly. "Yes, to both."

He sealed their engagement with a deep, passionate kiss.

He took her hand again. "You don't feel forced to marry me, because of Grace's safety, do you?"

205

"Oh, no, Reed. I'm doing this entirely for the love I feel for *you*, and the life we will build together, *not* for my love for Gracie."

"That's the job I have to offer you, by the way. Be my wife? Help me build a life?"

"Absolutely."

She leaned forward as he put his lips to hers once more. Poppy may have come to Hope Springs out of love for Gracie, but it was her love for Reed that compelled her to stay.

About Julia Daniels

Julia Daniels writes stories of happily-ever-after. When she's not writing, she teaches children with special needs. She's living the dream in rural Nebraska with her husband and two teenage kids. For the Love of Grace is her first work with Prairie Rose Publications. She can be found on Twitter: @ScribeJulia and Facebook: https://www.facebook.com/JuliaDanielsAuthor

Winner Takes All

By Meg Mims

Cora Peterson's plan to beat her rival at a picnic auction brings about a surprising end and an unexpected love...

Chapter One

Cora Peterson smiled at her basket covered with a blue-checkered cloth. The scent of warm apples mingling with cinnamon and sugar wafted throughout the kitchen. Today, her pie would fetch a good price at the Fourth of July Picnic and Barrel Auction. She hoped it would also redeem her after last year's fiasco.

"Mm, what is that?" The wooden screen slammed behind her older brother when he waltzed in from the barn. Elmer reached a hand toward the cloth, but Cora smacked his fingers with a wooden spoon. "Ow! I just wanted a peek."

"That would cost you five dollars."

"Five dollars? Ha. You're dreaming if you think anyone would pay five dollars for a measly apple pie."

"This year, I'm going to beat Maybelle Winslow."

"Good luck with that."

Elmer stalked out of the kitchen. His boots clattered on the stairs and half-drowned out his shout. "You better be ready to go in ten minutes. I've harnessed the team, so get the hampers out on the back porch for me."

"I'm ready." Cora untied her apron and hung it on the hook by the door. "My pie will bring at least three dollars, wait and see," she muttered aloud. "Maybelle Winslow's raisin custard brought three dollars one year, and it hadn't even set properly. This pie will bring a lot more. What man can resist apple pie? And this one's extra special."

Then again, she didn't have the same reputation as a good cook and baker like Maybelle. Or was it her rival's hourglass figure that drew the men like flies over spilled honey? Cora smoothed her skirts. Maybelle's dark hair, china blue eyes and long lashes that she batted half-a-dozen times helped, too. But men usually focused on her overly-large bosom instead of her face. And Maybelle

207

lapped up any attention like a thirsty dog. Cora straightened her collar. Twenty years old, and her flat chest hadn't blossomed an inch.

What did that matter? She knew her effort at baking this year was flawless. Two years ago, her rum cake had fallen between here and the picnic area, so it only fetched two bits. But Maybelle's pecan pie, despite a burned crust, had brought in two dollars. It wasn't fair. And last year, Cora had walked home early out of embarrassment. Elmer whistled as he entered the kitchen, buttoning the sleeves of his fresh shirt.

"You didn't switch salt for sugar this year, did you?" He winked. "I had to bribe Billy Cooper with twice what he paid so he wouldn't complain—"

"Oh, shut up."

"Billy was able to buy Maybelle's shortcake, you know, with my money. And I didn't even get one single strawberry. He went off with her and that bowl of whipped cream."

"It's not my fault. She didn't have to go anywhere with whoever buys her desserts."

"Hmph. I suppose that's true."

"She must have saved some of the best berries, since most of them were sent to Long Grove for their Strawberry Festival back in June."

"I only wish I could have won that," her brother said.

Cora knew Elmer loved strawberry shortcake more than anything in the world. She had to wonder why Maybelle had gone off with Billy; he'd followed her like a lovesick puppy the rest of the summer. She'd finally grown tired of him, getting her brother to warn Billy to stay away from her. But Maybelle had boasted at church last week that she was making her best dessert ever for the auction. Cora was desperate to beat her with the highest bid.

"I'm calling this 'Mile High Apple Pie'," she said, although her brother looked skeptical. The heavenly scent tickled her nose. "What? I used a whole bowl of apples, mixed with sugar, flour, and cinnamon, and flipped it over into the bottom crust. Then I covered it with a top crust, brushed it with egg and sugar, too. It looks beautiful."

Elmer leaned over and raised the edge of the blue-checkered cloth. "Woo-wee. That does look and smell mighty good, Cora. But Maybelle's making a chocolate cake."

"Chocolate?" Her heart sank.

"With buttercream frosting and raspberry filling."

"Raspberry–how do you know that?"

He grinned. "I've got my sources."

A COWBOY CELEBRATION

Cora marched to the sink and wrung out the wet dishcloth, then hung it to dry. "My apple pie is perfect. The pastry is flakier than Mama's biscuits used to be."

"Then it should fetch a few dollars. Don't worry. I've got a few friends coming to play a game of baseball," he said, and whistled his way outside. "They'll be hungry. I bet one of 'em will go for pie." The screen door slammed again, *thwack*.

"You ought to fix that," she yelled. "I've asked you three times."

Cora stalked over to the hallway and picked up her new hat–a darling straw boater with streaming blue ribbons. She jammed the hatpin into the pile of braided and looped dark red hair behind her head. Thankfully, not carrot orange—like her grandmother—or so Mama always said. Cora turned away from her image, wishing freckles didn't mar her pale complexion and silly upturned nose. Why couldn't she be buxom and dark-haired, or even blonde?

Instead, she was thin and clumsy. Always running into a door frame, or jarring her hip against the table's edge. Cora refused to wear the spectacles that would help, or so the doctor told her. Far-sighted, he called it. But she would not perch them on her nose to help her see things closer. Not even for reading. They looked awful with those round wire frames and spindly ear pieces that rubbed her skin raw.

If she wore them, she'd be laughed at by all the young men and remain a spinster the rest of her days. Cora wanted to marry. She wanted to have her own home, a husband, and children... what woman didn't? Poor Elmer. He'd been saddled with her since their parents had been killed in a railroad accident. Her brother had hoped to study law, but now was stuck farming like their father in Cady Corners, Iowa. A one-street village surrounded by farms, northeast of Long Grove–also a small settlement, but at least the railroad ran through it. Here in Cady Corners, they were too close to the Mississippi. In her opinion, anyway.

They'd nearly been wiped out the year Pa and Ma died, with spring flooding the worst anyone had seen–eighteen feet. That's why Cora wanted a home west of this village, away from any chance of losing so much. She couldn't bear another flood.

And that meant marrying a farmer, or someone's cousin, or one of Elmer's friends, who worked either in Long Grove or one of the towns in the surrounding county. Cora wouldn't mind starting over somewhere close enough to visit Elmer. Her friends, too. And this picnic was the best chance for all the young ladies to meet young men and begin courting.

209

Cora fetched her gloves and carried the picnic hampers to the back porch. Then she fetched her pie, safe in its separate basket. Once he nestled it between the two heavy hampers, Elmer helped her into the buggy. Her best dress nearly caught on a sharp edge. Cora fussed over the pale blue linen skirt, its scalloped hem showing the eyelet ruffle of her best petticoat, and then adjusted the large poufs of her sleeve tops.

"You promised to bend that edge down the last time that happened."

"I forgot. Is that a new hat? It looks nice."

"Thank you, but don't change the subject. Fix that rough edge, or you'll be sorry."

Elmer let out a long-suffering sigh. "If I had a hammer, I'd do it now."

"Stop the buggy then, and I'll go fetch one from your tools."

"Oh, hush. We'll be late enough for the events."

Cora glanced back at their two-story frame house, white with green shutters, shaded by oaks and elms, the large red barn, the neat chicken coop, the acres of corn and oats. Would Elmer find a wife who would be content here? Hopefully, after she was married. Who would her brother court? He hadn't yet, despite being talented, smart, and funny. Elmer had carpentry skills, too, and was good with horses and any animals; stray dogs and cats followed him all over the farm. Cora knew he'd make a wonderful husband.

At twenty-five, he was ripe for marriage. Elmer had turned their farm around from barely scraping along to prospering with corn-fed hogs and a few bumper years of corn and wheat. With the help of his hired hands, of course. Cora knew Elmer's wife would not want to share a home with a spinster sister, though. She'd just have to set her cap for a man, and pray harder.

"So, who are these friends coming to play baseball?" she asked Elmer, and winced when the buggy lurched over a series of dry ruts in the road.

"Tom Price, Bill Cooper, and a bunch of others. Remember the Swede who's working for Ben Bergman at the sawmill, the one I invited for dinner?"

"Oh. Yes, I remember."

"You don't sound real happy about Nik—"

"You wouldn't understand," Cora interrupted, her face hot, "because you're used to my burned biscuits and ruined cooking. I felt terrible! Making chipped beef for company, when that roast should have been fork tender."

"He ate it, didn't he?" Elmer laughed. "Good thing Nik couldn't understand too much English. He's a little better, now. Don't get your knickers in a knot."

"Hmph. And you never invited him again to prove I'm not that bad a cook."

Her brother shrugged. "Lundquist keeps to himself mostly, from what I hear, and he's been working overtime for Ben Bergman. Not sure why he came to Iowa. Most Swedes go to Minnesota, but who knows? He's a nice fella. Real polite. I talked him into playing ball."

"It's always about baseball with you."

Cora clung to the buggy's side when the horses swerved around a sharp curve. She had felt so self-conscious with Niklas Lundquist in their home. He was taller than any man she'd met before, taller than Mr. Bergman–but a decade younger, perhaps the same age as Elmer. Bigger too—hands, feet, shoulders—and those blue eyes had taken in everything during his visit; their tiny dining room with its lace curtains and linen tablecloth, the china and flatware, the stuffy parlor where Nik had not spoken more than 'ya' or 'nay' either. Polite, perhaps, but aloof.

"—hit the ball a mile when we had our last practice," Elmer was saying with clear satisfaction. "We'll beat the DeWitt Devils this year. Wait and see."

"What did you come up with for a name?"

"The Timber Wolves."

She sniffed. Cora wasn't surprised, given their rough-and-tumble ways. Last year, Elmer and his friends had played three innings before a melee broke out over a bad call. None of the other picnic-goers had a piece of raw meat left from their picnic lunch, so she could not treat his black eye; she had to tear her good petticoat to wrap his broken ribs. She was prepared this summer. Cora had wrapped the meat in butcher paper she'd saved, stuck it between the chunks of icy lemonade, and brought an old flannel shirt.

Just in case. But he'd better behave himself, along with the rest of the Timber Wolves.

Wolves, hmph. More like wild savages.

Chapter Two

Niklas Lundquist wished he had stayed back at the boarding house, but hiding on such a fine summer day would be *vanligt dum*. His boss, Mr. Bergman, told him to enjoy the picnic and meet people in the village. So here he was.

He eyed the short, wiry man in an odd getup. *"Vad är*—what is hat?" Nik asked, wishing he'd practiced his English more before coming to this event.

The man grinned. "A Stetson. Wanna try it?"

Nik solemnly took the wide-brimmed black hat with its feather trim and placed it with care on his blond head. It did not fit. Ever since he'd clunked himself on the top of his skull with a double blade ax, at ten years old, he could never wear anything but knitted hats. He had been lucky to survive such a blow. His father had said, *"Alla höns hemma."* Nik had never done such a stupid thing again, not after that insult. He had all his hens in the house now, given his decision to take ship and seek prosperity here in a new country.

He handed the hat back to the man. *"Tack."*

"Uh, sure." The man grabbed his arm and led him to his horse. "This here bridle is the best harness for a cowboy. How do you like this saddle? Gussied up with silver studs."

Nik could tell the young man took pride in his fine bay. He rubbed the horse's flank and checked the teeth, then stepped back. Two other men in similar hats, red neck scarves, plaid shirts and rough trousers grinned at him. They acted silly, and jostled each other with joking words Nik did not understand. The men also gestured toward several pretty young ladies who carried baskets toward a long table, setting out pies, cakes, and other *bakverk*. Nik did not think they meant them any harm, but fumed in silence at their disrespect.

"Look-ey that brunette. I could sure rub those cat-heads all night."

"Ha. You'd be lucky to tumble with the skinny red-head," the other whispered.

Nik wanted to punch the man in the nose for that comment. He knew from the joke talk at the sawmill what was meant by a 'tumble.' And the red-headed woman was his friend Elmer's sister. While he was tempted to give them both a lesson in manners, Nik turned his back and walked toward the meadow. Elmer Peterson had been first to greet him when Nik arrived in the village. The young

A COWBOY CELEBRATION

farmer seemed to be well-liked and popular, and the leader of the group of friends who would be playing "baseball" today.

"Come on, boys, it's show-off time!"

The leader of the cow-boys–which seemed an odd name for men, since they did not resemble cows–herded his group and their horses toward the grassy open field. Nik watched along with the excited crowd of villagers when the cowboys screeched and yelled, riding hard and then throwing ropes over a post at the field's edge; they twirled the ropes over their heads or alongside their horses, which seemed pointless. Where were the cows?

"Hey, Nik. Good to see you." Elmer Peterson gripped his hand firmly and then pointed at the men racing along the meadow. "They're tearing up the grass. Won't be easy playing ball today if they keep that up for their hour of fun."

"*Ja.*"

He wished Mr. Bergman had organized an ax competition, or tossing a heavy log, to prove these cow-boys they were not so strong and agile. That was not important. Bergman knew his men were skilled, and so did the villagers. Elmer voiced his wish, however.

"Too bad you and the other workers at the sawmill aren't showing off today. See how fast two of you could saw through a tree," he said, shading his eyes. "What's this about the mill making doors, sashes, and window frames now more than planed lumber?"

Nik nodded. "*Ja.* Money is good. Better—better—" He raised one hand higher.

"Profit? I guess so then. Bergman knows the business."

He nodded again. His boss was intelligent and shrewd. There was little timber left on the ridge to the east of the village; if Bergman wanted to make doors, sashes and windows, then his job was to follow orders. Nik would work until he earned enough money to travel. He wanted to cut timber in the Pacific Northwest and farther north into Canada, but he couldn't find the words to put his thoughts into *Engelsk* to explain. He didn't know if a farmer like Elmer Peterson who worked the fields would understand.

One of the cowboys ran alongside his horse and jumped on, and then off, back and forth. The man hung from the saddle horn, lifting his legs off the ground, and then twisted around, and jumped backward onto the horse, who was smart enough to ignore him. Another cowboy stood twirling his rope, back and forth, stepping in and out of the circle. The crowd clapped and whistled, clearly happy with the display. He noticed that Elmer's *syster* Cora smiled and

213

laughed until the dark-haired 'cat-head' woman moved to her side and whispered something.

"It's called Mile High Apple Pie, if you must know," Cora sniffed.

"What kind of apples? Last year's, I would think."

"So? They're Northern Spy."

"Hmph. Sour as anything, no doubt, and full of worms," the brunette said.

Cora Peterson turned so fast she bumped into him. Nik stepped aside, but she did the same thing. He felt stupid, stepping in the other direction, but again matched her move–which seemed to make her angrier. Her blue eyes snapped fire at him.

"Please, Mr. Lundquist, may I get past you?"

"*Jag beklagar.*"

"Excuse me?"

Nik shook his head, wishing he hadn't said anything, and stepped to the right–she had done the same again, though. Frustrated, wanting to cool her temper, he reached out his large hands and planted them on her shoulders; holding her in place, he moved out of her way and then let go. She burst out laughing. Cora waved a hand before her flushed face.

"I'm sorry—oh! That was funny."

He nodded, smiling too. She wasn't angry at him, good. Nik thought he'd been too forward and wondered if she would complain to her *broder*. But Elmer was laughing too, heading their way. Once he joined them, Nik apologized again.

"Speak English," Elmer reminded him. "But don't be sorry, that wasn't your fault. Are you ready to play ball?"

"*Ja.* I am ready for ball."

Cora smiled up at him. "Baseball, you mean."

"Nik, you remember my sister, Cora," Elmer said.

She rewarded him with a pretty curtsey, so Nik bowed. His face flooded with heat from his neck to the roots of his blond hair, and he wanted to kick himself. He must resemble a native they called a savage Redskin. He admired her fairness, the freckles sprinkled over her nose, and her cheeks resembling pink flowers. She was taller than the other village girls, but her blue dress hugged her slender figure. He spied a few reddish curls peeking beneath her hat.

Perhaps he would bid on her apple pie. The meal she'd cooked for him and her brother had not been so good, except for what Elmer called 'cobbler'–juicy and sweet with luscious peaches and cream. She seemed very nice and polite, even if she was thin instead of plump like the cat-head woman, who giggled too much to his liking. Cora. The name seemed to fit her, too, for some reason. Nik remembered his *Tant* Corinna, a family favorite.

He'd heard about today's auction and how it was run. The ladies took pride in their baking, like his own sisters and *moder* back home. Nik had brought plenty of money and had a sweet tooth that topped anyone in his family.

Elmer held out a straw hat. "It's hot out there in the meadow. You might need this."

Nik shrugged and placed it on his head, but it slid off. "*Nej. Liten.*"

"Well, it does seem a bit little. Come on, then," Elmer said. "Hobble those horses, boys! Let's play ball. The Timber Wolves against the DeWitt Devils."

A group of men from the other town whooped and hollered, earning admiring glances from the ladies. Nik followed Elmer and Cora, grateful that he'd been asked to play this strange running game of baseball. He'd played twice before to practice; the village men used a long wooden stick to hit a horsehair-stuffed ball as far as possible. His calloused hands never hurt much after catching balls hit to him in the field. He could easily cover a wide area and throw to those guarding the "bases," or so they called the wooden blocks set in a diamond shape. An odd game, but better than standing around listening to others.

Nik didn't mind sweating in the hot sun. He was used to it.

Many of the ladies glanced at him with open admiration, but he was too shy to introduce himself or speak to them. Nik enjoyed the sun and wind, though, after enduring the long and snowy winter back in Sverige. His family disliked the long months of darkness. He preferred the crisp cold nights best, watching the color dance of green, red, and purple shimmering over the northern horizon, and the infrequent bright sunlit days of skiing along a track of animal prints hunting fresh meat.

Perhaps he ought to have moved to Minnesota. The winters were similar, from what he'd heard, and many communities had plenty of people from Sverige. But Nik had met Ben Bergman in New York when he first came to this country, and accepted his offer of work. He was a fair man and paid better wages than he'd expected. Nik had time to make his way across this country, seeing the sights. With enough money, he could go wherever he wished.

For now, he was content here in the village of Cady Corners. Nik had no idea what "corner" meant in this very strange language. Cady had been a blacksmith who first set up shop here long ago, from what Elmer had explained. Nik thought it odd the villagers would honor a man who had

WINNER TAKES ALL—MEG MIMS

abandoned his smithy to head west. Then again, *he* wanted to go west.

Perhaps it wasn't so odd, after all.

The group of village men gathered on one side of the grassy field, while the men from DeWitt stood on the other. Elmer checked his pocket watch, glancing around in worry. Some of the men talked in low voices. Nik glanced a few times at Cora Peterson. She chatted with other young ladies near the *bakverk* table; they pointed out several items. Nik had enjoyed apple tarts back home. He jumped when someone prodded him from behind.

"Nik, can you pitch?" Elmer sounded worried. "My friend Tom Price hasn't shown up. We're ready to start the game, and we need someone to pitch."

"Pitch? What is pitch?"

"Like this."

Nik followed him to the small mound of dirt, in the center of the diamond shape, between the three bases. Elmer threw the ball toward Billy Cooper, who caught it after a bounce. "*Ja?*" Nik asked, puzzled.

"No, throw it all the way without bouncing. I'm not so good," Elmer said. "Throw it so the man can hit it. Or throw it so he swings and misses. That's the best way."

Finally, he understood. Nik had watched Tom pitch at practice, while making sure all the other men stood guard at the bases or out in the field. Elmer ran out to where Nik would have stood, and then waved, as if signaling him to begin. One of the DeWitt Devils came forward with the wooden bat on his shoulder. The crowd watched on the sides, some of the ladies holding parasols for shade from the hot sunshine, calling encouragement. Nik shut out all the noise, in the same fashion he did at the mill, to concentrate.

He threw the ball and grinned when the player swung hard and missed. Nik threw again, with a bit of a spin on the ball–surprising himself at that. Billy Cooper caught it and threw it back. The man who stood behind the "catcher" held up two fingers.

"Two strikes!"

"How can I hit it when he's spinning it?" the man with the stick complained.

"Just pay attention, son," he said and waved his hand at Nik.

This time, the man swung and hit the ball straight at Nik, who somehow managed to catch it against his stomach. *Oof.* His belly stung; he rubbed his shirt and winced. Someone from the crowd ran to him, the town *Läkare*, the one they called *Doktor* Kirchner, who had visited the mill when there'd been a

216

bad accident and tended the injured men. Nik waved him away, his face hot with embarrassment.

"*Jag är inte sårad*–I am not hurt."

"All right then. Lucky man."

The game began again, with Elmer catching the ball hit by the third DeWitt player and then throwing it to one of base guards to tag the runner. The man behind Billy called him "out" to much grumbling by the DeWitt Devils. Nik did not understand much, but marched off the field with the Timber Wolves, who took their turn at bat next, in a whirl of confusion. Elmer handed Nik the bat and pointed at the two men standing on a base.

"See them? If you hit the ball out to where those horses are, they'll all score. You can, too, if you make it around the bases before they fetch the ball and throw it back. Okay?"

"*Ja*. Okay."

Nik rubbed his hands on the seat of his trousers and stepped up to the plate. He squinted into the bright sun, holding the wooden stick high. The other team's pitcher threw the ball at his shoulder. He barely jumped out of the way.

"Hey! No fair," Elmer yelled. "You're not allowed to hit the batter!"

"Sorry."

The man did not sound sorry at all, grinning like a fool. Nik waited for his second throw, which was wild and nearly hit him in the head. This time he ducked, swearing under his breath, along with half of his team. Elmer stormed out to the pitcher along with the older man who stood behind the catcher; the man claimed he was "um-pire" and scolded the DeWitt Devils for their bad behavior. The Timber Wolves yelled and stomped their feet before the game resumed. The pitcher didn't laugh any longer, and Nik knew he had thrown it on purpose to hit him. Angry now, he waited for the third pitch. The man threw it the right way this time.

Nik swung the stick. *Whack*! His hands stung, and he watched the ball sail toward the horses. It dropped past them, in fact. Without thinking, Nik ran–the stick still in hand–around the bases while the crowd cheered and clapped. He caught up to Elmer's friend Billy, who had stumbled on the rough ground. He grabbed Billy by his shirt collar and set him upright. Then they ran toward the "home" base, although Nik had no idea why it was called "home". The pitcher let Billy through but blocked the base, glaring at Nik.

"Go on back to third."

"*Vad*? *Varför*?"

"Throw the ball," the man yelled, glancing past him.

Nik turned to see one of the other team members fire the ball at him. He swung the stick and hit it before the pitcher could catch it, with the same jarring force. This time, the ball sailed over the trees beyond the field. The rest of the DeWitt Devils ran out to meet the Timber Wolves with raised fists. Nik stood in the middle of the men, stick in hand, watching Elmer tackle the catcher. The two sprawled on the grass, kicking and punching.

He shook his head at this crazy game. "*Jag förstår inte.*"

"What did you say?"

The man who asked, the burly and dark-haired pitcher, didn't wait for Nik to answer. He punched Nik in his already-sore belly. Roaring with anger, he dropped the stick and connected his fist with the pitcher's jaw; his opponent flew backward and tumbled into another pair of fighters. Everyone was taking part, with Nik in the midst. He swung out in all directions, landing punches to noses, jaws, bellies, until a shrill whistle blast halted everyone. The men looked up, groaning in pain or holding white handkerchiefs to their bloody noses.

Ben Bergman held his hands in the air. "That's enough! Stop all this fighting!"

Nik straightened to his full height, respectful of his boss, but the pitcher tackled him backward onto the ground. Somehow, Nik hooked an ankle around the burly man's leg and rolled over, holding him down, but someone else crashed into them both. Grunting, Nik found himself assaulted with punches by two sets of fists.

"Stop right now!" His boss hauled the two men back, allowing Nik to slowly rise to his feet. "If any of you keeps at this, I'll have the county sheriff arrest you."

"All right, all right," the burly pitcher said, and spat at Nik's feet. "Dumb Swede hit the ball twice, which is against the rules."

"You kept him from scoring that home run," Elmer said, pushing his way into their circle. "Do you call that fair?"

Bergman brushed dust from his shirt sleeves. "Whatever happened, it's over. Take a break for lunch. We'll have the auction after."

"What about the game? We have to finish—"

"If you want to play ball and fight for the rest of the afternoon, that's your business. But the ladies are upset from all this violence."

"Understood, Mr. Bergman. Come on, boys."

Elmer waved to his players, including Nik, who limped his way after the Timber Wolves toward the picnic area. Bergman stayed behind, talking to the burly pitcher and the DeWitt Devils. Nik didn't care. Somehow he'd twisted his knee. His ribs hurt, his eye had swollen almost shut, and his jaw had a knot the size of the ball he'd hit over the trees. He wondered if someone had fetched it. Then again, what did it matter? He wasn't sure he wanted to continue playing such a stupid game.

Listening and learning *Engelsk* might be less painful.

Chapter Three

Cora shook her head in disgust. Both her brother and his friend Niklas Lundquist looked terrible–their clothes dirty, their knuckles skinned red, their faces bruised and swollen. She handed one chunk of raw meat to Elmer, who slapped it against his right eye. The other, she handed to Nik, who sat cross-legged on the ground. He refused to meet her gaze and covered his swollen left eye with a deep sigh, muttering in Swedish under his breath. It sounded like he was complaining, but perhaps he could be thanking her.

"You're welcome. I don't understand why you boys have to fight over every little thing," she said. "It's just a game, for heaven's sake! It's not that important."

Elmer snorted. "It is when we have fifty dollars riding on the outcome."

"Fifty dollars?"

Nik looked confused, as if he didn't understand the conversation, but Cora figured he must be aware of the arrangement. Gambling on the outcome of a silly baseball game! Immoral, and plain stupid. She was glad Mr. Bergman had stopped play.

"Well, go wash up. You're not eating a bite until you do."

Elmer groaned when he scrambled to his feet. He held a hand out to Nik, who accepted his help. Once they returned from pumping clean water and washing at the horse trough, Cora set plates before them heaped with fried chicken, along with a mound of corn pudding, potato salad, wedges of johnnycake, baked beans, bacon and green beans. She added pickled eggs and onions. She didn't care if they had trouble eating with their sore hands and mouths. Let them suffer. Niklas fixed his one blue eye on her.

"*Tank*."

"You're welcome, again." Cora smiled at him, amused by his beet-red face. "Would you like beer or lemonade? Ginger water?"

"*Vatten*, water. *Var god*."

"It is very good. From our well," she said, "with fresh ginger grated in for flavoring."

He only nodded his blond head. Niklas Lundquist wore his hair longer than most men in the village. It curled above his ears but fell over his plaid shirt collar. A darker lock waved over his forehead–perhaps no one told him about Cady Corners having a barber. Nik didn't seem to understand or speak much

A COWBOY CELEBRATION

English, given his halting answers. He certainly wolfed his lunch as if he'd never eaten before. She knew fried chicken was her specialty. Her mother had taught her well. If only she'd learned the trick of flaky biscuits.

Cora thought Nik handsome enough, and nice, but he certainly didn't seem interested in her. He glanced at Maybelle Winslow a few times, who simpered and giggled not too far from their picnic blanket. She sat with a group of other church friends, along with her parents.

Billy Cooper walked over to Maybelle. He hadn't given up hope, apparently, but she pointedly ignored him. "Mind if I sit with you—"

"I *do* mind, Mr. Cooper! As I told you, we are no longer courting."

His cheeks aflame, Billy fled the picnic area. Cora felt sorry for him. She finished her lunch and filled both Elmer's and Nik's plates once more from the hampers. Let them stuff themselves. That way they'd be too full to play baseball, or fight.

She did admire Nik's strength, however, in hitting two home runs–although they had only counted one in the score. Cora smiled. The Timber Wolves must be desperate to win that bet, given last year's game when they hadn't scored a single run. She hummed to herself. Once she'd wiped the empty plates, she loaded them back into the hamper. Cora walked to the pump, washed her hands without splashing her linen dress, and then slowly returned to search for the last piece of raw meat. She reached out to her brother.

"Here, Elmer."

"Nah. Give it to Nik. His eye is real bad."

Cora slapped her brother's hand away from his swollen nose and tipped his head up. "You boys, fighting like rabid dogs. And over what? A silly game."

"We didn't start it!"

"Hmph."

"How are you feeling, Elmer?"

Cora gritted her teeth, hearing that sickening sweet voice behind her. Maybelle Winslow crouched down beside her brother, showing off her puffed-out bosom, and eyeing Elmer's swollen nose and cheek. She clucked like a mother hen, fussing over the hard bruised lump on his forehead, too. Cora thought her fake concern disgusting.

"Mr. Lundquist is in worse shape," she pointed out.

"Oh, is he? What a shame." Maybelle only glanced once at Nik, who didn't seem to be all that aware they were talking about him.

Cora marched over to the blond Swede and held out the raw piece to him. "For your eye. That one is too old now. Go on, take it. It's fresher."

He held out the old graying hunk. "*Fräsch?*"

"Yes." She plopped the new meat over his eye. "It's also beef, the same as the other. Beef from a cow. See? It's colder."

"*Biff?*" He winced in pain, fingering his swollen eye. "Cow. *Det är kallt.*"

"Uh-huh. Cold."

"*Ja.* Cold."

Maybelle giggled. "You're funny, trying to talk to him. He doesn't sound smart."

"How would you know that?" Elmer scowled. "Niklas Lundquist is a good man and a hard worker. He's only been here a few months in the States. He's picked up a lot of English since he arrived."

"I didn't mean–I'm sorry." She scrambled to her feet, clearly disappointed. "Well, it's nearly time for the auction. I'd better go check on my cake."

"Yes, make sure it hasn't melted and slid off the plate," Cora said.

Maybelle gasped at that and looked hurt.

"You should apologize," her brother scolded. "What's with you two, anyway? Why can't you get along?"

"Oh, that's rich! I could say the same thing about you and your Timber Wolves, fighting with the DeWitt Devils."

"It's all right, Elmer. Your sister has never liked me."

Maybelle flounced off, which was fine with Cora. She still smarted from that nasty insult about wormy apples. And she'd been secretly pleased that the buttercream frosting had not lasted in the heat, despite Maybelle's frantic efforts to set the glass platter on a bed of ice chunks. Cora's pie looked wonderful in comparison. All the villagers and church women would forget about her fallen rum cake and last year's salty rhubarb pie. Libby Bergman, the president of the Ladies' Auxiliary, had complimented her apple pie in front of everyone today.

All the ladies in Cady Corners listened to Libby, the older sister of Ben Bergman–who owned the biggest business in the area. Cora thought she was quite pretty with her brown hair and eyes, different from her dark-haired, blue-eyed brother, and wondered why Libby had never remarried. The widow was successful county-wide as a talented seamstress and dress designer, ran the Ladies Auxiliary, and backed many charity functions.

Cora fetched the lace parasol she'd bought from Libby and raised it above her head. "Maybelle's right, it's almost time for the auction. I hope you're still hungry, Elmer."

"We will be." He patted his stomach and grinned at Nik. "This will be fun.

Do you know what an auction is?"

"*Auktionwerk, ja.*"

"Sounds the same. Where things are on sale, and people bid?"

"Bid?"

"Yes, like I say a dollar. You would say two, and then I'd bid three."

Cora bit her lip at Nik's puzzled expression until he raised his eyebrows. "*Ja?* Bid, dollar. *Kroner.* It is money."

"Money, that's right," Elmer said with a laugh. "Come on, then!"

Cora and Niklas followed him toward the long table, where people who'd finished their picnic lunches gathered. A few families remained on their blankets, finishing their meal, so Reverend Rausch announced the auction would take place within fifteen minutes. Cora slowly walked along the table, eyeing the mouth-watering display. Cherry, blueberry, strawberry and gooseberry pies covered with pale or brown lattice crusts sat between a variety of fruit cobblers, mincemeat and chess pies, cookies of all kinds, and glazed cakes sprinkled with nuts.

Maybelle's cake looked a mess beneath its glass dome. The matching plate sat atop a glass bowl of water; the original swirls of frosting had left streaky gobs down the cake's sides. Other ladies clucked in sympathy, but Cora couldn't help feeling a surge of satisfaction. Her Mile High Apple pie remained a mound of goodness, the top crust golden, sprinkled with sugar crystals, the fluted edge perfect. Excited, she tapped her foot while waiting for Libby Bergman to finish speaking to the minister.

Reverend Rausch finally waved to a young boy, who rolled a round wooden barrel forward. The two of them stood it on end. The minister rapped a hammer on the barrel, which no one heard due to the large crowd's chatter. Once Ben Bergman stuck his fingers into his mouth and whistled shrill and long, everyone quieted down.

"All right, the Fourth of July picnic was delicious–let's give a hand to the Cady Corner ladies," Bergman shouted. After the loud clapping died down, he signaled the minister.

"Yes, it's time for the Barrel Auction. Bring on the first item," Reverend Rausch ordered. Libby Bergman handed him a slip of paper and a pie tin. "Looks like a wonderful triple berry pie, baked by Miss Hannah Mueller. Who will start the bidding?"

"Why didn't you start with your pie?" Elmer asked, but Cora shook her head.

"No one wants to go first and end up with a lowest bid," she said. She folded her parasol, and nearly poked her brother in the eye. "Men never expect the first dessert to be all that good. We draw straws, and this year Hannah lost."

Only Hannah's father bid on the pie, raising it from two bits to fifty cents. Hannah looked crestfallen and blinked back tears when none of the young men stepped forward. The seventeen-year-old wore her blonde hair in a braid over her head, with an outdated blue hat pinned on one side, and her ruffled blue dress looked more suitable for a schoolgirl. Cora remembered her own first effort and how low the price had been. She noticed Libby Bergman whispering something to her brother. The minister raised the hammer, but Ben Bergman raised a hand to interrupt.

"I'll bid two dollars."

"Thank you, Mr. Bergman! Any other bids?"

Although no one else stepped forward, Hannah beamed and delivered her pie to the mill owner. She quickly returned to stand beside her father, however. Bergman handed the pie to Libby, who in turn gifted it to the Reverend Mrs. Rausch. The minister's wife gasped in surprise and gratitude. Cora smiled, knowing that Libby was well-liked for her thoughtfulness and her hard work for the Ladies Aid group. She turned back to the auction. A peach pie had brought fifty cents, followed by three others that each brought in a dollar.

Several cowboys joked and laughed, outbidding each other for one iced cake that reached three dollars. The auction sped up, with men from Cady Corners and DeWitt bidding. At last, Cora noticed that Reverend Rausch held Maybelle's glass-domed cake plate.

"People, we have a special buttercream frosted cake, with a raspberry filling," he read off a slip of paper, "baked by Miss Maybelle Winslow. You better believe this cake is special. Who will start the bidding?"

Billy Cooper gave a whoop. "A dollar!"

Everyone laughed, although Maybelle did not look happy in the least. Other young men muttered to themselves. One stepped up, the catcher who played for the Timber Wolves. He doffed his flat cap and raised a hand.

"I'll go over that with another two bits."

"Jim Kelly bids a dollar twenty-five on this cake," Reverend Rausch said. "Any others? Going once—"

"A dollar fifty!" Billy Cooper grinned wide and stuck his thumbs under his suspenders. He swaggered in a small circle. "Even if the frosting's all melted, and the cake is just a bunch of crumbs, I'll take it!"

"How dare you insult my cake," Maybelle screeched.

Cora fought back laughter, although she didn't blame her rival for being

A Cowboy Celebration

upset at Billy. But to her shock, Elmer marched over and shoved Billy aside. Cora gasped, covering her mouth too late to stifle it. Maybelle looked triumphant.

"Four dollars."

"Sold!" The minister banged his hammer on the barrel, perilously close to the plate. The cowboys snickered. "Come and retrieve your prize, Mr. Peterson!"

Her brother plunked the gold coins down on the barrel. Reverend Rausch handed the glass-domed plate over to Elmer, who smiled at Maybelle. She slid her hand into the crook of his elbow and started to lead him away. But Billy Cooper suddenly blocked their path.

"Hold on—"

"Next up, it's a Mile High Apple pie, baked by Miss–oh, dear," Reverend Rausch said when he dropped the slip of paper. It fluttered to the ground.

Cora rushed to retrieve it, but the breeze caught and sailed it further. She reached out to grab it and then leaped backward in fright, dropping her parasol. Niklas Lundquist had stamped his boot down, an inch from her fingers, on the paper. He snatched it up and offered the slip to her, but she ignored him and whirled around.

"I baked that apple pie," she called out to the minister with a frantic wave.

But Reverend Rausch had set her tin down on the barrel and didn't hear her. He stepped over to Billy Cooper and her brother, who each had a tight hold of the cake plate. They pulled and pushed, back and forth. Cora stood with her mouth agape. Elmer's friends egged him on; the cowboys yelled, whistled, and stomped their feet. Maybelle had shrunk back against Libby Bergman, who slid an arm around her waist and drew her further away.

"She doesn't like you," Elmer hissed at Billy, who cursed aloud.

"None of that, now," the minister chided, but Billy spat.

"You didn't give me a chance to bid again," he yelled. "I'll pay five dollars for this cake! Now, let go, Peterson."

"It's not for sale!"

"Let go of that cake, Mr. Cooper," Reverend Rausch said sternly.

Billy twisted and jammed his elbow into the minister's stomach, which sent the older man reeling backward in pain. He hadn't lost his grip in the tug-of-war with Elmer, who kept his hold on the glass plate and dome. Nik rushed over with an angry roar.

"*Det är respektlöst!*"

Cora had no idea what he said, but cheered with everyone else. The big

Swede's left hook had caught Billy Cooper right on the nose. Unfortunately, Maybelle's cake plate flew up into the air. The dome flipped and then conked Reverend Rausch on the head. Cake and melted frosting slithered over him before the plate crashed down, as well, and broke in two. He howled in pain, and his petite wife rushed to his side.

Maybelle shrieked. "My cake! It's ruined—"

That enraged Elmer, who butted his head into Cooper's belly. The two men crashed into the middle of the long table; all the women shrieked, grabbing what they could, trying to save their desserts–but the majority slid into a heap on top of the two men who bit and kicked each other. Laughing children dove into the melee and grabbed what they could reach, and then ran off with their prizes. All the cowboys did the same, clearly figuring the auction was ruined. Several women pummeled them, yelling in protest.

"Hey, you can't take anything without paying!"

Their husbands jumped into the fight, shoving their wives to safety, although a few kept screaming, kicking the cowboys, and pulling their clothing or hair. Cora had grabbed her parasol and dashed forward to save her apple pie. Unfortunately, she smacked into Ben Bergman, who had made a beeline from the opposite direction to break up the fight. Cora rolled onto the grass, the breath knocked out of her. Bergman fell on top of her.

"Oo-oof!"

"Watch out, you big dumb Swede! Get outta the way—"

Crack!

Nik had stepped right on her parasol and looked down in shock. "*Jag är ledsen!*"

She watched, dazed and helpless, as a cowboy punched him. Nik's long arms pin-wheeled before he crashed to the ground by the barrel. Someone else collapsed against its other side, tipping it–and dumped her Mile High Apple pie onto his blond head.

Chapter Four

Nik licked the sweet syrup that trickled down his nose and dripped onto his upper lip. "*Kanel. Väldigt bra.*"

"My pie!"

Cora had risen to her feet with Ben Bergman's help, although his boss seemed woozy and unsteady. Ignoring him, she raced over to Nik. He'd already reached upward, hoping to rescue whatever he could of Cora's *bakwerk*, fully aware of her dismay. She stared, her blue eyes filling with tears, her lovely mouth open, her teeth white; she looked so vulnerable and lost. He blinked his one eye–but bits of apple and juicy syrup stuck to his eyelashes and half-blinded him.

Nik leaned forward, desperate to shove the apples and crust back into the tin instead of letting it all slide sideways onto the grass. He saved most of it, although the crust's edge was broken up and his hands felt sticky and wet.

"*Ja.* It is not good."

"What? You think my pie is—"

Sobbing, Cora dashed out of sight, her hat ribbons streaming behind her. Confused, Nik hurriedly scraped apples and pastry off his hair and into the round tin. Maybelle stood laughing, pointing at him, her cheeks red, her eyes streaming. Why would she laugh at a terrible accident? Nik did not understand that woman at all. But what had he said wrong? Why was Cora crying? She had disappeared, however, into the crowd.

He scooped apple bits from his shirt into his mouth, savoring each bite of their tartness, the cinnamon syrup and flaky dough. *Utsökt*, the best *paj* he'd ever tasted. Somehow, Nik managed to get to his feet. He had saved most of it, and now avoided the last of the fight despite a few cowboys punching each other for fun. He had to find Cora and learn what he said to upset her. And pay money for the pie, since he had eaten about half of it already. He carried the tin to the hampers, set it down, and covered it with a napkin.

Ben Bergman, many ladies, and the minister had regained order. Elmer and Billy Cooper were the only men still rolling around on the ground, but Nik hauled his friend up by the collar. Another young man from the Timber Wolves dragged Cooper backward.

"Enough, Billy! We gotta play the game yet and win that bet."

Ignoring them, Nik helped Elmer stagger back to the picnic blanket. "Oh,

227

my head," he groaned. "Where's Cora? Is she all right?"

"*Nej*, she is not. But–*jag vet inte vad som är fel.*" Frustrated that he could not express it in *Engelsk*, Nik wiped his sticky hands on another clean cloth napkin. "I must go. *Jag kommer att hitta henne och göra denna rätt.*"

"What? Speak English!"

He only shook his head and stalked off. First, Nik washed his hands, face, and head at the pump, shaking off the excess water, dousing his shirt as well, until he felt clean again. Despite being damp, he walked around the crowd to find the minister. Reverend Rausch stood among a larger group of frantic women, although Cora was not with them. Nik scrounged in his pocket and pulled out the largest gold coin. Ben Bergman had explained the different values of this country's money–dollar–when he earned his first wage at the sawmill. This gold piece must be plenty to pay for the wonderful pie that had landed on his head–and in his stomach. Nik grabbed the man's hand and pressed the coin into his palm.

"For the *äpple bakwerk*. Miss Peterson. *Hon gjorde det*–she—"

"She baked the pie? The Mile High Apple pie, right?" Reverend Rausch's eyes popped at the sight of the gold coin. "That's a ten dollar eagle. Are you sure, son?"

"*Ja*. Ten dollar."

Nik darted past him before the minister could reply. Despite his one eye that had swelled shut, he caught sight of Cora's straw hat and blue dress out in the meadow. He raced after her, ignoring the pain in his ribs, his long legs pumping hard, his chest burning; he panted for air and slowed down, holding his aching side. Limping fast, Nik finally overtook her. Cora's face was hidden by her straw hat, but he stepped in front of her and halted. She dodged him, however, marching in a different direction, her head high, her face still wet with tears.

"Go away. Go away!"

"*Hur mår du?*"

"What?" She stopped this time and looked up at him. "What is it?"

"*Vänta, vänta!*" Nik bent over, breathing hard, hands on his knees.

"What do you want? You said my pie wasn't any good—"

"*Nej, nej*! I—*det var bra*. It is good, good!"

"I don't believe you." Cora whirled around, but he caught her by the elbow and turned her around. "Let go of me. You're hurting my arm. And you stepped on my parasol, too. It was brand new and very expensive!"

"*Jag är ledsen*. Sorry. Sorry!"

228

A COWBOY CELEBRATION

She smoothed her dress sleeve, her blue eyes flashing with anger. Flustered, Nik rubbed his hands together and stood before her. If only he was not such a big stupid ox. He didn't know how to offer to pay for her fancy umbrella, or how to reassure her it was an unfortunate accident. Nik hadn't seen it on the ground, not with the angry cowboy threatening him with upraised fists; he wanted to take her into his arms, wipe her tear-stained cheeks, take the pins out of her hair, unbraid it and let the waves of reddish curls fall over her shoulders...

Nik pulled her forward, praying she would not resist, hoping Elmer would not kill him for touching his sister. He leaned down to kiss her gently on the lips. And waited, fearing for her reaction, but she seemed to melt against him. Her pretty blue eyes fluttered open.

"*Hur mår du?*" Nik wished she would say something. Anything.

She blinked, clearly confused. "Why—what?"

This time he kissed her again, longer, less gentle. But Cora planted her hands on his chest and pushed hard. Nik backed away, but he kept smiling in hopes she would understand. He only meant to console her. She looked more surprised than angry, that was good. And she glanced around, as if afraid. Perhaps of who might be watching? He could understand that. She must want to protect her reputation as a lady.

"Sorry."

"Why would you–I don't understand." Puzzled, she touched her reddened mouth. "Do you always kiss someone when you're sorry?"

"*Kyss? Ja.*"

Nik smiled again. Cora slapped him hard across the face, and marched back to the picnic grounds. His cheek stung for several minutes and his flesh felt hot. Baffled, Nik felt like a fool. He followed her, but at a safe distance; Cora's sudden reaction and anger sent a clear message. He'd tried so hard to make up for what had happened. He felt badly that her pie had been ruined, but not that he'd eaten it. He would talk to Elmer and pay for her umbrella.

What else could he do? What did she expect of him? Had he misunderstood what she wanted? He thought she'd enjoyed that kiss. So much so that Nik had grown bold and kissed her a second time, showing his interest. He did care for Cora, but he did not know how to explain his feelings. Perhaps he ought to have asked her brother first for permission. Nik had no idea of how *uppvaktning* worked here. Didn't she want a suitor? Confused, he shook his head.

Women. They were the same here, or back in Sverige.

Determined, Nik marched over to the picnic blanket and sat by the hamper,

229

ignoring everyone, no longer caring about the baseball game, or the auction, or the cowboys who hooted and hollered. He stopped thinking about Cora and ate the mound of juicy, syrupy apples and pastry until not a crumb was left.

After all, Nik had paid a lot of Kroner for the privilege.

Chapter Five

Cora touched her lips, her face aflame. He'd kissed her. Not once, but twice–and the second time had sent delicious shivers throughout her entire body. Good heavens. No other man had dared do such a thing. Elmer had never broached the subject of what she would do if a man wanted to court her. After their parents died, she assumed he would have to give permission. And she'd once overheard Jim Kelly asking if she was interested. Her brother had flatly refused, however, and warned him against staring at her like a wolf.

Cora had felt uneasy by that habit. When she'd asked Elmer about Jim, her brother was just as uncomfortable explaining about his sordid reputation– roving hands and more. Heavens above. What would Elmer say about Niklas Lundquist?

Nik's one blue eye had gazed into her own with clear admiration. He'd looked so funny, his blond hair damp, along with his cotton shirt plastered in spots against his muscular shoulders and chest. Heaven help her.

Perhaps she ought to have slapped him twice.

But Cora also felt terrible. Confused, too. She straightened her hat, honest enough to admit she'd enjoyed that longer kiss and wanted more. His arms felt so right around her. She felt safe. Admired. Loved? Or was he just trying to get under her skirts, like when Elmer accused Jim Kelly? She'd heard that much, although Cora didn't believe it. Until she'd asked a few girls at church, and heard the warning about Jim's reputation. They cautioned her to stay far away.

No wonder he was courting a girl in DeWitt.

"Cora! Cora, wait!"

She whirled around to see Hannah Mueller running toward her. Cora bit her lip. Had she seen what happened in the meadow? But Hannah looked flustered, her brown eyes sparkling, her face flushed pink, and grabbed her hands in excitement.

"Congratulations!"

"What?"

"Your pie! You had the highest bid."

"What?" Cora pulled away. "Why? It was ruined."

"That foreigner, the Swede. He paid ten dollars, a gold eagle!" Hannah laughed at her confusion. "It fell on his head, remember? But he paid for it. Libby Bergman told me that most of the cowboys chipped in money to pay for the desserts they tried to steal. Your brother's bid for Maybelle's cake was the highest, you know, up to that point. She boasted about that during the fight. You should have heard her..."

Cora tuned her out, thinking hard. Niklas Lundquist had paid ten dollars for her Mile High Apple Pie? A gold eagle! Her heart leaped into her throat, wondering at that, until she suddenly stopped cold. Wait. Had he claimed those kisses, thinking he had paid plenty of money and deserved more than dessert? Is that why? The nerve of him! How could Elmer be friends with such a man! To take advantage of her—but then again, Nik didn't seem the type like Jim Kelly, staring at women when he thought they weren't looking. Roving hands, and more...

"—are they? Cora, you haven't heard a word I said!"

She blinked. Hannah had shaken her arm, startling her out of her racing thoughts. Cora swallowed hard. "I'm sorry, what did you say?"

"I asked you if your brother is courting Maybelle."

"What?" Cora shook her head. "No, why would you think that?"

"Because they're over there, sitting under that tree." Hannah pointed behind her with a sly smile. "I'd say you're wrong, the way they're acting right now."

Cora's mouth fell open. Was she seeing things? No, that was definitely Elmer with her rival half on his lap! Maybelle allowed a quick kiss before she pulled away, however, with a giggle and a shake of her finger. He grinned. Elmer leaned forward to say something and then scrambled to his feet. Maybelle held out a hand; he pulled her up with a quick hug, and then led the way toward the meadow where the other Timber Wolves and the DeWitt Devils were heading. Many of the men had young ladies or wives accompanying them.

"Uh, I'd better go."

Stumbling, Cora rushed back to the picnic blanket and hampers. Nik was gone. She didn't see his tall figure among the baseball players milling around, either. Her pie tin had been washed clean and wiped dry, and sat on top of its basket. Puzzled, she peered in every direction for his blond head. Cora had never seen him wear a hat, and hadn't understood why until he tried on Elmer's spare straw hat; clearly it was too small. Nik was a giant compared to most of the village men, but she'd never felt afraid of him. Or uneasy, like with Jim Kelly.

The top of her head reached his shoulder. Cora liked that. She'd often sensed how other men didn't appreciate looking at her straight in the eye. Nik treated her with gentleness, without acting awkward, or making her feel gangly and unfeminine. Maybe she'd been wrong about his intentions. Cora wished

A COWBOY CELEBRATION

she hadn't been so impulsive, thinking the worst of him, and even slapping him when he may have been trying to comfort her.

After all, he did bid on her pie.

And Nik had eaten three helpings of that peach cobbler a month-and-a-half ago. Cora wished Elmer had invited him again for supper. He must have been lonely, not knowing any families, except for the Bergmans and his fellow mill workers. Where was Nik? Had he left the picnic? She had no idea where he lived. Probably the boarding house, and Cora shuddered at the thought. Mrs. Wyatt had a reputation for providing the least she could for the most money; her cooking was decent, but she did not keep that neat a house, nor changed the sheets often. Or so Hannah had once told her. Then again, Hannah loved gossip.

Cora marched over to the meadow. "Elmer? Elmer Edward Peterson!"

Her brother was huddled with the other Timber Wolves. He glanced up and waved, as if signaling her to wait. Impatient, she approached Maybelle Winslow. Cora didn't smile, but she tried hard to sound friendly in her tone.

"Is it true you and my brother are courting?"

"As if you really care," Maybelle said, her cheeks flushing red.

"I *do* care. Hannah Mueller asked me, so I'd like to know the truth." Cora had softened her tone, although Maybelle didn't meet her gaze. "Is it true?"

"Yes, we've been courting for a month. Elmer's been so secretive, thinking you wouldn't approve. I kept telling him your opinion didn't matter, but he's sensitive."

"As long as you treat him right, and appreciate him, then I do approve. But don't take Elmer for granted, Maybelle. He is sensitive, that's true. Don't break his heart like you have so many others. Or treat him like Billy Cooper."

"Billy Cooper! Hmph. I told him last summer I wasn't interested." Maybelle looked furious at first, but then sighed. "I've been waiting since then for Elmer to pay attention to me, so I tried to make him jealous. And I'm sorry now. But if—if he's serious, and asks me to marry him... I don't know if Elmer will."

She worried her bottom lip with her teeth, clearly uncertain. Cora laughed. "Oh, I'd say you have a good chance of being asked. Once Elmer makes up his mind on something, he's set. You ought to know him well enough by now."

"That's true."

"What are you saying about me?"

When her brother tapped her shoulder, Cora whirled around. "Oh, nothing."

"Have you seen Nik Lundquist? He disappeared a while ago. Haven't seen

233

him since, and none of the other boys have either."

"He's hard to miss, though," she said. "He must be somewhere."

"True." Maybelle shrugged. "Maybe he thought there wouldn't be a game, since so many men fought earlier. I heard some say they were too sore."

Elmer groaned. "We need to win that bet! And we won't be able to without Nik. Cora, can you walk around and see if you can find him? I've got to get back in case they restart the game before everyone's ready."

He stalked toward his team at the far end of the picnic area. Cora wished Elmer had asked Maybelle instead, but she turned and headed in the opposite direction. Better to just confront Nik and get it over with if she must.

Where would he have gone, and why? Nik knew about the baseball game. Was he too injured to play? He hadn't acted as if his swollen eye would prevent it, given their encounter. Her face burned once again. Cora hooked a strand of hair and pulled it away from her eyes; her attempt to catch it behind her ear and tuck it into a pin failed. She gave up and walked faster, studying the various families sitting on blankets or resting in the shade.

The blazing sun beat down on her head. If only her parasol hadn't been broken in two. Elmer was sure to protest her replacing it, after it cost her a dollar. They couldn't spare much until harvest, when Elmer could sell the corn and oat crops, pay off the harvesters, pay off some of the loan for farm equipment, and the grocery bill. Cora ought to have salvaged the lace, at least, but hadn't seen her parasol since the fight. She'd have to hunt it down.

But her hunt for Nik ended sooner than she expected. Cora caught sight of his blond head above a crowd of villagers watching another cowboy demonstration–this time, while they raced down Main Street. She hurried toward him, but he moved fast; she lost sight of him when Billy Cooper suddenly gripped her elbow. He jerked her to face him.

"Is it true your brother's courting Maybelle?"

Cora licked her lips nervously. His anger was clear, and she fought to pull away from his tight hold. "Let go!"

"Not until you answer me," he hissed and then cursed. "Tell me!"

"Yes—"

"*Lämna henne ensam!*"

Billy howled in pain and let go of Cora's arm. She jumped back in fright, since Nik had hauled the other man away from her by his shirt collar. Billy ran faster than a hare on the prairie, down Main Street past the small hotel, Schneider's General Store and Post Office, the dry goods shop, and the old blacksmith shop. Cora glanced up at Nik, whose reddened face had not faded despite the concern in his eyes.

"I'm all right," she said, even though he hadn't asked.

"*Ja*. Good." Nik smiled. "I—I pay. For parasol."

"No, no. You don't have to do that."

"I break, I pay."

Cora changed the subject, since she could tell he would be stubborn about it. "What about the baseball game? My brother was worried you wouldn't help them win."

He looked surprised at that. "Baseball game? *Jag kommer att hjälpa*."

Nik held out his arm, ignoring the other villagers who had been observing them. Cora tucked her hand into the crook of his elbow and tried to hurry him away from the village, past the picnic area, toward the meadow where the game had already started.

"There he is! Come on out into the field, Nik," Elmer shouted.

Cora gestured to where her brother stood past the shortstop. "I guess Tom Price did show up after all," she said, and nodded to the man who rocketed a pitch past the batter. "He wants you in the outfield. Over there."

"*Ja*. I go." Nik hesitated, although the batter had smacked the ball past the second baseman. He took both of her hands in his. "*Kommer ni domstol med mig?*"

"I don't understand what that means."

"*Uppvaktning?*"

She shook her head. Confused, Cora watched Nik point to Maybelle, clearly frustrated by his inability to make her understand. He pointed to Elmer next, and then Maybelle–and then she understood. Or so she thought. Her heart skipped a beat, as hope and excitement rose inside her. Did he really mean that? Cora suddenly stood on her tiptoes and kissed his mouth. His eyebrows shot up in shock, but he broke into a wide smile.

"Yes? Like Elmer and Maybelle, you mean? Courting? Getting to know each other, spending time together?" She smiled back. "I could help you with your English, too."

"*Engelsk. Ja*. Courting."

Cora pushed him a little, gently. "You'd better get out there to right field. There's two men on base, do you see? Go on, help them win."

"Win."

Grinning, Nik ran out between the first and second basemen, at the same time as the next batter hit the ball in his direction. She gasped, unable to yell a warning; he twisted, reached up a hand, and caught the ball before tumbling to the ground. But Nik had not dropped it. He rose to his feet, still holding the ball, and heard the other Timber Wolves yelling and waving. Then he threw it to the first baseman, before the runner, who'd taken a lead, could get back to the base.

"He's out! Double play, that's three outs," the umpire called. He motioned the DeWitt Devils away from home plate. "No arguments or fighting, or you forfeit the game!"

Grumbling, the men marched out to the field. Elmer, Tom Price, and the other Timber Wolves surrounded Nik, slapped him on the back, and followed him to the side of the field. Cora walked over to join Maybelle and watch the rest of the game.

"So. I guess next year you won't bring a frosted cake to the auction."

Maybelle blinked. "Elmer loves chocolate—"

"He likes strawberry shortcake best. Come on, hit a home run!" She waved at her brother who'd stepped up to the plate. "With whipped cream."

"I'll remember that." Maybelle giggled. "I have to admit your pie looked the best of all the others. It must have been wonderful, if the Swede paid—"

"His name is Niklas Lundquist," Cora interrupted. "And I heard how much he paid for my Mile High Apple Pie. I hope it was worth every penny."

Cora smiled to herself. She had a feeling Nik would agree.

About Meg Mims

Mystery author Meg Mims earned a Spur award for her first novel, Double Crossing, and a Laramie Award for the sequel, Double or Nothing She and her co-author, (writing as D.E. Ireland), also earned a Malice Domestic Agatha Award nomination for the first book of the Eliza Doolittle & Henry Higgins Mystery series for Minotaur Books. Meg loves writing about the historical west, and sweet contemporary romance with dog and cat rescues. She lives in Southeastern Michigan with her husband and a Malti-poo.

Visit her website at www.megmims.com

A COWBOY CELEBRATION

Recipes

RECIPES

Lily's Berry And Apple Crisp Cobbler
Submitted by Lorrie Farrelly

Preheat oven to 375°

Fruit ingredients:

6 cups mixed fruit: tart apples, sliced and mixed with any berries, fresh or canned
1/3 cup sugar
1 teaspoon lemon zest, grated
1 tablespoon lemon juice

Topping ingredients:

¼ cup flour
½ cup oats
pinch of salt
2/3 cup brown sugar
1 teaspoon cinnamon
1/3 cup cold butter

Optional:

Whipped or clotted cream, or ice cream

Butter a 9" X 13" baking pan. Toss all fruit ingredients together and place evenly in the pan.

In a large bowl, combine the dry ingredients for the topping. Cut in cold butter to make coarse crumbs. Spread over fruit mixture.

Bake in preheated oven at 375° for 30-40 minutes or until lightly browned and bubbly. If desired, serve with whipped or clotted cream or ice cream.

Serves 8, unless Luke Cullinan is visiting. He'll eat the whole pan by himself.

RECIPES

Buttermilk-Crispy Chicken
Submitted by Linda Carroll-Bradd

¾ cup buttermilk
2-3 plump garlic cloves, crushed
1-1-1/2 lbs skinless, boneless chicken breasts
¾-1 cup panko breadcrumbs
2 tablespoon flour
½ rounded teaspoon paprika
¼ rounded teaspoon dry mustard powder
¼ rounded teaspoon dried thyme
¼ tsp hot chili powder
½ tsp ground black pepper
3 tbsp vegetable or olive oil

Pour the buttermilk into a wide shallow dish and stir in the garlic. Slice the chicken into chunky slices, about 4" long x 1.5" wide. Lay the chicken in the dish and turn it over in the buttermilk so it is well coated. Leave in the fridge for 1-2 hrs, or preferably overnight.

Meanwhile, heat a large, non-stick frying pan and pour in the panko crumbs and flour. Toast them in the pan for 2-3 minutes, stirring regularly so they brown evenly and don't burn. Tip the crumb mix into a bowl and stir in the paprika, mustard, thyme, chili powder, pepper and a pinch of fine sea salt. Set aside.

When ready to cook, heat oven to 350° (moderate-high temperature). Line a baking tin with foil and sit a wire rack (preferably non-stick) on top. Transfer half the crumb mix to a medium-large bag. Lift half the chicken from the buttermilk, leaving the marinade clinging to it. Transfer it to the bag of seasoned crumbs. Seal the end of the bag and give it a good shake so the chicken gets well covered (you could do all the crumbs and chicken together if you prefer, but it's easier to coat evenly in 2 batches).

Remove the chicken from the bag. Heat 1 tbsp of the oil in a large, non-stick frying pan, then add the chicken pieces and fry for 1½ mins without moving them. Turn the chicken over, pour in another ½ tbsp of the oil to cover the base of the pan and fry for 1 min more, so both sides are becoming golden. Using tongs, transfer to the wire rack. Repeat with the remaining seasoned crumbs, oil and chicken.

Bake all the chicken on the rack for 15 mins until cooked and crisp, then serve warm or cold.

RECIPES

Knee-Deep Dried Apple Stack Cake
Submitted by Agnes Alexander

This cake recipe was handed down from my great-grandmother. I was told she got the original recipe from her mother-in-law who was a Scottish immigrant. Various versions are fairly well known in the south so I'm sure others made it, too. I'm also sure it was tweaked through the years, but is the way my mother made it.

Cake ingredients

¾ cups shorting (Old recipe called for lard, but my mother used Crisco)
1 cup sugar
1 cup molasses
3 eggs
6 cups All-purpose flour
2 teaspoons baking powder
½ teaspoon baking soda
1 teaspoon salt
2 teaspoons ground ginger
½ teaspoon cinnamon
½ cup buttermilk
1 teaspoon vanilla

Cream shortening and sugar; Add molasses and mix well. Add eggs, one at a time beat well after each egg is added.

Sift together all dry ingredients; Add dry ingredients alternately with butter to the creamed mixture. Beat well after each mixture. Blend in vanilla.

Dump dough onto floured surface. Work in enough flour to make dough easy to handle. Knead well. When dough is ready, divide into 12 equal balls. (The easiest way to do this is to divide the dough in half – then divide the halves into halves again. This will give you 4 equal parts. Now divide these 4 into thirds. This will give you 12 equal balls of dough.)

With your hand press each ball evenly into a lightly greased 9 inch round cake pan. Bake at 350 for 12-15 minutes. Let cool slightly and remove from pan. (The length of time it will take you to bake all 12 layer depends on how many cake pans you have.)

240

RECIPES

Ingredients for filling between layers

3 lbs. dried apples
1 ½ to 2 cups brown sugar
1 cup white sugar
1 Tablespoon cinnamon
(Other spices such as allspice, etc. can be added if desired)

Stew all ingredients together on med. to low heat until soft and easy to mash. When done, mash well. If filling is too juicy – drain.

When cake layers of cake are all cool, place 1 layer on plate. Spread filling on top, then add another cake layer. Continue spreading filling between the thin layers of cake as you stack them. Leave top layer plain. Place in tall cake plate with lid or use stock pot to cover cake. Best if made 2 – 3 days before serving so the apple flavor can seep into the cake.

RECIPES

Lip Smackin' Good Corn Bread
Submitted by Beverly Wells

2 packages (6.5oz.) Betty Crocker Cornbread & Muffin mix
1 stick butter (soft)—can use light
8 oz. sour cream
8 oz. can cream corn
8 oz. can whole kernel corn
2 eggs

Preheat oven to 350'

Beat eggs with whip till blended. Mix: all ingredients. Pour into greased 9x12 pan

Bake approx. 30 minutes or until golden brown. Overbaking dries it out, under will be gooey.

Wait 10 minutes to cut. Serve—Mm mm, lip smackin' good!

Refrigerate leftovers. Microwave 10 seconds or so to reheat. Always serve warm as honey or butter will taste so much better on it. May make smaller batches or larger, just portion accordingly—may to have change bake time.

**If you prefer to use *corn bread meal* then add the standard dry ingredients called for in corn bread recipe, and then all moist ingredients from this recipe.

** Homemade Sour Cream: ¼ cup milk, ¾ tsp. White Vinegar, 1 cup heavy cream, stand 10 min., store 24 hours at room temp. covered. Chill till used.

RECIPES

Green Corn Fritters
(A great way to use early or unripened corn on the cob)
Submitted by Angela Raines

1 pint young and tender green corn, grated
3 eggs
2 tablespoons milk or cream
1 tablespoon melted butter, if milk is used
1 teaspoon salt
1 teaspoon baking powder
Flour enough to thicken
(optional) depending on your taste
1 teaspoon ground mustard powder
1 tablespoon ground chili peppers of your choice
or any other seasoning of your choice.

Set out ingredients in order. Beat the eggs well, add baking powder, add the corn by degrees, with the milk and butter, thickened with just enough flour to hold it all together. Have a kettle of hot lard or lard and butter ready. Drop a large spoonful of the corn mixture into the fat, and fry to a light brown. Drain. Can be served warm or cold.

RECIPES

Ma's Molasses Cookies
Submitted by Julia Daniels

1 cup unsweetened flaked coconut
1/3 cup unsalted butter, softened (not melted)
1/3 cup granulated sugar
1 large egg
1/2 cup Light/cooking molasses
1 1/2 cups rolled oats
1 cup flour
1/2 tsp allspice
1/2 tsp salt
1/4 tsp nutmeg
1/4 tsp ground cloves
1 tsp baking powder
1/4 tsp baking soda
1 tsp vanilla

Preheat oven to 325* and spray two cookie sheets with cooking spray (or grease them). (I am a BIG parchment paper fan!)

In a medium mixing bowl, cream the butter and sugar together.

Beat in the egg.

Beat in the molasses evenly.

In a larger mixing bowl, stir together all the dry ingredients. Add the wet mixture to the dry, including the vanilla and the coconut. Stir together till a nice batter forms.

Drop the batter onto the cookie sheet (about a ½ dollar dollops), about a dozen on a sheet (they do spread).

Bake for 15-20 minutes. (I always have to shift cookie sheets from top rack to bottom during baking- your oven may be different)

You'll know they are finished when the center is firm. DO NOT OVERBAKE!

Makes about 2 dozen

RECIPES

Cora Peterson's Mile High Apple Pie
Submitted by Meg Mims

DOUBLE CRUST for pie
3 cups all-purpose flour
Pinch salt
1 cup lard
6-8 tablespoons cold water

In a bowl, combine flour and salt. Cut in lard until mixture resembles coarse crumbs. Sprinkle in water, a tablespoon at a time, until pastry holds together. Shape into a ball; chill for 30 minutes. On a lightly floured surface, roll dough to 1/8-in. thickness. Transfer to a 10-in. pie plate. Flute edges; fill and bake as pie recipe directs.

Yield: 2-10-inch crusts, which you will need for this very tall pie.

APPLE PIE ingredients

12-16 Northern Spy apples, or any preferred such as Jonathan, MacIntosh, etc. or a mix.

1 cup plus 2 tablespoons of sugar
1/4 cup plus 2 tablespoons of flour
3 teaspoons (or more, if preferred) cinnamon
3 tablespoons butter
1 large egg, for egg wash

Toss apple slices (thick best) with 1 cup sugar, flour and cinnamon in a deep round bowl. Place your pie dish (with one crust, of course, very carefully!) UPSIDE DOWN over the bowl AND FLIP. The apples will be mounded nicely. Cut butter and shove into various spots or place on top, cover with top crust. Flute edges, cut vents. Lightly beat egg and brush over top crust, mix up remaining sugar and cinnamon, sprinkle on top.

In a very hot oven (400 degrees, our ovens today), bake for 50 minutes to one hour -- or try baking at 450 degrees for 10 minutes to brown crust, then reduce heat to 375 and bake for another 50-60 minutes.

Made in the USA
Middletown, DE
14 August 2015